AN. WILLIS

UNDER GLASS AND STONE

This is a work of fiction. All characters and events in this work are fictitious. Any resemblance to real persons, living or dead, is coincidental.

Under Glass And Stone (Byrne House #1)

Copyright © 2020 by A.N. Willis

All rights reserved. No part of this book may be reproduced or transmitted in any form or by any means, electronic, mechanical, photocopying, recording, or otherwise, without prior written permission of Observatory Books. If you would like to use material from the book (other than for review purposes), please write to observatorypublishing@gmail.com.

Produced by Observatory Books
Denver, Colorado

First edition April 2020
Print ISBN 978-1-7343597-1-8
Ebook ISBN 978-1-7343597-0-1

For my writing group:

*I couldn't have done it without you,
and it definitely wouldn't have been
so much fun.*

UNDER GLASS AND STONE

Part 1
Do I Know You?

1

THE DAY MILO FOSTER DISAPPEARED, NO ONE could say what he'd been doing up in the tower. A few neighbors even insisted he'd never gone inside Byrne House at all. But Evelyn knew what she'd seen. She would never forget the discordant whiteness of Milo's face, small and pale as a fish in the round mouth of the tower window. Later, when Evelyn reported the sighting, she left out her unsettling first impression: that it was her own face she was seeing, about to be swallowed up by the mansion.

For as far back as she could remember, maybe ever since she'd been tall enough to see above the sill, Evelyn had liked to watch Byrne House from her second-floor bedroom across the street. When Evelyn was little, her mother asked why the sprawling Victorian fascinated her. Viv Ashwood was making Evelyn's bed and pretending to be focused on her task. But Evelyn could tell by the slow rhythm of her mom's hands that Viv was listening carefully.

"Is it because of Nana?" her mom prompted. "Is she still telling you those stories?"

He'd gotten trapped behind the walls, Nana had whispered. *They could hear him knocking.*

"No," Evelyn said. She didn't want to get Nana in trouble. But it wasn't just the bedtime stories, not really. "It's because of my dream. I'm trying to find the part that's missing."

Her mom had gotten very still and very quiet. She hadn't asked again.

Even now, at seventeen, Evelyn would glance over at the tower whenever she passed by her window or when she turned onto the street on her walk home from school. And always before she went to bed at night. It was a little ritual, an itch to scratch. It wasn't because of the dreams anymore —her nightly dreams of Byrne House had eventually turned to a nightmare and then morphed into something worse. Something she didn't like to think about. But those dreams had stopped years ago and still she watched, unable to say why. She knew better than to mention the habit around her mother.

Until the day Evelyn saw Milo, the tower window was always dark. A hole punched into the stone. Reginald Byrne lived alone in there, a forgotten king in his walled-up castle.

Evelyn never saw anyone go in or out of Byrne House's wrought-iron gate except the cleaning lady. And Mrs. Lake only came the last day of each month. She'd walk over from her own home several streets away and stay all day. Then she'd reappear just as darkness fell, red curls tucked into a wool cap, bag hitched into her side as she marched down the mansion's front path. An official emissary returning from a journey into a foreign land.

On July 31—the day Milo would disappear and all the trouble would start—Mrs. Lake spent only a few minutes inside the mansion before she ran back out, screaming.

Up until that moment, Evelyn had been lying in bed, immersed in a horror novel. Her window was open, curtains lifting and falling with each breath of wind. Evelyn's room was tiny, just big enough for a twin bed and an antique secretary desk that doubled as a dresser. Her collection of vintage and thrift-store clothes was tucked carefully inside. She also had a narrow closet, but she certainly couldn't put her clothes in there. *That* was where she stored all her books.

"Help! Please, help!"

Evelyn froze, and her hands tightened on her book. The cry had come from the street. Then there was a slamming door. Evelyn tossed her book on the bed and rushed to the open window.

Mrs. Lake was running across Byrne House's yard, crying. She yanked open the iron gate and ran into the street, then started turning back and forth like she couldn't make up her mind where to go.

A bike turned onto the avenue. Immediately the rider had to swerve to avoid hitting Mrs. Lake. Evelyn recognized his closely-shorn brown hair and chunky black-frame glasses. It was Milo Foster. He must've been on his way to visit his grandma. In one fluid motion, Milo jumped off the bike and left it lying by the curb. He went to Mrs. Lake, who kept shouting and gesturing at the house behind her.

Milo seemed to get the gist. He ran up the mansion's front steps and tried the door. It wouldn't open. He said something else to Mrs. Lake, who was sobbing actively now. She pointed him to the side of the house. Milo ran in that direction.

All this had happened in the span of a minute, maybe two. Evelyn grabbed her phone and ran downstairs. By the time she got outside, a handful of neighbors were streaming out of their homes. Several held phones to their ears.

She paused at the sidewalk, looking up at the mansion. She couldn't explain her hesitation, only that something seemed different. Strange. Her pulse seemed unsteady, too fast. Now too slow. Then, from the corner of her eye, she spotted movement near the top of the tower.

It was gone. The tower's round window was just reflections laid on top of black. Nothing there.

Her eyes traced the mansion's rough stone facade and the curve of the porch railing. Then back to the tower with its cone-shaped roof.

There—the curtains in the tower's highest window were shifting. Now, an oval of white appeared within the larger black circle. Like the opening of a milky, reptilian eye.

A face.

For a surreal split second, Evelyn imagined she was seeing her own reflection, though the angles were all wrong.

But then she saw the square-frame glasses, and the illusion dissipated. It was Milo again. Why had he gone inside? Was Mr. Byrne alright?

A siren whined, the pitch climbing. An ambulance with flashing lights skidded down the road. The loiterers on the street scattered toward the park, and the ambulance's tires squealed to a stop a few yards from the Byrne House gate. A patrol car pulled up a heartbeat later.

She'd only glanced away for a moment. But when Evelyn looked up at the tower window again, Milo's face was gone.

She hurried across the street, joining the group standing by the mansion's front gate.

"Everyone back, please!"

One of the officers was waving the neighbors away from the mansion. Reluctantly, the crowd relocated to Walter Park, where they'd still have a clear view of the goings on.

Evelyn crossed over with her neighbors. She saw Ms. Foster—Milo's grandmother. Joyce Foster was sitting on a park bench beside Mrs. Lake, the cleaning lady who'd recently run screaming from Byrne House. Mrs. Lake was speaking into a phone while Ms. Foster patted her leg.

When she spotted Evelyn, Ms. Foster stood up. "Goodness, Evelyn! It's all just awful!"

They hugged, and Evelyn inhaled her neighbor's clean-laundry scent. Ms. Foster had pulled her long white hair into a ponytail. She'd asked Evelyn to call her Joyce, but Evelyn couldn't think of her grandmotherly neighbor as "Joyce." Ms. Foster was the resident social butterfly of the streets surrounding Walter Park. Evelyn had always liked her because she bore a strong resemblance to Evelyn's own grandmother, though Nana Stanton had been more the quiet and intense type.

"What happened?" Evelyn asked.

"She's had a shock," Ms. Foster whispered, nodding her head at the cleaning lady. "She hasn't been making much sense."

"Have you seen Milo?" Evelyn asked. "Has he come out yet?" But Ms. Foster had knelt beside the cleaning woman again, and so she didn't hear.

A couple of detectives had now arrived. One was a woman wearing a navy windbreaker and a necklace-badge. She took out a small notebook and flipped it open. The other, a man who was squeezed into a gray blazer, came across the street to Mrs. Lake.

"Ma'am, you're the one who found him?"

"*Him?*" Evelyn said to Ms. Foster. "Does he mean Mr. Byrne?"

Ms. Foster stood and hugged Evelyn to her side. "We'd better wait for the official word. But it doesn't look good."

The detective guided Mrs. Lake across to the mansion. To give a witness statement, Evelyn assumed, based on the police shows she'd streamed. She didn't know much about such things in real life.

An SUV pulled up and double parked beside the ambulance. A young woman got out, ribbons of dark hair flying. She clutched her phone. "Where's my father? Where is he?" The woman's eyes darted around, large and frightened, and Evelyn felt a pang of sympathy as she realized who it was. Daniella Byrne. She'd gotten here fast. Evelyn wondered if Mrs. Lake had called her.

She hadn't seen Daniella or the other one—the younger brother—since they'd left for boarding school years ago. Everyone said Daniella was a genius, graduated from college when she was just eighteen. The Byrne siblings would be in their twenties now. They hadn't been back to Byrne House in all that time. Not until now.

The windbreaker-wearing detective ushered Daniella toward Byrne House's door. Evelyn watched Daniella's sheet of chestnut hair disappear into the mansion, where Mrs. Lake had also gone.

Evelyn glanced up to the tower window. Scratching that familiar itch. She thought of Milo's face, the strangeness of seeing him there, and how quickly he'd gone. Both real and not-real, like this entire day so far. Blurry at the edges.

Milo had been Evelyn's classmate since forever. He was the backbone of the academic decathlon team; quiet, kind, but also easygoing and cute. He straddled both the popular and the brainier crowds at school. But aside from that, Evelyn hadn't known him well until this summer.

Starting in late May, Evelyn and Milo had spent several afternoons a week helping clean out Ms. Foster's overstuffed attic—Milo because he was a dutiful grandson, and Evelyn because it was easy to pass off to her mother as a summer job. Ms. Foster wanted to write a book about the history of Castle Heights, but she had so much material she didn't know where to start. She'd been collecting old photo albums, boxes of newspapers, and treasure-filled antiques from her neighbors for years. Evelyn, of course, always kept an eye out for anything related to Byrne House. She wanted corroboration of her Nana's creepy but vague stories about the place. Tales of children gone missing, lost lovers driven mad. They had dragged crate after crate out of the attic in the past two months.

At the end of each day, she, Milo and Ms. Foster would sit down in the dining room and comb through their finds over pitchers of iced tea. Evelyn wasn't great at striking up new friendships, but she could imagine Milo becoming a good friend. And now that Milo had actually been *inside* the mansion? Evelyn couldn't wait to talk to him. She just hoped Mr. Byrne was alright. And that Milo wasn't, somehow, in trouble. But maybe the police just needed to interview him, like they were Mrs. Lake.

"Have you seen Milo?" Evelyn asked Ms. Foster again.

The older woman looked confused. "Was he here? I wasn't expecting him today."

Evelyn explained what she'd seen earlier in the day: Milo arriving on his bike and running into the house, presumably from the back door. How she'd seen him in the window. As she spoke her anxiety increased. Was he still in the house? Why would the police be holding him? He'd been justified in going into the house, surely. Mrs. Lake had been screaming for help.

"I wouldn't worry," Ms. Foster said. "If Milo's a witness, they'll need to find out what he knows. Then we can ask him all about it," she added slyly.

The afternoon wore slowly on, and Evelyn got more and more worried. The police finished interviewing Mrs. Lake and several of the neighbors and released them. Word went around: Mrs. Lake had found Reginald Byrne unconscious, and she'd panicked. But there were no other details.

Evelyn walked around the block, getting as close to the yellow line of police tape as she dared. She even asked an officer if he'd seen a boy in thick-framed glasses. But there was no sign of Milo.

Finally, the EMTs rolled a stretcher with a body-shaped lump on it, covered with a thick plastic sheet. The murmurs around her confirmed it. Reginald Byrne was dead. Nobody knew yet what had happened to him.

But Milo, Evelyn kept thinking. *Where is he?*

The EMTs packed the stretcher into the ambulance, clamped shut the doors, and drove away. No more flashing lights. A couple of officers milled around the lawn, but they looked like they were just chatting.

Evelyn went back to Ms. Foster in the park. "I still can't find Milo."

"I'll just try him." Ms. Foster pulled up his number on her phone. Then held it to her ear.

"Is Milo answering?" Evelyn asked. Her chest was starting to squeeze, tighter and tighter. She kept thinking of the pale face in the window. The pale plastic sheet lying on the stretcher. The images flashed one after the other, faster and faster. She struggled to breathe.

"No." Ms. Foster turned off her screen. "But he leaves his phone at home half the time. Or forgets to charge it." She looked around and then pointed to the uniformed man and woman still in front of Byrne House. "Why don't we just check with one of those officers? They'll know."

Evelyn and Ms. Foster crossed the street. The two uniformed officers saw them and ambled over to meet them by the mansion's gate. Ms. Foster explained the situation to the officers. But they just shook their heads. They hadn't seen any teenage boy, and no one matching his description had been detained as a witness. Though they offered to double check inside Byrne House, just in case.

"I know I saw him in that window," Evelyn said to one officer while the other went inside the mansion to check. "And what about his bike? He left it by the curb at the end of the street. He couldn't have gone home." Evelyn turned to point out where she'd seen Milo drop the bike. Way down at the other side of the block. But the street was empty.

Milo's bike wasn't there.

"Where was it he left his bike?" the officer asked.

This made no sense. Evelyn ran down the sidewalk and back again, scanning for any sign of it. She couldn't remember when she'd last seen it. The bike had seemed so unimportant. She hadn't given it a second thought until now.

"He left it by the curb down there," she said. "A red mountain bike with white lettering. But it's not there anymore."

Ms. Foster chewed her lower lip. "That *does* sound like Milo's bike …"

"We'll make a note of it," the officer said.

Again, Evelyn thought of the body under the sheet. "What happened to Mr. Byrne?" she asked the officers. "Was his death, you know, suspicious?" She didn't want to say the word *murder*.

"We can't give out any information." The officer looked at her pityingly. "But there's no reason to be concerned. Guy getting on in years…these things happen."

His partner jogged down the front steps of the mansion to join them. "I walked the entire house," he reported. "Didn't see anybody inside who didn't belong."

"Are you sure?" Evelyn asked. "You definitely checked the tower?"

Ms. Foster tugged at Evelyn's elbow. "We've been out here all afternoon. I think we could all use some rest. I'll have Milo call you later to let you know he's alright."

Evelyn said a half-hearted goodbye and walked back home, doubting herself more with every step. She had seen Milo in the tower, she was sure of it. But why did that bother her so much? Milo had taken his bike and gone home, he was fine. He had to be. She'd just missed him. Yet she still felt dread coming from the deepest part of her, a place too dark to see.

"Don't look," she said to herself as she jogged up her porch steps. "Just this once, don't look." But just as she opened her front door, she turned back. Her eyes connected with the round black window.

She wanted not to look. But she always did.

August 6, 1898
Byrne House

Dearest Mary,

I must first apologize to you for not writing sooner. As you might have guessed, I have not had many happy things to write to you about. You and I have never lied to each other, even to ease the other's mind. Life in Denver has been hard. Much harder than I imagined when I left you and set out on my own the day I turned nineteen. But I hope—no, I am <u>sure</u>—that my luck has changed. I have met someone.

In fact, I think I am in love.

I know you're already skeptical. 'Silly Ada,' you will say, 'don't fool yourself into seeing Cupid's wings in lust's shadow.' I'd expect no less of my stern elder sister. Easy for you to say with a dashing husband in your bed. (You see? I am still playing our old game, trying to make you blush.) So please let me go back to the beginning, to give you a clear picture. Indeed, so much has happened that it would do me good to set it all down and consider it myself. In some ways, it feels much too miraculous to be true. But it <u>is</u> true. It must be, for this is no dream. I am wide awake.

My first difficulty was the governess position that your dear Christopher secured for me in one of the fine homes of Capitol Hill. Unfortunately, the pay was far lower than advertised. So I immediately set out to find new employment. But I quickly learned that jobs are scarce here, especially positions in reputable households. When I asked again after the governess position, I found it had already been taken.

You know I'd be the last to hold grand notions about myself. I ask no pity for our family's downcast fortunes, or where they've led me. But am I so naive to have thought an educated young woman—who can recite Emerson, conjugate French verbs, and (almost) fudge her way through a Beethoven piano sonata—might earn a decent living?

I shouldn't complain. As I've told you, my luck has since changed. But I've come to realize just how precious a warm bed, a good meal and a shelf of books can be. I'm filled with gratitude that you and Christopher sheltered me for so long despite the strain on your finances, and I can only hope that one day I'll repay you. If only father hadn't died. If only we'd received the pension that the church had promised him.

But—to continue with my story.

A girl I met at the employment office, Daisy, told me about a boarding house on the outskirts of town where young ladies could rent a room for a very cheap rate. With no other options to speak of, I moved that night to the extra bed in Daisy's small room.

This is the point that my story gets harder to tell.

In addition to our rent, we girls were expected to work in the dining club next door. You will probably guess that this club catered to men, and served alcohol and allowed gambling. It served only well-dressed gentlemen, and the proprietress claimed to tolerate no inappropriate behavior from the customers. But she turned her head more than I think was wise. There was an innuendo of seediness to which the men seemed drawn. Even some of the girls, for that matter. But I won't speak more about it. Suffice to say, I navigated the place as best I could.

After a few months, a fever confined me to bed. Daisy worked extra hours to cover my rent in addition to hers. When I finally came out of it and returned to the dining club, I noticed a man with beautiful blue eyes and a charming smile sitting alone at one of the tables. I remembered serving him before. Daisy said he'd asked several of the girls about me in my absence.

He called me to his table.

I was on my guard at first, but he simply ordered a bourbon. At the end of the night, he left a silver piece on his table for me. He left without a word, without even an improper glance. Each night for the next two weeks, he was there. He would only order drinks from me, and left another silver piece on the table each time. By then, some of the other girls were jealous and told the owner about him. She cornered me in my room and demanded the money. She said I could either return the "stolen" silver to her, or take my belongings and sleep on the street.

I was ready to hand over the silver when we heard a knock at the door.

Daisy stood there with a woman I had never seen before. She told me she was Mrs. Trilby, the housekeeper for the young man who had given me the silver pieces. "Mr. Simon Byrne," she said, "wishes to hire you as a maid." I refused, of course, but the housekeeper assured me that Byrne's intentions were honorable. I'd live in his house under her protection. And it was true that I'd not seen anything threatening in his behavior toward me. So, reluctantly, I agreed.

I packed my meager belongings and boarded Mr. Byrne's carriage, his housekeeper the only other passenger in attendance. The congested city quickly receded, replaced by gentle foothills and woods as we moved south. The mountains were an ever-present border to the west. We passed the time silently; Mrs. Trilby was rather stern, but nodded with approval when I mentioned our late father's vocation.

"Prayer will serve you well at Byrne House," she said. When I asked her to elaborate, she said that there was little else to do. "The master's home is a large estate, and isolated." Mrs. Trilby straightened the fingers of her gloves.

It is a tic of hers. "We have rules that must be observed. It is imperative that you stay in the house at all times. It is dangerous to go wandering."

As you may imagine, this sort of talk only increased my unease. I asked Mrs. Trilby to explain what dangers one could meet on Byrne's estate. But she would not say more.

After a half-day's journey, the road began to descend along a gradual slope. A tower of rough-hewn stone appeared, and then the shoulders of a great house isolated on a barren stretch of plain. Its windows winked in the sun like blinking eyes, watching my approach. I could not tell if it watched in welcome, with indifference, or with some darker intent. In fact, I felt an unsettling chill, as if I had tread upon a grave.

I laugh at myself, now that I know more about Byrne House. A building is defined by the people in it, and so far I have found them all to be kind enough. If perhaps a bit aloof.

For the first few days, I saw nothing of my new master. His house is enormous, one of the largest I've ever seen, yet much of the house is still under construction. The sound of hammering echoes even in my dreams. Mrs. Trilby and the butler together manage an entire staff of maids, servers, cooks and footmen. There are so many that I don't even know all their names yet. The house is three floors and rooms beyond my count—many of them closed to me on Mrs. Trilby's orders.

On my third day here, Mr. Byrne appeared while I was dusting a parlor.

I gasped to see him in this new context. His skin was paler than I'd remembered, the half-moons darker beneath his eyes. He seemed a man with many worries on his mind. But he was far handsomer, too. His expression was more open here, in his home, than it had been in the dining club.

"Miss Ada," he said, with utmost sincerity, "would you do me the pleasure of joining me for dinner?"

These were more words than he had ever spoken to me before.

We dined in his study, at a small table set before a roaring fire. Bookcases surrounded us, a comfort only my sister could truly appreciate—imagine, even more books than Father once had in his library!

Mr. Byrne told me about his work in the mine on his property here before he made his fortune. He told me about his family, too—parents who left him an orphan, and a brother who is distant in both body and spirit. I told him about our family, too. Our whole sad history. And not only this; we discussed literature, philosophy. We lost all track of time.

Oh Mary, how can I explain to you what I felt as that night progressed? The sense of friendship and connection, after so many months trapped inside of my own head?

Mr. Byrne understands what it means to begin again from nothing, to feel that a clean bed, a hearty meal and a bit of kindness are the greatest luxuries. And he has lofty ambitions: to build a community here united by a common sense of purpose. I humbly believe that Father would approve.

I see something in him, Mary, when I look into his eyes. Like a reflection of the best aspects of the city itself—vast and exhilarating, the promise of excitement, the triumph of dreams over circumstances.

There is darkness there too, of course. An undercurrent of pain, regret and longing. And if I dare say it—dangerous desires. It is sometimes enough to make me afraid, more of myself than of him. For who has not felt that same darkness deep within?

I suspect that I have much to learn, both about myself and Simon Byrne.

But now, finally, to the most pressing matter. Simon—as I call him now—asked me to marry him just a few hours ago, this very night. The proposal was certainly not expected, and I can hardly believe how rapidly my fortunes have changed.

I do care for him. And I cannot deny the attraction I feel. I think that I will say yes. But I need your advice, sister. In person, if it's possible.

Simon has asked me to invite you to visit us for as long as Christopher can get away. He would like to arrange the wedding to coincide with your visit, though I haven't yet decided on that. But I do look forward with greatest anticipation to the day you meet him. For I owe him everything; he has saved my life in every way.

I have no good reason for my lingering doubts. I am convinced that, once you are here to witness his kindness and affection, I will accept his offer without the slightest hesitation.

All my love,

Ada

2

OF ALL HER NANA'S BEDTIME STORIES, THE ONE about Ada Byrne was Evelyn's favorite.

Once there was a girl named Ada, who fell in love with two brothers: first Simon, a charismatic businessman, and then Walter, a young inventor. She nearly broke her heart trying to choose between them. But of course, Ada could marry only one. She made her choice, and devoted herself to her husband. Mind and body, heart and soul. Together, they lived in a grand house, almost a castle. They had a baby girl.

But Ada's husband was ambitious. He dreamed of creating something that would astonish the world. His small, precious family was not enough. His dreams turned to obsession. By the time Ada realized the danger, her husband had wandered too far.

Remember, Ada loved him. She vowed to save her husband. But when she tried to follow him, Ada got lost, too. And by the time her husband realized his terrible mistake, it was too late.

"Did Ada's true love ever find her?" Evelyn would ask, cuddling against her grandmother's side. She'd often ask about the other parts of the story, too, but Nana just as often refused to explain. This was the only question that Nana always, always answered.

And her Nana would say in her hoarse whisper, "He tried to bring Ada back. But her mind was gone, forever wandering. Because that was easier than facing the truth."

Evelyn didn't understand. She was only six years old, and truth was something you told. Not something you could see.

Her Nana would say, "Listen to me very carefully, Evelyn. If you face whatever you fear the most, no matter how bad, no matter how frightening, you'll take away its power. Then it can't hurt you. That's what I want you to always remember, even when it's dark. Promise me."

Evelyn nodded faithfully, believing every word.

Later, when she was years older, she'd realize how strange it was that Nana told a child such stories. She figured that Nana had wanted to teach her how to be brave. Nana must have seen some weakness inside of her, something that needed to be patched over and shored up. And it worked, or so Evelyn thought. She was never afraid.

But after Nana died, when the nightmares started, Evelyn learned the truth. It hadn't been her bravery but her grandmother's steadfast presence that kept the fearful things away. When you were all alone and dared to look into the dark, sometimes the bad things looked back.

Her mother was waiting for her when she got home. Viv stood at the base of the stairs, blocking Evelyn's way up to her room. "Where have you been?"

"I dunno. Outside." She brushed past her mom. "I'll order some dinner."

"I *saw* you. You were over at Byrne House talking to those police."

So she knew about that. Crap.

"Whatever happened over there, it has nothing to do with us," Viv said.

Evelyn looked at her mother. People always said that Viv was Evelyn's mirror image. Same oval face framed by blunt bangs, and sapphire eyes beneath prominent dark brows. Viv sometimes still got carded when she ordered wine at restaurants. *Oh, you must be sisters.* Evelyn didn't get it.

To be fair, she sometimes wore her mom's old clothes from the '90s; long-sleeved flannels and oversized denim overalls. But in her mom's face she saw only the permanent dark under-eye circles, the hard twist at the edge of Viv's mouth. Her mom had won a seat on the city council two years ago, on top of her already demanding position as a consulting school administrator. Now Viv spent her days trying to solve other people's problems since she couldn't solve her own daughter's. And as for Evelyn's dad, he was in Baltimore three weeks out of four these days, opening a new office for his company. No doubt his daughter rarely crossed his mind.

Evelyn went to the kitchen, scrolling through the bookmarked takeout menus on her phone. "Mr. Byrne died. But I guess you don't care."

"Why were *you* talking to the police?" Viv asked.

"I just thought I saw something."

Don't say it, she told herself. It would just end badly, like all the other times she'd opened her mouth even though she knew she shouldn't. *This was why Nana didn't like explaining herself. Somebody always got pissed off about it.*

"Why would you have seen something at Byrne House? You didn't go over there, did you? Evelyn, *look* at me."

Evelyn slammed her phone on the counter and spun around. She was still smarting from confusion and self-doubt, and her mother kept poking at the raw spot. Sometimes, no matter how hard she tried, she just couldn't stay quiet.

"I thought I saw Milo Foster in the mansion's tower window. And now, nobody can find him. But Ms. Foster doesn't think it's a big deal, so it's obviously *not important*. Okay?"

Viv stared at her daughter, breathing hard, visibly trying to stay calm. That muscle in her neck was twitching a warning. "We've talked about this so many times. Your obsession with that place isn't healthy. You know that."

Evelyn felt her defiance slip. She looked at the tile floor.

"I'm sure it was upsetting with all the activity, the police and the ambulances, over at that house today," her mom said in the kitchen. Years away from where Evelyn's mind had gone. Viv lifted Evelyn's chin with her fingers, made their eyes meet.

"Ev, we can't go down that road again."

Evelyn felt exposed. Her weakest, ugliest parts in full view. She pulled away. "It was *one time*. It's been almost three years, and I've been fine."

"The doctor said that it could happen again if we weren't careful."

She could still feel it. That horrifying helplessness, lying paralyzed in her bed. Hearing the voices cry and plead, so loud Evelyn felt the tearing in their throats. She'd woken up from a nightmare—*that* nightmare, the one about Ada Byrne—and suddenly she was surrounded with screams. Disembodied voices full of pain and despair.

They were coming from the mansion.

She couldn't explain it but she *knew*.

Their voices became hers, and she screamed them out until her parents came running and didn't stop until her vocal cords gave out.

A sleep hallucination. That's what the doctor called it. Brought on by the stress of freshman year and a childhood of too many scary bedtime stories told by Nana Stanton. Evelyn was supposed to relax more, avoid potential triggers. As if the problem was in her brain. As if it was *her fault*.

Back in the kitchen, Evelyn broke for the stairs. Hungry or not, she couldn't stand another moment of this.

"Evelyn. Stop."

She kept going. Turned the corner, started jogging up the stairs. The old wood protested.

"Stop. Right now. Hand over your phone."

She stopped mid-step. "You cannot be serious."

"I pay for it. That means I own it. Your phone is a stressor, and I'm removing it. Now give. Me. Your. Phone." Viv stood by the bottom step and held out her hand. "If you make me force this, then you won't get it back."

Screaming curse words inside her head, Evelyn stomped down the stairs and thrust out her phone. Viv palmed it without another word. She headed toward her office.

"I wasn't hallucinating!" Evelyn shouted after her.

She didn't just mean the sighting earlier that day of Milo in the tower.

3

SOMETIMES, WHEN EVELYN BOLTED AWAKE IN THE middle of the night, the whole world seemed like a hostile, unknowable place. A place where the sun might never rise again. But her rational mind knew that morning would come, and when it did, suddenly things would be right. No matter how frightened she was or how hard it was to breathe with darkness crawling over every inch of her, it would end. She just had to hang on.

Now, with Milo missing for two whole days, really *gone*, she wasn't so sure. The sun was sinking fast on another day, and this nightmare could just keep going on and on forever.

Evelyn was sitting on her front porch when Silvia Reyes's Tesla SUV pulled up. The two friends had a standing date on Sunday nights. Silvia slammed the driver's side door closed and ran up the walkway. She was still wearing her tan equestrian pants and tall boots; she must've come straight from riding practice. She gave Evelyn a fierce hug.

"This is all so crazy," Silvia said. "It doesn't even seem real."

Evelyn struggled not to cry. So much and yet so little had happened in the last couple of days. There were posters up all over the neighborhood: last spring's yearbook photo, black and white, a hesitant smile. *Have you seen this boy?* There were talks of a candlelight vigil, a fundraiser, unofficial search parties. Evelyn, for her part, had spent hours on the computer to no effect. She had never felt so powerless.

They sat down on the bench on Evelyn's porch. Usually on such nights, they'd share a peanut butter and banana smoothie and dish about ex-boyfriends, the latest school gossip or their most fervent hopes for after college. In other words, things that they couldn't tell anyone else.

Silvia took a brown paper bag from her purse and held it out. "I thought we needed something a little stronger than a smoothie tonight."

Inside the bag were a couple of Snickers bars and two cans of White Claw. Evelyn smiled, maybe her first in the last two days. She hardly ever drank, but tonight, she needed to escape a little.

"Assuming your mom's hard at work?"

Evelyn snorted. "You assume correctly." Silvia popped the tab and took a swig. She held it out. Evelyn took a sip and coughed when the spiked bubbles went down the wrong way. Silvia grinned and clapped her on the back. Evelyn laughed at herself. She almost felt like a human again.

"Thank you," she said. "I guess I needed this."

Silvia was a real-life version of a Disney princess: compassionate, a friend to all animals—horses especially—and of course gorgeous, complete with long, flowing black hair. Her perfection should've been infuriating, but Silvia was so sincere that you couldn't help loving her. Silvia was the kind of friend you could call in the middle of the night because you couldn't sleep. The kind who'd take you seriously when no one else did.

Things had been a little different ever since Silvia had started dating Jake Oshiro. She and Jake fought all the time, and sometimes Jake was all Silvia wanted to talk about. But Evelyn knew that her friend would be there whenever she really needed her. Like now.

"I can't understand why no one's come back to search the mansion again. There could be evidence or something."

Silvia tilted her head back and forth noncommittally. "But what could they find? Milo took his bike and got lost on the way home. That's what everybody's saying. Jake thinks so, too." Silvia took out her phone and thumbed through various screens, apparently verifying that Jake hadn't sent further updates.

"No offense, but Jake wasn't there. He doesn't know what I saw."

Viv still hadn't given back her phone, so Evelyn had been forced to use the family's ancient laptop, which Viv probably forgot existed. Using the grimy old keyboard, she'd told everybody she could think of about seeing Milo in the Byrne House tower. She'd posted to Tumblr and SnapChat; she'd used the "send us a tip" contact form on the police website. She'd even tried emailing local news. Nobody was listening.

Evelyn had the same feeling of dread every time she looked across the street at the mansion. She was positive that Byrne House had something to do with Milo's disappearance. The problem was that she couldn't explain *why*.

Silvia offered another sip of the hard seltzer to Evelyn. But Evelyn shook her head.

"I know what you must be feeling," Silvia said. "How can somebody be right here and then just vanish? You want an answer. We all do. Maybe you even blame yourself because you think you were the last to see him. But that doesn't mean..."

Silvia continued to speak, but Evelyn was distracted—a beat-up hatchback had just driven past Evelyn's house. It was Ms. Foster's car; Evelyn would know those "Coexist" bumper stickers anywhere.

Ms. Foster stopped in front of her house on the far edge of the park. A few seconds later, an unmarked police car followed. It parked at Ms. Foster's curb. Two detectives got out of the sedan—the same detectives Evelyn had seen at Byrne House on Saturday.

"Evelyn?" Silvia murmured. "Are you listening?"

"Those detectives are back." Evelyn's stomach twisted with both anxiety and eagerness. She knew their names now from a news article she'd read: Ruby Penn and Clifford Tyson.

Detective Penn had interviewed witnesses outside Byrne House and jotted notes in a small notebook. Detective Tyson was the big one, wearing the same blazer that stretched taut across his massive shoulders. They looked sweaty and tired.

The three of them started toward Ms. Foster's door.

Right away, Evelyn knew what she had to do. "We have to go over there," she said.

"*We?*"

Evelyn got up and headed for the street. Silvia ran, her footsteps loud as she caught up. "Ev, wait. Can we finish talking please? I didn't say what I need to say."

Silvia was probably worried about Jake. He was Milo's good friend, after all, so no doubt he was upset. But discussing Silvia's boyfriend would have to wait. Evelyn crossed the road and started to cut across the park, making a straight line toward the Foster residence.

Evelyn charged up the steps. Silvia was on her heels, still asking her to wait. But then Evelyn knocked on the frosted glass, and Ms. Foster's outline appeared.

The door cracked open, emitting a stream of cooler air. Ms. Foster peeked out. She was wearing her favorite yellow knit top with its ever-present ink stains on the sleeves. The top looked more rumpled than usual, and her eyes were bloodshot.

"Oh, hello girls. This isn't the best time. What can I do for you?"

"We saw you were back. Are you okay?" Instantly, Evelyn regretted it. What a stupid question. Nothing was okay.

"I—" Ms. Foster's voice cracked and she shook her head, blinking fast. All Evelyn could think to do was reach out. Ms. Foster returned the hug tightly.

Evelyn swallowed hard to keep back the tears. "Do the police have news?" she whispered.

"Nothing but questions," Ms. Foster said. "And God-awful paperwork. I'm trying to handle things for Milo's parents."

A throat cleared from farther in the room. "We just need another minute of your time, Ms. Foster," Detective Penn said. She'd taken off her jacket, and had the sleeves of her peach-colored shirt rolled up. Detective Tyson looked on from behind her, his eyes lasered onto Evelyn like she might be a suspect in any number of crimes. Both of them stood by Ms. Foster's dining table, which had papers spread out over its surface.

Evelyn stepped out of the entryway. This was her best shot at getting the police to listen. She had to take it, no matter how nervous Tyson made her. "Excuse me Detectives, but why haven't you searched Byrne House?" she asked. "I mean *really* searched, not just glanced around. The mansion was the last place Milo was seen."

Beside her, Silvia sighed and rubbed her forehead.

Detective Penn took a moment to straighten the papers on the table. "I can't give out specific information, but we're doing everything we can."

Evelyn tried to keep her tone respectful. If she could explain herself clearly, they'd have to listen. Right? "But I don't think you are. I've reported to several officers and online that I saw Milo in the tower window."

The detectives' expressions were completely blank. She might as well not be speaking at all. "Ms. Foster, Silvia, tell them," Evelyn said. "I've been saying this since Saturday."

Ms. Foster hesitated and glanced at the detectives. Silvia didn't even look up from the ground.

"Sweetie, no one denies Milo was there," Ms. Foster said. "Mrs. Lake remembers talking to him, and they think it was Milo who broke the window in the back door. But we simply don't know what happened after. His bike—"

"But what if his bike was stolen?"

"You're Evelyn Ashwood?" Detective Tyson suddenly asked. His voice was surprisingly quiet, and for some reason that made her even more nervous.

"Yes." *Is that good or bad?* she wondered.

Detective Tyson shot a gruff look at his partner. Penn gave a small shake of the head. Then she crossed the room toward Evelyn.

"We appreciate your information," Penn said. "But several officers did another search of Byrne House first thing this morning. My partner here led the team himself. They walked the entire house and the grounds. There was nothing to find."

This morning? She couldn't see how she'd slept through something so important. "But how can that be? Did you bring a forensics team?"

"It would be best if you wait outside," Detective Tyson said.

Panic and frustration bunched into a ball in Evelyn's throat. "No, I'm *not* waiting outside. Why can't you just search Byrne House again, but more carefully this time? If there's even the slightest chance it would help find Milo—"

"Look, Miss Ashwood." Detective Penn frowned. "You've caused enough distraction from our investigation already. Let us do our jobs without unnecessary interference." She turned away, walking back toward the dining table and its stack of papers.

Silvia opened Ms. Foster's door. "Ev," she whispered. "Let's just go."

"I'm not going anywhere," Evelyn said. "Something strange is going on, and it all comes back to Byrne House. What if Milo is *still in there?* He could be scared and hurt.

Why won't you listen?" It was like they knew something that she didn't. What were they hiding?

Ms. Foster walked across the room to the bathroom, holding her hand over her face. She was starting to sob. *Oh God*, Evelyn thought. *I only wanted to help.* Her whole body went rigid with fury and shame.

"Please close the door on your way out," Penn said without glancing up.

Silvia had gone out on the porch, and the detectives were making themselves busy. Ignoring her. Evelyn began backing toward the door. She recognized Detective Penn's jacket hanging in the entryway, the one that Penn must have taken off when she got inside.

The top edge of a notebook peeked out from an inner pocket.

The detectives were still turned away, talking quietly to one another. She couldn't possibly do it. They'd know it was her, or at least suspect. But while her mind was denying the very idea, Evelyn was already sliding the notebook free from Penn's jacket. Unable to breathe, she quickly turned and walked out the door.

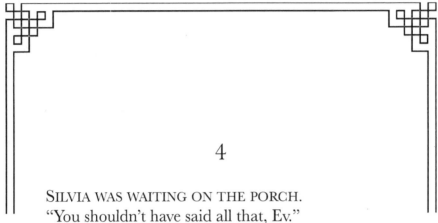

4

SILVIA WAS WAITING ON THE PORCH.

"You shouldn't have said all that, Ev."

"I didn't mean to upset Ms. Foster."

Evelyn tucked the notebook into her jeans pockets. Her hands were shaking. She could hardly believe what she'd just done. *What if Penn notices the notebook is gone? What if Tyson storms out here and arrests me?* But just as equally, she wanted desperately to know what the notebook said.

She started walking briskly back towards her house. Silvia kept up alongside. "I don't just mean upsetting her. I mean that stuff about '*it all comes back to Byrne House.*' Making it sound like a conspiracy."

"I can't believe you're on their side." She just wanted Milo to be okay. And the police weren't doing their jobs. Why couldn't Silvia see that? Why wasn't her supposed *best friend* listening to her?

"Their side?" Silvia's face flushed red. "Evelyn, not everything is about *you*."

Evelyn stopped walking. For a terrible, endless moment, she couldn't speak. "Excuse me?"

"That came out wrong." Silvia closed her eyes. "We're all scared for Milo. But you're...well, you're kind of weird about Byrne House," she said in a small voice. "As in, obsessed with that place. Light can play tricks. Anyone with your history, I mean, it's understandable."

Evelyn's throat had tightened like a fist was around her neck. "You think I would make this up?"

"This is what I wanted to tell you earlier; you need to let this Byrne House thing go. People are starting to talk." Silvia looked away. "I really am sorry."

Evelyn started down the street again. "It's fine," she said over her shoulder. Even though it really, really wasn't.

She'd confided in Silvia about the bad dreams, about the terrible episode three years ago, when she was fourteen. About her sense of connection to the mansion across the street, no matter how strange that might seem. And Silvia had always taken her seriously. At least, Evelyn had thought so. Maybe Silvia had never believed a single word.

Evelyn was so tired of nobody believing her, nobody listening. Not just the past few days, but her whole life. *You just imagined it, Evelyn. You need to let it go.* It made her feel weightless, like every dismissal took another little piece of her. Eventually she'd just float away.

"You're right," Evelyn forced herself to say. "I'll just…I don't know, put it out of my head or something." Stop thinking about it, right? Like that was so easy.

"Want to come to my house?" Silvia offered. "We could still have smoothies."

"I need to think for a while. I'd like to be alone."

After a few more awkward moments, Silvia got into her SUV and left.

Keeping her eyes on Ms. Foster's place, Evelyn pulled the notebook from her back pocket. Already she regretted taking it. What had she been thinking? She'd been so angry, so sure that the police were hiding something. Now, she realized how she'd look if anyone found out.

You're obsessed with that place, Silvia had said. *People are starting to talk.*

The street was quiet and dark. Night had settled in. She retreated farther into her yard, positioning her body behind the elm tree. "Screw it," she muttered to herself, and opened the notebook.

In the dim light, Penn's tight cursive blended together. Evelyn flipped to the last page with writing on it and held it up, trying to catch the moonlight. She saw the words, *Byrne House*. And further down the page, *Evil memories. I hear their screams. Coming from the dark.*

Evelyn's breath quickened. She flipped the pages again, trying to understand why Detective Penn would have written these words. But the shadows on the street were stretching out, shapes distorting. Her skin crawled with unseen eyes. She heard the voices in her memory. The screams.

"*Enough.*" She squeezed her eyes closed and pressed her fingers to her temples. "That's not helping."

She heard a noise. Her eyes jolted back open.

Over on the other side of the park, Detectives Penn and Tyson had come out of Ms. Foster's house. They stood on the porch—Tyson glancing around at the street, Penn fiddling with her jacket. Either they knew the notebook was gone already, or they'd know soon enough. She had to get rid of it before the detectives came asking questions.

But I was right, Evelyn thought. Her heart was thumping in her chest. *There's something written here about Byrne House. Something important.*

That meant she could be right about the rest of it, too.

Still watching the detectives on Ms. Foster's porch, Evelyn made her decision. Keeping to the shadows, she ran toward Byrne House.

5

SHE TURNED THE CORNER AND SLOWED DOWN, gasping. Headlights roved over the street. She ducked behind a hedge just as a car drove by. But she couldn't tell if it was the detectives.

As the quiet returned, Evelyn's heart began to calm. She was on the far side of Byrne House, beside the iron fence that bordered the mansion's overgrown gardens. She glanced up, eyes tracing the familiar rise and fall of its roofline. Only a few of the third floor windows were visible from this angle. Gray clouds winked in the glass. The house looked deserted. She was pretty sure that Daniella and Darren Byrne, the grown children of poor late Mr. Byrne, had not yet returned. *But you missed the police search this morning*, she thought. What else might she have missed?

Indecision made her chest ache. Now that she was here, she didn't know exactly what to do. She wasn't sure she could get into the grounds, much less inside the house itself. But there had to be a way.

A car idled somewhere nearby. The notebook was still in her hand; she stowed it for now in her pocket. She began to creep slowly along the fence, carefully watching the street between the gaps in the hedge. Headlights swung across the street, and again Evelyn bowed her head, hiding in the shadows near the fence. She lost her balance, and the metal bars of the fence rattled.

She was leaning against a padlocked gate. Between the iron slats of the fence, she could see a narrow path snaking into the gardens toward a stone structure. The stable. Her

Nana had told her that the building once housed the Byrnes' horses and carriage. For ages the stable had been closed up, abandoned.

But now, there was a light coming from one of the filthy stable windows.

She blinked her eyes and looked again. It was definitely there. A soft, flickering yellow light, like a candle.

Trembling, Evelyn reached between the bars and tugged on the padlock. It was fastened tight. She leaned in as close as she could, pressing her cheek to cold wrought-iron. A sickly-sweet smell enveloped her, like rotting flowers. The flame shuddered in the small square window.

She was absolutely sure. Someone was inside the stable.

Her first instinct was to run back to Ms. Foster's for help. Or maybe she could wave down the detectives in their car. But how stupid would that be? She still had the notebook. And you know what? She'd steal it again if it would somehow help Milo. She was very much *in this*. Neck deep. More than she even rationally understood. No way to turn back now.

She moved along the fence until she was sure she'd be out of sight of anyone on the street. Then she grasped one of the brick columns of the fence and scrambled up, scratching her palms. She cursed when the gauzy fabric of her blouse caught on something and ripped at the hem. It was vintage from the '70s, not the best uniform for climbing. But she'd never imagined she would end up here tonight.

She crouched on the small square atop the column. From the street, her form would be obscured by the trees growing near the fence. But at this vantage point, Evelyn could see farther into the Byrne House grounds than ever before.

Between the mansion and the stable, rows and rows of hedges formed a pattern. A maze. And in the middle stood a white sculpture of a woman, all alone in a sea of dark green.

Deja vu sunk all the way to her bones, turning her numb. It was the statue from her dream. *Ada Byrne,* Evelyn thought. One of the mansion's flower-shaped stained glass windows framed the sculpture's head from behind, like a brilliantly colored halo.

She couldn't really be thinking of going past this fence into the actual Byrne House grounds. Toward the maze and the cold white statue at its center.

Could she?

She didn't need her mother here, with her nagging reminders of *doctors* and *triggers* and *stress,* to know this was a terrible idea. She never should've come near Byrne House at all.

But Milo …

Evelyn leaned forward as far as she dared, balancing precariously on the fence column. She was studying the dirty stable window so intently, watching the dance of the tiny flame, that she didn't notice movement in the shadows of the garden. She didn't hear the quiet snapping of twigs or the crunching of long-dead leaves.

She didn't realize anyone else was there until a voice whispered, "Hey!"

Two eyes were looking up at her.

Evelyn jerked in surprise. She reared to one side, away from the face. But her knee slipped forward off her perch, and then she was falling into sharp branches. Falling into the nightmare-dark on the Byrne House side of the fence.

October 3, 1898
Byrne House

Dearest Mary,

I finally received your letter. It was misdirected by the post. I am sitting down straight away to write to you, in the hopes that this letter will reach you before your confinement begins. I, of course, am ecstatic that I will soon have another niece or nephew to dote upon. You expressed such kind regrets that your news will delay your visit, but I want you to forget about me and focus entirely on your task ahead. Besides, I have Simon's library, don't I? You know that I can sustain myself for quite some time on a meaty <u>Works of Shakespeare</u> or a <u>Collected Poems of Emily Dickinson</u>.

The only thing I lack is Simon's company. His business takes him into Denver frequently, sometimes for days. He often returns exhausted and troubled. Simon tells me that I don't understand these things, but I wish he could delegate some of his duties to assistants.

In truth, I am still endeavoring to banish my doubts about our impending marriage. Somehow, we have ceased to discuss whether I <u>will</u> marry him, and instead speak only of <u>when</u>. But unless his business slows down, I can hardly see how he will have time.

But I wish to be cheerful for you. We have something new to look forward to, as of late. The household is excitedly awaiting the arrival of Simon's brother, Walter. He has been traveling abroad, doing important medical and scientific research (Mrs. Trilby tells me—I've tried not to show Simon how nervous I am about his brother's return by asking too many questions). But as the co-owner of the estate, Walter calls Byrne House his home. I hope he will approve of me. I suspect that Simon shares my worry; he grows more nervous about Walter's return every time I see him.

I'll keep you and the baby in my prayers each night. I thank our Lord that you have a husband like Christopher to look after you. Otherwise, I promise I would have commandeered a wagon to be at your side, or even come on horseback if I had to. Please tell Christopher to write me as soon as there is any news.

Always yours,

Ada

October 20, 1898
Byrne House

Dear Mary,

I have not slept for forty-eight hours now, but I can't lie still long enough to fall asleep. So I'm turning to you. Since I can't sneak into your bed like I did so often when we were girls, I do so in writing. I hope that this letter to you will allow me to empty my head and rest, even for an hour or two.

Walter arrived two days ago. We'd been expecting him for over a week, but each day brought no word. Simon grew restless with waiting and insisted on going into town. One day later, a carriage arrived with Walter inside. He was in a terrible state, convulsing with fever. He couldn't even sit upright. The driver was afraid of catching disease. He kept a handkerchief pressed to his mouth and refused to stop to rest his horses.

The servants panicked. They managed to get Walter onto a couch in the drawing room, but scattered after that. I found Mrs. Trilby standing over him, trying to decide what to do. I only hesitated a moment. I thought of you, Mary, and how you cared for all of us after Mother was gone. I told the butler to carry Walter to one of the bedrooms right away, and to summon the doctor, while I prepared cold compresses for Walter's burning skin. I told the cook how to make the medicine like Mother showed us. For the first time, the servants looked at me with something like respect.

I sat by Walter day and night and gave him the medicine, one dose every hour and a half. The doctor finally arrived, pushed me aside, and ordered new medicines and treatments. But after he left to see to another case, I resumed my post.

Aside from the deep tan of his face and arms, Walter looks so much like Simon at first glance. But the more I watch him, the more I notice small contrasts. I've studied the lines of Walter's face and the curve of his mouth, both by sunlight and the candle. Walter has such a calm expression, so different from the sharp curl of Simon's upper lip. I hadn't realized until I had a subject for comparison, but Simon's smile has a certain harshness to it. I hope that doesn't sound ungrateful. I couldn't help but make the observation. Even in the throes of his fever, Walter's face is untouched by worry or doubt. I wish I could say as much for myself.

In the early hours of this morning, Walter turned to me and opened his eyes for a few minutes. He has the most unique emerald eyes, ringed with gold, without the blackish-blue depth of Simon's, but still very beautiful. Walter reached out and took my hand, as if he knew me. He said nothing, but slowly lifted my hand to his lips and kissed it. After a while he turned his head and closed his eyes again.

Luckily, the rest of the household was asleep. I wore my dressing gown and had my hair down on my shoulders, so I can't imagine what Mrs. Trilby would have said if she'd seen us.

I think Walter is past the worst of it, now. The only thing that worries me is why Simon has not come home.

I sent a servant to Denver on horseback immediately upon Walter's arrival. But the boy saw nothing of Simon in his Denver office, nor the nearby hotels and lounges that he frequents.

I don't know what to make of it. The message I sent was very clear about Walter's illness, and the danger he faced. Even the most pressing business should not have kept Simon from his brother's sick bed.

I feel exhaustion overcoming me. Thank you for indulging me, Mary.

I'll sleep now and hope that by this evening, Walter will be stronger and Simon will be at his side.

All my love,

Ada

6

Dust was in her nose and mouth, acrid as rusted metal, choking her. It was pitch black down here, damp and cold. A world that never felt the sun. Desperate voices grasped at her, sharp as claws digging into her skin, demanding to be heard. Help me, please, let me out of here! *She didn't know who the words belonged to, her or them. They wouldn't leave her alone.*

Evelyn's chest spasmed with coughs. She felt hands grab hold of her. There was somebody else here, telling her not to be afraid.

She opened her eyes, blinking away grit. "Where am I?" she whispered, but already it was coming back. She'd fallen. In the confusion, she'd thought she was underground. But that must have been panic screwing with her head.

She was inside the Byrne House fence. She hurt everywhere, especially her elbow and legs. Someone was kneeling over her. But her vision was still hazy.

"Milo?" she asked, and started coughing again. She kept expecting to taste dirt in her mouth, but nothing was there.

"Hey, it's okay. Take a second to breathe." He touched her cheek, brushing something away. His face leaned closer and came into the light.

He wasn't Milo.

A wide, jagged scar ran from his eyebrow down his cheek, twisting one corner of his upper lip into a permanent smirk.

Evelyn screamed, and the boy let go and sat back on his heels. "Who are you?" she demanded.

"Not so loud." He made a shushing motion, holding a finger to his mouth. "I was trying to *help* you. You were screaming. Which is a really bad idea, considering you're trespassing."

"And you aren't?" Whoever he was, she'd never seen him before. Clearly he didn't belong here any more than she did. Evelyn sat up, scooting a few inches away from him. Her blouse had slipped off her shoulder, so she put it to rights.

He chewed at the scarred part of his lip. The rest of him was coming into focus as her eyes adjusted. Around her age, dark brown hair in need of a cut. Large eyes, long nose.

"You're looking for the guy who's missing?" he asked. "Milo Foster?"

"How do you know that?"

He smirked and his scar accentuated the sarcasm. "Well you *did* say his name five seconds ago."

That was a fair point. But he hadn't answered her question. "What are you doing here?"

"Can't I be here for the same reason you are? I'm looking for Milo."

"And why should I believe that?" Evelyn got up, ignoring the pain, and brushed herself off. "I should call the cops on you right now. In fact, I will." She stuck a hand into her pocket, remembering only then that her mom still had her phone.

He laughed and stood. He was tall, but he slouched like he was trying not to be. "If I get in trouble, then so do you."

More than you know, she thought, feeling the lump of the notebook in her pocket where her phone should be. "Do you even know Milo?"

"I heard about what happened. I'm guessing he's a friend of yours?"

"Yeah, he is," she said. "I was the last person to see him before he disappeared. I still don't get why *you're* here."

"Wait. You're her. You saw Milo in the tower." He peered at her more closely. Recognition lit up his eyes. "You're *Evelyn*."

A tingle ran over her body. He'd said "Evelyn" like it was more than just a stranger's name.

He took a step toward her, eyes intense. "I'm Alex Evans."

Alex reached out like he was about to touch her. But then he stopped. He seemed to be watching her reaction, as if his name was supposed to mean something to her.

"Do I know you?" Evelyn asked. She had no memory of anyone named Alex Evans. Or anyone with that scar.

He tilted his head. "*Do* you?"

"Stop that. Stop answering my question with another question."

He just continued to fix her with that same purposeful look. Like he was trying to beam thoughts into her brain. She shook her head to clear it. "I don't know you," she insisted. "Tell me why you're here."

Alex held up his hands, surrendering. "I'm really here looking for Milo. I was just checking out that old shed—stable, whatever—when you climbed the fence and perched up there like some ninja Hello Kitty. Cute, but not exactly subtle."

She cringed. So much for being sneaky and unobserved. "So you're the one who lit the candle in there?"

Alex stuck his hands in his pockets, and screwed up his lips. "No, I saw that too. The doors are padlocked, windows painted shut. I can't explain it. Look, if we're here for the same reason, then we might as well stick together. You shouldn't be wandering around here alone."

She shifted her weight. Whoever Alex Evans really was, he didn't seem like an immediate threat.

"Fine, we'll stick together," Evelyn said. "But you go first."

When he walked, Alex limped every time he stepped onto his left foot. The same side as his scar. She took a sidelong glance at him and found Alex looking right back.

Just as he'd said, the stable door was locked tight. The flame still wavered in one of the windows, coming from an antique oil lamp set into the wall. All she could see in the room was a fossilized bale of hay, years-worth of dust, and narrow wooden stalls. There was no sign of anyone in the room or any clue as to how they could've gotten in. Or better yet, *why*. All the other windows were dark, too dirty to see much inside.

"Who'd want to light an oil lamp in an old stable?" she asked. "Trying to start a fire?" She'd been talking to herself, but Alex answered.

"So we're dealing with the world's worst arsonist?"

She allowed a small smile. "Fine, what's your theory?"

"About the lamp? Or about what happened to Milo Foster?"

Alex held her gaze, and she felt a thrill of excitement. Right now, despite everything, she wasn't afraid. She wondered if she should be.

"Both."

Alex leaned his back against the stone wall of the stable. "I don't know who lit the lamp, or why. I'm adding that to my long list of 'weird shit that doesn't make sense about Byrne House.'"

She opened her mouth, but Alex held up a hand. "Hold on, I'll never finish if you keep asking more questions. So—Milo. Maybe he took his bike and disappeared on his way home like the police say he did. But maybe they're wrong."

"Exactly! He could still be in the mansion."

He looked doubtful. "Inside? I guess that's possible. But here's my theory. Milo did leave the mansion." Alex dropped his voice to a whisper. "But he never made it off the Byrne House grounds."

"You mean, he's out *here*?" Evelyn wrapped her arms around herself. The wind was picking up, turning the night cold. "Why would you think that?"

Alex looked at her for a long, drawn-out moment. Then he shrugged. "Because I know things about this place," he said. "I know Byrne House. And I'm pretty sure you do, too."

"What the hell is that supposed to mean?"

Alex rolled his neck. He was trying to think of a way out of answering, she just knew it. "And *do not* answer with a question," she added. "You can't say something like that and not explain."

He pushed off the stone wall. "Alright, you want to do this? Then let's do this." He held up his flashlight, searching. "I can only explain by showing you. Then maybe—well, come on. It's this way."

He took off down the path, and Evelyn could only follow. They skirted around the hedge maze—she averted her eyes from Ada's statute—and headed deeper into the gardens, where the tallest trees grew. The sensations of her old nightmare began to close around her like rising water.

Evelyn's feet stopped moving. *I can't*, she thought. She was hyperventilating. *I can't.*

Alex retraced his steps back to her. "You okay?"

Evelyn didn't get the chance to respond.

A flashlight beam swept over the gardens. "Stop right there. Hands on your heads." A police officer was standing on the other side of the maze, near the garage. His badge glinted gold in the moonlight.

Instead of obeying, Alex turned to face her. "You have to come with me."

No, no, no. This couldn't be happening. She'd be grounded for a month. Grounded till college. Then she remembered the lump in her pocket, and realized it might get so much worse. Detective Penn's notebook. Oh my God, they were going to find the notebook.

"Move away from each other, hands where we can see them," another officer shouted.

"Come *on*." Alex switched off his flashlight, grabbed her arm and ran. Evelyn tripped over her feet and nearly went sprawling before she regained her balance. Alex was pulling her into the thick brush, away from the paths and the officers. Branches smacked into Evelyn's face and scratched her bare legs. There was shouting behind them. Alex changed direction, ducking through an old stone archway, looked back and forth briefly, then darted again.

Finally he pulled her into the shadows. The voices and footsteps of the police had faded. She could barely see.

Evelyn was panting, trying to catch her breath. "Where are we?"

"Back corner of the property," Alex whispered to her, moving her hand until she touched stone. "I'm going to boost you over."

"But what if they're waiting on the street? What if they see me?"

"They won't," he said. She saw a faint glint in the darkness as he smiled. "They'll be too busy with me."

"With *you*? What are you going to do?"

He didn't answer. Instead he wrapped his arms around her hips and lifted her upwards. She clamored onto the top of the wall and crouched there. She was still concealed by a couple of tall trees. She looked back down at him. His face was turned up to her, eyes bright. He didn't look scared at all, not like she felt. He actually looked like he was having *fun*.

Who are you? she wanted to ask. *Why are you protecting me?*

"Don't worry about me," he said. "Just get out of here."

Whoever he was, he could fend for himself. She took his advice and left him behind.

She was all the way home, all the way in her bedroom with the door locked behind her, when she realized it—the notebook wasn't in her pocket anymore. Somewhere, she'd dropped it.

7

Evelyn sat up in bed. She'd heard a noise. Like tapping on her window.

Her heart was racing. The clock on her desk read *2:17 a.m.* She was disoriented—she'd been having the dream. The one about Ada Byrne.

She hadn't had that dream in years.

Her bedside lamp was still on. After all that happened last night, she'd been afraid to sleep in the dark. But the dream had come anyway, for the first time since freshman year. The dream of seeing Ada's statue in the Byrne House gardens and then disappearing into nothingness.

Tap, tap, tap. There it was again. Somebody was out there.

The curtains were open, the glass a slick mirror of her own frightened face. If someone really was out there, they could see straight in. Evelyn reached for the light switch and flicked it down. She plunged into darkness and held back a scream. Then blood rushed to her face.

"You are kidding me," she whispered.

Alex Evans was sitting on the roof of the porch, looking in at her with an amused expression.

After getting back home last night, she'd brooded over everything that had happened on the Byrne House grounds: seeing the light in the stable; meeting Alex; running from the police. Losing the notebook.

She'd watched from her bedroom window, utterly powerless, as the police had led Alex out of the gardens in handcuffs.

The police kept Alex on the front lawn for about an hour, until Daniella Byrne and another man—Evelyn had never seen him before—showed up. Then, incredibly, the police had let Alex go. The mystery man yelled at Alex for a while, and then Daniella gave Alex a hug. Daniella Byrne had actually *hugged* him. Like they were family or old friends. Then Evelyn had watched Alex get into the car with Daniella Byrne and the angry guy and drive away.

And now, here he was. Out on her roof.

Evelyn ran to the window and opened it a crack. Crisp night air flowed into her room, sweet with lilac and grass. "Are you insane?" she whispered. "What are you doing up there?"

Alex put a hand to his chest, playing at being offended. "After I came all this way to return your property?" He pulled Detective Penn's notebook from his jeans pocket.

"How did you get that?" she demanded.

She'd panicked last night after she got home, when she realized the notebook was gone. She'd been vaguely worried about fingerprints and that sort of thing, in case the police found it on the Byrne House grounds. But at least if Penn came looking for her notebook, then there was nothing in Evelyn's house to find.

"You dropped it when you climbed over the fence," Alex said. "Though I guess it's not really *your* property."

Evelyn made a disgruntled sound in her throat. "You looked at it."

Alex wiggled the notebook in front of the glass.

She pushed up the window the rest of the way and grabbed for the notebook. Alex held it out of her reach. She lost her balance, falling forward. She ended up halfway out the window, hands braced against Alex's shoulders, their noses almost touching. Alex smiled like he was trying not to laugh.

Maybe it was the dim glow from the streetlight, but his scar looked different up close. A smooth, soft curve along his cheek. Evelyn had an overpowering urge to touch it. To know the story behind it.

"How did you get your scar?" she asked, voice barely audible.

"I ... fell."

Alex's shoulders moved as he breathed, but the rest of him was still. Watching her. She pushed herself back into her room, her entire body humming.

I don't know him, she kept thinking, but in her head it sounded like a question. She doubted she'd forget someone like him and not just because of the scar. Alex was lean and long-limbed, with a nose that was a little too large, and eyes slightly too far apart. But all together, the features worked better than they should. Handsome wasn't exactly the right word. *Compelling.*

The silence between them stretched. Finally, Alex held out the book. "I only glanced at it. I thought since you, uh, appropriated it, you should be the first to read it. You've got skills. I'm impressed."

Evelyn took the notebook and set it on her desk. She'd have to find a good place to stash it. "How'd you hide it from the police?"

"You have your secrets, I have mine." Alex moved his hands in a magician-like flourish, and suddenly he was holding her notebook again. He gave it back. This time Evelyn tossed the book behind her, onto the bed. She'd study it after he was gone. She wasn't sure yet how much she should share with this boy.

"I told the officers about the light in the stable," Alex said. "Convinced them to take another look around."

"And they didn't see any sign of Milo," Evelyn said. It wasn't a question because she could already read the answer in Alex's expression.

He shook his head. "But that doesn't mean there's nothing to find." Alex's eyes grew intent. He inclined his head and lifted his eyebrows, like he was inviting her to come outside.

"You want me to go with you to Byrne House? *Now?*"

He shrugged one shoulder. "Only if you're quieter this time. It was one of the neighbors who called the cops on us before."

She almost laughed. But too many things didn't make sense.

"How do you know Daniella Byrne?" she asked.

"She's a distant cousin. *Very* distant. I swear it's not that interesting." Alex rolled his eyes. "Technically my brother William and I own half of Byrne House. Daniella and Darren own the other half. It's this whole complicated family history thing. William and I live in New York; we just got to town yesterday. To sort out the estate. That's when I heard about Milo going missing."

A branch of the Byrne family she'd never heard about. That seemed surprising after an entire summer of research at Ms. Foster's. "Why didn't you tell me this last night, when we met?"

"I don't know," Alex said softly.

"Why did you go to Byrne House looking for Milo?"

"Because of you. I mean, I read online that someone—*you*—saw him there. And then he disappeared. I wanted to help." He held out his hands, as if asking, *What more do you want from me?*

Then he closed his eyes and sighed. "Look, I'll go by myself if you don't come with me. I was serious when I said I wanted to find Milo. But there's more to it than Milo Foster. A lot more."

She did want to go with him. Just take off into the night, following wherever he would lead. And that scared her.

"Thank you for bringing me the notebook. You should go now. Please."

"Evelyn—"

She shut her window and turned her back. She was breathing so fast and shallow she was almost hyperventilating. *I don't know him.* But some part of her responded to him as if she *did* know him. And that wasn't possible.

Evelyn switched on her desk lamp and opened Detective Penn's notebook. She flipped hastily through the pages, trying to force Alex out of her mind. She'd already seen the words on the last page, but now she flipped back through, trying to find the first mention of the name Byrne. She turned the pages slowly, deciphering Detective Penn's tight scrawl.

Writing on the walls of the second floor hallway. Suicide note? Penn had asked at the top of a page. *But cause of death unclear. ME says could be natural.* And then, further down, *Call lab tomorrow.*

Then the detective had jotted down what Reginald Byrne had written, over and over: *Leave this house. Evil memories here. I see them. Hear their screams, coming from the dark.*

I won't let them take me.

Evelyn snapped the notebook shut.

Night had transformed her room into an unfamiliar place, the shapes all out of proportion. The tangle of linens atop her bed made her think of Mr. Byrne's body under the sheet. There was no way she could sleep tonight. She regretted sending Alex away. Now she was all alone in the dark, terrified of what might be waiting.

She went to the window. Alex was standing on the sidewalk, staring over at the mansion. No matter how confused she felt about him, Alex was the only person who seemed to share her suspicions about Byrne House. He'd never even met her before last night, and yet he'd believed her when nobody else did. That had to count for something. Right now, she needed an ally.

Evelyn opened her window and climbed out into the night.

Carefully, she worked her way down the elm tree in her front yard and jumped to the grass. Alex ran over to meet her. "The notebook," she began. "I read it."

Alex hushed her. "There's someone in the park," he whispered. "See?"

Evelyn turned to look. A slender, male silhouette stood between the trees. His shoulders were hunched, and he seemed to sway in place. Then he took a lurching step toward them, then another. He reached the sidewalk and fell into the street.

Alex and Evelyn ran towards the figure. Alex turned him over and light brown hair slipped across the person's unconscious face. Evelyn brushed the hair away from his eyes and gasped.

"It's him." His face was scraped up, and she almost hadn't recognized him without his glasses. But she knew the curve of his cheekbones and the shape of his lips.

It was Milo Foster.

October 28, 1898
Byrne House

My dearest Mary,

I received Christopher's letter. Please thank him for his kind words. I'm surprised that the baby hasn't come yet, at least as of the date Christopher wrote. But perhaps you are already holding the little dear as I write these words. I haven't forgotten you in my prayers.

Simon is still nowhere to be found. His friends and associates in Denver claim no knowledge of where he is. Or, as I suspect, they know but have no intention of revealing his whereabouts. I have no firm reason to suspect Simon or his friends, but certain details surfaced in the past few days that give me pause. First, the butler let slip that Simon packed half his belongings from his room before he left for town. Second, he left the estate's accounts in disarray before he left. Walter was shocked when he saw the books. Several lines of credit had been drawn, and Walter still cannot tell where the money went.

I should have told you before that Walter is doing very well. He recovered quickly from his illness. After my last letter, I continued to sit by his bedside for a few more days, until I realized that he spent far more time watching me than resting. Now I see him at meals, and when he feels strong he joins me outside for a walk on the grounds. The gardeners are busy planting trees and plants of every description on the bare grasslands surrounding the house.

Walter and I spend the evenings in the library. Each night Walter tells me more about his travels and the new scientific work he's undertaken since returning. He loves to show me different rock and mineral specimens that he says came from his own mine beneath the house. Each night he chronicles his discoveries in his journal. I love to watch him sitting at his desk in the corner, concentrating. He will sometimes write for an hour without a single pause. I would expect the effort to completely exhaust him, but he seems invigorated by it.

Walter also told me his plans for the Byrne estate. He showed me the blueprints for the mansion, and described all his improvements on the original architect's design. Work on the house and grounds has tripled since his arrival here. His lawyer and friend, Mr. Henry Stanton, also arrived from Denver yesterday to help put the affairs of the estate in order. His wife Rebecca and their children will join him shortly. I very much look forward to their companionship. I asked Mr. Stanton discretely whether he'd had any news of Simon in Denver. But he's heard nothing.

I am so ashamed, Mary, of what I feel now. Just weeks ago, I believed myself in love with Simon. I thought I might become his wife. But now I wonder if I have any ability to judge a man's character. Could it be possible that I was so grateful to Simon for taking me away from that awful boarding house that I chose not to look too closely at my savior?

I dread what will happen if Simon never returns. Where will I go, after having lived unmarried under the same roof with Simon and now Walter? For no one in this household still believes me a maid. Their judgments and assumptions are clear in their glances. But the thought of Simon coming back is almost worse. My love for him is decaying with each passing day. No, that isn't right. It was never real at all. The illusion is simply evaporating away.

Ada

8

The next thirty-six hours were a blur of waiting rooms, questions, exhaustion and elation. But no answers.

After finding Milo Monday night, they sped him to the ER. Alex drove because Ms. Foster couldn't stop crying, and Evelyn navigated from shotgun. Time seemed to stop while she sat in the waiting room, holding Ms. Foster's hand while Alex tried to wheedle news from the nurses. The next thing she knew, the waiting room was a mob of people—the rest of Milo's family, his classmates, all the neighbors from around Walter Park, even Detectives Penn and Tyson.

"Evvy, is it true?" Viv asked when she rushed through the glass doors. Ms. Foster had made Evelyn call her mother on their way to the hospital. But Ev had already planned out what she'd say.

"Milo was in the park. I saw him from my window."

"And you didn't come downstairs to wake me?"

"I just...went after him. I wasn't thinking." Evelyn's eyes met Alex's across the waiting room. The Byrne siblings and Alex's brother—William—had arrived, too. But she figured that this wasn't the best moment to introduce her mother to Alex.

Viv turned around, following Evelyn's gaze. When she turned back, her expression seemed oddly frozen. As if seeing the Byrne family at such a close distance was too much for her. Presumably she recognized Daniella and Darren Byrne. Evelyn wondered if Viv had ever met Alex and William Evans or their parents.

But before Evelyn could question her mother, Viv asked, "Do you know that boy?"

Evelyn could hear the familiar tension in her mom's voice—that slight waiver that signaled danger ahead.

"The one with the scar?" Viv added, nearly whispering.

"Um, I don't think so," Evelyn said. "Should I?"

Viv cast another glance over her shoulder. Alex sank into a chair, hunching like he knew he was being examined and wanted to escape. Evelyn didn't blame him.

"I want you to stay away from him," Viv said. "Away from all of them."

"*That's* what you're concerned about right now?"

Evelyn knew who her mom meant by "them." The Byrnes. *I'm not the one with the obsession*, she thought. Viv had zeroed in on Alex because he was attractive and interesting and also had something to do with the Byrne family, and Viv was pathologically overprotective. Despite all her protests, maybe she *wanted* Evelyn to still be that scared little girl, cowering under her blankets and calling for her parents. Viv wanted to matter.

"Whatever," Evelyn murmured. She paced the room for a while, and then went over to sit with Silvia, who'd just arrived with her boyfriend Jake in tow. Jake was too busy on his phone to even say hello.

By morning, the waiting area was still full, but quiet and tense. Milo's family had been ushered into some other room. Silvia dozed in the chair beside Evelyn.

"I wish they'd just tell us already."

It was Jake who'd spoken. He was sitting on Silvia's other side. Like Evelyn, he hadn't slept a single moment. Instead, he'd been having an extended staring contest with the wall. Though he'd taken a bathroom break to re-spike his hair. Evelyn was surprised he'd said anything at all; without Silvia, she and Jake rarely had much to say to one another. Theirs was a mutual, if quiet, loathing.

"Tell us what?" she asked.

"What the hell happened so we can get out of here. Not like Milo cares if any of us is sitting here, waiting. It's not doing him any good. And I've got things to do."

Quite the charmer, this one. Evelyn had never been able to understand Silvia's attraction to him. "Then why don't you leave?" she asked.

"Can I?" Jake glanced down at Silvia. He stayed put.

Finally a young doctor came out, looking exhausted. "I've been given permission to tell you," she said. "Milo Foster is awake."

They all cheered and cried. Slowly, more information trickled out. Milo was severely dehydrated, with some bruises and cuts that needed treatment, but nothing too serious. Evelyn asked to see him but was refused—by both her mom and the hospital staff. Milo would spend some time secluded with his family getting much needed rest.

By the time Evelyn looked around the waiting room for Alex again, he and his family had gone. But when she got home, Evelyn found a scrap of paper folded up in her shirt pocket. *Meet me tomorrow morning in Walter Park, 10:00AM*, the note said.

The note wasn't signed. But Evelyn knew it was from Alex.

She found Alex sitting at the base of the statue of Walter Byrne. The stone figure was small and thin, almost frail. Walter held a large open text, and he bent over the book as if it weighed him down. Sitting beneath the statue, Alex looked equally pensive, chin resting on his hands. He stood when he saw her, but his worried expression remained.

"Thanks for the note," she said.

Alex nodded. "I didn't know how to reach you otherwise. Without climbing up to your window again, anyway."

Actually, she didn't think she would have minded, as long as her mom continued to be a heavy sleeper. But Alex didn't need to know that.

"How's Milo doing?" Alex asked.

"Stayed overnight again at the hospital, and he's supposed to head home today. But Ms. Foster said he has no memory of what happened to him. The doctors aren't sure he ever will."

Neither of them said anything for a little while. They both sat down beneath the statue and watched as the park filled up with kids. She could smell the citrusy shampoo on Alex's still-damp hair. It was less than a month until school would start. Evelyn wondered where Alex went to school. She didn't even know where he lived or what kinds of books and movies he liked. But if she asked all these questions, Alex would probably just stare meaningfully at her. As if she was already supposed to know the answers.

She got up and twirled her hair into a knot. She started to pace in front of the statue. Her skirt swished around her legs—a sixties, Bohemian kind of style, though only a modern throwback instead of a vintage original.

"I think we should team up," Alex said in a rush, like he'd been holding the words in. "Find out what really happened to Milo."

She stopped walking and looked at him. "Why us?"

He laughed sheepishly. "Because I'm new in town, and I need a hobby? Because you're a pretty girl and I'm a guy who wants an excuse to hang out with you?"

She felt blood rushing to her cheeks and a not unpleasurable tightness in her chest, though she knew he was only trying to distract her. Given what she'd seen of him so far, this was not a boy who lacked confidence.

"Why *us*?" she asked again.

His grin slid away. "Because I'm starting to think that we might be the only people who can," he said.

She watched Alex closely, wishing she could see inside that head of his.

The detectives had asked Evelyn surprisingly few questions at the ER. They'd mostly seemed annoyed that, once again, Evelyn was tangentially involved with their case. The detectives probably wanted to find a meaningless explanation for Milo's missing days so they could move on to something else. *Milo fell off his bike*, they could say. *He hit his head...*

It sounded reasonable enough, didn't it? Lots of people would accept it, especially when most of the other possibilities were *scary* and *disturbing* and *wrong*. Castle Heights would breathe a sigh of relief and move on. But Evelyn wasn't sure that she could. Not anymore.

"You still think Milo's disappearance is somehow tied to Byrne House, right?" she said. "Just like me."

Alex nodded slowly. "Right."

It was exactly what she wanted to hear. Why did she still feel so uneasy?

"You told me that you know things about Byrne House," she said. "Okay, then. Take me back to the gardens and show me what you claimed I 'need' to see."

Alex got up so they were face to face. "I don't think that's a good idea. Daniella and Darren are going to start moving their things over from the hotel soon. And my brother is already pissed at me about the trouble I caused with the police." Alex looked up at the trees, like he was searching for another excuse to add to the list.

Evelyn stared at him in disbelief. A couple of nights ago, Alex had sat outside her bedroom window and asked her to come with him. *It's not just about Milo Foster*, he'd said. *There's a lot more...*

"Alex, you know something important about Byrne House. I know you do. Please, tell me the truth."

A pained look crossed his face. Alex's eyes met hers, trying to say something that she couldn't understand. She'd never been that good at reading people, and Alex was a tougher case than most. "Alex. *Please.*"

He debated another moment or two. "They're just weird memories," he said at last. "Things I probably just dreamed. But …"

"But?"

He exhaled slowly and closed his eyes. "But sometimes I'm not so sure."

Evelyn waited. The sun was inching its way across the sky. A bead of sweat trickled down her chest.

"I came to Byrne House when I was a little kid for my great-grandma Clara's funeral." Alex's eyes moved to hers again. He was hesitating. She nodded for him to keep going.

A breeze ruffled Alex's hair across his forehead. "I've always had strange memories of that trip. Dreams that don't exactly seem like just dreams. Will and my mom never wanted to hear it, said it was my imagination. My dad was the only person who'd listen to me." Alex opened his hands and looked down at his palms. "My dad always believed there's more to the world than we know. It's like sleight of hand. Just because you don't see something doesn't mean it's not there."

"You had dreams?" Evelyn prompted. The word echoed in her head. *Dreams. Dreams.*

"Yes and no." Alex held her gaze intently. His posture relaxed as he spoke. "After Clara's funeral, I looked around the mansion a little bit. I went down in the basement but there wasn't much there. Storage rooms, locked doors. So I went outside to the gardens. There's this hedge maze back there. Did you see it the other night? And a statue in the middle. Kind of like this one of Walter, but a woman."

"Yes." She sounded breathless. "I know. The statue of Ada." *Like my dream,* she thought. *My nightmare.*

"I remember wandering in the gardens," Alex continued. "That happened, but I've also dreamed about it. And in the dream version, I get lost."

Her mouth was dry when she spoke. "I dream of the maze, too. I dreamed of it just last night."

Alex's eyebrows shot up. "You did?"

He waited for her to say more, but she couldn't. She was remembering. Seeing images that she'd never be able to forget.

He went on. But he spoke slowly now, hesitating with each word. "Everything gets dark, like I'm… underground."

She sucked in a ragged breath. *The tower-well.*

The dream was always the same. Evelyn would be standing in the middle of a forest with the steep roof of Byrne House looming above. A dense maze of trees. A light flickered between the branches, coming from the house. The tower was there too, but this dream-version was inverted. A bottomless well. That's where she always ended up, no matter how carefully she stepped. Down, down, into the dark.

How was it possible that they'd dreamed the same thing?

Alex looked worried. "Hey. Are you alright?"

"I'm fine." She glanced past him at the mansion. The answer had already come to her, just as soon as she'd asked it—they'd had the same dream because of Byrne House. *The mansion had made them dream it.*

"Tell me the rest," she insisted.

Alex cleared his throat and continued. "In my dream I'm feeling my way, and my hands brush against something cold. Metal. I find a handle. It's a door. But it won't open. It's a locked metal door, with a triangular keyhole. I know I've seen it before. And since I've been back here in Castle Heights, I remember where. The door in my dream is exactly like a locked door I saw in the Byrne House basement when I was six years old. That day after the funeral."

Chills spread across Evelyn's skin. *A metal door with a triangular keyhole.* She'd seen one too, just like Alex described. But it hadn't been at Byrne House.

Alex lifted his hand, and Evelyn thought he might put his arm around her. But he scratched at his scar instead.

"Anyway, after I touch the metal door, the picture in my head—dream, whatever—it goes blank. Maybe it's something that really happened to me. Or maybe it's not. Either way, I've always wanted to know what it means. I guess that's what I was trying to say the other night. There's more to Byrne House than what you can see on the surface."

That much, she already knew. She remembered the screams, the pleading she'd heard coming from the mansion that night when she was fourteen. The night of her supposed "sleep hallucination." She'd been dreaming of Ada Byrne's statue and the inverted tower right before that, yes. But then she woke up. Those voices had been *real*.

She decided to take a chance.

"What if Byrne House is trying to tell us something?" she asked.

She waited for the laughter. The rejection. But it didn't come.

"Let's say that's true. How do we find out what it's saying?"

She wasn't sure. But she knew a good place to start.

"Come on," she said. "There's some things I need to show *you*."

9

THE BASEMENT WAS DARK. "WAIT HERE," SHE told Alex, and began to feel her way across the room.

The basement walls were slightly bumpy under Evelyn's palms. She searched out the old oil lamp with her fingers. It was mounted into the plaster of one wall, the only antique light fixture left in the whole house.

Evelyn felt the jut of metal she'd been looking for. "There you are," she whispered. "Be good, now." Sometimes the lamp was fussy and didn't want to light. But today, it behaved. The oil-soaked wick ignited in the flame of her lighter, and Evelyn fiddled with the valve until a soft glow fell over the basement.

She felt warmth behind her and knew Alex was standing there, just a couple of feet away. It was strange to have him here, in this place where she was almost always alone. Just to fill the silence, she said, "Sometimes I come down here when I can't sleep." Only on those nights that insomnia took up residence in her brain, rifling through her darkest thoughts.

"Does that help?" Alex asked, eying the cobwebs hanging from the beams.

"You'd be surprised."

Evelyn took a moment to inhale the familiar scents of oil and earth. Just being down here, she felt calmer than she had in days. Stacks of dusty boxes sat next to her dad's forgotten collection of Colorado Rockies memorabilia and her grandpa's old tool chest. The light reached the exposed brick wall at the back corner of the room, marking the edges of her nighttime universe.

Evelyn's home had been built in the 1890s, a decade after Byrne House went under construction. But where the mansion was stained glass and meandering gray stone curves, the outside of the Ashwoods' home was simple lines and rust-red brick. Evelyn's living room featured the same ornate fireplace and cherry-stained wood floors as when Viv grew up here, when her last name had been Stanton, not Ashwood. And it had been the same for Nana before her. The kitchen and bathrooms were newly renovated, as well as most of the second floor. Viv had even purged several irreplaceable antiques before Evelyn could stop her. But the historic touches remained here and there, despite Viv's efforts to modernize.

There were plenty of recent transplants in Castle Heights, of course—like Ms. Foster, who'd only lived here for the short period of thirty years or so—but a surprising number of families had been here for generations. Like Silvia; her ancestors had emigrated from southern Mexico before Colorado was even a state, and her great, great-grandparents had moved into Castle Heights at the same time as Evelyn's.

And Alex, too—he was linked to Byrne House by his family. And possibly in ways that she didn't yet fully understand.

"How much do you know about how Castle Heights began?" she asked Alex.

Alex shrugged. "Not much."

"Some of it I learned in school. Then there are the stories my Nana used to tell me." She began to recount what she knew.

Like Evelyn, every child who'd grown up in the neighborhood knew the basic story. Castle Heights had started its life over 130 years before as a mining claim filed by Walter H. Byrne. Walter had meant the name "Castle

Heights" ironically. It was just a few square miles of flat land south of Denver that no one else wanted. Which was perfect for Byrne because he had little of his small inheritance left to pay for it. He'd lost his share to failed business ventures.

But fortune smiled upon Walter in his new home. He found valuable minerals on the land, enough to build his very own castle and marry his beloved Ada. Finally, he could focus on his true ambition: his inventions. He built an innovative sewer system in their burgeoning community, years ahead of its time, and had a hand in the design of every home. Though Denver had grown over the years and slowly surrounded Castle Heights, the neighborhood had always remained isolated and unchanged.

Fewer people knew that Walter had a brother who also helped build Castle Heights. Simon. Walter's legacy overshadowed the lesser Byrne, probably because of Walter's doomed marriage and early death. Nothing like tragedy to make people remember you.

Alex listened quietly to her story. He followed as she went over to her grandfather's old tool chest. She pushed it around so its back was showing. There was a hollow at the bottom of the chest, something she'd discovered as a kid looking for a hiding place. She reached into the hollow and pulled out a small plastic case. Her keepsake box.

"My great, great-grandparents knew the Byrnes," Evelyn said. "They were friends. My family has lived in this house ever since."

She opened the lid and took out the stack of pictures resting on the top. Once, they'd belonged to the Stanton family collection. "My Nana," she explained, handing Alex the first picture. It was Nana Stanton, standing stoically outside this very house when she was seventeen. Her hair was a silky wave of chestnut instead of the white that Evelyn had known later on. Nana was actually Evelyn's great-aunt; she had raised Evelyn's mother from a young age after Viv's parents died. Nana had never married. She'd remained a Stanton her whole life.

"My mom and dad back from their honeymoon," she said, flipping through more photos. "My Uncle Sammy skateboarding on the sidewalk by Walter Park." Without realizing it, she'd been speaking in a quiet, reverent voice. She tried to quickly pass over a snapshot of her at about six years old. But Alex plucked it from her hand.

"It's you," he said, using the same hushed tone. "I remember…"

"You remember?" Evelyn asked.

"Being that age."

He was staring so intently at the photo that Evelyn snatched it from him.

"Yes, and if you make fun of my SpongeBob shirt I will hurt you."

There were more photos beneath, much older, yellowed and brittle. Generations of Stanton family members that Evelyn knew only from their faded images. And in all of them, regardless of the photo's age, there was Byrne House towering behind them like a sharp-peaked mountain.

When Evelyn was younger, she'd liked to keep all kinds of family photos in her bedroom so she could look at them whenever she wanted. After a while, she'd separated out the pictures with Byrne House and kept them right by her bed. It just felt nice to see them and to run her fingers over their slick surfaces. She'd pretend to be these other people living in this sepia-toned, simpler version of the view from her window. But after the supposed hallucinations when she was fourteen, her mom took the mementos away. "It's not good to dwell on the past," Viv had said. But Evelyn had found the trash bag and carried it back from the curb. The pictures had lived inside the old tool chest ever since. She loved the patina of old things, the way every scrape or stain or chipped layer of paint whispered a story. The past was a mystery, and Evelyn liked mysteries. There were clues and there were *answers*, if you could only find them.

One by one, Evelyn placed the photos in a stack on the floor. She reached the last item in the keepsake box, a clear plastic sleeve with a newspaper clipping inside it.

She handed the sleeve to Alex so that he could read it.

It was a very old newspaper photo from the *Castle Heights Register*. Two smiling couples stood on the steps of a church. *January 22, 1900: Mr. and Mrs. Walter Byrne celebrate the christening of their daughter Clara at Sacred Heart Church, attended by the godparents, Mr. and Mrs. Henry Stanton, and their two children.* Both women in the photo held babies—the Byrne child dressed in a long, white christening gown. Mr. Stanton clutched the hand of a small boy.

Evelyn had found the clipping in Ms. Foster's attic just this summer. "Please, can I keep this?" Evelyn had asked that day, nearly tap dancing with excitement. It had taken a surprising amount of cajoling, but Evelyn finally convinced Ms. Foster to settle for a photocopy and let Evelyn take the original.

"Clara Byrne—the baby is my great-grandmother," Alex said. "The one who died when I was six. And these were your ancestors?"

"Right." Mr. and Mrs. Henry Stanton. The original owners of this house. And here they were, best of friends with the two people responsible for building Castle Heights itself.

"So that means…Byrne House and your house, they're linked. Our families are linked."

"*Exactly*," she said. Alex understood what nobody since Nana—not her parents, not Silvia or even Ms. Foster—had ever truly understood. Evelyn *had a reason* for her fascination with Byrne House. It was practically fate.

Alex's eyes locked with hers. "Evelyn, you didn't have to show me this to prove we have a connection."

There it was again, that funny sensation in her throat. She searched his words and his face for some hint of sarcasm. But there was none. *What if he kisses me?* she suddenly thought. Her brain didn't think that was such a good idea, but the rest of her clearly was in favor.

Then he cracked a smile. So he'd been teasing her after all. She turned away to hide her embarrassment.

"That was all just the introduction," she said. "*This* is what I really wanted to show you."

They moved onward, to the far end of the basement. Here, a brick wall cut across the corner at an odd angle. For a long time she'd wondered why this wall was exposed brick instead of the white plaster that lined the rest of the basement. And the bricks were uneven in spots, the mortar too thick here, and too thin there, as if whoever built it had been in a hurry. Her mom claimed not to know anything about it. It was just a wall.

Evelyn had thought so too. Until she found a loose brick one day, a few years ago, and pulled it free.

Now, Evelyn took a flashlight from the tool chest and moved a large cardboard wardrobe box out of the way. She plucked the original loose brick, and then the two more she'd managed to pry out. That left a small hole in the wall, just large enough for her to fit a flashlight inside while leaving enough room for her to see.

The flashlight beam winked off of metal.

"See it?" she asked.

Alex stooped to look. "Unbelievable," he breathed. "It's exactly like the one I remember at Byrne House."

The first time she'd used a flashlight to look behind that shoddy brick wall, she'd found a hidden door. A solid face of rusted metal set into the plaster of one of the foundation walls of the basement. A matching metal frame surrounded the door, several inches thick on every side, with rivets the size of nickels. Beneath the thick doorknob was a distinctive, old-fashioned keyhole shaped like a triangle at the top. Just like the one Alex had described.

Someone had built a wall in front of that door to ensure it could never be opened. This hidden door was like a glimpse into her nightmare-world, a place that both called to her and terrified her.

Alex stood back. "Can you open it?"

"I assume it's locked." And she'd never been quite brave enough to pull down more bricks and find out.

"It looks that way. But have you *tried?*"

Now or never, she thought. With Alex here, the secret door wasn't so scary. She could hide the damage to the wall with boxes, and thankfully her parents never came down here.

Evelyn found two screwdrivers in her grandfather's tool chest. She and Alex went to work, sending a shower of powdery mortar onto the floor.

After about half an hour of effort, Alex went to the tool chest and brought back a crowbar. "Stand back," he said. He tapped the end of the crowbar into the bricks one by one, creating a cloud of dust. The bricks gave way and tumbled down behind the wall with muffled thuds. They left a narrow square, just big enough to crawl through.

Evelyn shone the flashlight into the newly open space. Dust hung in the air. Alex crawled forward through the hole and stood up. "There's room for us both," he said, his voice muffled. "Wow this is weird."

Evelyn followed, wiggling through the hole. She cursed herself for wearing a skirt today. She brushed the dirt from its gauzy folds as she stood.

There was room but just barely. Alex was running his fingers over the door's metal frame. Evelyn crowded in beside him and pressed her palm to the door's tarnished center. Ice cold. She pulled her hand back quickly.

Evelyn tried the door's handle, but it wouldn't budge. Alex had no luck either. He crouched down and pointed at the lock.

"Do you see this?" There was a plug of mortar blocking the keyhole, solid as cement. Even if she had a key, she could never have opened it. "Somebody really didn't want this door to open," Alex said.

"It had to have been someone in my family."

He stood up, his arm brushing against the side of her body. Now Evelyn was pressed against him, shoulder to wrist. She could feel his pulse beating, like it was responding to hers.

"You have mortar dust on your face," he said. He lifted his hand to brush the bits of sand from her cheek. Evelyn inhaled, holding her breath. "And there's more here," he said, quieter this time. His thumb brushed her lips. It was getting very warm in the small space that they shared.

She'd had a couple of boyfriends, as awkward and unsatisfying as those experiences had been. But that was a long time ago. Too many guys at school knew about her incident freshman year; remembered the school days she'd missed and the rumors that spread. Not to mention her fondness for all things vintage when her classmates only cared about what was new. For the past three years, Evelyn had lived on the periphery of the Castle Heights social world, with Silvia her only link to a normal high school existence.

But Alex didn't know her past.

This time, she *definitely* wanted him to kiss her. No—she wanted to pull him closer and kiss *him*, mortar dust and all. She turned her body to face him. She took a step forward, leaning in.

Then her foot hit against something on the floor and she tripped, crashing into him. Her elbow slammed into his ribs. They landed hard against the wall. Her knee hit something softer, and he yelped with pain. She looked down.

She'd kneed him in the crotch.

"Oh my god, I'm sorry," she said. "There's something down on the floor. I tripped on it. I am *so* sorry." Agonizing seconds passed as they maneuvered, trying to stand upright again.

"I'm fine," he managed to say, though his voice was strained. "Were you going to say something else, right before? Or…"

"Nope." The moment was gone. Or rather, she'd destroyed it. Obliterated it, along with any desire he might've felt to ever kiss her.

"What's on the floor?" Alex asked.

"I can't bend down to get it. Could you go out first? I mean, if you're okay."

"All good. Don't worry about it." Alex crouched and began backing out through the wall. She squatted and found the thing she'd tripped on—a small, dark cube.

She gathered her skirt, trying to decide on the least awkward way to get out. Alex would be watching. So butt-first was not happening. She pushed the cube in front of her and crawled toward the light.

"What is it?" he asked.

When she was out, she brushed off the dust with the heel of her hand and carefully lifted the top. An old-fashioned key sat inside, thick and ornate. Beautiful. It had a triangular shape at its top, a possible fit for the metal door right in front of her. Of course, thanks to that plug of cement, she couldn't try the key on this door.

But just maybe—

"The door in Byrne House's basement," Alex said, at the same moment that Evelyn realized it. "That key could open it."

Evelyn had thought her mom was still at work. And even if she wasn't, Evelyn assumed her mom would stay calm until Alex left, despite the warning at the hospital. But when she and Alex opened the basement door, Evelyn found her mother making tea in the kitchen. Viv gasped in surprise at first, and then her face tightened into a murderous glare.

"What is going on?" her mother demanded.

Evelyn put the key behind her back. She felt Alex lift it out of her hand. "Um, mom, this is Alex," playing innocent. "I think you saw him in the ER? He's visiting Castle Heights."

Viv purposefully averted her eyes, refusing to look. "I *told* you, Evelyn. I want him out of here. *Now.*"

"*Mom.*"

"I'm sorry. I'll go." Alex bolted for the front door.

"Wait!" The door slammed, and the house reverberated. "What the hell was that? You didn't have to be so rude."

Viv was so angry she was shaking. "Why don't you ever listen? What do I have to do to get through to you?"

"Byrne's not even his name. It's Evans."

Viv flinched. "I never want to hear *either* of those names again."

Evelyn felt something tearing inside of her. *Us. Them. Stantons. Byrnes.* "Why does it matter so goddamned much?" She honestly wanted to know.

The slap came so quick, Evelyn heard it before she felt it. Her cheek stung like a sunburn. Evelyn gasped, choking on tears.

"I didn't want to do that." Viv backed away, looking even more shocked than Evelyn felt. She went to her purse and came back holding Evelyn's phone.

"You're giving my phone back? Like that makes up for you humiliating me? *Hitting* me?"

"I'm giving you a chance to prove yourself. Next year you'll be off on your own. Act like it." Viv wiped away tears, smearing her mascara. "But you have to listen, Evelyn. You are not to see that boy. Ever. Please trust me, this is for your own good."

"You're treating me like a child. I can't wait to get out of this house, because when I do, I am not looking back."

"Maybe by then, you'll have grown up enough to understand."

Clutching her phone, Evelyn ran for her room. Viv followed her upstairs and tugged the curtains over Evelyn's window. "You're grounded until school starts. Don't test me."

Evelyn didn't respond. She sat at her desk, scrolling through her phone, her head a swirl of dark and furious thoughts.

10

EVELYN HAD A TEXT WAITING WHEN SHE WOKE UP in the morning. Ms. Foster asked her to come over as soon as possible. Milo wanted to see her.

Without writing back, she stuck her phone in her desk drawer and hurried to get dressed. Her mom was working today as usual and wouldn't be home until dinnertime. Not that Evelyn wanted to see her mother ever again. But no doubt Viv would be checking the location of Evelyn's phone all day. Viv's ploy was beyond obvious—she'd loaded the phone with trackers and spyware. That meant leaving the device at home. A month ago, Evelyn would've thought losing her phone was akin to losing a leg. And perhaps it was, but she'd already started to adjust. She'd just have to find ways to work around it.

It was brilliantly sunny outside, and little kids were playing in the park. In the rich light, Byrne House's stone turned to a flat gray, diminished amid all the blues and greens.

Milo was sitting in Ms. Foster's living room with playing cards spread over the coffee table before him. "Look who's here!" Ms. Foster said with exaggerated cheer.

Milo looked up and his expression didn't change. His brown eyes were older and a thousand miles away. "Hello, Evelyn."

"Hey. How are you?"

"Fine," he said automatically, but everything about him told a different story. He'd lost weight, and he hadn't shaved the few days' growth of whiskers on his cheeks. He had new glasses, square black frames that were similar to the old ones, and yet looked out of proportion now. Like a costume.

Ms. Foster ushered Evelyn to an armchair and began bustling around the first floor. She'd redecorated a few years ago in a style that Evelyn lovingly thought of as "Victorian boudoir." Thick curtains, velvet throw pillows, gold patterned wallpaper. From the kitchen, Ms. Foster brought a plate heaped with scones and a pitcher of iced tea. Evelyn helped pick up the playing cards to make room on the coffee table. Milo watched from the love seat.

"There," Ms. Foster said, settling into her own chair with a sigh. "Isn't this just like old times?" Then her lips drew in like she'd tasted something sour. Her eyes glistened. "Well. Help yourselves, please."

Evelyn took a scone and some tea. Milo just sat there with his back very straight. He'd picked up the deck of cards and was shuffling them in his hands. Ms. Foster set a glass in front of him, and he barely looked up.

"Thanks," he mumbled.

Ms. Foster looked around desperately. "Oh! Here's what we need." She reached over to the bookcase behind her to retrieve the pint of Captain Morgan she kept there for "spicing up" her tea, as she liked to say. She splashed a bit of rum into her glass. "Anyone else? I won't tell." She held out the bottle and winked.

This had never happened before. Evelyn lifted her eyebrows. "Um …"

Milo broke the tension. He rolled his eyes, the most emotion he'd shown so far. "Grandma, can I just talk to Evelyn alone for a while? *Please*?"

Ms. Foster seemed surprised, and then relieved. She smiled at Evelyn. "Of course. Yes … I'll just be in my room taking care of some things." She bustled around another moment and then grabbed her glass and went upstairs. She'd taken the bottle of rum with her.

They were both quiet until they heard the door to Ms. Foster's room click closed.

"How are you really?" Evelyn asked.

Milo's stoic expression faltered. "Not so hot. It might be easier if I remembered what happened. The doctors say I was talking while I was unconscious, saying weird things. They wouldn't repeat any of it. I think my parents asked them not to."

There was a flare of angry heat in Evelyn's stomach when she thought of her mother. "What *do* you remember?"

Milo shuffled through the playing cards. "I was riding my bike over here, I remember that. I wasn't doing anything else that day, and I thought … maybe you'd be here at my grandma's." Their eyes met briefly, then he looked away again. "I remember swerving, almost hitting someone in the street. And that's it."

"Nothing about Byrne House? Or the tower?"

"Nothing. That's part of why I wanted to talk to you. I heard you saw me from your window. What was I doing in the tower?"

Evelyn set down her iced tea. Her hands were slick with condensation. "I wish I knew."

"My grandma said you yelled at the police."

Evelyn smiled, and then smiled bigger when Milo grinned. "Thanks," he said. It was a glimpse of the Milo she knew, the boy who got more funny and animated the more time you spent with him. Once, she'd thought he might have a crush on her. But he never gave any sign of wanting more than friendship, and Evelyn realized that was just his way—Milo genuinely liked people. He was so kind. She hated that he was hurting.

They sat in silence for a few minutes, but it was a comfortable quiet. Milo sat back in the love seat, his body relaxing. He glanced at the stairs, and then said in a whisper, "There's another reason I asked you here. I have something I want to show you."

Milo put his hand under the love seat cushion and pulled out a newspaper clipping inside a plastic protective sleeve, not unlike the one she'd shown Alex just yesterday. He scooted to make room and waved Evelyn over. She joined him on the love seat.

It was another clipping from the *Castle Heights Register*, which wasn't surprising—it was one of Ms. Foster's favorite sources for local history. A lurid headline in old-fashioned lettering topped the page: *Stanton Child Finally Found, Raving From Mysterious Illness!*

"It's about a kid," Milo whispered, "nine years old, who went missing inside Byrne House in 1900. Elijah Stanton."

Stanton—her mother's family. Evelyn quickly read the brief text.

After having gone missing a fortnight ago, Elijah Stanton was found last night by his father, Mr. Henry Stanton, Esq. The boy had been last seen playing at Byrne House during a family visit, and is believed to have wandered off into nearby wilderness where he contracted a fever of unknown origin. He is currently receiving treatment in Denver for delirium. Sources told the Register that his illness is not contagious, but check future articles in this paper for updates.

"I think I've heard about this boy," Evelyn murmured. "There was a story my Nana told me …"

It was the bedtime story that frightened Evelyn the most, a little boy who was lost inside Byrne House. Nana had stopped telling it partway through, saying she'd changed her mind. She'd save it till Evelyn was older. But after several nights of pleading, Nana had relented. *He'd gotten trapped behind the walls*, Nana had said. *And he couldn't find the way out. For days, they heard him knocking.*

Evelyn shuddered. The story had scared her so much she'd made Nana sleep with her. Viv had been angry when she found them in the morning. It was the only time Nana ever apologized for telling a Byrne House story. And she'd never repeated it.

"I didn't think that particular story was real," Evelyn said. What more about her neighborhood—about her own *family*—did she not know?

"Where did you find this?" she asked.

"My grandma had it in one of her binders."

Ms. Foster had it? But why wouldn't she have shown it to Evelyn? It not only related to Byrne House, Evelyn's favorite subject, but to Evelyn's ancestors. Maybe she thought it was too gruesome.

"'Delirium,'" Milo read, pointing to the clipping. "Am I just exhausted, or does this Elijah Stanton article sound a little like what happened to me?" He shifted anxiously on the love seat.

"It does, in certain ways," Evelyn said, her mind a million places at once. *A boy missing, last seen at Byrne House, found ill ...*

Milo leaned his head close to hers. "Evelyn, you know more about Byrne House than anyone I know. I want to find out what really happened to me. I was hoping you could help me." Milo looked at her earnestly with his milk-chocolate eyes.

"Of course I will," Evelyn said. She'd introduce him to Alex. Share what they knew so far. Which, admittedly, wasn't much.

The doorbell rang, and they both jumped. Ms. Foster's door opened upstairs. Milo tucked the article back under the cushion.

"Oh, they're early," Ms. Foster said, coming down the stairs.

Evelyn got up to answer the door, but Milo touched her hand. "Wait, I have something else, too," he rushed to say. But he didn't get the chance to finish. Ms. Foster opened the front door.

"Surprise, the party patrol has arrived," Silvia said, beaming. "Ev, you're here already! Perfect!"

Silvia and her boyfriend Jake stood on Ms. Foster's porch holding balloons. Milo turned a deeper shade of red and made excuses about being tired. But they wouldn't take no for an answer. That, and Ms. Foster practically pushed her grandson out the door. She was the one who'd called Jake. And to Jake's credit, he'd gathered more friends and picked up supplies for their impromptu welcome-home party.

"You're coming, right?" Milo asked Evelyn on the porch. The others had already run to Jake's Camaro. It was parked out front, with pizza boxes stacked in the backseat. Caitlin Meyer had come too, one of Silvia's friends.

Usually, Milo was the sunny, optimistic presence at the Foster house. Evelyn hoped this was a temporary change. Both because she wanted to see Milo his truly happy self again, and because she wasn't sure how long her supply of cheerfulness would last with Jake and Caitlin in tow.

Evelyn mustered a convincing smile. "Of course. This'll be fun."

They took over a picnic table in Walter Park and ate sausage pizza, Milo's favorite. Jake entertained them by recounting the instances—not once, not twice, but *three times*—that random people had asked him for anime recommendations. "Because of course the guy with Japanese grandparents watches freaking anime."

"You should've told them *Full Metal Alchemist*," Milo said. "Love that show." They all laughed, though Caitlin argued that *Death Note* should be first on anyone's list.

Silvia hugged Evelyn around the shoulders. "I've missed you. Did you get the texts I sent?"

"Sorry," Evelyn said. "I only just got my phone back. My mom's been worse lately than usual, and I'm pretty sure she's reading everything on my phone now."

Caitlin snorted. "That's why the rest of us have used WhatsApp since middle school. Have you seriously not heard of that?"

Evelyn smiled wryly in reply and made a mental note to research some new apps.

She and Caitlin had never been close. She *wanted* to like Caitlin. Cait planned to be a U.S. Senator someday, and she was always front-and-center at any protests downtown, shouting down injustice while waving a pithy sign. Evelyn respected her; admired her even. But too often, Caitlin used her barbed sense of humor against Evelyn. "God Ev, you're so clueless," she'd say whenever Evelyn missed some political reference. Or when Evelyn hadn't heard about the latest outrage on whatever social media site she had yet to join. But freshman year—after Jake showed up at Silvia's quinceañera and suddenly they were a couple—Evelyn and Caitlin finally found common ground. Neither of them could stand Jake.

His family lived in a fancy house at the edge of the neighborhood, and Jake drove a classic 1967 silver Camaro to school. It was gorgeous, the kind of car Evelyn would dream of having—but to Jake it was just a second-rate hand-me-down from his dad. He rarely said two sentences without mentioning "the Club," as in the Castle Heights Charity Club, so named because members' sky-high dues went to vaguely charitable causes while they pounded the tennis courts or held events at the downtown opera.

Yet Jake hadn't always been so conspicuously superficial. Evelyn had known him since kindergarten, and she remembered a boy who made up silly dances at recess, who once cried when they saw a dead squirrel on the sidewalk. He'd changed when they hit high school, suddenly prowling the hallways with the soccer guys and wearing a practiced smirk. He was hot, no doubt about it. But Evelyn didn't get what else Silvia saw in him. Maybe Silvia still saw that sweet little boy from recess, though Jake had left that part of him behind.

But Silvia was also Ev's closest friend, and that meant putting up with both Caitlin *and* Jake.

"Who is *that*?" Caitlin sat up, looking at the street.

A U-Haul truck had pulled up in front of Byrne House. The *who* in question was Alex. He'd just gotten out of the passenger side of the cab and went around to open the cargo door. He reached up for the latch, and his t-shirt inched above the waistband of his jeans, revealing the fine trail of hair on his stomach. Alex looked over at the park, and caught all three girls watching him. He grinned and started walking over.

"Whoa, his *face*."

"*Cait*," Silvia hissed. "Don't be mean."

"What? Scars are sexy."

Evelyn gritted her teeth. The last thing she wanted to do was introduce Caitlin to Alex.

But here he was, combing his fingers through his messy hair. "Evelyn!" he said, smiling. Then he made a show of glancing around. "Your mom's not here, right?"

"Uh, no," she mumbled. "Sorry about yesterday." Silvia looked curious, ready to ask what happened, so Evelyn quickly introduced Alex to the others. Milo and Jake had now joined the circle.

"My grandma said you helped me get to the hospital," Milo said quietly. "Thank you."

"Of course." Alex smiled, but Milo didn't return it. There was an odd tension to the moment that Evelyn couldn't decipher. But Caitlin broke it.

"What're you up to over there at the mansion, Alex?" Caitlin asked. "You can call me Cait, by the way."

"Moving day, part one," Alex said, pointing his thumb at the mansion. Darren and William were walking up the porch steps with boxes.

"I met your brother at the Club," Jake announced, a little louder than necessary. "Along with your cousins. The Byrne family's larger than I thought."

Caitlin commenced rolling her eyes and mouthing, "*The Club*" with her tongue sticking out.

Alex stuck his hands in his back pockets, laughing. "We're a twisted family tree."

Jake ignored Caitlin. "You should come by the Club sometime," he said to Alex. "Most of my soccer team are members."

Alex shrugged noncommittally.

Thankfully, Silvia changed the subject. "You're moving into Byrne House, Alex?"

Alex glanced at Evelyn. "Nah, for now I'm stuck in the hotel with my brother. But I was told to make myself useful."

Caitlin had moseyed around the edge of the group until she was next to Alex. "If you're staying for a while, you might be here for the kickoff dance," she said. "It's this awesomely awful Castle Heights tradition right before school starts. We might do a hotel afterparty this year."

"Not happening," Jake cut-in, to Evelyn's relief. She was feeling hot suddenly. "I always host the afterparty," Jake said. "Plus I'm having people over this Sunday night, if you all want to come. Now that Milo's back, we can get on with the rest of our summer." He clapped Milo on the back.

"Nice, Jake," Caitlin said. "You're a sensitive one, aren't you?"

Jake looked ready to deliver a snappy comeback, but his phone rang. He hurried to silence it. "I gotta go," Jake mumbled. "Nice you meet you, Evans. See you Milo." Jake waved a distracted goodbye to the girls and jogged toward his Camaro. Silvia watched him go with a forlorn expression.

I guess Jake already used up his one good deed for the day, Evelyn thought.

"What was *that* about?" Caitlin asked as Jake drove away.

"Jake's been really stressed," Silvia said. "Something's been going on at his dad's work. Maybe that's it."

Silvia tried to rally her spirits, but the good mood from earlier was gone. Alex said he should head back to Byrne House to help his brother, and Silvia said she was needed at home.

"Can we exchange numbers first?" Caitlin asked, holding out her phone to Alex.

He looked over at Evelyn, his eyebrows lifting like he was asking for permission. Did he *want* to give Caitlin his number? *After you kneed him in the junk yesterday? And your mom ordered him out of the house?*

The pause was getting awkward. Evelyn shrugged, though jealousy had left her light-headed. "Sure," Alex said to Caitlin. He didn't sound enthusiastic about it, which was a small consolation. A very small one.

"See you later, Evelyn?" Alex asked.

She nodded, though she wasn't sure about the next step in their plan. He still had the key they'd found. They needed to get into Byrne House. But only Alex could make that happen.

She couldn't resist a last look at him as he walked across the grass. He'd slid his hands into his back pockets as he strode across the street, his shoulder blades broad and curving under his shirt. The ever-present limp on his left side was almost undetectable.

Longing hit Evelyn like vertigo, like the first rush of a fever. The intensity took her by surprise. In her heart, Alex was already hers. True, yesterday had been a disaster. But she'd thought she could fix things. Take her time, be sure about how she felt. She hadn't counted on Caitlin getting there first.

Caitlin was watching Alex, too, with a possessive intensity in her eyes.

A few minutes later, Alex was out of sight and Caitlin had gone home. Evelyn and Milo were alone in the park. They walked to a sunny patch of grass. Evelyn leaned against a tree.

"I should get going. Technically I'm grounded at the moment. My mom might call to check on me." When it came to escalation, Viv did not have an end point. Evelyn preferred her defiance to go undetected.

"Can we talk later?" Milo asked.

Evelyn told him to come by, as long as her mother's car wasn't out front. She didn't want a repeat of her mother's freak out when Alex was over. *Ugh, don't think about Alex.* Of course, telling herself that would guarantee she thought about him pretty much every second for the rest of the day.

"Wait, one more thing." Milo touched her elbow. Evelyn turned back. "I was trying to give you this earlier." Milo took a flattened bundle of papers from his pocket and held them out.

"Some of Ada Byrne's letters. My grandma won't miss them for a while. I thought you might like to read them."

November 15, 1898
Byrne House

Dear Mary,

Let me send my congratulations in another letter. I long to see you and kiss your sweet son for myself. But such happy thoughts have no place in this letter. Every fear and suspicion has been confirmed.

Simon has returned.

I should begin with the visit I received three days ago. I told you about my friend Daisy, who helped me find a room and job when I was utterly desperate. Three mornings ago, Mrs. Trilby summoned me from my room just after I finished dressing. I could tell immediately that something was wrong. She said a woman was there to see me. Her mouth was drawn up, as if the words disgusted her. She showed me to a parlor on the second floor that no one ever uses.

My friend Daisy was waiting there for me. She stood when I entered, and I saw with shock the dirt smeared on her ragged skirt, the holes in her shawl, and the grime in her unkempt hair. I almost didn't recognize her. She burst into tears as soon as she saw me and hid her face in shame. I asked what happened, but she cried for several minutes before she could form a single word of reply.

She finally told me her story. She had lost the job at the saloon (yes, it was a saloon, I am not too proud to admit that now) where we worked. She moved from place to place, calling on every friend and favor that she had. I won't repeat how far she descended. The Lord knows the truth, and only He can judge poor Daisy.

One day, not long ago, Daisy heard a familiar voice. She looked up and saw Simon.

Daisy told me that while Simon was courting me here at Byrne House, he continued to visit the saloon in Denver nearly every week. His tab and gambling debts grew so large that the owner eventually refused to serve him. When Daisy saw him next, just a few days ago, Simon was destitute. He was begging for more money from a moneylender. Daisy saw Simon at the card tables just hours later. She followed him for several nights and each night saw him enter a dank hotel, a notorious resting place for the low people of Denver. He was usually not alone.

I gave Daisy some money and arranged for a carriage back to town. In the days after Daisy's visit, I kept to my room. I sent a message to Walter that I was sick. And I <u>was</u> sick, but more in spirit than in body. I couldn't bring myself to tell Walter the truth about his brother. I believed that Walter suspected some of Simon's vices, but he had no idea of the extent.

But yesterday, Simon appeared.

I'd ventured out of my room to have dinner with Walter. First we heard shouts. Then Simon ran into the dining room, his hair wild and his clothes dirty and disheveled. The butler followed close behind. Simon stared from me to Walter and back again. His lips curled into a vicious sneer. Simon called me a terrible word and demanded to know why I was still in the house. Walter stood and hit him across the face. Simon lay on the floor, his skin caked with dirt and now blood. Then Walter asked the butler to take me from the room. Even after I reached the hallway, I could hear Simon laughing.

Mary, since I wrote the above, more has happened. About two hours after Simon's appearance, Walter called me into the library. Walter told me what Simon revealed to him. It confirmed every bit of Daisy's terrible story. Simon fell into debt while Walter was away. As the date of Walter's return grew near, Simon became desperate. He took money from the estate's accounts in the hopes of recouping the funds by gambling. When he lost everything, he chose to lose himself in Denver's underworld rather than come home to face Walter and me.

Walter has agreed to give Simon enough money to settle his debts in exchange for Simon's entire interest in the Byrne House estate. Mr. Stanton will draw up the necessary legal documents tomorrow. Then Simon will leave.

The only missing piece of Simon's story is why he showed any kindness to me. I can't account for it. Perhaps he saw some reflection of his own suffering in me. In any case, whatever regard he felt for me was nothing compared to his compulsion to destroy himself. I don't expect to sleep tonight, knowing that Simon is in this house. It sickens me to think that I believed myself in love with that man—that I didn't see the truth that should have been plain.

I asked Walter whether I should go as well. I am almost too ashamed to write this, but he begged me to stay. He says he loves me, Mary. I can't imagine why he thinks I deserve any consideration, much less his affections. He knows the truth about how Simon met me, but he said it means nothing to him. He must feel some kind of deluded gratitude to me for my role in his recovery. I think the only proper choice for me is to leave Byrne House. I'll wait until Simon is gone, and then arrange for a driver to come fetch me in the night. I think I'll spend a few days with you and Christopher in Leadville if you'll have me. Then I can decide where to go and what to do.

With all my love,

Ada

11

EVELYN PUSHED UP THE WINDOW SO HARD IT thumped against the frame. She cringed, thinking too late of her mother asleep downstairs.

"You couldn't have texted?" she asked, whispering but still trying to convey her frustration in her voice. She hadn't heard from Alex since they'd seen each other at the park yesterday. Her messages on WhatsApp had gone unanswered. She couldn't help wondering—okay, obsessing—over whether or not he'd been texting Caitlin. Or whether he'd taken that key they found in Evelyn's basement and decided to use it without her. Whether he'd forgotten about her completely.

Yet here he was, sitting once again on the roof of her porch. It was reckless. She glanced over her shoulder, checking that her door was locked.

He tilted his head. "I could have texted. I *should* have. I'm sorry. But this seemed more efficient."

He held out the key with the triangular top. She didn't take it.

"What does that mean?" she asked. "You're giving it back? You don't want to…" She waved her hands, not saying the rest: *You don't want to find out what Byrne House is telling us? You and me?*

He averted his gaze. "I'm giving you the option. It's not too late to back out. Your mom was pretty adamant."

She shook her head. She was still pissed off at him for going quiet and then showing up this way. But looking at him now, in his simple black t-shirt with his head leaning against the window frame, she didn't want him to leave.

There was too much she wanted to tell him, and too much she still needed to know.

She'd spent all afternoon reading the letters that Milo gave her. She'd been fascinated by Ada's account of her early days at Byrne House. Yet the letters cut off so abruptly—when Ada fled the mansion after Simon's return. Evelyn knew that Ada eventually ended up marrying Walter, but how? And why had Ada's story eventually turned so tragic, fodder for Nana Stanton's unsettling stories?

Byrne House held the answers. If she wanted to find out what really happened to Milo—and to Mr. Byrne, to Alex, to her, maybe even Ada—she had to get inside.

"I'm going into Byrne House to unlock that door and find out what's behind it," she said. "Whether you come with me or not."

Again, Alex held out the key. She took it from his palm.

"Are you in?" she asked.

For a moment, he just looked at her. She was wearing leggings and her dad's old Nirvana tee, her usual bedtime ensemble.

Then he nodded.

"For now, the back door is just patched over, so it's not hard to get inside," he said. "But I don't know how long that'll last. Darren and Daniella are planning to move in permanently soon. We're running out of time."

"You don't have a house key? I thought you partly owned the mansion, too."

"It's not like *I'm* going to live there. Neither is Will. Besides, I have zero say until I turn eighteen. Which my brother reminds me daily."

Evelyn sat on her desk. The night air was warm and still; there was no breeze tonight. She leaned closer to him, keeping her voice low. Her mom hadn't heard them yet, but they had to be careful. And her mind kept wandering to Caitlin—wondering if Alex had really *wanted* to trade numbers with her.

Evelyn perched on her desk, inches away from Alex on the other side of the opening. His eyes were dark green, and he had a tiny mole beside his left ear. Not that she was staring.

She looked back at the key in her hand. Like he said, they were running out of time. She knew what she had to do, though she was still stalling, still trying to talk herself out of it.

"You sure you couldn't just ask your brother or the twins for permission to go into the mansion?" she asked.

Alex laughed again, softer this time. "Does *your* family take you seriously about stuff like this? Or do they start questioning your sanity?"

"Good point." She tossed the key in her hand, pretending to be cavalier though she was nervous as hell. "If they might fix the back door to the mansion soon, then we'd better go tonight. If you're up for it."

His grin was slow, and it gave her a thrill at the center of her chest. "I thought you'd never ask. Let's go."

The night was cool, one of those summer nights that reminds you that fall is coming soon, and winter is inescapable.

Keeping to the shadows, Alex and Evelyn silently circumnavigated the Byrne House grounds until they reached the back side. They climbed the wall, carefully waded through brush and twisting paths, and emerged at the mansion's still-broken back door. Alex had already loosened the boards that patched the broken window. He reached in to turn the latch, and then they were in.

Alex switched on a flashlight, holding the beam low to the ground. They were in the kitchen. Evelyn smelled cleaning fluid and cardboard, but that didn't fully cover the tang of ancient garbage and stale dust. Mrs. Lake's monthly cleanings must not have been enough. A bile-colored refrigerator hulked in the corner, and beside it a grease-stained stove. Open moving boxes were scattered over the counters and table.

"We've been packing up the old stuff," Alex whispered, tipping a box full of cloudy glassware to glance inside. "Will keeps saying the mansion needs a lot of work. He wants to restore it so it's exactly like when it was built. Darren's been talking about a security system. Good thing they haven't gotten around to that."

"Right," Evelyn murmured back. She was anxious, sweating in the black hoodie and jeans she'd put on. Now that they were inside the mansion, she could barely speak. She'd waited so long for this. Alex seemed to be dealing with his nervousness the opposite way, by filling the silence with talking.

"This way," he said.

They stepped out of the kitchen and into the main hallway. It was long and wide, with a ceiling so high Evelyn could barely see it. The paneling on the walls was unbroken by doors, dark and smooth as the inside of a wooden coffin.

Evelyn glanced toward the front door at the other end of the hall. A grand staircase opened up from there, leading to the rest of the house. To the tower on the third floor. She doubted she'd be brave enough to venture into the mansion at all if Alex weren't here, but even his presence wouldn't make her risk a trip to the tower tonight. *Not yet*, she thought.

"Door to the basement's over there," Alex whispered. "I scoped it out yesterday. I couldn't go far, though. Will's always hovering like he thinks I'll steal something. He didn't want me to come on this trip at all. But it wasn't really his choice."

"Then why'd you come to Castle Heights in the first place? No offense."

"It's complicated. William's not my biggest fan, but he watches out for me, anyway." Alex glanced at her. "Besides, I wanted to see this place again. See if the things I remembered…were still here."

The floors spoke under their weight, warning the house of their presence. But nothing stirred. Alex opened a narrow door that Evelyn hadn't seen. It was paneled to blend into the wall. They descended a twisting staircase. At the bottom, they entered another long hallway, this one with stark white walls. The plaster glowed yellow in the flashlight beam. An electric cable ran along the length of the ceiling, with naked bulbs hanging every few feet. They decided not to turn the lights on. Too risky that it would somehow be seen from outside.

The floor sloped downward a bit as they walked. The air got colder, smelling of earth. They turned down a new basement hallway. Curved archways opened off of the new passage on either side: alcoves for storage, all piled high with boxes and furniture. After several minutes of walking, the hallway started to curve to the left. Then a split appeared, and they followed a narrower side passage.

"I don't remember anything like this," Alex said. "We must've taken a wrong turn."

They backtracked. It was a maze down here. And every step they took carried them farther away from the exits.

After several more minutes of wandering, Evelyn thought they were lost. But finally Alex shined his flashlight into an alcove, and they saw the metal door at the end of it.

"There it is," Alex whispered. "I knew it would be, but…it seemed more like a dream for so long."

Evelyn checked the keyhole. It wasn't blocked like the one in her basement. But it had that same triangular shape to the top of the hole. She tried the old-fashioned key. Her breathing was loud in the small space.

Tumblers clunked inside the door, moving the bolt out of the way. Evelyn tugged on the door handle, but it wouldn't open.

Alex dug into his pocket and pulled out a tiny can. "WD-40. I came prepared."

She held the light while Alex sprayed oil onto the hinges. Alex had also brought a screwdriver, which he ran along the cracks between the door and the frame to dislodge some of the rust. He wrapped his hands around the handle. The door creaked and groaned as he pulled, but didn't open. Alex pulled again, harder this time. Evelyn could hear the door fighting to stay closed. It must not have been opened for decades.

"Let me help." She set the flashlight down, leaving the door deep in shadow. She pressed in next to Alex and grasped the bottom of the door handle, while Alex moved his hands up to the top to make room.

"Okay," Alex said, "one, two, three, *pull!*"

They grunted and yanked the door. Metal shrieked, grinding against metal. The door let go of the frame and burst open, sending them crashing back against the wall of the passage. The flashlight rolled a few feet away. Evelyn scrambled up and grabbed it, aiming the beam at the now open doorway.

The light hit a short set of stairs and bounced off white plastered walls. The stairs led down into a wide room. It was so big Evelyn couldn't see the far wall—it just ended in shadow.

"Come on." Alex jogged down the steps. Evelyn followed, and the metal door clanked shut behind them.

No going back now.

Evelyn didn't really understand until later: there are some things you can't un-know. Some things you can never forget once you've peeled back the layers and seen what's hiding underneath.

Part 2
The Mirror

12

Evelyn pointed the flashlight upwards. The walls curved together into a vault. Glass-topped sconces jutted from the wall every few feet.

"Do you have a lighter?" Alex was examining one of the sconces. His voice echoed against the hard surface of the ceiling.

Evelyn fiddled with the knob on the light. It looked identical to the oil lamp in her basement. "Nope. And I can't tell if it has any fuel in it, anyway." She wiped the dust from her fingers against her jeans.

A few yards away, a huge wooden beam cut horizontally across the arched ceiling. Thick wood posts supported the beam on either side, and one post held up the middle, forming an angular "M" shape. Evelyn's flashlight hit the outline of another wooden support up ahead. After that, the cavernous space faded into dark, out of range of the light.

"This is … not exactly what I expected," Alex said. "I'd been thinking dungeons and casks of Amontillado."

Evelyn laughed nervously, but the echoes took her laugh and spun it back to them, turning it frantic.

They walked toward the first wooden support. Alex looked up at the rough, splintered surface of the beam as they passed underneath.

"Could this be part of Walter's mine?" Alex asked.

"I don't think so." She'd grown up in Colorado; she'd been to mines-turned-tourist traps plenty of times as a child. The shafts were always rocky, cramped. "It's like a train tunnel. But where does it lead?"

They started walking. Without a conscious decision, they'd both reached for the other's hand.

They followed the gentle curve of the passage for several minutes, until they came into another cavern-like area. Here, the tunnel split into three branches. Evelyn moved the flashlight into each branch in turn. The first two looked the same as the tunnel where they stood, at least as far as the light touched. But the third tunnel was much lower and narrower, and filled almost to its top with crumbling bricks, dirt, and rock. The vault above sagged, earth and thick roots trailing down from above.

"I guess these passages aren't as stable as they look," Evelyn said.

Alex nodded, his eyes fixed on the caved-in branch. "You want to head back?"

"We can't." Going back was impossible now, even if she'd wanted to. She had to know where this would lead.

Alex smiled knowingly. "Then we'd better mark our path, so we don't get lost." He dug into his pockets again, and this time came out with a box of Tic-Tacs. He dropped a few into the passage, marking where they were.

"Breadcrumbs," he said.

Evelyn shrugged, thinking uneasily of how the rest of that particular fairytale went.

They picked the far left branch at random. For what seemed like forever, they walked through an identical series of sconces and wooden posts, Alex dropping mints every few yards or so.

"Does your phone work?" Evelyn asked. As usual lately, she'd left hers at home, in case it would be recording her location.

Alex checked. "Nope. No reception."

They walked slowly, no clue where they were heading. Evelyn's mind was going to all sorts of frightening places, but Alex was the first to say it out loud.

"Do you think Milo was down here?" he asked.

Of course she'd been thinking it. She'd also been remembering the newspaper article Milo showed her about Elijah Stanton. The boy who'd gone missing over a hundred years ago. But it was so awful to think of Milo lost down here. Her heart naturally resisted it. "But how could he have gotten all the way here from the tower?" she said. "And through a locked door?" A door that, as far as Evelyn could tell, hadn't been opened in years.

"Maybe there's another door. And someone else has a key." Alex's grip on her hand got tighter. "The same someone who moved Milo's bike."

"But who would be sick enough to do something like that? And *why?*"

A square shape appeared on one side of the wall ahead of them. As they approached, the shape materialized into a broad wooden door. It was placed partway up the wall, with a set of stairs leading up from beneath. Thin, black metal bars stretched out in the shape of a cross from a circular handle in the middle. The bars extended across each of the four sides of the door, pinning the door in place against the tunnel wall.

Evelyn ran the flashlight over the door's surface. It had no keyhole.

"We can't still be under the mansion," Alex said. "We've walked far enough to be a block away by now, at least."

They continued down the tunnel and another wooden door appeared, followed by another on the opposite wall. The tunnel started to curve, and more square doors appeared every few yards as they walked. They chose random branches as the tunnels split and split again, leaving Tic-Tacs to mark their route. A few times the passages dead ended, and they had to backtrack to try another.

Alex shook the plastic Tic-Tac box. "I'm running out. And the tunnels curve so much I can't tell what direction we're going in anymore."

"It's probably just more of the same up ahead," Evelyn said. "But what *is* all this?" Neither of them could hazard a guess. They followed their makeshift breadcrumbs back to the first square wooden door and up the short set of stairs to reach it.

"Well ... do we open it?" Alex asked.

Evelyn bit her lower lip. "Do it." They'd come this far. They couldn't turn back now without answers.

Alex gripped the circle and turned. The ugly screech of metal filled the chamber. The handle turned a series of levers, which in turn pulled the iron bars inward bit by bit. With a shuddering thud, the handle turned the rest of the way and the bars retracted from the edges of the door, just enough to allow the door to swing freely.

Alex pulled the handle, and the door moved toward him. In Evelyn's bones, she could feel the horrible scream of the hinges as they moved. The door swung out. It was huge, nearly a half-foot thick, constructed mostly of wood but with a sheet of dark metal bolted to its inner face.

Something shot out of the space behind the door and onto the tunnel floor. She jumped back and fixed it with the flashlight beam. It looked like a boot. Alex went to fetch it and brought it closer to the light. A ski boot. The boot looked new. The green decals on the sides were hardly scratched.

Evelyn shone the flashlight beam into the open doorway. There were more boots sitting on a shelf along one wall. Skis and a snowboard leaned against the opposite side, next to a bunch of camping supplies, tools and the wooden handle of an axe. One of the skis slid toward the tunnel opening and toppled out. Like the boot, the ski looked fairly new. A few seasons old, at most. Alex picked up the ski and put it with the boot.

It was just a storage room, one you might find in any random Castle Heights home.

"But how would anyone get down here?" Evelyn asked. "It seems like a weird place to store your gear."

"Evelyn." Alex's voice had a new edge to it. He was leaning into the storage room. "Get the light over here. You need to see this."

The beam shone against the tarnished metal walls as she brought the flashlight closer. There was a door in the wall directly opposite. It was identical to the one in Evelyn's basement, down to the riveted metal frame and the keyhole below the thick handle. Her hand drifted toward the key in her pocket. She already knew that it would match the lock.

"Do you see the inside of the door to the tunnel?" Alex said. "It's completely smooth from this side. No hinges, no handle, nothing. I'll bet that when this door is closed, you'd have no idea it even *is* a door."

Evelyn tried to process the meaning of what Alex had said. Her mind fought against the obvious conclusion. But the evidence was there in front of her eyes. "It's a false wall. That metal door on the other side leads into someone's basement. Someone's home. And they have no idea what's out here."

Alex was already backing away from the room. He pushed the wooden door with both hands. The storage room with its ski equipment disappeared behind it. Alex turned the circular handle and the metal bands popped into place with a loud snap.

"All these wooden doors down here ..." Evelyn was thinking out loud. "They could all lead into people's houses." She didn't remember metal-lined storage rooms in other Castle Heights homes, but she didn't spend a lot of time in people's basements. She was pretty sure she'd never seen one in Silvia's cellar.

But somewhere down here, there could be a storage room with a false wall that led into *her* basement. And some past member of her family had plugged up the lock, made sure that fake storage room wouldn't open. Was it because they knew about the false wall and the tunnels beyond?

Evelyn's lungs couldn't get enough air. "I think it's time to go back now."

"Agreed."

She and Alex followed the trail of Tic-Tacs back through the tunnels. They reached the large, open space where the three passages had branched, and immediately, Evelyn knew something was wrong. In the passage that led back to the Byrne House basement, light flickered against the tunnel walls.

One of the oil lamps was lit.

She and Alex stopped abruptly, holding tight to each other's hands. "Evelyn," Alex whispered. "I thought you didn't have a lighter."

"I don't."

Evelyn's mouth had gone dry. She stared hard into the glowing passage, and the edges of her vision feathered into static. Someone else was down here in the tunnels with them. Were those footsteps she was hearing? Or was it just her imagination?

She didn't want to find out.

Alex tugged on Evelyn's hand and they went into another passage, a branch where they hadn't been before. For a brief moment, Evelyn considered going through one of the square doors, hiding in a storage room. But she dismissed it—they'd be trapped there unless they went into the home it connected to. What if they got caught? How would they possibly explain?

"Wait, stop," Alex said. "Listen."

Evelyn's entire body shook with each beat of her heart.

Footsteps. Definitely footsteps.

Alex's eyes flew to hers, and she saw her own terror reflected there. They were being followed.

"What if it's whoever took Milo?" Evelyn whispered.

They ran blindly, minds wiped clean by panic. Neither of them thought of breadcrumbs now. The flashlight beam ricocheted over the vaulted ceiling and white walls and more of the oversized square doors with circular handles. The passage kept curving, and Evelyn felt like she was running in an endless spiral. She choked back a cry when they hit a dead end and had to double back. The only thing keeping her together was Alex's hand clasped around hers.

Finally—miles later, it seemed—a smaller door reared out of the shadows, blinking in the light. It looked like the one into Byrne House's basement. The tunnels must have curved back around to the mansion, bypassing wherever they'd seen the flickering light from the oil lamp.

"Is this it?" Evelyn asked. "The right door?"

"It has to be." Alex took the key from Evelyn's trembling hands. He threw the door open, and they went inside.

This was not the Byrne House basement.

It was a tomb.

13

WHITE MARBLE CAUGHT THE FLASHLIGHT BEAM.

They were in a circular room with a domed ceiling.

Water stains made web-like patterns in the plaster. Roots poked through fine cracks in the dome, furred with spiders' webs. A stone table sat in the middle of the chamber, and atop the table was a sarcophagus covered in intricate designs. Carved, inhuman faces blinked in the light like creatures awakened from an ancient sleep.

This is wrong, Evelyn thought. This place…it was filled with death.

Evelyn turned back to the metal door. But Alex had already shut it, and there *was* nowhere else to go.

They were trapped. Trapped in this cramped, dim space underground.

Alex was breathing heavily. Evelyn could feel dust settling on her, itching in her nose. She kept the flashlight beam pointed down and waited for the horrible sound of an old key rattling in the metal door. Whoever was out there, following them here.

But it didn't come.

She was still tense, waiting, but more worries continued to settle in. She had no clue where they were. She assumed they were still beneath Castle Heights somewhere. But Castle Heights didn't have a graveyard.

Evelyn inhaled shallowly. She'd never been claustrophobic, but there had to be layers of rocks and dirt over their heads, pressing down on the dome. The air was stagnant and thick. It wasn't like being in her own basement, even in that tiny space between the brick wall and the metal door. That was her home.

She couldn't help thinking of that caved-in tunnel. Every nerve ending in her body seemed to be pulsing with alarm. Alex's phone didn't work, and that meant no calls for help.

"We need to get out of here," she said, trying to keep her voice calm. "I don't think it's safe."

Alex squeezed her shoulders reassuringly, then let go. "Maybe there's another way out. Either that or we wait and go back the way we came."

She did *not* like the second option. Evelyn swept the light over the room again. The sarcophagus had a lid on top and looked sealed. She wondered who could be buried inside, assuming it was occupied. She shuddered.

Alex made a circuit of the room. "Here! There's another door on this side."

The top of the door frame was visible over the sarcophagus. Narrow and metal, like the one they'd come through. Evelyn began to cross the room, and she stepped on something brittle. It made a popping sound. She moved the flashlight beam down to the floor.

The sound had been bones breaking. She'd just stepped on the hand of a skeleton. It was sprawled on the floor beneath the stone table, empty eye sockets staring up at her, arms reaching from inside a tattered coat. Evelyn screamed and reared back. She dropped the flashlight. Instantly, the light went out. The burial chamber plunged into darkness.

She slumped onto the floor, knees too wobbly to stand. Her mouth opened but no air came in, only darkness. She was choking on dirt and dust and terror. From very far away, the rational part of her mind told her to stop this. *They're just bones.* But she couldn't quiet the hysteria running circles around her head.

They're coming, oh they're coming. The voices. The screams. They're coming for me out of the dark.

"Hey, it's okay." She couldn't see Alex but his warmth was suddenly everywhere. Alex crouched over her, and his hands found her face. "Evelyn, listen to me. You're going to be okay."

But his voice shook. Alex was scared.

She could hear it in the empty spaces between his words. And it wasn't just because of the tunnels, or the footsteps, or this terrible room full of death—it was the darkness. Alex was afraid of it, too. Somehow, she knew.

Alex sat beside Evelyn and wrapped her in his arms. She focused on his heartbeat. It came rapid-fire at first—*boom, boom, boom* against her ear—but it began to slow. Gradually, Evelyn calmed down too.

"I'm sorry," she said. Her cheek was still pressed against Alex's chest. "I freaked out."

"It's alright. We've both had enough."

They got up and began feeling their way along the curved wall.

An ache remained at the base of Evelyn's skull. A deja vu kind of sense that she'd been remembering something without knowing what it was. But she felt it there, throbbing like an empty tooth socket. A void in her memory. *Something happened to me*, she thought. *Not the voices when I was fourteen. Something else happened and I don't remember it.*

Maybe she didn't *want* to remember it.

She kept feeling her way along the wall. A piece of the plaster gave way beneath Evelyn's touch. She gasped and pulled her hand back.

"What is it?" Alex asked.

"I don't know."

She thought of the brick wall in her own basement, and the discoveries she'd made behind it. Maybe this wall concealed something too. And after her embarrassing weakness a moment ago, she wanted to prove to herself she was still brave. She reached out again—cautiously and slowly—and found a gap in the wall. It had regular sides, like a small rectangular niche. A hiding place. Her fingers touched soft fabric sitting inside the space.

"I found something," she said.

There was a solid, heavy thing inside the fabric, with a protrusion at one end. Like a handle. She pulled it out of the niche, fabric covering and all.

"I don't know what it is." At the very least, she could use it as a weapon.

"I have to find the flashlight," Alex said. "I'll never get the door unlocked in the dark."

Evelyn stood with her back to the wall, holding her new weapon-thing like a bat. It felt good in her hands. Solid.

It took forever for Alex to find the light, but he finally got the door open. A bunch of furniture was piled on the other side of the doorway. Was it another storage room in someone else's home? They both hesitated.

"What do you think?" Alex asked.

"Anywhere's better than where we just were."

While Alex was pushing an old couch out of the doorway, she held up the heavy object she'd found in the burial chamber. A velvet bag covered the thing, with strings at the top. The fabric was filthy, caked with dust. She pulled the long drawstrings apart and was startled to see dark blue eyes looking back up at her—her own eyes.

A mirror.

"Oh, thank you baby Jesus. We're back." Alex pointed beyond the furniture to an archway, which led in turn to a long corridor. Naked bulbs hung along the ceiling. They'd made it back to Byrne House.

Relieved, she tucked the mirror away again. "Let's keep going," she said. They still had to make it through the basement, upstairs, out of the house and the gardens. It felt like such a long way.

Alex was rubbing at the scarred part of his lip. In the low light, the old wound cut a jagged line down his cheek.

"If everything seems quiet, then we will." His voice was barely audible. "Otherwise …"

He didn't finish, but Evelyn understood. The sane, daylight world had upended the moment they stepped into those tunnels. In this new, dark universe, nothing was certain. They were living second by second, breath by breath. They stayed still, listening.

In Byrne House's basement, all was quiet.

Alex nudged her hand. "What did you find in there?" he whispered.

She stuck her hand in the bag and grabbed hold of the handle. The velvet bag fell away. It was an antique hand mirror with a filigreed gold frame. The meager light from the flashlight glowed in the mirror's tarnished glass, illuminating her face in the reflection.

Alex had stooped to pick up the velvet bag. "Look," he whispered, holding open the drawstrings.

A yellowed, folded paper was nestled into the bottom of the bag. Alex took it out. A word was written on the paper in tiny script. Alex picked up the flashlight so they could see the writing. *Mary*. He carefully unfolded it and held the cursive lettering in the light.

Dearest Mary,

Everything is worse than my last letter. Byrne House is now a prison to me. I doubt the strength of my will to carry out my plan, but I don't know how I can get Clara and myself out otherwise. I have no other option but to see this to the end. You must keep the mirror hidden until you next see me. Even my room is no longer safe from him. Please pray for me, dear sister.

Ada

"Ada Byrne?" Alex asked. "She actually wrote this?"

Evelyn nodded. She remembered that Alex hadn't read Ada's other letters. She'd have to show him later. But this new letter didn't fit with the others; clearly Ada had written more letters in between, but they were missing.

And it looked like this letter had never made it outside Byrne House at all.

Evelyn held up the mirror again. It wasn't opaque like most mirrors. The glass inside the frame was translucent, so she could see both herself and the storage alcove in front of her. Yet it wasn't really clear, either, the way a window would be.

A pale shadow blurred across the glass.

Alex took in a sharp breath. He'd seen it too. Evelyn looked behind her, wondering if the mirror had reflected something there. But the far reaches of the storage alcove were inky black. She looked back to Alex. She opened her mouth to speak.

That's when they heard someone speak.

"Dany?"

The overhead lights in the corridor flickered on. Alex grabbed their flashlight to switch it off, and he and Evelyn retreated against the back wall of the alcove.

A man appeared in the hallway. Evelyn recognized him immediately—William Evans, Alex's brother. William was tall as Alex but broad-shouldered and filled out, his hair slicked back with product.

He leaned forward, peering into the alcove where they were hiding. Alex grabbed Evelyn's wrist. She held her breath.

A woman laughed, and William spun around.

"*There* you are," she said, her voice light and teasing. "You got a head start on me. I've been looking for you everywhere."

Alex put his lips against Evelyn's ear. "It's Daniella."

Evelyn's eyes went wide. What were William and Daniella doing here in the middle of the night? They were supposed to be at the hotel. Had they followed her and Alex?

Could it have been one of *them* in the tunnels? But why?

Daniella's long, dark hair appeared. "Did you find what you wanted?"

"The painting? Not yet. Maybe you're right. Your dad got rid of it."

"That would be a shame." She stifled a yawn.

He stepped in closer, running his thumb along Daniella's shoulder. The gesture was intimate. Daniella didn't react.

"We could come back tomorrow instead," William told her, "if you're too tired to be rummaging through antiques."

"I didn't think you *actually* wanted to meet here for the antiques."

William's eyes darkened, and one side of his mouth ticked up in a sly grin. Then he pushed Daniella roughly against the wall, directly opposite Alex and Evelyn's alcove. He kissed her.

Alex and Evelyn looked at each other in shock. "Oh my God," Evelyn mouthed. Will and Daniella were *cousins*. Alex mimed gagging.

Daniella pulled his hips against her. She moaned. Cloth rustled. Daniella was pulling up William's shirt. Were they going to do it right there in the basement hallway?

Evelyn and Alex crouched deeper into the shadows behind the furniture. Evelyn's skin burned all over, and not just from embarrassment. She clamped her hands over her mouth, ready to burst out laughing. Alex stared at her like she was insane. But after the night they'd had, this was just so absurd.

The makeout session finally stopped. "Did you talk to Alex yet?" Daniella said.

William grumbled, adjusting his shirt. "I told him he has to go home in time for school to start. But so far, Mom hasn't agreed to take him back. What am I supposed to do?"

Evelyn felt Alex go still. He was staring hard at the ground, his jaw tight.

"I'm not saying he has to go right away," Daniella said, leaning her back against the wall. "I feel bad for him. He just seems lost."

William braced his arm above Daniella's head. "Alex is so self-centered he wouldn't know what he was looking for even if he found it."

Evelyn thought about reaching for Alex's hand, but he'd tucked his fists against his sides.

"What about *your* brother?" William asked. "He's been even harder to get rid of. He hates me, you know that right?"

Daniella huffed. "Our father died less than a week ago! Darren needs time to mourn, even if he won't admit it. I—" Her voice broke. "*I* need time."

"Dany." William leaned his forehead against hers. "I'm sorry. I just want to be with you. We've waited so long." They kissed, soft and slow. "But if you want," he said, "we can wait a little longer."

"Thank you."

"As long as we can sneak away to get some privacy," William added. "Meet me here again tomorrow night?"

"We'll see." The smile had returned to her voice. Their footsteps faded as they moved down the corridor.

For another fifteen minutes—which felt like an eternity—Evelyn and Alex sat silently, waiting for the coast to clear.

Finally, Alex stood. "Let's get out of here."

They snuck through the basement, checking constantly to make sure William and Daniella had really gone, then up the stairs into the kitchen. The house was quiet and dark, as if no one had been there all night.

Evelyn and Alex made straight for the back door. Outside, in the clean, night air, Evelyn took a full breath. They were out. They were safe.

A young man emerged from the shadows, blocking their path. He was short and stocky, with messy blond hair.

"Alex," he said, smiling. "I don't know why we're all paying for hotel rooms. Nobody seems to stay there, anyway."

Alex swore under his breath. "Hey, Darren."

14

"What are you up to?" Darren Byrne asked, still smiling like they were casually meeting on the street in broad daylight. Not at three in the morning on private property.

"Um…" Alex slung an arm around Evelyn's shoulders and pulled her closer. "What do you think a guy and a girl do alone in the middle of the night?"

"*Alex.*" Evelyn swatted his arm away, even as she realized what Alex was doing. Luckily, her reaction probably made his claim more authentic. The jerk.

Darren's smile didn't falter. "Didn't happen to see your brother and Daniella inside, did you? They're not at the hotel. I thought they might've come here."

"I *did* see them, in fact. Why are you following them around? In the middle of the night?"

Now, Darren's composure cracked. He shuffled his shoes and looked down. "I suppose I was worried about Dany. For…certain reasons that you don't need to concern yourself with." He looked over at Evelyn and his eyes brightened. "Sorry, I'm being rude." He offered his hand. "Darren Byrne."

Evelyn had to switch the drawstring bag holding the mirror to her left hand. They shook. "Evelyn Ashwood."

"The famous Evelyn Ashwood," Darren repeated. He glanced at the drawstring bag. "What've you got there?"

Evelyn held it against her chest. "My purse." *Please let him think it's full of condoms and a hash pipe or two*, she thought. The mirror was an interesting antique, but it was really

Ada's letter she wanted. She didn't want Darren to claim ownership and take it away. And then start asking questions about where she'd found such a thing.

"I'm famous?" she asked skeptically.

"Around Castle Heights, anyway. You helped find Milo Foster. That was awful, how he was missing?"

"Alex helped too," Evelyn said.

"So they say, so they say." Darren shrugged and yawned. "What d'you say we walk you home, Miss Ashwood?"

"I can walk her myself," Alex protested.

Evelyn agreed. "Thanks, but—"

"My sister would be furious if I didn't see you home. I think you and Alex have probably had enough fun—*not* that I'm judging. Your reputation is safe with me."

Alex snorted, which Evelyn thought was unhelpful. "Thank you?" she said. *I think?*

"Don't worry about it." Darren kept smoothing down the cowlick by his temple. "I got up to much worse at your age," he said. "Believe me."

"Are you going to tell my mother about this?" she asked.

Darren cringed. "Not unless you tell my sister I was checking up on her," he whispered back, leaning toward her. "You might want to find other friends, though. Alex is a handful."

"I can hear you," Alex said. "I'm right here."

They started toward Evelyn's house. Alex dragged his feet behind them, huffing every few steps in protest. It was a good act. He was every bit the petulant younger cousin. Evelyn wondered if his heart was beating anywhere near as hard as hers. Thank goodness it was Darren who caught them and not William or Daniella in the basement. She had a feeling that his older brother wouldn't buy Alex's act nearly as easily.

"I think I remember you from when we were kids," Darren said. "You're probably, what, seventeen now? I haven't lived in Castle Heights for a long while."

That reminded her of why he'd returned. Darren's eyes were exhausted. Evelyn chided herself for being so self-absorbed.

"I'm really sorry about your father."

He brushed at his cowlick again. "Our dad shut us out of his life a long time ago. He's had heart problems for a while, but his cleaning lady wrote us that he was really getting sick. I was trying to patch things up. I just wish I'd had more time." He glanced back at the mansion in disgust. "Losing our father hurt my sister a lot worse. Our mom had already left, and now him. He wouldn't even let us come see him. He—"

Suddenly, Darren stopped and put a hand to his forehead. He was squeezing his eyes shut. "Ah, damn it."

"Are you okay?" Evelyn asked.

Alex rushed over, the petulant act gone. He put his hands on Darren's shoulders, steadying him. "You need to sit down, man?"

Darren shook his head, gritting his teeth. He dug into his pocket and brought out a bottle of capsules. He shook one into his hand. Swallowed it dry.

After another minute Darren said, "I'm good. It's passing."

Evelyn looked to Alex for an explanation. He hadn't seemed surprised by Darren's episode. Alex just gave her a reassuring half-smile.

"Actually, Alex, why don't you take Evelyn home the rest of the way?" Darren asked, clearly still in pain. "I think I should get back to the hotel."

"I can drive you," Alex said. But Darren shook his head and walked away.

"What happened?" Evelyn whispered when Darren was out of earshot.

"He gets these bad headaches. Migraines, I guess. Sometimes he passes out if he doesn't take his medicine. But he seems okay now."

Alex and Evelyn watched Darren walk back toward Byrne House. There, he got in his car and drove away.

※

They sat on the roof of Evelyn's porch beneath a blank sky. There were stars out there somewhere, millions of them, but she couldn't see a single one. She hugged Ada Byrne's mirror to her chest inside its velvet bag. It was after four in the morning now, the air dewy and cool, and Evelyn thought she might never sleep again.

She and Alex were sitting close enough that their hips were touching. Alex let his knee brush against Evelyn's. She inched her arm over until her wrist touched his thigh. Neither of them had said anything for a while.

Alex settled back against the window and looked up at the sky. "William started packing the moment he heard Reginald Byrne had died. I guess now I know why—Daniella. No wonder he got me my own hotel room. The two of them have been getting busy, apparently."

"Aren't they kind of related?" Evelyn asked. It was easier to talk about William and Daniella than the rest of what they'd seen tonight.

"A bunch of times removed, but yeah, kinda weird." Alex shook his head at the sky. "As far as I know, they hadn't even seen each other for years. Not since Will was nineteen, and I guess Dany would have been around thirteen, at the funeral. Will's a lot older than me, and it's not like we've ever been that close, but still … He's always been there for me when nobody else was, so I thought we had a basic understanding. Shows how little I really know him."

"Do you think William will send you back home?" She now knew home for Alex was an apartment on the Upper

West Side. He'd mentioned it in passing. She couldn't picture it. Evelyn hadn't even traveled outside Colorado before.

"You heard my brother. My mom doesn't want me to come back." Alex hunched forward, resting his elbows on his knees. "I did something stupid, and it hurt a lot of people that I care about."

She set down the mirror on her other side. "What did you do?"

Alex was quiet for a few moments. He glanced over at Evelyn. "You sure you want to know?"

"You don't have to tell me. But, yeah. I do want to know." Evelyn paused. The predawn sky was so blank, the street below as still as a painting.

"I want to know you, Alex," she said, so quiet she could barely hear it herself.

He took a slow inhale. Evelyn held her breath with him until her lungs burned, but he kept waiting. Finally, he exhaled and started to speak.

"My dad had a stroke last year. He got pneumonia in the hospital, and that was that. I got into trouble a couple times, got suspended from school, so suddenly I was home alone every day. I found all these prescription bottles in my dad's bathroom cabinet. My mom threw away almost all of his stuff, but she'd forgotten those. So one morning, after my mom left to meet her friends, I opened the bottles and swallowed all the pills inside.

"Afterward, everyone thought that I either lost my mind and didn't know what I was doing, or I just wanted attention. But it wasn't like that. I was just so angry and sad and so damned tired of feeling it. I hated my dad for dying, and Will and our mom for getting over it so fast, and myself for *not* getting over it. I thought it would be easier for all of us if I were gone. After the hospital, my mom couldn't deal with me. All she did was cry and drink and call herself a bad mother. She sent me to live with my brother instead."

Evelyn reached out for his hand. Alex turned his palm upward and wrapped his fingers around hers.

"Do you still feel the same way?" Evelyn asked. That it would be easier if he were gone?

"I still miss my dad. But I'm glad I'm here. If that's what you mean."

"I'm glad you're here, too."

She wanted to run her palm across his wrist and up his arm to feel what that skin was like. But she kept her hand still, afraid he would pull away. And afraid that she herself would because the closeness was simply too much.

Alex had experienced things that she couldn't imagine. It was frightening to think of being so desperate. But he'd made it through.

They sat awhile, and she felt safe despite everything else they'd seen that night.

"Who do you think was down there with us?" she whispered.

They'd both been avoiding this conversation. Soon, morning would come like it always did. But now they knew about the tunnels. They'd heard those footsteps. A permanent darkness, following them into the day.

"Somebody who has another key," he said. "Somebody who knows what really happened to Milo."

She nodded. "Daniella and William were there tonight. So was Darren."

"I really don't think…" Alex drew his hand away and ran it through his hair. "Well, I guess I don't know any of them that well, even my brother. But kidnapping Milo? Sneaking around those tunnels? Why?"

And then there was the light they'd seen in the stable. And the strange dreams, the voices. Too much that didn't make sense.

"We won't tell anyone," Evelyn said. "Not yet."

There were plenty of reasons they should call the police right now. The tunnels could have something to do with

Milo's disappearance, and those false walls meant the entire neighborhood was vulnerable. There could be more entrances and exits all over Castle Heights, more antique keys. *And someone else had been down there with them.*

But this secret—the tunnels—was too monumental to just unleash it on the neighborhood, consequences be damned. Nothing would ever be the same. People would panic. The police would take over, and they'd screw up the investigation just like they did with Milo, and Evelyn would never get answers to any of it.

"But we have to tell Milo," she added. "He deserves to know."

Alex looked at her sharply. "I've heard about stuff like this. If trauma caused his memory loss, then it might cause even more damage if we make him face the truth before he's ready."

He sounded like a psychology article on HuffPost. "You heard this *where?*"

"I don't know. Maybe I read it in a magazine someplace. That doesn't matter. What matters is, it's way too risky."

She'd never heard of anything like that, but Alex was insistent. He said Milo could have a breakdown or go catatonic. It was hard to imagine, but reluctantly Evelyn nodded her assent.

"So for now, we try to figure this out on our own." She tapped her fingers on the gold mirror. The letter from Ada was folded underneath. One more mystery about Byrne House that she wished she could solve.

Alex yawned and took out his phone. "I should get back to the hotel. Thank goodness for Lyft."

"You could sleep in my room." Evelyn heard herself saying it, like someone else was speaking. Someone whose mother wasn't Vivian Ashwood. "On the floor, I mean. Obviously."

Alex raised his eyebrows. His gaze lingered, waking nerve endings all over her body.

"I'd better not." He glanced away and cleared his throat. "My brother told me yesterday that he booked me a flight home. My school starts back at the end of the month. It's not clear where I'm going to live yet, but he was pretty insistent. That gives us three weeks to figure this out. Unless … anything else happens first."

"Right." Three weeks until the end of August, and then they'd tell the police.

Unless anyone else disappeared before that.

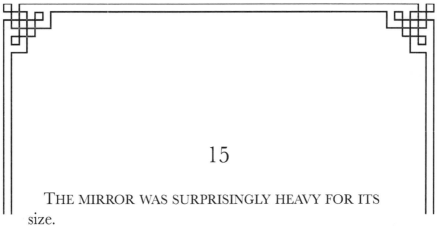

15

The mirror was surprisingly heavy for its size.

She held it in her palm, enjoying its solid weight against her skin. Alex had climbed down her tree about an hour ago. The sky was lightening in her window. It had been twenty-two ... no, twenty-three hours since she last slept. But Evelyn was still lying awake on her bed and staring at Ada's mirror in her hand.

She'd tried briefly to sleep, but a barrage of memories had assaulted her and kept morphing into other things: the footsteps in the tunnels now belonged to Milo, pleading for her help. The skeleton turned to stone and looked just like Ada Byrne. Evelyn reached for Alex but he kept pulling away, and Caitlin watched it all, laughing. Then everything played again, again, infinite repeat. Alex, the tunnels, Milo. *And Alex. Alex and Alex and Alex.*

It was easier to think about Ada Byrne, wondering how long the mirror had been inside that secret compartment in the burial chamber. From all the dust and dirt it had collected, probably a very long time.

And that note. *Byrne House is now a prison to me*. What could be so important about a mirror that Ada would want to keep it hidden? And from whom?

Evelyn held up the mirror. Her blue eyes stared back, and her hair stuck out around her face, a mess of tangles from lying in bed. At the same time, she could see her secretary desk in front of her. It was disorienting, like looking in both directions at once. Forward and behind.

Another image flickered across the mirror's surface. A little girl. Evelyn blinked, and the girl disappeared.

Had she imagined it?

She leaned forward, staring harder, and the desk suddenly began to swirl and blur in the glass. The swirls started to catch in places, trying to take a shape. All at once the little girl's image reappeared and spread across her vision until Evelyn could see nothing else.

A little girl's face, framed by a halo of curls. She's asleep on the bed, eyelids fluttering, holding tight to the edge of the blanket.

A woman sits in the chair by the desk, fighting back tears as she watches her precious girl sleep. The woman bites her thumbnail—she's chewed her nails down to nubs—and yelps. A dot of blood wells on the tip of her thumb.

On the bed, the girl stirs. Whimpers.

The woman rushes to the girl's side. The girl snuggles against the woman's stomach and drifts back toward sleep, toward the darkness of dreams. "Sleep, baby," the woman whispers. "I'll be here."

The images flooded into Evelyn's brain, filling her up to bursting with wholeness and contentment. Love. It surrounded all of her at once, like she was floating in a vast expanse of water, and nothing else existed but the girl and that woman. A woman who looked exactly like Evelyn herself.

Then the image fled and Evelyn's fingers opened, dropping the mirror with a thud onto the carpet. She sat heavily on the bed, head swimming with euphoria. But the feelings didn't stop. Instead they blossomed, unfolded until Evelyn was so crowded with them that she couldn't think, couldn't breathe as they multiplied out, spinning into the tips of her fingers and toes. She held onto consciousness, treading water, for another moment before giving in completely to the comfort of darkness washing over her.

Knuckles rapped on the door. "Evelyn? Are you up?" The doorknob rattled, but it was locked.

"Mhrm," Evelyn said, half unconscious. She tried to sit up. She was partway off the mattress, her legs falling to the side. Her back ached, but her head ached even worse. She pressed her palms to her eye sockets and felt the blood pounding between them.

What the hell happened?

The lock popped, and her mother appeared holding a wire coat hanger. Evelyn had locked it last night before she'd snuck out with Alex.

Alex. The tunnels ... *the mirror*.

"Are you feeling alright?" Viv asked.

"I don't know." Evelyn looked down and saw the mirror on the floor. She shoved the mirror under the bed with the heel of her foot.

Viv didn't say anything about it. She was pacing the tiny room, looking at the window. She pulled the curtains closed. "You don't *know*? Evelyn, it's the afternoon. I left that note asking you to get some groceries, and there's still nothing in the fridge. I told you I'd be working extra this weekend. I should be able to count on you."

"You only left that note last night. I'll take care of it."

"No, I left it on Friday. What did you do all yesterday while I was gone?"

She sat bolt upright. "Wait, what day is it? Is today Sunday?"

"Of course." Her mom lifted an eyebrow. "Are you *sure* you're alright?" Viv put a hand on Evelyn's forehead, which Evelyn swatted away.

"I'm fine. Just...tired."

It was *Sunday*? The last she knew, it had been Friday night. No, make that Saturday morning, after she and Alex had returned from the tunnels. She'd slept for an entire day?

"I'd assumed you were still angry with me and hiding in your room. But you must have been exhausted—probably from spending so long at the hospital the other night." Viv sighed and sat beside Evelyn on the bed. "I know it's not fun being grounded. And I'm sorry I've been so distracted with work. Why don't you come downstairs? We can order some groceries together on Prime Now. Maybe watch a movie?"

Her mom was trying. That counted for something. But the thought of food made Evelyn nauseous. "I don't feel good. I just want to lie down."

As she spoke, Evelyn's mouth filled with cold saliva. She ran past her mom to the bathroom, slammed back the lid of the toilet, and retched out a bitter stream of bile. She sank down onto the floor and hugged her knees to her chest.

"Evelyn, what is going on?"

She kicked the door closed. "Just go away Mom. Please."

"You're sick. Why won't you let me help?"

Her mom wasn't trying to help. She was trying to assert control, as usual. "I can handle it."

Viv lingered outside the door for a while longer, but Evelyn kept refusing to let her in. Finally, Viv gave up. She said she'd head to the grocery store herself. She mumbled a few words that were probably supposed to sound comforting and left.

Soon the nausea passed, and Evelyn's stomach calmed.

She stooped over the sink and brushed the bitterness from her teeth and tongue. A layer of oily sweat coated her face in the bathroom mirror. Lines etched across her cheeks from her quilt. She looked ridiculous. She laughed at herself, and realized she looked like both of the people in the mirror's vision. She had the same eyes and cheekbones as the woman, but the same constellation of freckles as that little girl from the vision.

That girl was me, Evelyn realized. *And that woman was Mom.*

Evelyn didn't remember anything like that—her mom holding vigil in her room at night. Rushing to Evelyn's side, all compassion and no judgment. It didn't seem possible that Viv ever cared so much, yet demanded so little in return.

But it had seemed so real.

And the way the vision had made Evelyn feel. So happy, that the word "happy" didn't even begin to describe it. And it was more than that. Underneath that happiness was a feeling of such simplicity, like every other thought or feeling she ever had just disappeared, swallowed up by the love between that little girl and her mom. A connection Evelyn hadn't shared with her own mother for years.

Ada's mirror was more than it seemed. And despite the headache and the nausea, Evelyn wanted more.

She had to try it again.

The basement stairs swayed as she went down. Beside her grandfather's old tool chest, Evelyn found a clear place to sit. Once she was comfortable, she held up the mirror with both hands and aimed at the brick wall.

She wanted to test the mirror, see what it could do. And she wanted that feeling again. Like all her troubles and fears had been wiped away, papered over by the consciousness of a different person, a different time. For even that brief moment, she wanted to be someone else. One of the people in her old photos.

Come on, she thought. *Come on.* She waited for something to happen.

Wispy, smoke-like swirls appeared in the mirror, glowing in contrast to the darkness. The focus of her eyes relaxed and passed through the glass as the swirls shifted in and out of form. Evelyn thought she saw movement over near the brick wall. The silhouette of a man. But then he was gone, replaced by a woman's bowed head. The images moved and changed, and each time that she tried to hold onto a shape and return her focus to the mirror, the image disappeared.

Fragments of emotion—fear, fury, heartbreaking anguish—seemed to whirl in her mind, like debris in a storm.

Evelyn closed her eyes, then opened them again, letting her eyelids droop. She tried to relax.

She focused on one of the swirling emotions, the most prominent. Despair. A new picture appeared: a man on his knees. His outline sharpened, the image growing until it spread across her eyes. As if she was dreaming, though she was still wide awake.

A man in torn dark trousers kneels in the corner of the basement, an unfinished brick wall beside him. He is exhausted, stiff with pain. His body is still here, but his soul is gone. Elijah, *he thinks.* My precious son. *He left Elijah out there in the darkness, far beyond the wall he's constructing to keep the remnants of his family safe. The woman today—Mary—she brought the letters, tried to make him interfere. But that would be no use. He told her she's better off forgetting. It's too late to do anything else.*

The man lays aside his trowel and pan of mortar to pick up something from the floor. A box. He stands to drop the box into the black space beyond the wall before returning to his mortar and the pile of bricks stacked at his feet.

The image suddenly dissolved. Evelyn couldn't hold herself up anymore, and her knees smacked against the ground.

Someone grabbed her shoulders. Someone else was here, in the basement with her.

16

"Evelyn, are you okay? Can you hear me?"

She pushed the hands away and sat up, gasping. Her heart was racing, palms sweating. She put her head between her knees until the basement stopped spinning.

Finally, she looked up into Milo's face.

"Thank God!" he said. "I didn't know what to do. You collapsed."

"Is it still Sunday?" she asked in a panic.

"Uh … yeah." Milo regarded her cautiously. "Are you alright?"

People keep asking me that. "I don't know." Evelyn rubbed the back of her head. But she hadn't passed out this time. Thank goodness for that. "What are you doing here?"

Milo knelt beside her. "You said to come by sometime when your mom was gone. I waited until she drove off. I knocked, but then I heard you scream. Your front door was unlocked, you know. That's not safe. Anyone could just walk in."

"Anyone, such as you?"

Milo grimaced. "I'm a little jumpy these days. I was worried about you." He helped Evelyn to her feet. Then he bent down. "What's this?"

He picked up the mirror from the ground.

"Stop!" Evelyn grabbed the mirror from his hand, and Milo stared incredulously.

Her memory of the vision, complete with all the wrenching fear and despair, crashed into Evelyn again. She fell hard onto the basement floor, pressing her knuckles into her temples. "It just keeps coming," she moaned. "He was so afraid …"

"Who?"

"Henry Stanton." Evelyn had recognized that poor, broken man. Her great, great-grandfather.

Milo knelt beside her. "Evelyn, please. Tell me what's going on. Does this have anything to do with Byrne House?"

She didn't know if she should tell him. She couldn't *think*. But if Milo could see it too, then at least she would know this wasn't all in her head. She'd be here to help if the mirror affected him like it had her.

Evelyn handed him the mirror. "It does relate to Byrne House, I think. And definitely Ada Byrne. But this is something you just have to see for yourself."

She told Milo to face the brick wall and to relax his focus. Milo looked from Evelyn to the mirror and back again, like he wanted to tell her just how insane this seemed. And he didn't even know the half of it. Boxes concealed the hole in the bricks and the metal door. *One thing at a time*, she thought. Evelyn said nothing more, and after another minute Milo held up the mirror and concentrated.

For several long seconds, nothing happened. Then Milo's entire body seized, like it was shot through with electricity. His eyes widened, staring through the mirror at the brick wall. Evelyn brought the velvet bag down over the mirror and pulled it out of Milo's grasp. Instantly, Milo fell back and crashed into the shelves behind him, his arms flailing.

She helped him sit up on the floor. His chest rose in spasms as he gasped for air. "What the heck was that? I saw someone, I saw … no, it was more like …"

"Like you were feeling it?"

He shifted forward, pointing at the bricks. "I saw him over there."

Evelyn exhaled with relief. It *was* real.

"Do you feel okay?" she asked. "Are you going to throw up?"

Milo squeezed his eyes closed, shaking his head. "I feel dizzy, but it's passing."

He'd fared better than she. Perhaps she'd helped by pulling the mirror away before the vision had ended on its own. Or maybe each person reacted differently to the mirror's power. "Tell me more about what you saw," she said. "There was a man? Was he putting up the brick wall?"

"The bricks weren't there at all. I saw two men arguing in front of a door. Their lips were moving but I couldn't hear anything. But I felt sad, too, sadder than I've ever felt in my life. And angry—well, I guess I've been that angry lately."

Milo tried to stand. But he swayed, putting his hands on the tool chest. "On second thought," he said, "maybe I don't feel so great after all."

While Milo sat down and rested, she got her photos out of their hiding place in the tool chest. She showed him the old newspaper clipping of the Stantons and the Byrnes at the christening. The same one she'd shown Alex not long ago.

"Was this the man you saw?" she asked, pointing to Henry Stanton.

"Yes." Milo took the picture. "And the other man's here too. Walter Byrne. He looked awful, like he hadn't slept in a year. Walter and Henry were screaming at each other. There was this black thing hovering around Henry. Like a cloud. He was heartbroken."

"Because of Elijah. His son."

"The boy from the newspaper article who went missing." Milo's eyes dampened, and he blinked. "Do you think all this really happened?"

Evelyn nodded slowly. "Yeah. I don't know how it's possible, but I think that mirror can show you the past." Not just the events themselves, but long-dead peoples' thoughts and emotions, too. It was incredible.

Milo picked up the mirror, holding it at arm's length. "Evelyn, where did you find this thing? What *is* it?"

She couldn't tell him that. It had everything to do with the tunnels. Even though Milo had sensed something about them in the vision of Henry, she didn't feel confident about telling him the full story yet. Alex's warning still worried her. But she could tell Milo part of it.

"I don't know what the mirror really is, or where it came from originally," she said. "But Ada Byrne had it. She was trying to hide it." Evelyn showed Milo the note that she'd found with the mirror. Ada's ominous warning. *Even my room is no longer safe from him.*

"Why exactly did you give me Ada's other letters?" she asked. "How did you know they were important?"

"I didn't. I just know how much Byrne House's history means to you, and I couldn't understand why my grandma would have kept them from you."

"Thank you." Evelyn couldn't imagine why Ms. Foster would do that, either. But she also felt an awful twinge of guilt. Because she was doing the same thing to Milo. She had to find some way to tell Milo about the tunnels as soon as she could.

"Alex Evans has been helping me look into Byrne House," Evelyn said. "I bet he can get us into the mansion so we can keep investigating." And Alex could help her find the right time to tell Milo the full truth.

Milo shuddered. "I'm not sure I want to go in there. And I *definitely* don't trust Alex."

Evelyn was taken aback. "Alex is a good guy," she said. "You just have to get to know him, and then you'll see—"

"Ev, no." Milo took her hands and blushed even deeper. "You can't tell Alex about this mirror thing. Alex is way too close to Byrne House. Doesn't it seem weird that he showed up in town right after I disappeared?"

She fought the urge to roll her eyes. "Alex and his brother came to Castle Heights because Mr. Byrne died. To sort out the estate. That's all."

"Think about it. I might be able to use this mirror to find out what really happened to me. What if we tell Alex, and suddenly the mirror vanishes? Or the Byrnes demand it back because it once belonged to their ancestor? You have to promise you won't tell him. *Promise.*"

The word *no* leapt to the tip of her tongue. But she held it back and considered. Evelyn did believe that Alex was on their side. She felt completely safe with him. *But should I?* she asked herself. How many times had she snuck off with Alex alone and told him things no one else knew? How much more would she give him if he just asked?

She wanted to trust Alex. But could she trust *herself?*

"Okay." Evelyn hated it even as she said it.

She walked Milo to the door. There, he stopped and turned to her. "Think you'll go to Jake's party tonight?"

She'd completely forgotten about that. "I don't know. There'll be so many people." People like Jake. And Caitlin. And the whole senior class. *Oh my.*

"Should we join forces? Take them on together?"

Milo was smiling hesitantly. Evelyn wondered for a moment if he felt more than friendship for her. Then again, she was often clueless about the male mind.

It was better to say no. Besides, she didn't have high hopes for Jake's party. Her well of optimism had officially run dry.

"Sorry Milo, I'm tired. A party is the last place I want to be."

17

EVELYN HEARD THE MUSIC BLARING BEFORE SHE even saw Jake's house. He lived in an imposing brick two-story on Orran Avenue, a mile away from her home. She'd run almost the entire way.

Milo waved to catch her attention. He was on the sidewalk in front of Jake's place. Silvia was crouched on the curb. Evelyn hurried over to them, trying to coax her hair back into its messy ponytail.

"Talk to her," Milo whispered.

Silvia looked up at Evelyn. Her face pinched into a sob. Evelyn sat down and wrapped her arms around her friend. "What happened?"

"He broke up with me." Silvia pressed her wet face to Evelyn's shoulder.

Jake, she thought. *I should have known.*

Half an hour ago, Milo had called Evelyn's phone. He apologized for waking her, though she hadn't been asleep. He said that Silvia was inconsolable. But she wouldn't tell anyone why. *You need to get over here*, he'd said.

"What can I do?" Evelyn asked Silvia.

"My purse is still in there," she whispered, air skipping in her chest. "My phone and keys. And a tampon. What if someone looks in there and sees it?"

Evelyn's heart was breaking for her friend. She hugged Silvia closer. "Silv, if somebody in that party doesn't know that girls get periods, they have bigger problems to worry about."

Silvia nodded. "It's just so humiliating. I didn't hear back from him all weekend, and I was trying not to worry too much. But then tonight, Jordan Davis was there, and …" She doubled over, crying into her bent knees.

Jordan Davis was on Jake's soccer team. Evelyn barely knew the girl. But she'd seen Jake flirt with Jordan a time or two. It wasn't hard to figure out what must have happened.

Evelyn couldn't sit still. Fury was building in her stomach. "I'll go inside and get your purse. Then we'll get out of here." Right after she trashed some fancy artwork in Jake's house.

Evelyn left Silvia with Milo and trudged toward the pounding music coming from Jake's backyard. She passed through the gate just as a senior boy jumped into the pool with a whoop, cheered on by a crowd.

She pushed her way through the mob and went inside, dodging a plastic cup in the hand of a dancing sophomore. All afternoon and evening, a strange pressure had been lingering in Evelyn's head. She'd dismissed it as more nausea, and then tiredness, but it wasn't that. It was like pieces of her had started to come loose, shifting around inside her skull, pressing against each other until she didn't feel completely like *Evelyn Ashwood* anymore. It was that mirror. The things she'd seen. She was overwhelmed by all she'd experienced in the last couple of days.

And now *this*.

She couldn't believe Jake had invited all these people and then chosen tonight to humiliate Silvia. And if Silvia forgave him, he'd just do it again. Maybe this was how Caitlin felt when she was out marching with her activist friends. There was so much wrong about the world. Kind people like Milo and Silvia got bruised and broken and *hurt*, and nobody did a thing to stop it.

A hand squeezed Evelyn's shoulder. She whirled around.

"It's you!" Alex said, shouting over the music. "Thank God. A few minutes ago I thought I saw you, and I grabbed that girl over there. She screamed at me. I thought she was gonna knee me in the crotch too but, you know, on purpose."

Evelyn cringed and looked. It was Jordan Davis, who gave them an extremely disapproving glare. Evelyn returned it, and then some.

"What's *that* about?" Alex asked. "Are you defending my honor?"

Evelyn was trying to figure out how to explain, but then Caitlin pushed through the group of sophomores. "Hey, what happened?" Caitlin said to Alex. "Jordan said you were molesting her or something?"

Alex groaned. "It's not my fault! She looks exactly like Evelyn from the back."

Caitlin noticed Evelyn standing there. Her lips twitched with annoyance, and her fingers closed over Alex's elbow. Caitlin smiled weakly in greeting.

Subtle, Evelyn thought. She chewed the inside of her lip. Her insides started to burn with rising fury. Caitlin and Alex were here. At Jake's party. Together.

Alex didn't seem to notice the tension. He leaned in to speak. "I'm glad you decided to come. Did you get Caitlin's text? We put the details in code, in case parental eyes were watching. But I couldn't tell if it went through."

"My phone's been acting up." She'd noted the "we" that Alex just dropped. It was buzzing around Evelyn's skull like the hornet that once got into her bathroom. What the hell did that mean, *we*? But she had other things to deal with right now.

Evelyn moved to the side to avoid a dancing couple. "I'm only here because Milo called me. I just need to find Silvia's purse. And Jake. Then I'm going."

Alex's face fell. "Why? What's going on?"

"Jake and Silvia broke up."

"Oh no." Caitlin's demeanor softened. "I'll help."

Caitlin and Alex went up to the second floor to search, while Evelyn headed downstairs to Jake's fancy game room in the basement.

Jake was there, bent over the pool table as he aimed his cue. A new rush of anger propelled Evelyn across the room. She tapped on Jake's shoulder. He glanced back, saw her, and deliberately ignored her. He finished his shot and then turned leisurely around.

Jake's easy smile brought a hot lump into Evelyn's throat. The words flew from her mouth. "You think we're all stupid, don't you?"

"Excuse me?" Jake's smile drooped at the edges, but then rebounded. He glanced sidelong at the other boys standing around the pool table—fellow soccer players, most of them fellow rich kids. They smirked along with him. Evelyn hesitated a split second, but it was too late to back off now.

"You think we're all idiots. That we don't know."

Everyone in the room stopped talking and turned to look. Jake's smile vanished. He dropped the pool cue on the table. "Go away, Evelyn. You don't know shit." A few people laughed.

Evelyn's cheeks burned hot. "You were cheating on Silvia. Weren't you?"

Jake's fingers closed over her upper arm, and he pulled Evelyn across the room into the bathroom. He shut the door behind them. "What the hell are you doing," he whispered, pushing her up against the vanity. He kept his tight grip on Evelyn's arm. "I didn't cheat."

"You're such a liar. At least have the decency to admit it."

"You have no idea who I am." Jake spit the words out into Evelyn's face.

She leaned forward, trying to hide the way her whole body was trembling. She stared straight into his dilated black pupils. "I see through you, Jake. You're that sad little boy from the playground, and you'll do anything to feel big."

His eyes flashed. He let go of Evelyn's arm and put his hand on the doorknob. "Get out of my house."

Jake opened the bathroom door and stormed out. Their audience scattered back a few feet to make room, then crowded around again. "Evelyn has a little problem with *making shit up*," he announced. Jake looked over his shoulder at her. "I don't know if you're delusional, or just that desperate for attention. But you need serious help." He shook his head, smirking, before turning back to the pool table.

Evelyn's hands started shaking. Someone snickered. Everyone was staring at her, and one by one their mouths opened and they all started laughing. The scene in front of her started swimming and blurring. She thought of Caitlin's hand on Alex's arm, staking a claim. And Silvia trying to hide her tears. And Milo asking for her help.

It was like seeing vision after vision in Ada's mirror, just observing without any control over what was about to happen. What she was about to *do*.

Evelyn ran after Jake, leapt onto his back, and dug her fingernails into his face. Jake yelped and spun around, slamming into the pool table. She lost her grip on his neck and tumbled onto the green felt, landing on a rock-hard ball. She hit her elbow on the raised edge of the table, and the pain threw her back into herself.

"What the *hell*?!" Jake shouted, pressing his hands against the indentations in his cheeks. "You bitch!"

Evelyn cradled her elbow. She couldn't believe what she'd just done, but she didn't regret it either. Jake glared at her, pink half-moons dotting his cheeks. She hadn't even drawn blood. Damn.

Alex appeared at the bottom of the stairs with Caitlin behind him. Caitlin held Silvia's purse by the strap. Alex's eyes got big when he saw Evelyn sitting on top of the pool table and Jake clutching his face. Caitlin's mouth fell open.

Alex pushed a gawking couple out of the way. He grabbed Jake's shirt in his fist. "What did you do to her?"

Jake opened his mouth to respond. But then a figure lurched into the room, slamming into the wall. Everyone turned.

It was Jordan. She'd just come out of a side bedroom. She looked dazed, bracing herself like she could barely stand up. She made a horrible, groaning noise.

A thin stream of blood trickled out of Jordan's nostril.

Someone finally tried going over to her, asking what was wrong. But Jordan waved her arms in front of her face. "No!" she cried. "No, no! Stop!" She looked up at the crowd of people around the pool table, and she let out a piercing scream.

Jordan suddenly dashed forward toward the pool table. Evelyn crab-walked backwards on the felt, trying to get away—that whole side of the room was retreating—but Jordan stumbled onwards. Jordan's lips parted. Vomit arced out of her mouth. Puke sprayed half the pool table. Drops of it splattered just inches from Evelyn's feet.

Jake's basement turned instantly to chaos. People were gagging, yelling, running for the stairs. "Call an ambulance!" someone said.

"No!" Jake said. "I'll take her, just—get out—everyone out!"

Evelyn couldn't stop staring at the mess. Alex lifted her from the pool table. "Time for us to go."

She kicked her legs. "Put me down!"

Alex let go, and Evelyn stumbled toward the stairs past him and Caitlin. She didn't want to see her own dismay reflected in their eyes.

18

Evelyn rubbed her hands against her jeans. She'd stopped to wash them—twice—before leaving Jake's house. It was all still so vivid. Jordan getting sick all over Jake's basement, the crazed look on Jordan's face. And before that, Evelyn's own confrontation with Jake.

I attacked him. That. Seriously. Happened.

Distantly, she'd knew she should be wary of walking alone at night. Alex had called up a ride share on his phone, offering to take everyone to their respective houses. But Evelyn had opted out. She couldn't take being cooped up right now. Or answering questions. She'd run right past her friends and headed toward home.

The street was dark and quiet except for her footsteps. She wrapped her arms around her sides.

Delusional, Jake had called her. Evelyn didn't even care what Jake thought, but still … He'd found the sore spot in her heart and jabbed it with a sharp stick.

But she suspected that Jake's obnoxiousness wouldn't have provoked her so much if this were any other summer. Between Milo, Alex, Caitlin, and the visions in Ada's mirror, Evelyn felt like she was just barely holding together.

She'd only been walking for a few minutes when a car drove up beside her. The backseat window rolled down, and Alex popped his head out.

"Ev, c'mon, get in."

"Evelyn!" Silvia shouted, leaning over him. "I heard, I mean—"

"Are you okay?" Milo interrupted.

"She getting in, or what?" The Lyft driver was looking on in confusion. Ev couldn't blame the guy. Nothing about tonight made sense.

"She's fine," came Caitlin's voice. "It's Jordan who's not. Did you guys *see* that?"

In a way, Jordan had saved her by drawing all the attention away. Maybe by tomorrow, nobody else who'd been in Jake's basement would remember what Evelyn did. *Though I doubt Jake will forget.*

Evelyn forced a smile. "We can all talk tomorrow. Just not right now. Please." She was afraid that, despite everything, Silvia would jump to Jake's defense. And she was in no mood to deal with Caitlin, certainly not with Alex around. She hadn't even really processed what she'd seen— Alex and Caitlin at the party together. Did it mean they were *together*, together? Or was it just a friends thing?

She rubbed her face with her hands. How had one night gone so completely wrong?

Alex tapped his hand on the car door, bringing her back to the moment.

"Evelyn, please get in?"

"It's not that far." She started walking again.

Behind her, there was more talking inside the car. Then a door opened and slammed. The driver zoomed off, and Alex jogged to catch up with Evelyn. "I'll walk with you. They're going home, though Silvia wasn't happy about it. I'm supposed to make you promise to call her tomorrow."

"This is completely unnecessary. I don't need an escort."

"Still doing it." Alex yawned, stretching his arms up into the air. His shirt rose. Evelyn glanced quickly away.

"Fine, you can walk me to the park." She wasn't ready to go home yet. If she walked back into that house and saw her desk and bed and all the so-called normal parts of her life, she'd have to admit that everything at Jake's party really just happened.

Alex stayed with her as she crossed the street and entered the park. "I'll wait with you until you're ready to go home," he said. "I'm not leaving you out here alone."

Evelyn shook her head, but she didn't argue. They sat down on a bench at the edge of the park. She felt Byrne House behind them, a shadowed presence at their backs.

"You think Jordan will be okay?" Evelyn asked. Jordan wasn't her favorite person right now. But getting sick in front of half of the senior class? Nobody deserved that.

Alex stretched his legs out in front of him. "Hope so. Jake took her to the hospital. We watched them drive off. Whatever she was on, it was a very bad trip."

"I guess." It reminded Evelyn of her own bout with nausea earlier. She grimaced at the memory.

Alex glanced at her sidelong. "So what exactly happened with Jake?"

"Don't wanna talk about it."

"Whatever you say, ninja girl."

Evelyn had closed her eyes so she couldn't see him. But she was pretty sure Alex was grinning.

The air in the park was mild, but she felt cold all the way to her bones. Like it was coming from within her, a block of ice at her core. Evelyn tucked her hands under her elbows.

"Are you okay?" he asked.

She nodded, her teeth knocking together.

"It'll pass. Come here." Alex put his arm around Evelyn's waist and pulled her closer, into the circle of warmth that always radiated from him. A different sort of ache began to creep through her insides. His chest rose and fell against her shoulder, and moonlight washed them in a blueish-white glow.

It was too perfect, too much of what she wanted.

"Why aren't you with Caitlin right now? You went to the party with her. She's obviously into you." *And she's beautiful and funny and clever. She's not bumbling around all the time, unable to find her way.*

"I barely know Caitlin." Alex's fingers shifted against the side of Evelyn's waist. "I'm right where I want to be."

She looked up at him. The night sky was bright above them, even though the moon was only half full. The light reflected off of Alex's green-and-black eyes like sun against glass. But darkness shadowed the side of his face closest to Evelyn, the side with the scar. After tonight—if Caitlin got her way—she'd probably never sit like this with him again, feeling his breath on her face and neck. It made her feel hopeless, but also bold. Like she could afford to be reckless.

She wanted to tell him the truth, about so many things. "Alex ..."

"Yeah?" His breath was sweet, slightly minty.

The words vanished from her head. Her thumb found the scar on his cheek and traced the raised skin. It was smoother, more delicate than she would have expected. It felt ... intimate. Alex's breathing changed, moving faster, as Evelyn's fingertips followed the scar down the length of his cheek to his mouth. His lower lip compressed beneath her touch, soft and yielding.

With her fingertips still lingering on his face, Evelyn sat up and brushed her lips against his. Alex's arm tightened around her waist, and he closed his mouth over her top lip, sucking gently, then the bottom. She'd pictured this kiss so many times alone in her bedroom, and now she knew. Her imagination was sorely lacking.

But then Alex turned away, and loosened his grip on her waist.

"This is a bad idea." His voice was low, almost drowned out by the chorus of locusts and crickets in the park. "I'll only be here a couple more weeks, and you and me—it's already so complicated."

At first the words didn't make any sense, like he'd spoken in a different language. But then her brain kicked in and began to translate. *Oh.*

"Bad. Right. I ... Sorry."

She didn't even know what she was saying. Evelyn got up and walked toward her house—slowly, methodically, like she might break apart if she tried to move too fast.

Alex didn't try to stop her.

19

Evelyn sat at the kitchen table and stared at the remains of her toast. She'd torn it into pieces and crushed it into gluey bits. Strawberry jam was smeared all over the plate, her fingers stained red. She squirmed in the wooden chair. Her tailbone was still sore from landing on that ball on Jake's pool table last night.

She was trying very, very hard not to think about everything that happened afterward.

Her mom came into the kitchen wearing a black pantsuit. She dumped her coat and purse onto the table with an exasperated sigh.

"Aren't you working from home this week?" Evelyn asked. Her mom had said something about taking a slight break after the long hours she'd been working lately. Evelyn found the least mangled piece of toast on her plate and took a tentative bite.

"Not anymore, thanks to the party at Jake Oshiro's house last night."

The bread turned to sawdust in Evelyn's mouth. "Party?"

"I got a call about a half hour ago from the school superintendent himself." Viv spoke in a clipped, official tone. She took a coffee mug from the cabinet. "A girl at Jake's party got very sick. She'd been dropped off at the ER, but someone called the police to Jake's house. A bunch of kids got ticketed for drinking."

"Really?" Obviously her mom didn't know she'd been there. If she had, Viv probably would have stormed into Evelyn's room earlier for an interrogation.

Viv's spoon clanked in her cup as she stirred in the instant coffee. She sat at the table across from Evelyn. "But that's not the worst of it. The girl who got sick? She's still unresponsive in the ICU. She might be in a coma."

"A coma? That's horrible." Evelyn pushed her plate away. Her stomach was threatening to reject what little breakfast she'd had. "Who was it?" she asked, since that would be the normal next question. Though she was sure she already knew.

"Jordan Davis. The doctors think she was high on something. A new designer drug, maybe. Evelyn, if you've heard anything, you'd better speak up." Viv had on her most serious expression, the one she saved for election speeches and disciplining her daughter.

Evelyn shook her head. She pictured Jordan's vomit splattering all over the pool table last night and forced herself not to react.

Her mom sighed. "Because it happened in my neighborhood, I need to get out in front of this. I'll be gone until tonight." She sipped her coffee and cringed. "And your dad just called—he's swamped with work in Baltimore, and he's not going to make it back this week like he'd promised. Just like him to bail when there's a crisis. I'm sorry to leave you alone again."

"It's okay." Evelyn got up and put her plate in the sink. She stared absently at it. A new, unsettling thought had just crept into her head.

Jordan had been acting really strange last night. Like she was seeing things. Jake was an idiot, but he wasn't usually the type to have anything more than pot at his parties. What if it was something else entirely?

Viv pulled Evelyn into an awkward hug. "I know this summer's been tough on us, Evvy. But it's just a little longer until your school's kickoff dance, and then the new semester will start. Lots of good things to look forward to."

Evelyn let her mom hold her, wishing that were true.

<hr />

Viv left for work just after nine. Five minutes later, as if he'd been waiting, Milo showed up at Evelyn's door.

"I brought bagels." He lifted up a paper bag. "I wanted to see if you're okay after last night."

"Still here. Mostly."

They sat down in the kitchen. He upended the bag, dumping out the bagels and a tub of cream cheese. "Have you talked to Silvia?" Evelyn asked.

Milo adjusted his glasses. "Yeah, I think she's good. Sad, but you know how it is. I heard what you did to Jake. Silvia laughed and cried at once when Caitlin told her."

Evelyn dropped her head to her hands. She really didn't want to think about that.

"What's wrong?" Milo asked. "Do you regret it? I mean, Jake's my friend but he totally deserved it."

"I'm just worried about Jordan Davis. My mom said—" Evelyn was about to tell Milo about Jordan's coma. But someone knocked on the front door.

Evelyn went to the foyer. Alex waved at her through the frosted glass. He grinned when she opened the door, casual as ever, like nothing had happened between them. *Just pretend nothing did*, she told herself. *There are bigger things at stake than your stupid little heart.* At least Milo was here. She didn't have to face Alex alone.

"Any more epic fights since last night?" Alex's smile fell when Milo appeared in the hallway behind Evelyn. "Hey, Milo. What are you guys up to?"

"We're ... studying," Milo said. He glanced at Evelyn, and she rolled her eyes. Milo clearly didn't have much practice with lying.

"In summer? That's dedication. Can I come in? Or am I interrupting this alleged study session?"

"Maybe we should ask Caitlin." Milo's voice rose when he said her name. "You sure you're allowed to be over here?"

"What are you talking about?" Alex looked at Evelyn like he thought she could explain Milo's hostility. But Evelyn wanted nothing to do with this conversation. She pretended to be deeply interested in the ancient water stain on the foyer ceiling.

"I just came to check on Evelyn," Alex said. "Things were kind of weird last night, but clearly you have it covered, Milo, so—"

"Alex, just come inside." She pulled him into the foyer, shut the door behind him and turned to face them. "Jordan is still in the hospital. She's in a coma. They think she was on some new drug, but at Jake's party? That seems unlikely."

"I saw Jordan not that long before she got sick," Alex said. "She was chewing me out for thinking that she was you. Seemed pretty sober to me."

Milo's eyes scrunched behind his glasses. "Then what was it?"

Evelyn bit her lip, looking back and forth between the two boys. How could she say this out loud? She had no proof whatsoever, only a creeping feeling at the base of her neck. A sense that a lot more was going on here than any of them knew.

"Evelyn," Alex said softly. "Jordan looks a lot like you. Especially from the back. You don't think …"

"I don't know *what* to think."

Jordan hadn't just been sick last night. She'd been afraid. She looked at everyone else in the room and screamed at whatever she saw. It was too much like Mr. Byrne's scrawling on his wall. *Evil memories. I see them.*

And what about those footsteps when Evelyn and Alex had been down in the tunnels? What about the hands that must have taken Milo's bike?

Jake's house was on the other side of the neighborhood from Byrne House. But the tunnels led all over Castle Heights.

"We have to tell each other the truth," Evelyn said. "All of it." Even the things about herself that she didn't want to tell.

"Ev, no," Milo said in a warning tone.

Alex was shaking his head with alarm. "Remember what I told you? The stuff about memory loss?"

He meant his fears about Milo reacting badly to the truth. "I know," Evelyn said. "But Milo deserves a chance to decide for himself." She turned to her friend. "Milo, there are things that Alex and I know that might have something to do with your disappearance. But there's a risk it could cause you more harm than good. If you're forced to remember a trauma before you're ready."

Milo's jaw tightened. "I don't care if there's a risk. You have no idea what this is like. I need to know." He scowled at Alex. "And you had no right to make that decision for me."

Alex held up his hands in surrender.

Evelyn went down to her hiding spot in the basement. She brought everything that she'd collected so far about Byrne House, the Stantons, and Castle Heights. She came back upstairs, dusty keepsake box in hand. Milo and Alex were still standing on opposite sides of the foyer, sizing each other up.

"We are *all* part of this," Evelyn said. "All three of us. The only way we're going to ever understand it is by working together. We're going to sit in the kitchen, and everyone is going to listen and be nice."

Alex sighed and stuck out his hand, offering to shake. Milo ignored it. "Fine," Milo said. "But he doesn't get any bagels."

Evelyn laid everything on the kitchen table, one by one: her family photos and the newspaper clipping about the Stantons' friendship with the Byrnes; the article Milo had found about Elijah Stanton's disappearance, which he'd kept in his wallet; Ada Byrne's letters to her sister, Mary; Detective Penn's notebook; the antique key; Ada's mirror and the accompanying ominous note.

Alex and Milo reached to pick up items they weren't familiar with. But Evelyn made them wait. "I'm not done," she said. She found a pad of sticky notes in her mom's junk drawer, and a ballpoint pen.

"My grandmother's stories about Byrne House—Ada Byrne losing her mind, a child getting lost," Evelyn said, writing at the same time on the pad. She peeled off the note and added it to the collection on the tabletop. "What else?"

"My disappearance for two days," Milo said, "which I can't remember." Evelyn jotted that down, and stuck the note on the table.

"The light in the old stable," Alex added, worrying his scar with his thumb, "which we still can't explain."

"You coming to Byrne House as a kid," Evelyn said to Alex, pen flying over the notes now, writing fast to keep up. "Seeing the metal door in Byrne House's basement."

"And the other metal door, hidden behind a brick wall in *your* basement," Alex said.

Milo put his elbows on the table. "What doors?"

Alex shot Evelyn a pointed glance. *Be careful*, it said. "We'll get there," Evelyn told Milo.

Hearing the voices when I was fourteen, Evelyn wrote. *And my dreams about Ada Byrne*. She peeled the note and put it down.

Alex and Milo both read it and seemed about to ask for explanations, but Evelyn shook her head. "We'll get there," she said again.

She wrote, *Jordan??* and added that note as well. The pad was getting thin.

They hadn't mentioned the tunnels or the footsteps or the burial chamber, but the antique key would lead into that. She'd go slow, and watch Milo's reactions carefully. It was a risk. But keeping secrets wasn't a viable option anymore. Really, it hadn't been from the start. All she'd found so far were more mysteries. More holes in all of their memories. She, Milo and Alex needed answers.

Evelyn sat down at the table. "Anything else?"

"Not from me," Milo said.

Alex looked away. "No," he said after a pause.

"Okay." She put down the pen and picked up the small bundle of Ada's letters. "Almost everything here on the table relates to Byrne House," she said. "And Byrne House *is* Castle Heights. So I'll start at the beginning. With Ada Byrne."

20

MILO HANDLED THE REVELATIONS WELL.

It was Alex who gave Evelyn the most trouble.

After reading Ada's letters aloud, Evelyn went over the newspaper clippings about the Stantons. She told them all her Nana's stories, and she showed them the notes in Detective Penn's notebook. Unable to speak above a whisper, Evelyn told them about the "sleep hallucination" three years ago. Milo had heard about the incident, but he only knew the rumors. The boys listened keenly and accepted every word. As she should have known they would. Lunchtime passed, but Milo's bagels sat untouched and forgotten on the kitchen counter.

Then, she came to the metal doors in the basements.

She told Milo about how she'd found one behind the brick wall in her basement, and later the hidden box with the key, and how the key unlocked the matching metal door at Byrne House. Milo just nodded along, not showing any unusual signs of distress or buried traumas or whatever Alex had been worried about. Alex stood up and leaned against the wall, arms crossed. He stared off into a corner while Evelyn spoke and said nothing.

At one point Milo got paler than usual when Evelyn recounted how she and Alex had run from the footsteps in the tunnels. But after a few deep breaths, Milo's color returned. He took off his glasses, wiped them, and nodded for her to go on.

They didn't discuss the full implications, though clearly they were all thinking of it: that someone in Castle Heights was responsible for Milo's disappearance. Might even—though Evelyn couldn't begin to explain how—be responsible for Jordan's sudden, strange illness.

Milo picked up the key. "So you're saying that with this, you could go into these tunnels and get inside anyone's house in the neighborhood? Through their basement?"

Evelyn shook her head. "It didn't look like there was a door to every house. The tunnels curve too much, and the doors are spaced too far apart. Besides, some people have finished their basements and covered up the doors."

"Right, like Jake's family," Milo said.

Which made her theory about Jordan less likely. "The tunnels are huge, though," Evelyn said. "There could be access to dozens of houses, or maybe even hundreds, depending on how far it goes."

Evelyn picked up Ada's mirror and removed the velvet bag. The filigreed gold frame caught the light as she cradled the mirror in her hands.

"I found this in the burial chamber in a hidden section of the wall."

"*Oh*," Milo said, nodding. "That part makes more sense now."

Alex turned to them. He'd been so quiet Evelyn hadn't been sure he was paying attention anymore. But now, Alex's eyes shone with fierce interest. "What part?"

Evelyn wet her lips, searching for the right thing to say. Alex had shared private, painful things with her. Yet she'd kept the mirror's power a secret. And now, he'd know that Evelyn had doubted him.

"The mirror shows you things," Evelyn said.

Alex's brow crinkled. "*Shows* you things? As in, other than your reflection?"

"Wait." Milo got up from his chair, palms down on the table. "First, Alex has to promise that he's with us, one hundred percent. He can't tell anyone else about this."

"Screw you, Milo." Alex went over to Evelyn. "Is that how you feel? You don't trust me?"

"I'm sorry," Evelyn began.

But Alex shook his head, dismissing her apology. "I'd never purposefully do *anything* that might hurt you. Believe me." Alex touched her wrist. "Please," he added.

Evelyn tried to swallow the bulge in her throat, but it remained firmly in place. "The mirror shows you things that happened ... in the past. Remember the note to Mary about keeping the mirror safe? This is why Ada Byrne wanted to hide it."

Alex didn't react.

Milo sighed, frowning. "She's telling the truth," he said reluctantly. "Through the mirror, I saw two men arguing in Evelyn's basement. Men that died decades ago."

Evelyn described each of her visions. She tried to describe every detail, even the nausea and dizziness. When she finished, Alex took the mirror from Evelyn's hand. She started to protest, but his eyes were hard and determined.

"I want to see this for myself."

Alex held the mirror up, aiming at the painting over Evelyn's fireplace. They'd decided to test the mirror in her living room amid a plush rug and soft upholstery, just in case Alex had the kind of powerful reaction that Evelyn did. They'd closed the curtains and dimmed the overhead light. Milo sat on a recliner off to the side.

"Okay, now what?" Alex asked.

"Don't look right at the glass," Evelyn said. "Look through it." She bent Alex's arm, bringing the mirror closer to his body.

"Can two people look at once?" Alex's eyes shifted to hers.

She took a step back. "I don't know what would happen. Milo and I will watch you to make sure it's going alright. Don't be nervous."

Alex's mouth curved up slightly. "I'm trying, but you described the nausea so vividly. I keep picturing Jake's pool table after Jordan was done with it."

"This isn't that hard," Milo said. "Just focus."

Alex concentrated on the mirror. His eyelids got heavy, and his shoulders relaxed. Milo sniffed and moved around on the chair. Alex's chin dipped. His focus on the mirror intensified. Then his lips pressed together into a thin line. Alex's throat made a reedy sound, like he was struggling to inhale.

Milo stood up. "Is he okay?"

Alex stopped making noise. His eyes started to bulge.

"I think we should stop now, Evelyn," Milo said. "Now!"

She closed the velvet over the mirror, pulling it from Alex's fist. He fell to his knees. "Milo, he's going to throw up!" Evelyn cried.

Milo grabbed the plastic-lined trash can they'd set aside and passed it to Alex. Evelyn put her hand on Alex's back and turned her head while he retched. *Really hope my mom doesn't come home now*, she thought. *This would be hard to explain.*

Alex pushed the trash can away and lay on the rug. His breaths came fast, the muscles around his jaw working as he fought a second wave of nausea. His eyes tried to close, but he forced them open. The bitter smells of bile and sweat permeated the room.

Evelyn knelt down next to him and touched his forehead. His skin felt cold, sticky and damp. "Close your eyes for a while," she said. "It'll help with the dizziness. I'll get a blanket."

Alex's hand shot out and grabbed her wrist. His head moved slightly side to side, once left and once right.

Milo sighed. "I'll take out the trash and get him a blanket."

"Thanks Milo. Linen closet, top of the stairs."

The stairs creaked as Milo went up. Alex pulled Evelyn's wrist to his chest and covered her hand with both of his. Evelyn used her other hand to smooth his damp hair away from his forehead. His chest was still heaving, gulping in air.

"Evelyn, last night— "

"Don't worry about it. Like you said, it was a weird night. I don't know what was wrong with me."

He closed his eyes and nodded. "Sure. Right."

Milo was coming down the stairs. Evelyn gently pulled her hand away from Alex's grip. They spread a red and green plaid blanket over Alex, and his breathing grew more regular.

"I think he might be asleep," Evelyn whispered.

"Nope," Alex whispered back.

"Maybe we should go to the park," Milo suggested. "Get some fresh air. Do you think you can stand?"

"Nope," Alex whispered again. His eyes were still closed.

Milo sat back down on the recliner. They waited for a while. After about five minutes, Alex opened his eyes.

"I saw Henry Stanton," he said, his voice scratching in his throat. "I recognized him from that newspaper picture. He was talking to a woman named Mary."

Ada's sister, Evelyn thought. "Could you hear what they were saying?" she asked.

"A little. I felt like I was getting thoughts and feelings from both of them at once. Everything was murky around them—"

"Like the air was thick, right?" Milo asked.

Alex nodded. "Yeah, kind of like that. Like watching a movie underwater. Their voices were flowing together ... it's hard to describe. And there were outlines of other people swimming around in the air too, other memories I guess. I think I could have seen those, too, if I tried really hard."

Evelyn wasn't sure what Alex meant by "underwater." Maybe visions in the mirror were different for different people.

"I got a general sense, though," Alex said. "Mary was begging Henry for help. Nobody at Byrne House would tell Mary where Ada was, and Mary knew something terrible had happened. But Henry refused to do anything. It was like he'd been carved hollow on the inside. Heartbroken. And Mary was so scared. I could *feel* it. She—"

Alex started shaking again. Evelyn tucked the blanket up to his chin and around his sides and rubbed his arms.

"That's okay," she said. "You should sleep. I'm sure that will make you feel better."

"No, I have to finish. One thing was really distinct, and I don't want to forget it. Mary gave Henry some papers. *Evidence*, she said. Letters from Ada that told what was really going on at Byrne House."

Letters, Evelyn thought. They couldn't be the ones Milo had given her. Those didn't even cover Ada and Walter getting married. Obviously, there were more.

"Mary begged Henry to read them," Alex went on, "because nobody else would listen. But he didn't. He put the papers behind a drawer in a blue cabinet." Alex pointed at a blank space on the wall. "It was right there. Henry didn't even want to *think* about those letters. Never wanted to see them again. It hurt him too much."

"I remember that cabinet," Evelyn said. "It was Nana's, something her parents had passed down to her. It had birds painted on it." Evelyn got up, realizing what this could mean. "The letters could still be in there."

But where is it? Evelyn hadn't even thought of the cabinet in years. It was an antique, a family heirloom. They must still have it somewhere. Unless …

Unless her mom had purged it, along with so much else of the Stanton family's history.

Evelyn flopped onto the couch, despairing. "I think it's gone."

"A blue cabinet with birds," Milo murmured. He suddenly grinned. "I know exactly where it is. It's in my grandma's basement."

21

EVELYN SILENTLY MADE HER WAY DOWN THE stairs. Voices—Ms. Foster's and Milo's—drifted from the kitchen.

Evelyn stepped onto the bare concrete floor. She'd never been down here. *We'll have to tackle the basement eventually*, Ms. Foster had said, *but most of that old junk belongs in a garage sale.* Knickknacks, books, and magazines towered in piles, and all sorts of boxes—plastic and cardboard and even wooden crates—were stacked high. Tall shelving units stood at angles throughout the space. Daylight filtered through the tiny windows near the ceiling.

The floorboards creaked overhead, and Milo's too-bright voice came through. "No, Grandma. Stay here. What about a sandwich? I'm starving."

Evelyn grimaced. Poor Milo. He might not last long. Better make this quick. She felt bad enough about sneaking around Ms. Foster's house; now she'd added corrupting Milo to the list.

He was supposed to distract Ms. Foster while Evelyn snuck down to the basement. At first, Alex had reasoned that Milo should go get the letters himself, but Milo turned all sorts of colors thinking about sneaking around his grandmother's house. "I only took the copies of Ada's other letters, and that article," Milo had said. "These are originals. I know we have to do it—but I can't. It feels like stealing."

Then Milo had glanced at Detective Penn's notebook on the table and back at Evelyn. The implication was obvious. Alex had laughed. "Our resident thief can do it."

Alex volunteered himself to stand watch in the park. He'd send an emergency text to Milo if Vivian Ashwood came home. Evelyn was still supposed to be grounded, which everyone except her mother acknowledged was ridiculous. She was seventeen, not twelve. But Viv could still make her life more difficult. Evelyn knew her mom well enough not to doubt that.

She carefully stepped around a tower of *Colorado Heritage* magazines, scanning for the blue cabinet. *It's not even stealing*, Evelyn told herself. *Those letters belonged to my family before Mom gave them away. And Ms. Foster kept things from me first.*

Pathetic excuses. And yet, here she was.

She knocked into a floor lamp with a stained-glass shade and had to grab hold of it to keep it from tipping. She passed a shelf of dusty, fabric-covered books. Milo had said the cabinet was back in the corner near the water heater. The light hardly reached over here. She crept forward inch by inch into the shadows.

Should have brought a flash— But then she stopped. White birds glowed against a sea of vivid turquoise-blue.

Evelyn pushed junk out of the way and crouched before the cabinet. She opened the small door on the cabinet's front, revealing four drawers. She'd played with those drawers endlessly as a child, hiding her toys inside, never suspecting there could be something already hidden for her to find. *What if the letters aren't here? What if Ms. Foster already found them?*

The top drawer pulled out smoothly. It had only dust and faded scraps of paper inside. Evelyn lifted it off the tracks to remove it altogether and checked all around the edges. She stuck her hand into the gap that the drawer had left.

Nothing.

The floorboards above creaked again. Her heart rate jumped.

Moving faster, risking a small amount of noise when the drawers slid along their tracks, she checked the next two. Still no letters. The voices upstairs had stopped, and there was more creaking. What were they doing up there? *We should have sent Alex as a distraction instead of Milo.* Her hands were clumsy, fingers cold.

The last drawer stuck. Evelyn pulled and the wood let out a terrible shriek. She cringed, pausing to listen for footsteps. She heard none.

She stuck her hand inside the cabinet and groped in the dark. Then, she found it. A small bundle of papers was tucked into the very bottom.

Evelyn grabbed the papers and replaced the drawers. Her breaths came fast and shallow. She closed the cabinet door and stood up. She was about to head back when a rectangle of deeper darkness caught her eye. There was something on the wall here behind the shelves. Evelyn reached out to touch it. She knew what it must be, but she had to be sure.

Her fingertips met ice-cold metal.

A door, flush with the wall, barely visible under knick knacks and newspapers and dishes. Evelyn pushed a chipped coffee mug out of the way on a lower shelf and found the old-fashioned keyhole with a triangular lock. Exactly like the one in her own basement, but the lock on Ms. Foster's door was not plugged. There would be a storage room beyond this door with a false wall behind it.

Another entrance to the tunnels.

She stumbled backwards in the dark. She'd known that many houses all over Castle Heights must have these metal doors, but it was awful to see it here, in a house where Evelyn had spent so many hours. Where she'd always felt safe.

The light changed suddenly, growing dimmer. It was probably just a cloud passing over the sun outside. Rationally, she knew that. But with the darkening of the room, Evelyn's bravery fled. Fear wrapped around her like a shadow.

She hurried for the stairs, tripping over stacks of things. *Quiet, quiet.* She'd almost made it when she lost her balance. Her hand glanced against a shelf. A glass jar teetered and in Evelyn's mind it shattered a thousand times before it even hit the ground.

Crash.

She ran full out, dashed up the stairs. But already the door at the top was opening. Ms. Foster stared down at her.

"Evelyn? What on earth!"

In a blink she was upstairs with Ms. Foster gaping at her. Milo stood in the living room, frozen with shock.

"What were you doing down there?" Ms. Foster said.

Evelyn groped for some kind of justification, anything, but her brain had gone completely blank.

"What's this?" Ms. Foster took the letters, which Evelyn had still been holding in her hand. Ms. Foster unfolded the papers and glanced through them. "Where did you find these?" She looked over at Milo and then at Evelyn. Understanding turned her expression hard.

"Your mother was right," Ms. Foster said. "You're obsessed."

"Grandma—" Milo said, but a glare from Ms. Foster quieted him.

Evelyn finally found her voice. "Those letters belonged to my family. Why can't I have them? Why have you been hiding other things about Ada and Byrne House when you knew I'd want them?

"I didn't even know about these letters. As for the rest— I can't talk about that. It's not my place."

"What did my mom say to you?"

Ms. Foster folded up the letters and put them in her pocket. "Go home now, please. Don't make me call your mother."

Tears pricked Evelyn's eyes, heavy on her lashes. But she didn't let them fall. Not on the street when Milo ran after her, or when Alex begged to know what happened. Not in her entryway, when the door slammed behind her, and she was alone with her agony.

She waited until she was in her room. Evelyn closed the blinds and crawled into her bed and under the covers.

Only then, silently, did she cry.

22

"I'M JUST SO, SO SORRY." IT WAS THE HUNDREDTH time Milo had apologized since yesterday. Evelyn didn't even bother to respond. She only blamed herself, not the Fosters.

Scratch that. She blamed her mother.

Milo and Evelyn walked side by side on the jogging track, going around in circles. In more ways than one.

Today's meeting had been Milo's idea, and Evelyn had chosen the school track. If her mom asked, Evelyn could just say she'd been getting some exercise. They were still waiting for Alex. He was supposed to be here by now.

"My grandma won't even say *why*," Milo said. "It's obviously hurting her. She's cried nonstop since yesterday, and it's not like her to just refuse to talk about something."

"It's my mom," Evelyn said. "It's partly those 'hallucinations' I had about Byrne House that probably weren't hallucinations. My mom thinks my 'obsession' isn't healthy. But it can't just be that." Evelyn was sure there was more. But demanding the truth from her mother would be worse than useless. It would be downright masochistic. Viv wasn't the type to back down.

"Could you ask your father?" Milo said.

They rounded the curve in the track and started back toward the school. *Where is Alex?* Evelyn wondered. "My dad and I don't exactly talk. And he's still out of town. Actually, I'm starting to think he won't bother to come back." He was probably sick of Viv's prickliness, sick of Evelyn's issues. It must be easier for him in that generic hotel room in Baltimore. No family, no history.

"I'm sorry," Milo said yet again. But his tone held so much kindness. Evelyn swallowed, not wanting to cry again. Especially over her father. She preferred not to think about him at all; clearly that was her dad's M.O. when it came to her.

A car door slammed. Alex's ride drove away, and he jogged over from the parking lot to meet them. "Sorry I'm late. I was stuck on the phone."

"With Caitlin?" Milo asked.

Evelyn bit the inside of her cheek. *Shut up, Milo. Please just shut up.*

"With my *mom*. Is that okay with you, Milo?"

"Can we move on please?" Evelyn walked out onto the grassy field and sat down cross-legged. The two boys did the same. "Alex is here now, so tell us your news," she said to Milo.

Milo rubbed his eyes behind his glasses. "It's about those detectives. Penn and Tyson. They came by my house this morning."

"What did they want?" Evelyn asked.

"They asked my parents to sign some papers giving the police permission to run tests on my blood samples the hospital took. Detective Tyson actually asked if I ever do drugs, which got my parents all worked up. Then the detectives wanted to know if I'm friends with Jordan Davis. But they wouldn't say why."

"So they think there's a connection between your disappearance and Jordan getting sick?" Alex said.

"*Obviously*," Milo said, but then shrugged sheepishly. "I mean, maybe. I wasn't in a coma ... I don't think."

That was just it. They didn't know what happened to Milo those two-plus days he was missing. Wasn't this a good sign? The police were actually still investigating.

"Tyson was asking about you guys," Milo said. "I told him you weren't at Jake's party. But Tyson was being all sarcastic like he didn't believe me. This was right after he implied that I'm a junkie."

Evelyn hugged her knees. "Whatever, forget him. The police are probably running tests on Jordan's blood, too. Maybe they'll find something."

"Like they'll tell *us*," Alex said. "The juvenile delinquents."

"And that's exactly why I called you guys today," Milo said. "I mean—not the delinquents thing." He rolled his eyes. "We can't get the rest of Ada's letters, so we need a new plan."

Milo paused and looked around, as if someone might overhear them. But the school grounds were deserted. "I want to take Ada's mirror into the tunnels you found. I need to find out if I was really down there. And why."

Alex looked at Evelyn, and she nodded her assent. With all three of them sticking together they'd be safe. Right?

Alex pulled at his scarred lip. "But we'd have to go through Byrne House, which is nearly impossible now. They've fixed the back door, and besides, Will and Daniella and Darren are there all the time. How would we get in?"

"But we *don't* have to go through Byrne House. My mom and my grandma went downtown to go shopping. They'll be gone all day." Milo pulled a house key from his pocket, and smiled guiltily. "I borrowed the extra key."

They went around the side of the house to Ms. Foster's backyard. Alex set their duffle bag on the grass. It clanked heavily. "I'll go inside first, just in case," Milo said. "Wait for my signal."

He unlocked the back door and tiptoed inside. After a minute, Milo waved at Evelyn and Alex in the window. Alex hefted the duffle bag back onto his shoulder.

They passed through Ms. Foster's bright kitchen. There was a fresh box of scones on the counter, and Evelyn felt a pang of guilt remembering all the happy days she'd spent here. Somehow this seemed far worse than sneaking into Byrne House, or even going into Ms. Foster's basement yesterday. Ms. Foster didn't trust Evelyn anymore, and here she was, acting like a criminal.

Milo must have seen her thoughts in her expression. He touched Evelyn's hand sympathetically. "Eventually, she'll understand. This is all for a good reason."

"Can we work through our guilt later?" Alex said. "Let's get this over with."

They were careful to lock the back door behind them and went down to Ms. Foster's basement. Milo and Alex moved the shelf that blocked the metal door. Ms. Foster would be sure to notice that, but if she got home before they'd returned, they were in trouble anyway. The quicker they could get into the tunnels and back out again, the better.

"Key?" Milo asked. Evelyn handed it over.

They opened the door onto a metal-lined storage room. Nothing except an empty wooden crate was inside. A copy of this same key must've come with each house when it was originally sold; maybe Ms. Foster had lost hers.

They stepped into the small, cold storage room and shut the door to the Fosters' basement.

This was the hardest part of their plan: getting through the false wall and out to the tunnels. As far as Evelyn and Alex had seen, these false walls were not meant to be opened from the inside. They could only be opened from the outside—by someone already in the tunnels. It would probably be hopeless if not for the fact that the door hinges were very old and very rusty by now. They'd made a quick visit to Milo's garage at home and raided his dad's extensive collection of tools. Evelyn had swung by her own house to get the mirror, which she was carrying in its drawstring bag.

Alex unzipped the duffle and extracted two crowbars. He handed one to Milo and told Evelyn to stand back. She argued that they were being sexist, but she did have to admit that the boys would get better leverage. They'd brought bolt cutters and saws, too, which thankfully proved unnecessary. Still, it took almost ten minutes. The mechanism holding the false wall snapped with a terrific boom. The wall sagged outward into darkness.

They waited, ears ringing in the silence.

Alex pulled out a flashlight and handed it to Evelyn. They trailed one-by-one through the gap, down the stairs, and out into the tunnel.

"My God," Milo breathed.

Evelyn held up the flashlight. They were in a passage just like the others she and Alex had seen. It curved away in both directions.

Milo craned his neck back to see the arched ceiling. "Look at this place. You weren't kidding. I thought maybe you were exaggerating a little but this is definitely huge."

Alex tied one end of a thick spool of string to the door handle. "So we don't get lost," he explained. "I'm out of Tic-Tacs."

She hoped they didn't have to go very far. She was relieved to see that Alex and Milo were still holding tight to their crowbars. It was broad daylight outside, but it was easy to forget that down here. *And Milo disappeared during broad daylight*, she reminded herself.

Evelyn held out the mirror to Milo.

Milo looked panicked. "I was hoping you'd do it."

"That's probably a good idea," Alex said. "One of us should see it first. In case …" He trailed off, but Evelyn understood. In case the truth was just as awful as they feared it could be. A madman kidnapping Milo, hiding his bike, bringing him down here for some sick reason ... The idea pushed down on Evelyn's chest like a weight.

"I'd rather it was you," Milo whispered to her. "Please?"

Evelyn nodded and drew the mirror out of its bag. *Don't think. Just do it.* Before her imagination started inventing morbid scenarios, and she lost her nerve.

She held up the mirror, not really sure how to go about this. The mirror seemed to show things that had happened in a particular place, and they were close to Byrne House. Maybe she'd pick up some sense of where to go. A little piece of psychic residue? Disembodied memory? That sounded like pure B.S.

Either it works, or it doesn't.

Smoke trails started to swirl in the glass. She saw a woman's silhouette, but it felt wrong, so she pushed the image away. *Milo*, she murmured to herself, searching with her mind for any hint of him. But nothing came. She concentrated harder on her memory from the day Milo had disappeared—his small, pale face in the tower window—and suddenly, she saw him. A boy with dark hair crouching against the wall.

But he was too young. It wasn't Milo at all. This boy couldn't be more than ten. Then, she knew.

She was looking at Elijah Stanton. The boy who'd been missing over a hundred years ago.

23

Elijah was confused. Terrified.

His consciousness flickered like a guttering candle. Elijah pulled himself up—he was such a tiny boy, so alone—and he ran down the passage.

Evelyn had to follow.

She ran after Elijah through the twists and turns of the passages. He was running blindly, but he was searching for someone, too. *Papa, Papa, help me!*

Finally Elijah couldn't run anymore. He collapsed onto the ground, barely conscious. Time passed, Evelyn couldn't tell how much. But finally, a man appeared at the curve of the passage and hurried to the small, prone form. The man's emotions flooded the space.

Evelyn fell headlong into the vision.

Henry Stanton kneels over the body of his son. He found the boy lying here after hours of searching the tunnels. In his haste, Henry nearly smashed the lantern when he dropped it to the floor and tried to wake the little boy. Now the boy's eyes are open, and he is breathing, which is more than the man hoped for after so many hours. He lifts the boy's head. The boy's eyes slide towards him, dull and almost lifeless. There is a brief light of recognition.

"I'm sorry, Papa," Elijah whispers.

Suddenly the boy screams and convulses. He holds out his small hands against an unseen assailant, trying to protect himself. Henry sees sheer terror in the boy's eyes. He hugs the boy close.

"There's nothing there son, nothing," *he says over and over.*

The boy clings to Henry's neck and buries his face. "I didn't want to see it but it wouldn't stop," *he wails.* "Even when I closed my eyes and covered my ears it was there. It's here now, just behind you. You can't stop it!"

"Elijah," the man says, trying to keep his voice steady. Tears are running down his face. "I know you did something you weren't supposed to. But no one is angry. Uncle Walter isn't angry. We just want you to come home. This is all a mistake, an accident."

Henry hears footfalls behind him. Another lantern appears, lighting another man's face.

Walter Byrne looks from boy to father. No surprise registers. He is sorry, wracked with guilt, but it couldn't be helped. After the boy swallowed it, there was nothing to be done, and the rest . . . the opportunity couldn't be wasted on emotion.

"You?" Henry says as he holds the boy. "You knew he was here, didn't you?"

"No," Walter lies.

The boy cries out again. He is shaking so violently his head smacks against the dirt floor. Henry struggles to keep his arms around his son. Blood begins to flow from the boy's nose and onto Henry's shirt.

Walter steps closer, holding his lantern out over the boy's convulsing body.

Henry lifts the boy into his arms and whirls to face the monster who once was Walter Byrne. He screams with despair and rage. Then he runs, holding his dying son, into the dark.

The room spun, and Evelyn fell to the ground.

Her cheeks were wet and cold from crying. A different presence lifted her, enveloped her. *Safe*, it said. She was safe and warm here. Evelyn didn't want this new vision to end. She was afraid to go back to the other one, the terrified little boy and his father, despair so black it was its own kind of death.

Eventually her head cleared, and she opened her eyes. She was cradled in Alex's lap as he sat cross-legged, his back against the tunnel wall.

"Hi." He smoothed the hair back from Evelyn's face.

Milo appeared beside Alex's shoulder. "Are you okay? You started running. We didn't know where you were going. And then you fell."

"I saw ..." Evelyn's breath caught in her throat as she tried to keep the tears down. "It wasn't you, Milo. I didn't sense you in the mirror at all."

"So I *wasn't* down here?" Milo's brows tightened in confusion.

"I just don't know," Evelyn said. "And I can't try again—not right now. Please."

"Then what did you see?"

"It was Elijah Stanton." Evelyn squeezed her eyes shut again, and Alex rested his chin on the crown of her head.

"Rest," Alex whispered.

"You don't have to tell us yet." Milo paced in front of them with his crowbar, eyes moving around the tunnel like a sentinel. It should have been reassuring, but it just reminded her of the potential danger here. "Should Alex or I try the mirror instead?" he asked.

"I don't think we have time. We need to go back." Evelyn tried to stand, but she fell back into Alex's lap. He caught her awkwardly.

"We're fine," Alex said. "It's only been ten minutes at the most. And I think we've used the mirror enough for one day. Unless you really want to, Milo?"

Milo thought a moment, then shook his head. "Later. We'll try someplace else. When Evelyn's feeling better."

"Okay," Evelyn murmured, leaning her forehead into Alex's chest. She was disappointed by her own weakness. She'd made a fool of herself after Jake's party and here she was doing it again. But Alex's presence was so comforting. She needed that right now.

"Talk about something else?" she asked. "Something boring and regular?"

Milo and Alex were both quiet for a while. Then Milo spoke up. "Um, the kickoff dance is this week. Do you know who you're going with, Evelyn?"

"Not really," she said. Her mom expected her to go, and that made her want to stay home in protest though it was usually fun.

"You're going with Caitlin, right Alex?" Milo asked. "I heard she asked you."

"I haven't decided. But I can probably guess who Milo wants to ask."

Milo shot Alex a look of disgust. "I really don't care what you think."

"Can you both stop? You're making my head hurt even more." Evelyn pushed herself up, wobbling a bit, and stood.

"Sure you're alright?" Alex uncrossed his legs and got up.

"Each time's been a little easier," she said. "With the mirror, I mean. I must be getting used to it."

"It'd be good if it works like that," Milo called from the other wall of the tunnel. He was leaning against it, staring into the depths of the passage, to where it disappeared into darkness. "Then maybe we won't need a bucket and stretcher every time Alex looks into it."

On the way back, Evelyn fought the urge to reach for Alex's hand. *No more of that*, she thought. *You're just embarrassing yourself at this point*. They reached the door to Ms. Foster's house and secured it as best they could after going back through. Milo scouted to make sure the house was still empty.

A few minutes later, they were back in Walter Park sitting beneath the statue. The sun was blinding after the dimness of the tunnels. Evelyn tried to blink the spots from her eyes, but they wouldn't go away.

"I'll tell you what I saw." She hugged her knees and looked at the grass. She would have to say this fast. Otherwise she might start crying.

"Elijah had been missing for almost two days, like the newspaper article said. His father, Henry Stanton, found him. Elijah was terrified of something, and he kept seeing it in his mind. Or sensing it. From what I could tell, it was like Elijah was looking in Ada's mirror, but there *was* no mirror. The little boy could just see it everywhere he looked. Memories, emotions. It was too much for him to take in at once."

"And he ... died?" Milo asked.

"He was having seizures, and his nose started gushing blood. Henry thought he was dying. Henry said that Elijah had touched something he wasn't supposed to."

Evelyn looked up at Alex. His eyes were fixed on her.

"Walter was there," she said. "I think he knew where Elijah was for a while, even before Henry found him. He'd tried to help at first, but it didn't work, and he was afraid to tell Henry. So Walter didn't do anything. The little boy was crying for his papa and Walter was just standing there."

Tears welled in her eyes and spilled onto her cheeks. Milo stepped in and put his arm around her.

"Henry blamed Walter for what happened," Milo said. "I felt that when I saw them in your basement. Walter felt sorry for something, but it wasn't clear why. Do you think Walter caused it? He killed his best friend's son?"

"No," Evelyn said, drying her eyes with her hand. "It wasn't intentional. But when Walter knew he couldn't help Elijah, he didn't go to Henry. He kept it secret. He was very ... blank. Henry had waves of emotion pulsing all around him, but Walter was just gray. I couldn't read what he was thinking underneath."

Alex tilted his head, thinking. "I might know a way to find out more. There's a bunch of Walter's journals in the Byrne House library. I've only been able to glance in there, but I heard Darren talking about them. Darren wanted to send the journals to some restoration place to be preserved, and Daniella had a fit. Irreplaceable family legacy, blah blah

blah. But I wonder if the journals might say something about Elijah. I'll try to get a look at them."

Evelyn was exhausted. She said goodbye and headed toward home. Milo insisted on walking with her—Alex had gone strangely quiet at that moment—but Evelyn was too tired to care either way.

In the pit of her stomach, she still felt Henry's agony. Elijah's terror. She wished she could sleep off these feelings like sleeping off an illness. She'd wake up and feel like herself again. But she was beginning to doubt that was possible. The other visions she'd had were still with her, too, like lingering bad tastes in her mouth. What if they never went away?

"Are you sure you're okay?" Milo asked.

Evelyn tried to smile and failed. "Just tired."

Milo took off his glasses and rubbed them on his sleeve. "I was wondering ... I just wanted to ask if you'd like to go to the kickoff dance with me?"

She couldn't think of a decent reason to say no. And if Alex was going with Caitlin, why not? "Okay," she said, shrugging. "Sure."

"Great." But he didn't sound that happy about it. Evelyn wondered if Milo had felt obligated to ask her because no one else would. Or maybe he just had something else on his mind.

Viv's car was still gone. They walked up the porch steps and stopped by the front door. Evelyn unlocked it and turned to say a quick goodbye. Milo was chewing anxiously on his bottom lip.

"What is it?" she asked.

"You didn't see me in the tunnels. With the mirror. Do you think that means I wasn't down there?"

It was hard to say. She didn't really know how the mirror worked. "I wish I could tell you."

"I'm just starting to think …" Milo stuck his hands in his pockets, shuffling his feet. "Maybe this whole solve-the-mystery thing isn't worth it."

"You don't mean that."

"But—" Milo glanced to the side. "Does it really matter?"

She was incredulous. *Of course* it mattered. Where had Milo been those two days? Why did Evelyn's mom and Ms. Foster treat her like an unstable mental patient? Who else had been down in the tunnels, and why?

"The police are doing their own investigation," Milo said. "Whatever really happened, I'm here, and I'm okay. The doctors will figure out what's wrong with Jordan. This stuff about Elijah Stanton or Ada Byrne—it's only making you upset."

A fist tightened in Evelyn's chest. "You think I can't handle it?" She'd been asking herself the same question, but it was so much worse to hear it from Milo. She'd thought he believed in her. He'd asked for her help.

"No, that's not what I mean. It's just, it's not like we can do anything to change what happened." Milo shoved his fingers into his hair. "I don't want you to get hurt."

"Don't worry about me." The tears were on their way back again, which infuriated her. "I'll talk to you later."

She went inside and shut the door before he could say anything else.

Milo's trying to be kind, she told herself. He was just worried about her. He hadn't really meant what he'd said about giving up. But still, the idea was a seductive whisper. *Just forget all the questions, forget the fear and the pain.* Cover it up and go back to how things were before.

But the wounds would still be there. For all of them. The *tunnels* would still be there.

24

Construction-paper leaves danced from the ceiling. "It's pretty, right?" Milo asked.

"Sure," Evelyn said in a monotone. The cafeteria glowed in fall colors, transformed with lights borrowed from the theater department. Nearly every Castle Heights High student was at the school tonight, the crowd noisy and exuberant. It was their last chance to enjoy vacation before the inevitable new term. Less than a week of summer break.

Milo put a tentative hand to the small of Evelyn's back and led her into the cafeteria. She felt hollow, like she was barely even there.

She and Milo had only texted a few times in the past days. But she and Alex hadn't spoken at all. Alex hadn't written her back. Not *once*. Their investigation was at a standstill. Supposedly it was because they didn't know where to go next for clues. Except back into Byrne House, which simply wasn't possible with the Byrnes and William always around. But Evelyn knew the real problem was her. The boys didn't think she was strong enough to handle it. *And what if they're right?*

"Should we dance?" Milo asked, jarring Evelyn out of her thoughts.

The music was already going, the bass throbbing in Evelyn's skull, and a few couples swayed on the dance floor. She smoothed down her dress—a lacy, long-sleeved mini that Viv had bought her from the best vintage boutique in town. A peace offering after their many fights lately. It was the most beautiful dress that Evelyn had ever owned, and she wasn't even excited to wear it.

"Maybe after we find Silvia. Do you see her?" It was going to be a long night. She could use all the friendly faces she could get.

"Not yet," Milo said. "She's probably still stuck in the line."

Chaperones had searched everyone's purses and coat pockets on the way in, while a couple of local police officers glared at each person as they walked through the doors. Even Detectives Penn and Tyson were there milling around, which seemed excessive to Evelyn. But lots of parents were worried. The school administration—at the urging of a certain City Council member, Evelyn was sure—had decided the doors would be locked during the dance, nobody in or out until it was over.

"There's Alex and Caitlin," Milo said.

They were dancing close together. Caitlin had worn a simple sundress, but she managed to look like an off-duty model. Alex's hands were on Caitlin's back, and Caitlin had a thumb hooked through a belt loop on Alex's pants. Evelyn couldn't stop staring at the way they moved in sync, at every place where Alex and Caitlin touched.

She'd always thought she could protect her heart. That she could stop herself from falling. But the agony of Alex ignoring her had made her realize it was already too late. For Alex, her heart had thrown itself right off the cliff. And now here she was, standing amidst the wreckage.

It hurt so damn much.

Evelyn finally turned away, and she found Jake standing right behind her. Jake's eyes were glassy, and he smelled like tequila. He took a slow sip of his punch.

"Go away," she said, right at the same moment that Milo asked, "How are you, Jake?"

Jake slapped his hand against Milo's shoulder. "Good to see you, dude. You keeping track of yourself any better these days?"

"Forget him," Evelyn said to Milo. "He's drunk."

Jake smirked, but his smile faltered at the edges. Jake's unfocused gaze lingered in Evelyn's direction, staring at the space just above her head instead of directly at her. Then he put his hand on Milo's shoulder again and leaned in. "Could we talk sometime, man? There's some things I need to say."

"About what?" Milo asked.

Alex appeared out of nowhere. He pushed Jake by the shoulder, and Jake bumped into a table, spilling his punch onto the centerpiece. Milo and Evelyn jumped back in shock. Caitlin trailed after Alex, covering her mouth in surprise.

"Stay away from Evelyn," Alex said.

"I didn't do anything!"

"Yet."

Jake held up his hands. "I don't want to be seen with you losers anyway." He brushed off his shirt and stumbled away.

Milo rounded on Alex. "Jake was trying to tell me something."

"And you were dumb enough to listen?"

"Jake's gone now," Caitlin said, tugging on Alex's sleeve. "Let's go dance."

Alex looked at Evelyn and seemed about to say something. "Don't pretend that you care," Evelyn said under her breath.

Alex looked sheepishly at the floor. Caitlin pulled his arm again, and this time he followed.

He'll be gone in a week anyway, Evelyn told herself. Back home to his fancy apartment in New York. At least she wouldn't have to see Alex all the time and want what she couldn't have.

Evelyn let Milo take her hand. She could either stand around all night being miserable or try to at least pretend to have fun. They found Silvia on the dance floor with her date.

Evelyn felt better as soon as she started moving to the music. She didn't even mind when the music slowed down, and Milo stepped in closer. He circled his arms around her waist. Evelyn closed her eyes, relaxing into the rhythm. When she opened them, Alex was staring straight at her. Evelyn felt a painful tug on her heart. Like a hook was impaled there, tearing as it pulled.

"You look great," Milo said. "Did I say that already?"

Evelyn smiled feebly. She glanced over in Alex's direction again. Caitlin had stepped back from him, and they seemed to be arguing in hushed voices. Then Caitlin spun and stormed off the dance floor, leaving Alex standing there with his hands in his pockets. Evelyn dropped her eyes just as Alex looked her way again.

Another slow song started. Milo didn't let go. Instead, he took a deep breath.

"So Caitlin told me," he said.

"Told you …?"

He flushed. "I wish I'd known a while ago. I mean, I'd hoped you did, but I didn't have the nerve to ask you to the dance until Caitlin said something."

No. Caitlin wouldn't. "What did she say?" Evelyn stammered.

Milo smiled shyly. "You know. That you like me?"

Evelyn just stared, not even trying to dance anymore. She couldn't move. Her whole body felt numb. Her lungs had ceased to exist.

"But it's good!" Milo said. "I mean, that's what I'm trying to say. I really like you too."

He was leaning toward her. Oh, God. Milo was about to *kiss* her.

Evelyn jerked back, bumping into the couple behind them. "But we're friends." As she said it, she knew: in the last couple weeks, Milo had become her *best* friend. The one decent thing to come out of this summer. And now that was ruined, too.

"Oh." His eyes kept getting bigger. "*Oh.*"

"I'm so, so sorry." Evelyn backed away from Milo and ran for the bathroom.

Her face burned maroon in the mirror. Evelyn rested her palms on the sides of the sink as a tear cascaded from the corner of her eye. What a mess she'd made. Of everything.

In the mirror, Caitlin swung open the bathroom door and walked inside.

Evelyn ducked her head and started washing her hands, hoping that somehow Caitlin wouldn't notice her. She grabbed a paper towel and looked up. Tears streaked down Caitlin's face.

"You just have to take everything, don't you? *Poor Evelyn.* All your little dramas. First Silvia, and now—"

Two freshman girls came into the bathroom. They stopped giggling as soon as they saw Caitlin's face in the mirror and whispered to one another.

"Milo told me what you said," Evelyn hissed at Caitlin, trying to keep her voice down. "That I'm into him? How could you do that to me?"

Caitlin's voice went up an octave. "Milo's crazy about you. I just wanted to help things along. But that's not enough for you is it?"

"I have no idea what you're talking about."

"You're dead to me," Caitlin said. "You are *cancelled.*" She went into the nearest stall and slammed the lock into place. The two freshman girls were gawking with their mouths hanging open. Evelyn scowled at them and left.

In the cafeteria, she found an empty table on the far side and sank into a chair. Her hair fell around her face as the music shifted to a slow song again, and couples materialized on the dance floor. She had no idea how she'd live through an entire night of this.

The chair beside her scraped on the floor. Alex. Of course. Because this evening just wasn't awful enough.

Alex sat down. "I need to talk to you," he said. "Is there someplace quiet we could go?"

Evelyn slid her hands under her thighs, refusing to look at him. "Is this about Caitlin? She said I'm cancelled. I don't even know why."

"Please, Evelyn."

"What do you *want*? You haven't spoken to me for days. Now you want to talk?"

"I know. I'm sorry."

Sorry. What a pointless word. "Go! Leave me alone!"

"I can't." Alex put his hand on her neck and traced her jawline with his thumb. "Let me make it up to you. If you won't talk, would you at least dance with me?"

She hated her heart for beating so hard, for the thrill it got just from Alex being this close.

Knowing she shouldn't, she led Alex to a deserted hallway just off the cafeteria. He touched the sides of her waist, and she lay her forehead against Alex's shoulder to avoid his eyes. He pulled her closer to him, so close she could feel the heat coming off his stomach and chest under his shirt. Exquisite torture, every second, but she couldn't pull away.

They swayed slowly to the music. Alex was wearing a green checked shirt that matched his eyes, and gingerly she touched one of the buttons. She'd never wanted anyone or anything so much. Her heart was beating so fast—flopping in her chest, gasping for air—she was sure Alex could feel it. But his heart was beating hard, too, his breaths quick and shallow against her ear. He'd stopped dancing.

"Evelyn, I've lied to you," he whispered. "About so many things."

She could feel his lips moving against her ear, but it didn't make any sense.

"I thought I had good reasons, but now …"

She lifted her head to look at him. The dimmed light of the hallway glinted off the green and black of his irises.

"I have to tell you the truth," he said. "About everything."

25

THE STAIRWELL WAS DARK, LIT ONLY BY A DINGY window. The door shut behind them with a click, dampening most of the noise of the dance, though the music still pounded like a faraway heartbeat.

Evelyn walked up the stairs to the first landing. She hugged her arms around herself.

"Are you cold?" Alex asked.

Evelyn turned around and bumped up against the window. "What did you lie about?"

She wasn't angry. Not yet. She just wanted to know. And she had that deja vu that she sometimes got around Alex, that feeling that maybe she *did* know the rest deep down. She was in the dark and something was there, coming for her, but she couldn't see it yet.

"*Tell me,*" she said.

Alex swallowed and looked up at the window. "When we ran into each other on the Byrne House grounds a few weeks ago, you asked if we'd met before. I let you think we hadn't. That wasn't true."

Evelyn nodded slowly. She didn't understand, but she also wasn't surprised. Hadn't she always felt it? That she knew Alex already, though she didn't know how?

"Why did you lie?" That wasn't the most important question. But it was the question she was least afraid to ask.

Alex raked a hand through his hair. "Because I already knew you wouldn't remember me. I was going to tell you, but the police showed up. And later, when your mom saw me in the ER—after we found Milo—she warned me not to *ever* tell you. She said if you found out it would hurt you. And it would be all my fault."

Evelyn braced one hand against the wall. "Are you saying my mother knew who you were? How?"

"My name. My scar." He flinched, his expression pure anguish. "Are you *sure* you don't remember? Anything at all?"

"Wouldn't I tell you if I did?"

Hot, angry tears sprouted from her eyes and burned trails down her cheeks. Alex took a step closer, and Evelyn pivoted away. She pressed her forehead into the cold cinderblocks in the wall, spreading her hands out to keep her standing. *What happened to me? Why can't I remember? Why why why?*

Alex smoothed her hair back and gently turned her head so she was looking at him. His eyes searched hers. "You were there, Evelyn. You were there when I got my scar."

The tears kept falling, but the rest of her went absolutely still.

"I told you about the first time I came to Byrne House. For my great-grandma's funeral? I was six?" Alex paused checking her reaction. She nodded. "That was true," he went on, "but there was more that I left out."

They sat on a step above the landing. He took a steadying breath and kept going.

"I met a little girl, a neighbor. Her family let her come over to play. I remember thinking how pretty she was. She had this funny laugh with her front teeth missing. Wavy brown hair, stormy blue eyes. You look almost the same as you did then. There's a few small differences." He nudged her arm. "More teeth."

They both smiled sadly. Evelyn's heart ached, too full of all the things she still couldn't name.

"The day I met you, it was raining. The grown-ups let us run all over Byrne House, playing some kind of game.

You and me, Darren and Daniella, with Will sort of babysitting us. Somehow we got the idea to go outside and splash in all the puddles in the gardens. Along the way, Daniella and Will disappeared, and Darren went to go look for them. Even then, he was tagging along after his sister. So it was just us."

Evelyn shifted her feet on the landing, trying to picture it. But her memory was as blank as the cinderblock wall opposite them. "What happened?"

"I don't know if it was your idea or mine. When I think about it now, it seems like it popped into our heads at the same exact moment, some weird telepathy. *Let's hide from them.* We picked the tallest tree on the grounds. An evergreen, the one that's higher than the roof now. We started to climb it. The branches were slippery, so we had to help pull each other along. The tree kept going and going. It felt like we climbed forever. After a while we heard shouting somewhere below us. We were both soaking wet, barely holding onto the trunk. I remember—you reached over to pick bark or leaves or something out of my hair, and you were trying not to laugh, and it seemed like the most amazing thing. I'd climbed into the sky with this wonderful girl and I didn't ever want to come down."

"But you did," she whispered.

Alex made a choked sort of sound. She put her arms around him, just holding on. The worst was still coming.

"This part really isn't clear to me," Alex said. "But I know it was my fault. I must have slipped. Or the shouting surprised me and threw me off balance. And I reached for the only thing I could think of—you. I remember the sky flashing between the branches, and this horrible crashing sound like the whole world was ending. The sun winked out. Everything turned black."

Evelyn squeezed her eyes closed. *Breathe,* she told herself. *Breathe.*

"We were underground," he said. "An old mine shaft."

She whimpered. She could taste the dust in her mouth, feel it in her nose. Choking her. The horrible claustrophobia she'd felt when she fell from the Byrne House fence and later in the burial chamber. It was the tower-well. The deep, dark chasm of her dreams.

That had been real.

Alex pulled back in alarm. "Evelyn? Are you okay?"

She tamped down the panic. Alex must have expected her to fall apart when she heard this, and that only made her more determined to stay strong. "I'll be okay."

Now Alex was the one freaking out. "We have to stop. I shouldn't have told you. I should *never* have told you."

"I'm *fine*. Tell me the rest." Then maybe the whole memory would come back. It was the confusion that frightened her. There was a big, dark hole in her memory, an open grave, and the rest of her was slowly crumbling and falling in. She needed to fill in that gap.

Alex's thumb traced a line along the top of her shoulder to her neck. Then down along her spine through her dress. After a couple more minutes, he spoke again, his voice a rough staccato.

"I was bleeding. You took off your rain jacket. Held it to my face. I think you'd hurt your ankle. We were both crying. There was a lot of dirt in the air from our fall, and you were coughing. And then something changed. The look in your eyes, the way you sat up. You put your arm out like you were waving something away. You kept asking, *Who's there? Who is that? What are they saying?* I told you I didn't know. There wasn't anybody down there. Just us.

"You pointed at the wall. There was a darker shape there, an arch, leading somewhere else. 'They're over there,' you said. 'Please, make them go away.' I crawled over to look. That's when I found the metal door, like the one we'd seen in the basement earlier that afternoon. I thought maybe it was a way out, but then you told me to get away from it. It was a bad place. You screamed and screamed, begging me to help make the bad things go away, and I couldn't do anything."

Evelyn put her face against Alex's shoulder, fighting more tears. It was a while before he could keep speaking.

"I asked for you in the hospital. My parents just said you were safe and that you couldn't remember what happened. I wanted to call you or something, to say—" His voice cracked. "To say I was sorry. But I wasn't allowed. I never knew why ... until a few weeks ago."

My mom.

The pieces began to shift in her mind like lenses sliding into place, and Evelyn's whole life came into a different focus. Viv had been lying to her for years, forbidding her from going near Byrne House, shaming Evelyn for her "obsession." The dreams of Ada's statue, the sleep hallucination three years ago—whether those voices had been real or some kind of flashback, Evelyn didn't know. But Viv must have known the reason for it. *All this time, Mom knew.* Viv had thought Evelyn was too weak to face it.

Well, now Evelyn knew the truth. Yet she still couldn't remember Alex or the fall or what happened in that mine shaft, much less explain what it all meant. The void in her memory was still there, a bottomless emptiness. *Maybe I am weak*, Evelyn thought. *My own brain's protecting me from it.*

"I'm sorry," Alex said again.

She let go of Alex, got up and walked across the landing. She and Alex had known each other a long time ago, apparently, but they weren't kids anymore. She couldn't cling to him like that would make everything better.

"Is that why you're telling me this now?" she asked. "You feel guilty?"

Alex stood and followed her. "I've wanted to tell you so many times. After what happened at Ms. Foster's the other day, when she took Ada's letters from you, I almost did. But I was afraid it would make things worse. Your mom said if I brought up what happened, and you weren't ready, it could mess you up. Even cause a ... breakdown or something." He looked away. "She said you'd had problems."

How humiliating. "So that's why you were worried about Milo 'reliving his trauma' too soon. That was about *me*."

Alex shrugged. "But then Milo did okay, even when we took him into the tunnels. So I thought maybe you could handle it, too. I know how strong you are. You're braver than me."

The compliments made her feel nauseous. "And after Ms. Foster threw me out of her house, you felt sorry for me."

"I have *never* felt sorry for you. It was never like that."

Evelyn faced the window. "But telling me the truth was the right thing to do, and so you did it. You don't have to feel bad anymore. You can go back to Caitlin now."

She felt him right behind her. Why wouldn't he just go? She'd had enough mortification for one night.

"When you kissed me in the park," Alex said, "I pushed you away because it *was* the right thing to do. I couldn't be with you that way with so many lies between us, but I couldn't tell you the truth. I had no choice."

She put her hands over her face. "Just stop. You don't have to explain."

"Evelyn, look at me. Please."

She turned around. He stood over her, so close his exhale tickled her forehead. But she still kept her eyes on the ground.

"My brother was right about me. I *am* selfish. If I wasn't, I would have stayed away from you like your mom said and never, ever told you the truth. We still don't know if it's going to cause you harm, and I hate myself for taking that risk. But I couldn't stand it anymore. I can't watch you dance with someone else, see him touch you."

Alex brushed his knuckles along her cheek, her neck. His fingers were hot on the skin of her collarbone. "I want to be the only one who's allowed to touch you."

The shadows in the stairwell shifted around her, closing in, turning everything upside down. This was exactly what Evelyn had wanted and she was afraid to trust it.

"The truth is, I'm not a good person," Alex murmured. "This is me being really, really selfish."

She lifted her chin, more to look at him than anything else, but he was already there, pressing his lips to hers. Evelyn's entire body responded, brilliant with electricity, sparking with flame. She opened her mouth to him, and their lips fit together. Alex's fingers slid into her hair, just as he pulled her closer to him with his other arm. The tips of their tongues met, so sweet and soft and achingly intimate.

"Show me selfish again?" she whispered. "I don't think I have it yet."

Alex laughed and wrapped her in his arms. "I told my brother I don't want to leave Castle Heights at the end of the summer. I want to stay. With you. If that's what you want, too."

"What about Caitlin?" she asked.

"We weren't really anything more than friends. I tried to tell her that I wanted someone else. She just didn't want to listen. I'll talk to her tomorrow, first thing."

He rubbed his nose against Evelyn's temple. "This is what you want?" he asked. "Me?"

"More than anything."

Alex dipped down to kiss her again. Soon they were both breathless and Evelyn's neck was aching from craning it back, though she hardly felt it.

She put her hand on Alex's chest, seeking out his heartbeat to prove to herself that he really felt the same way she did. *Alex is right here, with me, and he's really mine.*

"I wish we could get out of here," she said. "I don't know how I'll go back out there and pretend everything's the same and not be able to touch you. I feel like everyone will take one look at me and know."

Alex's eyebrow ticked up as he smiled wickedly. "We could stay in here all night."

A scream echoed through the stairwell.

They jumped away from each other. The sound had come from somewhere below. Alex jogged down the steps to the ground floor. He nodded toward the narrower set of stairs leading down into darkness. To the school's basement.

26

ANOTHER SCREAM ECHOED IN THE STAIRWELL.

"*No!*" a girl cried. "Stop!"

They dashed down the stairs. Evelyn's throat was getting tighter with every step. She pushed through the heavy double doors at the bottom of the staircase and into a tight, crowded room. A huge furnace occupied most of the space. Rust-colored water stains spread up the basement walls. The lights were already on, though several bulbs had burned out.

Beyond the furnace room, there was a dark hallway with closed doors. A moan came from that direction.

Alex was right behind her. "This way," Evelyn said.

They passed storage closets of cleaning supplies. The hallway veered left and opened up into a wide space filled with pipes and ductwork. A cylindrical water heater, and beside it, a huge cube-shaped object that Evelyn guessed was a generator. Everything was covered in dust, and the light was even dimmer over here. Concrete posts as thick as tree trunks broke up the space, creating ample opportunities for hiding places.

The sound was coming from this room. Muffled crying, like someone with a hand over a mouth.

"Hello?" Evelyn said. "Who's there?"

She took another step into the room, but Alex barred his arm to stop her. "We're in a *basement*, Evelyn," he whispered. "Maybe we should go get the police."

Evelyn's gaze darted wildly around the room. She hadn't really stopped to think. But Alex was right. They were still in Castle Heights, and those tunnels ran for miles, linked to who knew how many basements. She hadn't considered for a moment that the *school* could be vulnerable, but—

There it was, in a shadowed alcove at the opposite wall: a dark rectangle with thick rivets around its edge. A metal door exactly like the ones under Byrne House that led into the tunnels. Like the ones inside Evelyn's home and in Ms. Foster's basement.

And it was open, just by a crack.

Evelyn gasped and grabbed Alex's arm. She started to point. But the lights suddenly winked out. The entire basement dissolved instantly into pitch black.

Evelyn heard several things all at once. She and Alex had both shouted in alarm right when the lights shut off, but the other voice screamed, too—the girl who'd cried out earlier. Together their voices almost drowned out the sound of movement.

Someone was running through the basement. Hinges screeched, and a heavy door crashed shut.

The generator kicked in with a rumble, and the lights came back on. Evelyn didn't have to look. She knew the metal door was closed. Panicked thoughts overwhelmed her. But the girl's crying demanded her focus.

Alex and Evelyn ran towards the sound. They found the girl behind the generator, sprawled on the dirty ground.

It was Caitlin.

She was doubled over in a fetal position, bruises already forming on her pale arms. Alex pushed a plastic mop bucket out of the way and knelt on the floor beside her.

"Caitlin? What happened?"

She straightened up, turning her head to look from one side of the room to the other as if she'd heard Alex speaking but couldn't find him. Then she saw him and screamed again and fell backward. She covered her face with one hand.

"No, get away from me!" Her eyes jerked around the room before she squeezed them shut.

Evelyn was shaking almost as much as Caitlin. "It's Ev and Alex. We're going to help you." Her voice broke when she said Alex's name. Had Caitlin come down here to hide after Evelyn left her in the bathroom? And then, while Evelyn was in the stairwell with Alex ... *Please let her be okay.*

Evelyn touched Caitlin's wrist. "Did someone hurt you?"

Caitlin's eyes flew open, and she yanked back her arm. She stared with horror at the place on her arm that Evelyn had touched. "Get it off me! Oh God, what is this?" Caitlin scratched at her arm, long scrapes of pinkish white appearing on her skin. Her eyes rolled up to the back of her head and then she went limp.

Alex's terrified eyes met Evelyn's, and a silent communication passed between them. She knew Alex was thinking of Jordan and Elijah Stanton and even Evelyn herself, when she was six years old.

But someone was down here. Someone had done this to Caitlin. And then escaped through the tunnels.

Part 3
The Labyrinth

27

Alex and Evelyn created an uproar as they ran through the dance, Caitlin lying unconscious in Alex's arms. There were screams. The cafeteria glowed red—the emergency lights were on.

"Get out of the way!" Alex cried. "Move!"

The overhead lights flickered back on. Chaperones were staring in horror. Detective Penn pushed through the crowd, and pulled Alex and Evelyn into the front office. The detective immediately spoke into a radio. "I need an ambulance and backup units."

She put down the radio and knelt beside Caitlin, whom Alex had just laid on the carpeted floor. "Narcan!" Penn yelled to anyone who was listening. "Does the school have Narcan?"

"They think she's overdosed," Alex murmured to Evelyn. And maybe they were right. Despite all her suspicions, Evelyn had no clue what had made Caitlin react this way.

More school officials came running, and Alex and Evelyn were shunted off to one side. Within minutes, a paramedics team had arrived.

Detective Penn walked over. "You two, follow me."

She led them down a hallway. As they walked, the detective made a call on her cell phone. Evelyn could hear the other line ringing, and then a voicemail picked up.

"Tyson, where the hell are you?" Penn said.

She hung up and gestured at an open doorway. The Vice Principal's office. "Why do bad things always seem to happen when Alex Evans or Evelyn Ashwood are around? Notebooks go missing, *people* go missing, people get hurt?"

"That's not—" Evelyn began.

Penn held up a hand. "Save it. I need to head to the hospital. I have another officer coming to babysit you two. Don't move until Tyson gets here. You're going to tell him *everything*."

※

The automatic glass doors retracted. For the second time in less than a month, Evelyn and Alex rushed into the ER waiting room. It was packed with Castle Heights High students, all of whom stopped talking and stared as they crossed the room.

Milo and Silvia were already there. They got up from their plastic chairs. "Caitlin's parents just went in," Milo whispered. "Nobody will tell us what's going on."

Silvia took Evelyn's hand. She waited until the rest of the room began murmuring again, and then Silvia said, "We heard you guys were there when Caitlin got hurt. What happened? Where have you been?"

Evelyn couldn't find the words. They'd sat in the Vice Principal's office for over half an hour waiting for Detective Tyson. Finally, the patrol officer—who didn't seem to want to be there, either—agreed to drive them to the hospital on the condition that they'd consent to an interview with Detectives Penn and Tyson there.

Alex answered Silvia's question. "Police wanted to talk to us. We found Caitlin in the school basement. She was yelling and shaking and didn't make any sense."

Milo sucked in his breath. Alex nodded, confirming what Milo must have been thinking.

"The same thing that happened to Jordan Davis at Jake's party might have happened to Caitlin, too," Alex said. "And we're pretty sure someone was down in the school basement with us—he shut off the lights and got away before we could stop him."

"Or her," Evelyn added. "We don't know it was a 'him.'"

"But who would do something like that?" Silvia asked, one hand hovering over her mouth.

"How did he get away so fast?" Milo asked.

Evelyn only had time to whisper the word "door" when her mother came storming into the waiting room.

"Evelyn! Get over here. *Now*."

She had reluctantly called her mom during the ride over. But she didn't want to have this conversation without Alex beside her. She linked fingers with him. Alex just squeezed her hand and said, "You'd better talk to her alone. She won't listen if I'm anywhere near you."

She knew he was right. Evelyn didn't want to cause any more of a scene than they already had.

She and her mom went out to the parking lot.

Viv's first questions surprised her. "Are you okay? Are you hurt?" Viv's lips trembled.

"I'm fine, Mom. But Caitlin isn't."

"I know." Viv sighed, shutting her eyes. "I already spoke to her mom. Why do the police want to interview you?"

Evelyn shrugged. "Because we found Caitlin. I already told them—"

"We? Who's we?"

"Alex and me." Evelyn threw the words at her mother like a challenge.

"I already warned you about that boy."

Viv's tone was very low and very dangerous. But it made Evelyn smile cruelly. This was exactly what she wanted. The hospital parking lot wasn't the best place to hash all this out, but Evelyn didn't care. She could not hold this in another second.

"Alex told me the truth about what happened when I was a kid. How we fell on the Byrne House grounds, and we both ended up in the hospital. I know all of it now. You can stop lying."

Viv blinked at her, as if she didn't understand.

"And guess what?" Evelyn said. "The truth didn't make me have a psychotic breakdown. I'm fine. You've lied to me all these years and kept Alex from me, and I will *never* forgive you for it."

Evelyn went back inside, leaving her mom dumbstruck and alone in the parking lot.

William arrived not long after, his usually perfect hair disheveled and dirt on his designer jeans. William ignored Evelyn, pulled Alex aside, and yelled for a while about Alex's "astonishing irresponsibility."

Daniella and Darren Byrne walked in on William's heels. Daniella's eyes were sunken, and she clutched her purse to her chest. She noticed Evelyn's gaze and didn't smile.

By then, hospital security had cleared most of the curiosity-seekers out of the waiting room. That had included Milo and Silvia, but Evelyn promised to keep them updated. Her mom hadn't come back in from the parking lot, but their Prius was still out there. All Evelyn could do was sit in an uncomfortable plastic chair and think—actually, it was more brooding than thinking—and most of all wait. This night was far from over.

At one point, Detective Penn came to the waiting room to look for Tyson. She tersely reminded Alex and Evelyn not to go anywhere before she went outside and took off in her black unmarked sedan.

Almost another hour passed before Detective Tyson showed up.

The detective walked calmly into the waiting room. "Alex Evans and Evelyn Ashwood." He beckoned with his fingers. "Both of you, come with me."

William stepped in front of Tyson. "What do you want to talk to Alex about?" he demanded. "I'm his brother, and I also happen to be an attorney."

"I'm sure you are." Detective Tyson smirked and took a pad of paper from his coat pocket. "I'd just like to find out what he saw. He and Evelyn were witnesses to an incident at the school."

Viv rushed through the sliding doors into the waiting room. "Wait! I'm her mother. You're not speaking to my daughter without me."

Viv hooked her arm through Evelyn's and stiffened when she saw William was there. Then Viv audibly grumbled when she saw Daniella and Darren. *Wonderful*, Evelyn thought. *A roomful of people who can't stand each other.* And she and Alex were caught right in the middle of it.

"We heard Caitlin scream and we found her on the floor of the basement, flipping out," Alex said tersely. "I carried her back to the dance where we found Detective Penn. And then nobody could find *you*. Where were you exactly, Detective?"

Tyson wasn't fazed by Alex's question. Nor did he answer it. "How did the two of you hear Caitlin Meyer scream from all the way in the basement? Weren't you at the dance?"

Alex glanced at Evelyn. She felt everyone watching, waiting for one of them to respond. "We were in the stairwell," she said.

"You and Alex?"

Evelyn swallowed. "Yes." *We have to tell the police about the tunnels*, she thought. Yet she hesitated to give Tyson any more information than necessary. She didn't trust the smirk that kept appearing on Tyson's face. Why wasn't Penn here? Where had she gone?

"Now Alex, I'm confused about something," the detective said. "You're not a student at Castle Heights High. What were you doing there?"

"Caitlin invited me to go."

Tyson paused to scribble onto his notepad. His eyes shifted up again to Evelyn. "What exactly were you and Alex doing in the stairwell?"

Viv coughed loudly. "I don't see what that has to do with Caitlin's injury."

"We were just talking," Alex volunteered, and William waved his hand for Alex to be quiet.

Tyson looked to Evelyn, brows raised.

"Yes," she said. "We were talking."

Tyson's pen scratched on the paper for several seconds as he wrote. "Did you see Caitlin at the dance before you found her in the basement?"

"Yes, of course," Alex said.

Detective Tyson's pen paused. He smiled a little, as if they'd made some damaging admission. "Right. Because you went as Caitlin's date. And was Caitlin angry that the two of you were *talking* in the stairwell? Maybe she confronted you, Evelyn, said some nasty things? You were embarrassed? Angry?"

"You're twisting everything," Evelyn protested.

Viv pulled Evelyn behind her. "Alright, we're done."

Detective Tyson kept talking, obviously enjoying this. "And Alex, you got into some trouble back home in New York, isn't that right? Burglary? Assault?"

"Those records are sealed," William said. "This is harassment." Alex just looked at the ground.

Darren snorted. "Harassment, coming from Cliff Tyson? Who'd have ever thought. High school bully grows up to become a cop—isn't that a cliche?"

The detective turned and jabbed a finger in Darren's direction. "You still running your mouth after all these years? I've had enough of your—"

"All of you *stop*," Daniella hissed. "This is ridiculous."

Detective Tyson glared at all of them. "Fine. If we have more questions, I'll be sure to let you know."

"But," Evelyn started. "There's something bad going on in this neighborhood. If you would just—"

But her mother shushed her. "Evelyn, there's no point. We're going home."

Detective Tyson brushed past them out to the parking lot. Darren slumped into a plastic chair, while William grabbed Alex by the elbow and tugged him into a hallway, no doubt for another verbal lashing. Evelyn followed them with her eyes, worrying about what William was going to say. He wouldn't send Alex home, would he? Not now, not after Alex had finally told her the truth and they could be together. She needed to talk to Alex so they could decide what they were supposed to do.

Daniella held out her hand to Evelyn's mother. "I'm Daniella Byrne. We're neighbors, aren't we?"

Viv looked Daniella up and down, her face carefully blank. "Yes."

Daniella dropped her hand. "Do you know what's going on? The police, they can't be serious about suspecting Alex and your daughter."

Viv put her arm around Evelyn. It was more defensive than comforting.

"I mean, of course they didn't do anything," Daniella said. "I just didn't know if Cliff was being serious, or if he wanted to settle old scores and was using Alex and Evelyn to do it. We went to school together, Cliff Tyson and my brother and I. We had a falling out, I guess."

Darren laughed and crossed his legs, but he didn't elaborate.

"If that's what's going on," Viv said, "I'll make sure Detective Tyson's superiors know about it. He should be fired."

Daniella hugged her purse to her chest again. "But will they listen? Or will they think like Tyson, and bend the truth however they want to? There must be something more we can do."

Viv bristled. "I'll take care of my daughter. Why don't you worry about your own family." She sent a sneering glance toward Alex and William, who were still talking in the hallway. Evelyn let herself be pulled toward the exit door. It was clear that she and Alex wouldn't get to talk again tonight.

28

WHEN THEY GOT HOME, HER MOM CORNERED HER. "I know it's easier to hate me, but at least give me a chance to explain."

Evelyn sat at the kitchen table. Viv sat down directly across and folded her hands on the tabletop. The clock on the microwave said 3:35 am, but there wasn't exactly a perfect time to have this discussion. It would be awful whenever it happened. But it was also unavoidable, so it might as well be now.

"Then explain," Evelyn said. "Explain why you told me my dreams and my *obsession* with that place were some kind of sickness. Explain why you took away all my pictures with Byrne House in them, or why Nana had to tell me her stories about the mansion in whispers so you wouldn't hear. *She* thought I deserved to know the truth, even if it was indirectly."

Evelyn had started out speaking calmly, but now she was struggling not to scream or cry or both. "Explain why you sent me to doctors and told me it was all in my head, when the whole time you knew something terrible happened to me at Byrne House, and *I couldn't remember*." Evelyn couldn't say more without losing the little composure she still had.

"I was too scared to *let* you remember." Viv stood up and wiped a hand over her mouth. "After you got out of the hospital, I swore … No, I should start before that. I want you to understand why I did what I did. I love you so much, Evelyn. More than you could imagine."

Viv went over to the sink and poured a glass of water. Her movements were stilted.

Evelyn could see her mother's heartache reflected in the kitchen window. Every inch of this house was like that dark pane of glass—a seemingly inert thing that was teeming with memories and emotions and meanings if you knew how to see them. Thanksgivings spent at this table, dinner the night Nana died. Alex standing in front of the basement door. And thousands of versions of her mother, kind and terrible, impossible to reconcile.

It was too much. Evelyn closed her eyes, put her head on the table, and just listened.

"I should never have let you go to Byrne House that day. But my brother—your Uncle Sammy, do you remember him?"

Evelyn nodded. She had pleasant memories of her uncle, though they were soured by the fact that he hadn't spoken to the rest of the family in years. There'd been some catastrophic argument, and Viv had never forgiven him.

"Sammy was mixed up with the Byrne family somehow. He never had any sense. But anyway, he asked if he could bring you over to the mansion. There was a little boy visiting, around your age. Sammy thought it would be nice to bring you over to play. So I said okay. I'd heard the rumors about that place from my own grandmother—the kinds of stories Nana told you—but I never took them seriously. Besides, I was busy with some stupid, irrelevant project, and I thought Sammy would keep an eye on you. I've never regretted anything so much."

"What happened next?" Evelyn asked, still covering her face.

A chair pulled back, and Viv sat down. "I got a phone call hours later, and your dad and I dropped everything to rush to the hospital. You were so tiny in that bed. They'd …" Viv's voice had changed. She'd started to cry. "They'd strapped you down. You were hallucinating, trying to hurt yourself. Sammy tried to explain what happened, how you'd been playing with that Evans boy and fell into a mine shaft. It took over an hour for Sammy and the others to get you out of there. He said you'd been hysterical that whole time, completely terrified, and nobody bothered to call me, not even my own useless brother. I told Sammy I never wanted to speak to him again, and he obliged."

Evelyn sat up. She was trying to match up these events with Alex's story. "Did you see Alex in the hospital back then, too?"

Viv paused. "I spoke to Alex's parents," she finally said. "But they all went back to New York. I thought that was best." She licked her lips and went back to her story.

"The doctor insisted on sedating you. But then you wouldn't wake up. You slept for days. And when you finally regained consciousness, you wouldn't speak. A therapist told us that you were traumatized. You had nightmares so bad they made you wake up screaming, but you couldn't tell us what was wrong. I stopped sleeping and would sit with you all night, and stay with you all day. I tried everything I could think of, but you wouldn't say a single word. This went on for a solid week. I thought I'd really lost you."

Viv looked up and wiped her eyes, though the tears were still coming. "Then one morning you woke up," she said, "and you asked for chocolate chip waffles for breakfast. You acted completely like your old self, the same happy six-year-old you'd been before that awful day at Byrne House. It was a miracle. I had my baby back." Viv smiled wistfully. "I thought I did."

"But I wasn't really the same."

Evelyn's mother shook her head. "You still dreamed of Byrne House. You were fascinated with the place, and asked about it all the time. You have to understand, I thought if we told you what happened to you there we'd lose you all over again. I spoke to a therapist, and she agreed. We should minimize your exposure to reminders of the trauma."

"That's why you told Alex to stay away from me." Viv had probably told Ms. Foster, too. And it might explain even more. Evelyn got up, her chair clattering on the floor. "Did you say something to the detectives after I saw Milo in the tower?"

"I was trying to protect you. Nana thought it was better for you to face what happened, and your dad thought I was being too controlling. But they weren't the ones who'd sat with you, night and day, seeing you that way. Whatever you saw that day, it scared you so much you couldn't even speak. I was never going to let that happen again. I would have done *anything*."

"But you let people think I was crazy. *I* wondered if I was crazy."

"I just did the best I could." Viv stood up slowly and pushed in her chair. "I'm sorry, Evelyn. I drove my brother away, and then your dad, and now I've done the same to you. But I hope someday you'll see ..." She let the sentence drift away from her and looked at the floor, shaking her head. Viv turned to go to her room.

"Mom, wait."

Evelyn was trying to hold onto her righteous anger, but it was no use. She *did* understand, whether she liked it or not. She remembered the vision of her mother in her bedroom holding vigil while she slept. Evelyn could still feel the love that Ada's mirror had shown her. It was part of her, more real and more powerful than her resentment.

Viv had stopped in the entryway. Evelyn went to her mother and wrapped her in a hug. Viv sobbed into her shoulder.

As much as she hated it, Evelyn could understand why her mom lied. She could probably even forgive. But her mom would always be the same person. Imperious, stubborn, and overprotective. If Viv found out about the metal doors or the tunnels, she would send Evelyn away from Castle Heights.

That meant Evelyn had to keep lying, too, if she ever wanted to find out the rest of the truth.

29

"I'M SURPRISED YOUR MOM LET YOU OUT TO SEE me," Alex said. He'd come straight to the park when she texted.

"She's loosening up. A little." Evelyn stood, brushing grass from her jeans. It was morning, and dew had left damp patches on the denim.

She and Viv had come to an agreement. Evelyn was allowed to see Alex as much as she wanted, and Viv would stop spying on Evelyn's phone. In exchange, Evelyn would keep Viv appraised of where she was going at all times. Evelyn doubted that either of them would stay true to the bargain for long, but at least it was progress.

"My brother's done the opposite. He's wound himself up a million times tighter." Alex smiled, but he was obviously worried. Something had happened.

Evelyn pulled a leaf from the maple beside her and started bending it back and forth. "What did William say?" she asked.

Alex dug his teeth into his lower lip. "That he's sick of bailing me out. I don't know how Detective Tyson found out I'd been arrested, but that was true. The whole thing was stupid. After my dad died, my mom gave away his cigar box to a family friend. I was pissed, so I went to get it back. A neighbor saw me trying to break in and called the police." Alex shrugged one shoulder. "Not my best moment. Will could've let me rot, but he got me out of it. I don't blame him for wanting to get rid of me now. Half the time he sees me lately, the cops are involved."

"Wait, get rid of you?" Evelyn let the maple leaf flutter to the ground, her heart sinking as it did. "William's making you go back to New York?"

Alex closed his eyes. "My flight is Sunday."

"*Tomorrow?*"

"I don't want to go." Alex held Evelyn's face with his hands and kissed her. His mouth was soft and warm and reassuring. But he'd only said he didn't *want* to go. Not that he wouldn't.

"Are you kidding me?"

Evelyn's eyes flew open. Milo stood a few feet away, his mouth hanging open with shock. Silvia stood a few feet behind him, wide-eyed and very uncomfortable.

"It's been *one day*." Milo turned and ran.

"Wait!" Evelyn raced after him.

Milo stopped and whirled to face her, cheeks flushed and fists clenched. "*What*, Evelyn?"

"I'm sorry." She swallowed, catching her breath. "I never, ever would have wanted to hurt you."

Milo shoved his hands into the pockets of his hoodie. "I'll be okay. It's you I'm worried about. Alex was Caitlin's date yesterday, and the minute she's gone he's all over you. This is—"

"My business," she interrupted. "Alex and I have a lot more history than you know, and I'll try to explain it. But, Milo." She had to look away. It made her feel vulnerable to say this, but she knew Milo needed to hear it. "You're my best friend. I mean, I'd like you to be. Please?"

Milo nodded slowly. "Of course I will." He pushed up his glasses and rubbed his eyes. "Did you tell Alex what happened at the dance? How I thought—what Caitlin said—"

"He doesn't know anything about that. Can't we go back to being normal? Please?"

He sighed. "Then you have to be normal, too. None of *that* with him in front of me. For a while, at least. And we have to bring in Silvia. She knows something's up, and she wants to help."

"No way." After what happened to Caitlin, Evelyn didn't want any more of her friends getting hurt.

Milo held up his hands. "Fine, but you have to tell her. She can yell at you instead of me."

"I'll handle it." She and Milo walked back to the statue where Alex and Silvia were waiting.

"You're back," Alex said.

"Yep," Milo said, staring off into the trees.

At least they were speaking to one another. Evelyn took that as a good sign. She gave Silvia a quick hug and then sat down next to Alex at the base of the statue, though she kept some space between herself and Alex for Milo's benefit.

"We came to tell you about Caitlin and Jordan," Silvia said. "I got a call from Caitlin's mom a little while ago. They're awake. Both of them came out of their comas this morning."

"Seriously? That's amazing." Evelyn sat forward. "We should go visit Caitlin. See if she's doing okay."

Silvia cringed. "I'm going to see her this afternoon, but I don't think you should come, Ev. Caitlin doesn't remember how she got sick, but she remembers most of the other stuff. Like you and Alex dancing?" Silvia glanced toward Alex.

Evelyn felt a hot flush of shame, even though Caitlin's heartbreak wasn't really her fault. Of course Caitlin didn't want to see her. She'd be lucky if Caitlin ever spoke to her again.

"My mom said there's going to be a community meeting tonight," Milo told them. "To talk about Caitlin and Jordan and me. My mom said I have to go, but maybe you guys should too. It's insane that Detective Tyson was trying to blame you."

Alex pursed his lips. "So Caitlin doesn't know who attacked her?" he asked.

"You're really sure someone *attacked* her?" Silvia's voice had gone up an octave. "But why would anyone do that? You have to tell me what the heck is going on."

Evelyn tried to deflect the question, but Silvia would have none of it. Evelyn had rarely seen her friend so determined.

"You're always telling me to stand up for myself," Silvia finally said. "And you're right. I'm sick of being the last to know anything important. I don't care if it's dangerous. Let me be a part of this. Let me *help*."

"Alright." Maybe Silvia would see some connection that the rest of them had missed. Evelyn waved Silvia and Milo over to sit by the statue.

"This will take a little while to explain."

"So there's one of those creepy metal doors in the school's basement?" Silvia shuddered.

"We both saw it," Alex said. "Whoever attacked Caitlin went through the tunnels to do it."

Milo tapped his fingers against his leg. "They escaped through the tunnels, you mean. We don't know if they came into the school through the tunnels. It could have been someone who was already at the dance."

"Oh," Silvia said in a small voice. "I hadn't thought of that."

Evelyn hadn't either. But it couldn't be one of their fellow students. Could it? She tried not to picture Caitlin's wild, terrified eyes or the streaks of dirt on her skin.

"Thank goodness there's not one of those doors in *my* house," Silvia said. "How horrible."

They sat in tense silence. A few cars drove by. The sky was overcast, and Walter Park was deserted today.

"Let's think about what we *do* know," Alex said, stretching out his legs. "We have a bunch of people with similar symptoms. Caitlin and Jordan both seemed to be hallucinating."

"And it sounds like something similar happened to Evelyn when she was a kid," Silvia said. Evelyn nodded. She had already told Milo and Silvia about the mine shaft.

"Then there's Elijah Stanton," said Alex. "And the things Reginald Byrne wrote on the walls before he died."

"And me." Milo glanced over at Byrne House's tower. "I disappeared, just like Elijah. Then I couldn't remember what happened. Same with Evelyn, and Caitlin, and Jordan. That can't be a coincidence."

"Maybe Caitlin wasn't really attacked," Silvia said hopefully. "It could be a weird virus spreading around."

Evelyn wished she could agree. But she'd seen the door cracked open in the school's basement. She'd heard it slam closed. And she and Alex hadn't imagined the light or the footsteps when they first ventured into the tunnels. There was some connection between all these events, but too much was still missing.

"We need the rest of Ada Byrne's letters," Evelyn said.

Milo frowned guiltily. "I've tried, I really have. My grandma's being hard core about this."

"It's not your fault," Alex said. "We need Walter Byrne's journals, too, and I haven't been able to get those. They might say something about Elijah."

Evelyn threw her head back in frustration. Instead of focusing on what they didn't have, they needed to use the information in front of them. *Think like a detective*, she told herself. *You didn't read all those novels for nothing, right?*

"We know basements have something to do with it," Evelyn said, brainstorming out loud. "The old mine on the Byrne property is underground, so that's kind of like a basement. Then there's all the tunnels ... Jordan got sick in Jake's basement, too. Although, his basement is finished. So even if there was a metal door there, which isn't guaranteed, it could be covered up."

Silvia made a sound of surprise and snapped her fingers. "Jake's basement! There's one of the metal doors in the utility room, behind the water heater and furnace and stuff. I thought it was the bathroom the first time I was over there."

"Oh yeah!" Milo said. "You're right. I've seen it too."

Alex and Evelyn gaped at him.

"Milo, why didn't you tell us this before?" Evelyn asked.

He shrugged. "I don't know. I didn't think of it until now."

Evelyn rubbed her temples. "Then Jordan might have been attacked, too. Like Caitlin." She kept trying to make it all fit, but how?

Alex dug the heel of his shoe into the grass. "The tunnels aren't the only common factor here. Do you know if anyone saw Jake last night after we found Caitlin?"

Milo scoffed. "You can't think Jake had something to do with this."

"Jake would never—" Silvia began.

Alex held up his hand and started counting off his fingers. "One, we all know Jake has been having issues. Treating you all like crap, even though you were supposed to be his friends."

"Jake's going through some things," Silvia said. "But it's nothing to do with this."

Alex looked skeptical. "Two, Jordan got sick at Jake's house after they'd been hanging out together. Strike three, Jake had opportunity. He has access to the tunnels through his house, and he was at the dance. Bonus points, he's an ass. How can you rule him out? Maybe he was coming after Evelyn at the dance but found Caitlin instead."

Milo shook his head. "The timing doesn't make sense. And besides, I just don't think Jake could have done this. Yeah, he was awful to us, but put two people in a coma? No way. And what about my disappearance? Or Elijah Stanton? Jake was alive a hundred years ago?"

"Obviously not," said Alex to Milo. "I don't know how to explain Elijah or Evelyn or Mr. Byrne. But you, Jordan, Caitlin—the only thing you three really have in common, aside from just going to the same school, is Jake."

Evelyn didn't want to believe Jake was involved. But she also knew better than to think she could see into a person's heart and soul.

She stood up and paced. "If only Jordan or Caitlin remembered what happened to them. They could tell us in a minute whether it was Jake or someone else. We need a witness."

Alex scratched thoughtfully at his scar. He looked up at Evelyn, his eyes bright. "We have the next best thing to an eyewitness. We take the mirror to where they were attacked, and hopefully we'll be able to see it all unfold exactly as it happened."

"Mirror?" Silvia asked.

Evelyn groaned. She hadn't explained that part just yet.

"How would we get into Jake's house?" Milo said. "We can't break in from the tunnels; he probably has some kind of motion detector alarm. And the school will be crawling with police, especially the basement. They might even have set up video cameras for all we know. Not only that, how would we even find our way *through* the tunnels to those places? The tunnels aren't a straight shot. They zig-zag all over the place. And phones have no reception, so GPS is out."

This discussion was making Evelyn's head hurt. "Maybe we should just tell the police. Let them sort this out. If there's really an attacker out there—"

"*No way.*" Alex and Milo had spoken at the same time.

"So Detective Tyson can blame all of this on you and me?" said Alex.

"The police have been useless," Milo said. "They never even found anything from those blood tests. '*Inconclusive.*' And I don't trust Detective Tyson either. He's been a jerk every time I talk to him. Like he thinks I'm hiding things and my disappearance was all my own fault. He's never going to listen to us, and he'll make sure Detective Penn doesn't either."

"But—" Evelyn started.

She paused when she heard loud knocking. Across the street, a familiar figure was standing on Byrne House's front porch, pounding on the door. Mrs. Lake, the cleaning woman.

"I want a word with you!" Mrs. Lake said to the closed door. No one answered, and she began banging on the mansion's door again.

"What's she doing?" Milo asked.

"No clue." Alex jogged across the street. Evelyn, Silvia and Milo followed close behind.

"Ma'am? Can I help you?"

Mrs. Lake turned to Alex. "I'm here to see Daniella and Darren. I want to talk to them, right away."

"I don't think they're home."

"I already tried calling and they won't answer." Mrs. Lake pounded on the door one last time with her fist. "After all I've done for them, all these years, they had some lawyer send a letter to fire me. Probably the rest of my Castle Heights clients will drop me too when they hear that. I only kept cleaning this awful house out of respect for their mother's memory, but does that matter to them? Apparently not."

She thrust something into Alex's hands. "Here. Tell them that's all I had!" Mrs. Lake pivoted and marched down the path.

"I'm sorry about what happened," Silvia said as she passed, but Mrs. Lake only shook her head.

Alex was still on the wrap-around porch, looking down at his hand. Evelyn, Milo and Silvia went up the steps to join him.

The front door was made of shiny, almost-black planks of wood and brass hardware. It reminded Evelyn of a drawbridge into a gothic castle.

"What did Mrs. Lake give you?" Silvia asked Alex.

"Oh, these?" Alex smiled and opened his hand. A small ring with two keys sat on his palm. They were modern, stainless steel, like they could belong to any building anywhere. But by the excitement in Alex's eyes, Evelyn knew those keys wouldn't unlock just anyone's house.

Alex stuck the key into the mansion's lock and turned. The door creaked open onto a dim entryway.

"I guess since nobody's home, we should do them a favor and leave the keys inside. No telling who might get ahold of them otherwise." Alex stepped inside and then looked back over his shoulder.

"Aren't you guys coming?"

30

In the daylight, Byrne House's entryway was deceptively plain. The mansion's architectural style was similar to her own home. Curving wooden trims, high ceilings, floors aged to a deep patina. But as Evelyn looked closer, more and more differences emerged in the details. Evelyn put her hand out to touch the maroon wallpaper. It had tiny, almost invisible vines embossed on its surface. And subtle, abstract carvings decorated the staircase banisters.

"Beautiful," Evelyn whispered. She shouldn't be touching anything, much less admiring it. This house held dark secrets. But even knowing that, she was still drawn to it. There was so much history everywhere she looked.

Milo was hesitating by the threshold. "Aren't we going to get in trouble?"

"I'm inviting you," Alex said over his shoulder. "What'll they do to me? Send me home?" He ventured into the main hallway.

The subject of Alex leaving was not something Evelyn wanted to discuss. "Have you remembered anything about the day Mr. Byrne died?" she asked Milo.

He shook his head. "It's like I've never seen this place before, but also like I've been here too many times to count. You know?"

She did know. All too well. "You don't have to do this if you're not ready."

"No, I do." Milo let out a breath.

Alex stopped at a set of double doors, grasped the handles and slid them apart. The doors glided silently open. "The library," he announced.

Instantly, Milo's face lit up.

The scent of vanilla and rose hit them as they walked inside the huge room. Evelyn recognized it as Daniella's perfume. A stained-glass window lit the room with a rainbow of colors. Milo was already wandering amid rows and rows of books. The bookshelves stretched from the parqueted floor to the tray ceiling, all full.

"There's got to be thousands of books in here," Milo said with awe.

"Look at this," Silvia said, heading toward an open display case. "Crystals! They're so pretty!" She gently reached out a fingertip to touch one of the shimmery rocks.

Evelyn wandered through the stacks. There were so many beautiful, old books. They smelled of leather and memory. This was the kind of room Evelyn could spend days in without leaving. Months, even. *But this is Byrne House,* she reminded herself. *A trap always looks innocent at first.*

Evelyn turned a corner and found Silvia in a tiny alcove looking at framed photos on the wall.

"Ev, look at these!" Silvia said. "You'll love them."

The first photo had a typed caption beneath it: "Walter and Ada, July 1, 1899." The Byrnes stood in front of the mansion, though the building had scaffolding around it and the tower was only half-built. Walter looked serious, with sharp cheekbones and a thick mustache. To his right, holding tightly to his arm, stood a tiny woman with a round face and a bright smile. Ada. The crinkles beside her eyes made her seem like she was about to laugh.

It was hard to believe their lives had eventually turned so tragic. Evelyn wondered for the thousandth time what really happened to Ada and how much of Nana's stories were true.

The next picture was of Walter and his brother Simon. The two stood in front of the park, all the oak and maple trees just skinny saplings. Simon had the same cheekbones as his brother, but he was much taller and more handsome, with hooded eyes and a sly grin. But Evelyn knew from Ada's letters how much that grin concealed.

She remembered the note that Ada had enclosed with the mirror. *Even my room is no longer safe from him.* Had she been talking about Simon? Or could it be Walter, who'd shown such callousness to Elijah Stanton? Was there really one good brother and one bad as Ada seemed to think?

"I think I found them." Alex had stopped at a shelf of large, leather-bound books. They had handwritten dates and roman numerals along the spines. The soft covers were fraying at the edges, worn away in spots like they'd been read countless times.

Alex pulled down one of the volumes and flipped gingerly through its brittle pages. "These have to be Walter's journals," he said.

Milo plucked another journal from the shelf. He opened it, and dust floated up from its inside cover. "Look at the date here—1888!" He glanced through it with Silvia.

Evelyn read the dates on the spines until she found the first volume, marked with a large numeral I. On the inside of the front cover someone had written "May 1884 to March 1885." She thumbed through the pages, each so thin it was translucent. The tiny cursive was so slanted it was nearly illegible. Strange drawings were squeezed between the writing, too, in different configurations of circles, triangles and squares with equations beside them.

Evelyn chose another volume and another. She and her friends looked through the journals for several minutes hoping for some mention of Elijah Stanton or even Ada. But it was all notes about experiments and complex mathematical expressions.

Alex took the last journal from the shelf and flipped open the cover. "Volume twenty-four. It says this ends in 1901. There's a gap of over a year between this journal and the one before it. That means..." He paused, thinking. "Volumes twenty-one through twenty-three are missing. 1898 to 1900."

"Maybe he talks about Elijah in those?" Milo said.

"Or not at all," said Evelyn, disappointed.

Ada's letters, those Evelyn had read, were all from 1898. The other letters—the ones that Ms. Foster still had—must've come from that same missing period of time, around 1899 or 1900. What had happened to Walter and Ada during that time?

She put the journal she was holding back on the shelf. It seemed like everywhere they searched for clues, they'd only met dead ends—whether it was Ada's letters, Evelyn's own still-missing memories, or even the tunnels themselves. They had to keep pushing.

"We're going to the tower," she said.

She'd bring Ada's mirror along so they could finally start getting some answers.

"Actually, you're going to leave."

Evelyn spun to face the library doors. William and Darren were standing there. It was William who'd spoken. How long had they been listening?

"This house isn't a playground," William said. "You have no idea how valuable all these books are."

"How did you get in here?" Darren asked. Unlike William, he didn't sound angry. Just curious.

Alex walked nonchalantly toward them. "Mrs. Lake was here. She was pretty upset about being fired. I thought you'd want to know, and now you do. You're welcome."

He breezed past his brother and his cousin, waving for the others to follow him. But William's hand shot out and grabbed Alex's elbow. "How stupid do you think I am? Where's the cleaning lady's key?"

"Key?"

William patted Alex down and found Mrs. Lake's keyring in Alex's shirt pocket. He held it up. A single key dangled from his fingers.

"Oh, that." Alex sounded disappointed. But there'd been two keys on that ring earlier, when Mrs. Lake handed it over. Evelyn felt a secret thrill—Alex still had the other key.

William exhaled, and in that moment the two brothers looked more alike than not. "Do you think I *want* to be such a hard ass, Alex?" he said.

While the two brothers spoke, Darren shrugged at the rest of them. "Sorry folks. It's probably not the best time for a visit."

Milo and Silvia didn't waste any time. "We can go to my house and talk there," Milo suggested. But Evelyn decided to wait for Alex on the porch.

She sat on the stone porch railing. She was pissed at Alex's family for sending him back to New York. Frustrated with their secrecy. *My mother would fit in well here*, Evelyn thought. *Bet she'd be surprised to have so much in common with the Byrnes.*

The mansion's front door opened, and Darren stepped out. "Waiting for Alex?"

"Yes," Evelyn said cautiously.

"You've been spending a lot of time with him, haven't you?" he asked.

She'd thought Darren seemed nice enough before. But the way Darren was looking at her now—it made her uncomfortable. Like he wasn't just talking about the few times they'd run into one another. More like he'd been actively *watching* her.

"Why do you ask?"

He held up his hands. "I'm not trying to interfere in your business. But Alex and William both had issues back in

New York, and I doubt you know what you're really getting into."

"Are you talking about that stupid arrest? Alex explained what happened."

"I'm talking about how their whole family is in debt. Byrne House is an asset to William, and he's looking to cash in. He's been lying to my sister, and I think Alex knows." His voice had dropped to a whisper. "Look, Evelyn, I just think you should watch out for—"

William appeared. He clamped a hand on Darren's shoulder. "Dany's calling your phone."

Darren scowled at him with barely contained hostility. "I'm busy."

"It could be important. Go see what she wants."

Darren plodded back into the house, giving Evelyn one last look with an odd expression. Calculation? Indecision? Worry? It was hard to tell.

But William stayed on the porch. He put his hand on Evelyn's back and started ushering her down the steps. "There's a community meeting tonight at the Charity Club," William said. "A lot of people are worried about the illness that's going around. Will I see you and your mother there?"

Looking to cash in, Evelyn repeated to herself. *He's lying, and Alex knows.* Lying about *what*? If Darren had meant to unnerve her, he'd been successful. But should she believe him? She had no reason to trust his word.

"I don't know," she said. "Will Alex be there?"

William's hand was on the small of Evelyn's back, too large and too hot. "My brother will be at the hotel, packing," he said. "I know it seems like I'm being unfair, but this is for the best. Castle Heights isn't good for him. Too many bad memories."

She picked up her pace, eager to get away. How could someone like Alex have such a pompous jerk for a brother? She passed through the gate and closed it behind her.

William called out, "Evelyn." She looked back. He walked slowly toward her until he was standing on the other side of the gate. He rested a hand on one of the iron spikes at the top.

"This neighborhood isn't a very safe place these days," he said. "I hope you'll be careful."

31

ALEX TAPPED AT THE GLASS. EVELYN SLID OPEN THE window, anticipation blooming in her chest.

"Can I come in?" he asked, with only a hint of a smirk.

"You're early." It was only dusk. Someone might see him on the roof. But Evelyn didn't mind. Her mom, the detectives, and most of the neighborhood were at the Charity Club for their big community meeting. Her mom had instructed Evelyn not to go. Viv wanted to keep her daughter as far away from official scrutiny as possible, and for once, Evelyn agreed completely with her mother.

She had bigger plans tonight. They involved Alex, Ada's mirror, and Mrs. Lake's remaining key. She'd decided to ignore Darren's supposed "warnings." She trusted Alex. Whatever had happened in New York, it was his business. He'd tell her if he thought it was important.

Evelyn stepped aside so Alex could climb in. He pulled off his shoes, and Evelyn shut the window and then the curtains. It was the first time he'd ever actually been in her room.

He took a few steps toward her, and then collapsed onto her bed. He pressed Evelyn's pillow to his nose. "It smells like you," he whispered.

She laughed. "I smell like me too, you know." She kneeled on the bed.

Alex touched her knee and slid his fingers up along her jeans to her waist. Evelyn stretched out beside him. If Alex's brother got his way, this would be their last night together. Every single moment had to count. Part of her just wanted to stare at him, to memorize the way he looked: his hair falling across his forehead and onto her pillow, his green-black eyes studying her in turn. How could she have ever forgotten this boy?

Evelyn still refused to believe Alex was really going to get on that plane, but nothing was certain. She touched his cheek—the slightest bit scratchy and yet soft at the same time.

"If it's not clear already," Alex murmured, "I'm waiting for you to kiss me."

Evelyn's phone interrupted them. A notification from her private texting app. "That'll be Milo," she said. "He can wait a few seconds." She deserved one normal teenager moment, however brief.

The phone chimed three more times in quick succession.

"Apparently, Milo cannot wait," Alex said.

Evelyn grumbled and snatched her phone from her nightstand. She read the messages. "The community meeting just started. Detective Penn is answering questions, but our names haven't come up at all. Detective Tyson isn't there." She was relieved to hear that. She knew Viv had complained, so maybe Tyson was off Caitlin's case.

"What about my brother and the Byrnes?" Alex propped himself up on his elbow. He leaned over to kiss the side of her neck.

Despite the distraction, Evelyn managed to check with Milo. "Yep, they're in the front row. Same with my mom, on opposite sides of the room as usual. Plus Caitlin and Jordan, Silvia, even Jake ... Sounds like everyone's there except us."

The doorbell rang.

Alex lifted his eyebrows. "If everyone's at the meeting, then who's that?"

Evelyn got up from the bed. "I don't know."

The bell rang again.

It's Detective Tyson, she thought automatically. She wasn't even sure why that thought made her so uneasy. This was her house, and Alex had every right to be here. Tyson couldn't do anything to them except make empty threats.

Or so she hoped.

Evelyn left her room and crept down the stairs. The person at the door rang a third time, and then knocked. She gripped the banister and glanced back to make sure Alex was close behind.

"Who is it?" Alex whispered.

Through the leaded-glass window in her front door, all she could see were gray slacks. The person shifted his weight impatiently, and then reached out to knock again. Yellow. The person had a yellow sleeve.

Evelyn suddenly laughed at herself. It wasn't Tyson at all.

"Wait up there," she said to Alex. She jogged down the steps and opened the door.

Ms. Foster looked like she'd been crying. She clutched a large manila envelope to her chest. "You're here! Thank goodness. Oh Evelyn, I'm so very sorry."

Evelyn carried the manila envelope back up to her room, where Alex was waiting. He must have heard everything Ms. Foster had said.

"Is that what I think it is?" he asked.

Evelyn held the envelope in front of her. It had something thick inside. And yes, it was exactly what Alex thought it was. She fingered the clasp of the envelope.

Ms. Foster had apologized for keeping so many secrets. Years ago, Viv had told Joyce to avoid discussing Byrne House with Evelyn. And Viv made a more specific, more insistent request in the last few weeks: never tell Evelyn the truth about how she knew Alex Evans. Ms. Foster hated being stuck in the middle. But what could she do? As a fellow mother, she'd never go directly against Viv's wishes. So if Evelyn happened to come across a newspaper clipping about the Byrnes in the attic, Ms. Foster let it slide. She otherwise kept anything related to Byrne House locked away. When she found letters penned by Ada Byrne in the local library's archives, she kept them a secret.

And last week, when Evelyn had snuck in to steal a different set of Ada Byrne's letters—ones Ms. Foster hadn't even known about—the circumstances had seemed to confirm the worst of Viv's claims.

Evelyn had already guessed most of this on her own. But the details awakened new anger at her mother—until she found out that earlier that day, Viv had called Ms. Foster.

Evelyn's hardheaded, impossible mother was actually trying to fix what she'd done wrong.

In her room, she opened the clasp and upended the envelope onto her bed. The bundle of letters landed on her quilt. "The rest of Ada's letters," she told Alex. "Ms. Foster read them, and she had no idea what they meant. But she said I could have them back."

Those hadn't been Ms. Foster's exact words. In fact, she had said, "*I don't want them.*" Whatever these letters said, they'd been disturbing enough to frighten the older woman. "I suggest you give these to your mom," Ms. Foster had said, "since Milo tells me they belonged to your family anyway. None of it makes any sense to me."

Ms. Foster had hesitated. Then she added, "Milo said these letters could shed some light on his disappearance. I don't see how that's possible. What Ada writes—" She shook her head. "It's pure fantasy. Or horror, maybe. But if there's anything here, *anything*, that could help us find out what happened to Milo, you'll tell me?"

Evelyn had promised, and Ms. Foster left.

"Well, this changes things." Alex picked up the letters and unfolded them. "New plan?"

"New plan." But they had to read quickly. They had a lot to accomplish tonight, even more than they'd thought.

Evelyn sat down beside Alex and took the letters from him. She found the earliest one and began to read.

June 17, 1899
Byrne House

Dearest Mary,

We are finally home. In truth, we've been home for three weeks, but I'm sure you will forgive me if I treated the time after our arrival as a bit of a honeymoon. The view from the train was astounding on the way here, my husband tells me, but unfortunately I enjoyed very little of it. Little Walter was not kind to me. I was lying sick in my berth nearly the entire trip.

You and Christopher showed us such hospitality and kindness, but I didn't truly feel like a wife until I spent my first night in the tower bedroom as Mistress of Byrne House. I am very quickly getting used to that title.

Mary, I am trying desperately to keep this letter lighthearted, but you must allow me to give you the thanks you refused to hear in your home. I would be lost now without you. Your advice and understanding were my lifelines during that terrible time. When I arrived on your doorstep, you didn't turn me away as so many would have after the compromises I'd made. I don't regret any of it because it brought me to Walter, and he loved me enough to follow me after I ran. But I would never have accepted him had you not convinced me of my worth. I promise I'll leave it at that. Let me go back to telling you about my perfectly lovely life as Mrs. Byrne.

Walter was apparently very busy with his plans for the house and grounds during my absence. His vision for the house itself is still not complete. If you can believe it, there are far more projects now than I ever dreamed there could be. I'll admit, I am responsible for the addition of many of them. I've managed to persuade Walter (I'll leave to your imagination by what means) to undertake my plan of building homes for the staff, buildings for trade and services, parks, and a school for the children. We have too much land going to waste that can be put to higher use.

Mr. Stanton and his family have happily agreed to move here to join us full time after their new home is finished, just a few steps away from Byrne House. Their Elijah is nine years old, and they have a beautiful baby boy as well. Perfect playmates for Little Walter.

My husband is overseeing the work very carefully. I sometimes worry that his devotion is too taxing. Some days he is so exhausted, he can't get out of bed. He murmurs about people or things in his room that aren't there, as if he's awake but still dreaming. I am sure it's the lack of sleep. He hasn't had another episode like the one you witnessed. I keep telling him to demand less of himself, but I think this is the one area where my powers of persuasion are lacking.

Please give my love to Christopher and the children. I'll write again as soon as I can, but I'm warning you now that I don't anticipate having much time for correspondence. Walter wants me to work with the architect on plans for the school and I'm eager to begin!

Love always,

Ada

August 28, 1899
Byrne House

Dear Mary,

Walter is once again in his laboratory. The entire third floor stinks of pulverized rocks. His eyes are sunken and he jumps whenever one of the servants enters our room unexpectedly. He needs sleep; there is no way around it. Although my frame is taking on a rounder cast, I finally have more energy, and miss him so much during the day. He tends to fall asleep at his work table in the afternoon when we used to take walks outside.

My work on the school and other buildings for our little community has been delayed. Walter insists on changing the configuration of the streets, the arrangement of the buildings, and the various layouts of the homes time and again. Even the modern sewer system is being improved according to his design. I sometimes detect in him an obsessive tendency to control everything around him. Except for me, thank goodness.

I know my letters are increasingly critical of Walter, but I hope you don't interpret me incorrectly. I love Walter dearly. He is everything to me, and I know he will be everything to my Little Walter soon enough. Will you promise to come stay with me when Little Walter arrives? I can't bear the thought of doing it without you.

All my love,

Ada

September 5, 1899
Byrne House

Dear Mary,

I am so frightened I can hardly breathe, or even write this letter for the quaking of my hands. Walter had another of his fits. I found him in his tower laboratory after he failed to appear for dinner. He was slumped on the floor, partway underneath one of his work tables, with mineral samples and shattered glass equipment all around him. At first I wondered if he'd hit his head, or lost consciousness by some other means, but then I saw his mouth moving. I kneeled to the floor and lowered my ear.

He whispered, "Ada, it's all around us. Can you see it?"

I asked him what he meant. I was shivering with fear but I tried to keep my voice steady. I won't forget his next words, or the terror in his eyes when he said them.

"I see it all. The vital essence of all of us, of every living thing, every breath in and breath out, living and dying, love and sorrow—it's all here if you can bear to turn your eyes to it. We mustn't be afraid. We mustn't…"

Then his arms and legs stiffened and his eyes bulged for a moment before he began writhing like a man on fire. He screamed and cried out the most terrible things. His eyes rolled wildly in his head and his arms flailed, trying to catch the phantoms he saw in the air. I wanted to help him somehow, but he was so strong. I was afraid for Little Walter. And I couldn't go to any of the servants for help. Walter would never forgive me for allowing them to see him like that.

I finally ran to the corner of the room and waited for it to be over. More glass instruments smashed to the floor when he kicked the table. Once, he banged his head so hard against the floor I thought he had bashed in his skull. But he just kept shaking and muttering, and eventually he grew quiet.

Walter is awake now. I just came from our room.

He has been resting for the past day in bed. He told me quite a few things, far too much to put down in this letter. My head is swimming with all of it. Walter confessed that he has had these fits for years, ever since working in his mine beneath our home. Typically, he has no memory of these episodes, nothing but a shadow of insight that drives his research.

But the last few fits have been gaining in intensity. He said he has visions—both sublime and terrible—that he can now remember vividly. *Revelations*, he called them. He demanded that I bring him a pen and paper, and he is in there now writing furiously.

What troubles me is that Walter seems convinced that these visions are real.

I love my husband so dearly, but what he described today—it suggests his mind is dangerously close to the breaking point. Please tell me your impressions. I know that genius and madness tend to go hand in hand, but I cannot give up Walter to that possibility yet.

Ada

February 21, 1900
Byrne House

Dearest Mary,

When will you visit again? That is all I have been able to think about in these three weeks since you left Byrne House. I know I should be thankful you stayed as long as you did, but it's hard not to be selfish. It's so quiet in the house this afternoon that it unnerves me.

I was so hopeful when I saw Walter's joy after Clara's birth, despite her being a daughter instead of a son. But now he hardly looks at the baby. He said yesterday he's had the flash of an idea for an incredible invention, and even now he's upstairs polishing more pieces of rock for who knows what reason. As usual, he won't tell me more than that.

I'm sure it will end in nothing, like every other endeavor he's made in the last six months. At this rate, I may need to return to my vocation as saloon girl to pay the gas bills.

Henry Stanton's wife, Rebecca, comes to see me nearly every day now with her baby boy. Henry's business takes him into Denver more and more these days, so I imagine she's grown as lonely as I am. You remember their sad story, don't you?

She never speaks of Elijah, but I can see in her eyes that she thinks of him every moment. The housekeeper, Mrs. Trilby, tells me that Henry stopped making inquiries about the boy in Denver. I can't understand it. If they believe Elijah ran away, how can they stop looking? And how can they stop looking if they don't believe he ran away?

Ada

April 2, 1900
Byrne House

Dearest Mary,

Brace yourself. Something has happened that I never would have expected.

Simon has returned to Byrne House a married man. And rich, no less. You should have seen his little heiress wife step out of their fine carriage and take in Byrne House greedily with her eyes. Harriet comes from a very fine family in San Francisco, as I understand it, and I'm sure she has elaborate plans for her new life here. But she will learn.

In truth, though, any company is welcome. I suspect Walter himself wrote to Simon to beg his return to help with our financial situation, but my husband still hides in his laboratory. Even Rebecca Stanton stays away now, and before Simon came back, I hadn't seen the outside of my rooms for days. It was so terribly dull here until recently.

Will you take a wager on how long Simon can resist the temptation of Denver's gambling dens and loose women? I give him one week.

Love,

Ada

April 30, 1900
Byrne House

Dear Mary,

Henry Stanton came to Byrne House this morning. We hadn't seen him for over two months, so I was surprised to hear Mrs. Trilby announce him. He has changed, Mary. Gone is the handsome man I remembered, with cheeks that dimpled so attractively when he smiled. He's grown so thin and pale I wouldn't have recognized him on the street. I asked him to sit and inquired after Rebecca and their baby, but he refused to answer me. He wouldn't even meet my eyes. He demanded to see Walter.

Of course it took nearly half an hour for Trilby to find Walter. He was out in the gardens, doing Lord knows what. When Walter came into the parlor, Henry told me to leave.

I waited in the hallway with my ear pressed to the door.

Henry told him he'd had enough, that he couldn't spend a single day longer employed by Walter. Walter said nothing. I could hear my husband's feet shuffling across the carpet. I know his mannerisms so well by now. I doubt Walter was even listening.

Henry's voice grew agitated. "The least you could do is look at me, after what you've done."

Walter mumbled something that I couldn't hear. "Yes, an accident," Henry spat in reply. "As if your neglectfulness excuses you."

I can't imagine what he could mean. Walter has neglected us all, to be sure, and exhausted his fortune on fruitless research, but he is incapable of anything vicious. Yet Henry spoke to him with such contempt. And not only that. There was fear in his voice, as well. As if Walter was some sort of villain, and not his closest friend. Henry stormed out of the parlor so abruptly I had to jump away from the door as it opened.

Henry fixed me with his haunted gaze. "May God have mercy on you and your poor daughter, Ada." Then he left.

I went into the parlor and found Walter sitting in his chair by the fireplace. He seemed to be deep in thought. He said, "I'm sorry for what's happened, I did try, but it was the breakthrough I needed, that last piece to understand…"

"What did you do?" I asked.

He looked up at me. His eyes were wild and shining, like they are during his fits. But the rest of his body was completely still. He said, "I'm close, Ada. So very close. You will see. I'm almost there."

I have no idea what to make of all this. In the most practical sense, it means we no longer have Henry to look after our accounts and do business on our behalf. Walter is in no shape to take on these responsibilities. Do you think I should trust Simon to do it? My instinct tells me no, but my options are severely limited. I'll wait a few days before deciding what to do. Any insight that you could provide will be invaluable. You are the only thing in my life that I can still rely upon, Mary.

Love,

Ada

May 5, 1900
Byrne House

Dearest Mary,

I've struggled with how to write this. Whether to even attempt it. I'm sure you may think I've lost my mind after you read it. But I must tell someone, if only to convince myself that I am still living in the same world I thought I knew, and not in a creation of my own fantasy.

Walter woke me in my bed early in the morning several days ago, before the sun. I opened my eyes and saw him sitting on the blankets next to me. Moonlight shone through the window, illuminating his hand as it reached toward me. His face was completely in shadow. I held my breath, not knowing what influence might have swept over him. But he lay his hand gently on my shoulder and whispered to me,

"Ada, come. I'm ready to show it to you."

I followed him into the sitting room. He shut the door so we wouldn't wake Clara. From his pocket, he pulled a lovely hand-mirror with a filagreed gold frame. He gave it to me and told me to gaze *through* it, out into the room. That struck me as very strange. I only saw my own reflection, cast in the pale glow of moonlight. I was about to hand the mirror back, but Walter's expression was so earnest that I tried again. And he was right. There was no solid backing behind the glass, so it was translucent, like no other hand-mirror I've seen.

Then something else appeared in the glass. It started as a tiny bit of white and spread outwards, like branching crystals of frost on a window. I saw Walter and myself standing in that very room on our first night at Byrne House as a married couple. I heard us speak the same words we had that night. All of the hope and love and happiness I'd felt at that moment rushed back to me, as if the last year had never happened.

It wasn't just a memory, Mary. It was a glimpse into our past. But this time, I could sense, and even see, everything that Walter felt then, too. I know how it sounds. Impossible, unbelievable. But I can only tell you in the simplest terms available to me. That is what I saw.

It was so powerful that I lost consciousness for a time. When I woke, I felt the room spin around me, so much so that I couldn't stand. I was ill. But Walter held me, and told me everything about his research, and the breakthroughs he's made. All this time I wondered if Walter was losing his mind when he insisted that his visions are real. But I'm beginning to realize that he's right.

The mirror showed me what Walter sees in his episodes.

There are energies all around us that we can't see or hear or taste, but they're as real as the table I'm writing on now. It's terrifying but exhilarating at the same time. If I really tried to explain everything I saw and felt, you would think I'd finally given in to the stress of being mistress of Byrne House. But I'm convinced that I am sane, for now at least.

"How is this possible?" I asked him.

Walter explained that he'd traveled the world searching for a cure to the sickness he's endured for so many years. But not long after he returned home—after I nursed him back to health—he discovered the true cause of his condition.

The mine beneath Castle Heights.

Most of the minerals he found on his land were unremarkable, if still quite valuable on the market. That was how Walter amassed his fortune. But one day, many years ago, he struck a vein rich with very unusual crystals. He has no memory of what happened next, only that he awoke after hours of unconsciousness and found that he'd been ill. Simon told him that he must be overworked and exhausted, and did not give the incident much account. But later Walter came back to that same vein, only to suffer similar bouts of this fainting sickness. Walter's episodes began to recur outside of the mine as well. I suppose Simon's poor work ethic likely saved him from a similar misfortune.

The greatest irony? No buyer ever showed interest in those particular crystals. They were too impacted. Flawed.

It was just a few months ago that all of this, finally, became clear to him. He made incredible discoveries regarding his illness, though he couldn't explain those intricacies to me. He said his research came to a standstill, and he was forced to admit he'd never find a cure. But a glimmer of inspiration revealed the true potential of those rarest crystals he'd found in his mine. A recent vision drove him to transform them into the mirror. He only realized after he'd finished that he created this for <u>me</u>, so that I could finally understand him and see what he sees without enduring the full transformation that has nearly overwhelmed his body time and again.

"I should never have tried to cure my condition," Walter said to me. "It was never a curse at all. All this time, my dear Ada, my task should have been to open <u>your</u> eyes."

I can only imagine how all this will seem to you, Mary. It terrified me at first, but I've also realized what this means. Walter is truly a genius. I had no idea how much I'd lost my faith in him until now. I only hope that he doesn't pull away from me again. I couldn't bear it.

With hope that you will somehow understand,

Ada

July 16, 1900
Byrne House

Dear Mary,

I didn't receive a response to my last letter. I hope it was a mistake. I know that what I wrote may have shocked you. I'm afraid of what you may be thinking. Will you let me come to you, to see for yourself that everything I've said is true?

I would ask you to come to Byrne House, but I hate the influence that Simon has here. Since Walter and I reconciled, Simon has become an annoying mosquito in our ears, making innuendos and trying constantly to manipulate. Unfortunately, Walter is now completely dependent upon him. Walter's finances were in worse shape than I thought, and Simon agreed to pay our debts as a purchase price to regain half-ownership of Byrne House. He has free run of it now. As Simon's control over Byrne House grows, Walter withdraws again to his research. He lets me sit in the third-floor laboratory or library with him most of the time, but he often forgets I'm there. He even seems to be losing interest in the mirror.

I've looked into the mirror a few more times and each has been easier and more enlightening. One theory occurs to me again and again, but as yet I've been too timid to try it: what would happen if I changed the subject of the mirror's gaze? Focused it not on a place, but on a living person? I've tried to ask Walter for his opinion, but his eyes glaze when I try to describe my own experiments.

Simon's wife Harriet occupies herself with planning a masquerade ball for the end of the summer. I have never held a ball, or even a large party, at Byrne House. I don't know whom we would invite, really.

Unlike me, Harriet knows everyone and is determined to hold a grand affair.

She's planning it for the gardens, which are finally almost complete. Maybe a party will draw Walter back out of his shell.

With love,

Ada

September 22, 1900
Byrne House

Dearest Mary,

I know it all now.

I expected when Simon arrived here that he would try to weasel his half of the estate back from Walter, as he did. But I failed to see how intricately he had wound control of Byrne House around himself until it was too late.

Simon commands the servants. He demands to know what I am doing, where I go, and whom I see. I must seek his permission to leave the house. I even suspect he had something to do with the disappearance of Mrs. Trilby.

Mrs. Trilby has been housekeeper here for half a decade. I admit we did not see eye to eye when I first arrived, but in the last few months—especially after Simon's reappearance—she had warmed to me. I counted Trilby as one of my very few allies.

But a week ago, she vanished.

Simon has claimed she abandoned her post and even stole a set of silver candlesticks, but I won't believe it. I think Simon had Mrs. Trilby sent away because she showed me a bit of kindness. Nearly all the others have turned on me. One of the maids forcibly held me in my room today when I refused to follow Simon's commands.

But Simon's plans go much further than simply alienating me. I found out the truth this evening.

I knew Simon would summon me down to dinner at eight. So I was ready. At a quarter past seven, I brought the mirror with me in the pocket of my skirt and hid inside a rarely-used closet. I could just see the parlor across the hall from the crack between the closet doors. I knew that Simon and Harriet would sit and read in the parlor until dinner was announced. Simon's favorite chair was perfectly framed in the parlor doorway. I watched him for a while, sipping whiskey and reading his newspaper.

Then I held up the mirror and looked through.

I saw undulations of color eddying out around Simon's head, much like the auras that spiritualists describe. I felt his rage at losing his portion of the estate, the bitterness of learning I'd married Walter, and his disdain for his own wife. There were other women, too. Maids, the groomsman's daughter. I doubt I know more than a fraction of Simon's secrets even now. I could only seem to skim over the surface of his mind, sensing but not knowing the depths beneath.

Yet one thought was dominant over all the others: his plan for Harriet's masquerade ball.

He was thinking about it while he sat there pretending to read the front page of the *Denver Post*. He was imagining it, letting his thoughts of it nourish his hatred for Walter and for me. I was so sickened by it that I ran from the closet the first moment that Simon's back was turned and told the maid that I was too ill for dinner.

Simon plans to disguise himself in Walter's costume at the ball and seduce me. He relishes the thought of revealing himself afterwards and seeing the agony on my face after I realize what I've done. He thinks it will destroy Walter's love for me, what little there is left. After that, Simon plans to bleed away the last of Walter's fortune, and finally, when Walter is destitute and broken, take Byrne House fully away from him. Simon will never let me leave. He'd sooner see me dead.

But I have a better plan now, too.

I'll have a knife hidden underneath my costume at the ball, and when we're alone, I'll do what needs to be done to rid our lives of this twisted monster once and for all.

The ball is less than a week away. I have so much to prepare in that time, assuming that Simon doesn't tighten his grip around me even more.

I hope desperately that I see you again, Mary, but if something should happen, please ensure that Clara is taken care of. I don't trust Walter to see to that himself.

With deepest love for you, my beloved sister,

Ada

32

EVELYN GOT UP. THE LETTERS WERE SCATTERED across the bed. "We have to go find out what happened."

"Where? How?" Alex gathered the letters. "We're not going back to that tomb, are we?"

Definitely not what she had in mind. "The masquerade ball was held in the gardens. Whatever happened between Simon and Ada must have left a pretty strong impression there."

She grabbed her backpack. Alex got up, checking his phone. "Hold on," he said. "Milo says Jake just got up and left the meeting. Milo's going to follow him. He'll keep us updated."

"If the meeting's ending soon, then we'd better move." She swung her pack onto her shoulders and headed for the stairs. They'd already spent half an hour reading through the letters.

Alex went after her. His hand caressed the back of her neck. "It's probably really awful," he said. "The mirror doesn't leave anything out. You've seen that yourself."

Evelyn stopped at the top of the staircase. "What if no one else *ever* knew what really happened to Ada? Her suffering never goes away. It just *festers*."

"Are you sure you're not thinking of your *own* history with Byrne House? Your missing memories?"

That was possible. Evelyn had made the connection between Walter's blackouts in the mine and her own lost memories of falling as a child. But she still had to find out the rest of Ada and Walter's story. Maybe then, her own experience would make sense.

"Evelyn, solving Ada's mystery won't make you remember."

How do you know? she wanted to insist. But she didn't want to admit that Alex was right. It bothered her that Alex could read her so easily, and she couldn't do the same with him.

"I'd give you my memories." Alex brushed his hand down Evelyn's arm, and tingles spun out along her skin from his fingertips. "Do you think you could actually look into someone's mind using the mirror? Read their thoughts, the way Ada described? I'd let you."

Was he saying that because he still felt guilty about lying? *That's unfair*, she told herself. Alex was offering himself to her. But she couldn't accept it, not like this.

"I want to remember on my own." Evelyn wanted to prove to herself and to everyone else that she *could*.

Alex smiled teasingly, his scarred lip tugging upwards. "I could read *your* thoughts instead."

"You might not like all of it." She kept her tone light to hide the bitterness that crept into her throat, unwelcome.

"Yes I would. It's you."

He was trying to distract her, and it was working. "Please," she said. "I need to do this." Whatever Ada needed to tell her, Evelyn was going to listen. Simply because nobody else would.

He cupped her chin in his hand and kissed her slowly. When he started pulling back, Evelyn held his shirt with her fist. She deepened the kiss, lingering over his taste. It made her want to forget Ada Byrne had ever existed. Even forget that she had a past at all. But the truth remained what it was, no matter how much you tried to hide from it. Eventually—always—it would come for you.

"I'm going," she said.

Alex sighed. "Then I'm with you. But first, let Milo and Silvia know about the change of plans. The second anybody else leaves that meeting, I want to know about it."

The mansion stood over them, silent yet alert. Evelyn took off her pack and pulled out the mirror.

"Where would Simon and Harriet have held a big party?" Evelyn murmured to herself. She stood on the main pathway and scanned the gardens. Plants and trees packed every square inch except for the brick walkways and the maze. But the grounds probably looked a lot different back in Ada's time. Evelyn thought of the pictures she'd seen in the Byrne House library from when the neighborhood was still under construction.

Alex stood off to the side, quietly observing. Evelyn turned to a relatively clear area, free from mature trees, and held up the mirror. She sensed layers of feeling and energy there, but she kept her mind on the surface and skimmed through them quickly enough to realize she didn't sense Ada or anything like a masquerade ball.

She felt the same absence in other areas of the garden, despite the buzz of unrelated thoughts and emotions that pulled at her attention. Taking a breath to steel herself, she walked toward the labyrinth and fixed the gaze of the mirror on Ada's statue. Strong feelings emanated, a deep pall of sorrow clinging to the statue and spilling over onto the maze. She almost slipped into the memories there and had to close her eyes to break herself away. It was nothing about the masquerade ball.

When Evelyn turned the mirror to the rose garden, she knew.

"It's here." She inched between the thorny bushes until she reached a dense patch of plants. She waited until Alex was beside her. Then Evelyn opened her mind fully to the mirror.

Costumed revelers mill under an enormous white tent. Ada paces slowly along the edge of the crowd, holding her mask to her face and forcing herself to smile. At the center, Harriet basks in the attention of a laughing group of men. With predatory relish, they eye Harriet's barely concealed figure, draped in thin layers of blue silk.

Ada adjusts the corset of her Marie Antoinette costume. She can hardly breathe inside of it. She would have chosen a more practical dress, but Harriet picked it for her and wouldn't be swayed.

Ada knows Simon is there somewhere. Not here, under the tent. But in the gardens, watching her.

She recalls the note Walter sent her earlier that day. It said he would come to the party after all, after he finished his work, and would be dressed as a Roman emperor. She recognized Walter's handwriting. What could have gone through his head as he copied the note out for Simon? Did he even question it? Or did he simply do as Simon asked and turn back to his precious journal, now filled with more lunatic ravings than scientific reasoning?

Her mind turns to Clara, safely stowed with Ada's single trusted friend, the old seamstress who lives in a small house near the mansion. She has instructions and money to take Clara to Ada's cousin in New Mexico if Ada doesn't return. Ada swallows a pang of regret that she couldn't send Clara to Mary. But Leadville is far too close. It would be the first place Simon would look. On the other hand, if all goes according to her plan tonight, Ada will take Clara to Leadville herself, where she'll also find the mirror. She left it with one of the few kind servants to send to Mary, and by now it must already be on its way.

Ada feels a hand on her shoulder. She turns and sees a man dressed in flowing yellow and red robes, his head crowned with laurel, and his face covered by a golden mask bearing a grotesquely exaggerated grimace.

"Walter? I've been waiting." She presses her hand to her thigh, where the knife is hidden, feeling the cold blade against her bare skin. The man nods and holds out his hand as the music begins to play. She places her left hand at his shoulder and lets her mask fall as she gathers the billowing skirt of her dress with the other. He leads her through the

dance. She feels the slight pressure of his hand, almost teasing in its lightness, against the thick fabric of her costume.

This is a game to him. She thinks of the knife, solid against her thigh, giving her strength. "Where is Simon? I haven't seen him. Harriet is playing hostess alone."

"Simon is tending to business. He'll be here shortly."

She can tell he has been practicing the soft tones of Walter's voice.

The music ends. When she tries to leave the floor, she feels his fingers dig into the flesh of her upper arm.

"Dance with me again, Ada? I feel that I haven't seen you in weeks. I've been neglecting you. That's why I've come tonight. To pay you the attention you deserve."

They spin through the middle of the other smiling couples. Ada begins to feel lightheaded. When will he stop toying with her? She can't take another moment of his blue-black eyes staring at her through that mask. Did he really think she wouldn't know his eyes?

"Could I speak with you alone?" she asks, swallowing her revulsion. "You're right, I've hardly seen you, but everyone's eyes are on us here."

He pulls her close for a moment, then nods. He takes her hand and leads her out of the tent, away from the party and into a darkened corner of the gardens. They are far from the glow cast by the hanging lanterns that light the ball.

Ada looks up. The moon is a sliver of glass in the sky, the stars broken shards scattered around it.

"Here we are," he says. "What did you wish to say to me?"

"I've missed you."

He steps closer. "How have you missed me?"

"Your . . . touch." She smells the sweat evaporating from his skin. The pace of his breath speeds. He's excited. Acid churns in her stomach.

"Oh?" He runs his fingers along the bodice of her dress. He grips her by the hips and pulls her to him.

"I've missed you as well. I've missed the privileges you owe me as a wife."

He removes his mask, his face covered by darkness. His whiskers scrape the tender skin of her chin as he kisses her. His hands grope for her back and begin loosening the strings of her corset.

"Wait!" She overpowers the need to vomit that rises in her throat. "Someplace more secluded. Someone could see us here."

He leads her into the stable. The horses whinny nervously in their stalls. Simon kicks aside a rusted bucket and lowers her to the floor. A sliver of wood cuts into her back. He starts pulling up the edges of her skirt. She feels his palms on the slippery silk of her stockings. She kisses him to distract him, and her hand searches frantically in the layers of fabric, praying she will reach the knife before he finds it. Her fingers close around the handle and she rips it from its sleeve, grazing her thigh in the process. The pain sends a jolt of alertness through her body.

She brings the blade up and stabs it with all her strength into his torso.

His head whips back from hers, and he gasps. "You little bitch." Simon rolls away from her, snatching at the hilt of the knife sticking out of his side.

Ada tries to get up, but her skirts tangle around her feet. She scrambles onto her hands and knees and gains her footing. As she rushes toward the doorway, she feels Simon's fist close on her scalp and her head jerks back. Simon pulls her hair again to expose her throat and presses the blade against her windpipe.

"Impressive." His breath is hot against her ear. "I suppose I should count myself lucky that you have no aim. I, on the other hand, could cut out your throat with one flick of my wrist."

He drags the point of the knife up and down her neck, tracing the veins jumping under the skin.

"I can't imagine," Simon says, "how you could have known. I told no one about this, and I know Walter's mannerisms even better than you do. Perhaps you wanted to kill your own husband?"

"I wanted to kill you to rid this house of your disease."

He laughs. "Well, this makes things so much more interesting." He closes his eyes and licks her neck just above the drop of blood that trickles down from where the blade caught her skin.

"You know, I did love you once, Ada. In my way. I saved you from that hole you were living in, and how did you repay me? You took my pathetic, weak, invalid younger brother into your bed. Where you hadn't even allowed me. Did you think I had simply forgotten about that? You should have plunged this knife into my back when I walked through the Byrne House gate. Once I was inside, it was already too late for you."

He stepped back and yanked her hair to make her follow. "Let's go. I have just the thing in mind for—"

Evelyn blinked and dropped to her knees, the vision fleeing before her mind was ready. She looked up.

Simon was standing over her.

She fell back and almost screamed, but then she saw the scar. It was Alex. Just Alex. *And you're Evelyn. Not her.* She closed her eyes and shook her head, trying to cast out the imprint of Simon's sneering face, the sickening taste of Ada's fear.

Alex put a finger over Evelyn's lips and pulled her behind a tree. They were over by the stable, where Simon had taken Ada. "How did we get over here?" Evelyn asked. "We were in the rose garden."

"You started running," Alex whispered. "We ended up here. But I heard something in the bushes."

Evelyn looked around. The fence was right behind them, near the stable. She pointed and said quietly, "Let's get out of here."

"We can't," he said tensely. "You dropped your backpack somewhere. I think it was by the maze."

She swore. It had her phone inside. And her house keys.

Carefully, they edged forward, inches at a time. They reached the outermost hedge of the maze and crept alongside, bent over to stay concealed.

Deeper in the maze, branches rustled. Someone was in there. Evelyn held her breath, and Alex gripped her hand.

Milo's head popped up above the hedge. "Evelyn?" he whispered loudly. "Is that you?"

Evelyn and Alex both sagged against the ground in relief. "Get over here." Alex waved him over. "What are you doing in there?"

"I got lost." It took a few minutes of navigating the maze until Milo found them. He held up Evelyn's backpack. "Is this yours?"

"Yes! Thank you." She put it on.

"Silvia texted me five minutes ago," Milo said. "They're wrapping up the meeting early. I was at Jake's, and I came straight over here. You weren't answering your phones."

"We'd better go then," Alex said. They left the maze and stepped back onto the path. Alex glanced around, but the gardens were quiet again.

A short while later, they were sitting in Evelyn's backyard in the overgrown grass. It was a cloudy night, but the light by the back door was enough to see by. Her mom wasn't home yet. Evelyn was still trying to get her pulse to slow.

"What happened with Jake?" Alex asked Milo.

Milo had sprawled on his back in the overgrown grass. "I followed Jake to his house. I watched him go inside, and it didn't seem like anything was happening. But then Detective Tyson showed up. He knocked, and Jake let him right inside."

"*Tyson* was meeting with Jake?" Evelyn said.

"Yep. Don't ask me what it means. 'Cause I don't know. What did you find in the gardens?"

Evelyn and Alex summarized Ada's final letters for him —now, Milo sat up—and then Evelyn explained what she'd seen in the vision. Alex reached for her hand in the grass, where Milo couldn't see them touching.

"Ada tried to fight back," she said. "But Simon was ruthless. Ada didn't have a chance."

"Horrible," Milo muttered. He picked at a feathery stalk of grass. "I saw Ada's statue when I was lost in the maze. It seemed like it was symbolic or something. Ada in the middle of this labyrinth, trapped with no way to get back out again."

Suddenly Simon's last thought—an image of the maze —blossomed in Evelyn's mind. After Alex had taken the mirror and pulled her out of the vision, she'd assumed it was just one of her own thoughts about the gardens getting mixed up with those of Ada and Simon. But now she realized that was wrong.

"Simon was taking her into the tunnels. It's the labyrinth."

"What is?" Alex said. "What are you talking about?"

"It's a *map*." The image filled Evelyn's head, its curving pathways forming a web that her thoughts couldn't find their way around. "Simon had an image of the labyrinth in his mind because he was taking Ada there. The garden labyrinth is a map of the tunnels."

"I think you're right," Milo said. "The maze did feel like the tunnels. The curves, the dead ends. But how is that possible?"

"Because Walter designed the tunnels, just like he designed the garden maze." The intensity in their eyes sent a thrill down Evelyn's back. "We have ourselves a map," she said.

33

AT NOON THE NEXT DAY, WILLIAM LOADED ALEX'S suitcases into his Range Rover and checked out of the hotel. Evelyn knew because Alex texted her a play-by-play. Each message was another little cut across her heart. Then all four Byrne family members drove to the airport, William and Daniella in the front seat, Alex riding in the back with a sullen Darren. Alex's flight was set to take off in two hours.

Evelyn set down her phone, her mind a whirlwind of doubts. Alex had promised to come back, and that meant he would.

You hope, an annoying little voice snuck in. *He lied to you before.*

"Shut up." Evelyn unfolded her printout from Google Earth on her desk, welcoming the distraction, and got to work.

At four o'clock that afternoon, she stood and stretched. She'd spent hours tracing the grid of Castle Heights's streets onto a sheet of graph paper, muttering to herself as she worked. Then, she'd taken the aerial shot of Byrne House from Google Earth and laid the graph paper grid on top of it.

At first she'd hoped that the garden labyrinth and the neighborhood would match up according to their compass orientations, north to north, south to south. But it wasn't that easy. She knew that Byrne House was most likely at the center, and that her house, Ms. Foster's, Jake's, and the high school all must have access points into the tunnels.

Through trial and error, twisting the two pages back and forth, she found the only configuration that tied most of the points to a tunnel. Then she recognized the three branching pathways that they'd seen not far from Byrne House, just where they should be. This had to be it.

Now all she could do was sit on her bed, stare out her window, and wait.

Byrne House was dark and still, the way she'd always remembered it before the day Mr. Byrne died and everything changed. Bad things had happened, yes, but a lot of good had come out of it too. With Alex, all her mysterious dreams and weird obsessions finally made sense.

"He'll come back," she told herself. "He has to."

She wasn't even watching the mansion, not anymore. Maybe she never had been. She'd always been waiting for Alex.

Finally, he texted. *On the train. Almost to Union Station.* She allowed herself one quiet whoop of relief, and then quickly sent off messages to both Silvia and Milo.

Their master plan was officially in motion.

<hr />

Alex traced their path on the map with his finger. "So I'm guessing it will take a good half hour to get to Jake's house. Milo, what time are you supposed to meet him?"

They'd convened at Milo's house. Since Alex now had nowhere to stay—technically he was supposed to be on an airplane bound for New York right now—Milo had begrudgingly offered the guest room over his family's garage. Silvia came by Evelyn's house to pick her up, and Evelyn had told her mom they'd be at Silvia's all night.

So far, so good.

Milo knelt by the coffee table to study the map. "I told Jake one o'clock. His parents will be asleep by then. He seemed really anxious to talk to me, even more than at the dance."

They'd decided Jake's house would be an easier mark than the school. Evelyn would bring the mirror, sneak into Jake's basement, and find out what had really happened to Jordan. But that meant someone needed to distract Jake upstairs so he wouldn't realize Evelyn and Alex had snuck into his basement. Despite Milo's earlier failure with his grandmother, the distraction role had fallen to him. But thankfully, Silvia insisted on coming too so she could say a few choice words to her former boyfriend. Evelyn was glad. Silvia would keep Milo on track, and the girl definitely deserved a chance to tell Jake off.

"Will that work?" Milo asked Evelyn, looking up from the map. "Do you need more time to get there?"

"I could just yell at Jake for extra long," Silvia added, smiling. "He deserves it."

Alex laughed. "Please do. But I think we'll be okay." He glanced at his watch. "It's midnight. We should leave no later than five minutes from now, just in case it takes longer than I expect to get to Jake's."

The four of them piled into Milo's parents' truck and drove toward Castle Heights.

Evelyn and Alex were sitting in the backseat, fingers entwined. Her backpack rested on the floorboards, packed with everything they'd need: Ada's mirror, the key to the tunnels, their phones—to coordinate a pick-up afterward—and various other supplies.

But her mind kept going back to the airport, to the flight that Alex was supposed to be on right now. He'd sworn that his mom wouldn't start looking for him until tomorrow when he didn't show up to breakfast. But what then? Would Mrs. Evans demand Alex come straight home?

Would Alex listen?

She closed her eyes for a second, groaning to herself. *Focus, Ev. You have a job tonight. Focus.*

"We have a good plan. We'll be fine," Alex whispered, misunderstanding her expression.

"I know." Evelyn unfolded her map again to re-check their route. "Byrne House is definitely deserted?" she asked for the third time. She didn't want any surprises tonight.

Alex recited the same thing he'd said twice before. "I watched all three of them drive away from the Denver airport. I called Will an hour later while I sat on the concourse, pretending to wait for my flight. They were almost to Fort Collins."

Evelyn knew the rest. William had gone with the Byrnes to help them move the last few items out of their apartment, which was about two hours north of Castle Heights. Alex's older brother had also hinted that he would have a talk with Darren. He wanted Darren to renew his lease on the apartment and stay in Fort Collins instead of coming back to Castle Heights. Time to get rid of the third wheel. William planned to live at Byrne House permanently with Daniella—and only her. To Evelyn, it sounded like a lot of drama. But it would keep the Byrnes away from the mansion, and that was what counted.

Milo parked a few blocks away from Byrne House and turned off the car.

Evelyn folded the map and put it in her pocket. Alex slung the backpack over his shoulder. "Be safe," Silvia said. They jumped out of the car, and Milo drove away.

They scaled the Byrne House fence and ran for the back door. Alex used Mrs. Lake's extra key. Then, just like that, they were in.

Evelyn's pulse throbbed against her wrist, counting off the seconds.

Once they reached the tunnel entrance, Alex used an old paint can to block open their access to Byrne House's basement, just in case they needed a quick exit. He pulled two flashlights from the backpack and handed one to Evelyn.

"Are you ready for this?" he said.

Evelyn checked the map yet again in the beam of her flashlight. "I think so. It should be easy right? We'll be in and out."

"Exactly. No matter what, we stay together."

They started walking, following the twists and turns of the passageways. Now Evelyn's pulse was jumping in her throat, but not because she was about to break into Jake's house. Being down here in the tunnels made her a lot more nervous.

After what felt like an endless series of turns and stops to consult the map, they came to a long passageway with only a handful of wooden doors dotting its sides.

"This should be it," Evelyn said. The outermost tunnel at the edge of the neighborhood.

Alex set down the backpack and started digging around in it. Evelyn mounted the steps to the wooden door that would—they hoped—lead into Jake's basement. She put her bare hand to the circular metal handle. The cold shocked her. The tunnels seemed as damp and cool as always, but the door to Jake's house was frigid. Evelyn pulled her hand back, cringing.

She stood aside while Alex sprayed the hinges with oil and turned the circular handle. The metal bars holding the door retracted and snapped inwards, and the door began to swing open inch by inch. Evelyn shined her flashlight into the gap and saw rusted, metal-lined walls. Some old air filters and pieces of plastic piping sat in boxes on the floor of the storage room.

"You want to do the honors?" Alex handed her the antique key. Her fingers shook. She kept imagining Jake yanking open the door, his rage when he found her and Alex here.

Jake's upstairs. We're fine. We're fine.

Finally she got the key into place. The door opened onto another small room full of ducts, pipes, and a box-like furnace in one corner. The Oshiros' utility room, just as Milo had described it. She stepped inside.

Alex gripped the handle of the next door and opened it a crack. The hinges glided swiftly, making no sound. All was dark and quiet in Jake's basement except for a small square of light coming from the stairwell. Evelyn could see the edge of Jake's pool table at the center of the space. The door to Jake's bedroom stood open, and the light was out.

She slipped past Alex and turned right, passed the bathroom, and walked through the open door of the guest room. It was nearly pitch black inside. The room jumped into view as she turned on the flashlight.

"The mirror," Evelyn whispered. It was still in the backpack.

But instead of opening the pack, Alex grabbed her arm. Evelyn's eyes jerked upward to his stunned face. "What?" she whispered.

"I heard something. Down the hall. You stay here, I'll look."

"No! I'm coming, you said we stay together."

Alex's jaw clenched. "Stay here," he said through gritted teeth.

He turned off his flashlight and Evelyn did the same. The room went dark as Alex stepped noiselessly out into the hall. She leaned against the bedroom wall, letting her eyes adjust again to the dark, hearing only the sound of her own breathing.

Then came the sound of feet scuffling against concrete. A crash. She forced herself to run. She found Alex lying on the hard floor of the utility room beside the furnace.

"Alex?!" she whispered.

He groaned, holding his side. "Stuck me, my side. It burns. It's spreading all over."

Panic sent a jolt of energy through her system. She pushed Alex into the storage room and pulled the metal door shut behind them, closing off Jake's basement. Alex stumbled out and Evelyn jumped through the opening after him. The wooden door thudded closed. Evelyn turned the circular handle. The metal bands snapped back into place.

Alex stumbled down the stairs and fell to the floor of the tunnel in a heap. He was grabbing at his side and moaning. Evelyn hurried to him and ran her flashlight over his body. Alex's shirt looked dry. She stuck her hand underneath, feeling for wetness. He wasn't bleeding.

"Whatever it was, you're not cut. Now come *on*."

She helped Alex stand and started pulling him along the tunnel. He kept his back hunched over, clutching his stomach, tripping over his feet. They'd never outrun the attacker at this rate. Their only hope was that the person who did this to Alex was inside Jake's house right now instead of the tunnels.

She didn't have time to think about what that could mean.

Evelyn took a left into the next tunnel, praying that she'd studied the map enough times. Her memory didn't have the best track record, but it would have to do. She couldn't afford to stop and check the map. They had to *go*.

Alex suddenly dropped to the floor. "I can see her. She's here!"

He dropped into a fetal position and held his arms over his head. "Someone help her, help her." His voice rose into a cry. "*Have mercy, please! Don't leave me down here!*"

Evelyn rolled Alex onto his back and held his face in her hands. His eyes were unfocused, roving along the vaulted tunnel ceiling. "Alex, look at me. Whatever you're seeing, it's not happening right now. We're alone here, but we have to get home."

His pupils were dilated, the black nearly swallowing the green. "Evelyn," he whispered. "Please get me out of here. I can hear her crying and begging, please don't make me hear any more of this."

She helped him up again and braced his arm around her shoulder. She tried to walk, but he sobbed and fell back to his knees. "Alex, look at me. I'll lead us back. You just keep your eyes on me, okay?"

He stood and leaned on her again, this time keeping his face turned toward her. They stumbled on through the twisting passageways, the limp on Alex's left side unusually pronounced. Her speeding pulse began to slow as they turned into the last tunnel. Her flashlight beam hit the paint can. She pushed Alex through the door ahead of her. Only then did it dawn on her. Alex didn't have her backpack anymore.

Ada's mirror, the antique key, everything—it was all gone.

34

EVELYN DIDN'T KNOW HOW SHE GOT ALEX OUT OF Byrne House and through the gardens. But somehow she did it. By the time they reached the fence, Alex was strong enough to climb over on his own. They collapsed onto the sidewalk, chests heaving.

But how were they supposed to get back to Milo's? Their phones were gone, too.

"You're scared," Alex said. "What's wrong?" Then he answered his own question like he'd plucked it from her head. "The phones. The backpack. Oh no—Evelyn, I'm sorry. I'm so sorry. I must have dropped it."

She summoned every ounce of will to calm herself down. "It's okay." She'd take Alex back to her house.

"But your mom."

Evelyn nodded, only half aware that Alex had just responded to one of her thoughts. Nuclear explosions would ensue when her mother found out, but this was her only option. At least it was safe there. No way in from the tunnels. She helped Alex up, and they started down the sidewalk.

But they didn't have to go far. Milo's truck swerved onto the street and stopped at the curb.

"What happened?" Milo asked through his open window. Silvia looked on from the passenger seat.

Evelyn didn't try to answer until they were inside the truck, speeding back to the sanctuary of Milo's house. Never had she so wanted to get away from Castle Heights.

"Someone was in the basement with us," she said, tripping over the words. "They injected Alex with something." Evelyn met Milo's gaze in the rearview mirror. "Alex was seeing things in the tunnels."

Milo's eyes shot wide. "Seeing things, like you and Elijah and the others?"

Evelyn looked at Alex. He was lying against the seat, staring at her with a glazed expression. "I'm pretty sure," she said.

"Do we go to the hospital?" Silvia asked.

Milo and Evelyn both shook their heads. "What could they do?" Evelyn said. "They couldn't help Jordan and Caitlin. We just have to wait until it passes." What if Alex went into a coma? What would they do?

Silvia turned around to face the back seat. "We'd just gotten to the Oshiros' when Jake started acting all weird and looking down the basement stairs."

"I tried to stop him," Milo said, "but he started yelling at us to get out. We were so worried about you guys. We drove straight over here to the pickup spot hoping we'd find you. We've been driving around and around, losing our minds."

Evelyn tried to follow the trail of logic to some kind of conclusion. But she could only focus on Alex. He was sweating and kept closing his eyes, as if he was drifting in and out of consciousness. But he kept holding tight to Evelyn's arm like it was a lifeline.

In the room above Milo's garage, they laid Alex down on the couch. Evelyn sat beside him and pushed a cushion under his head. Alex was breathing more easily now but kept his eyes fixed on her. He hardly seemed to notice the presence of Milo or Silvia in the room.

It was a tiny rectangular loft, just enough room for a double bed against one wall and the couch on the other. Bright colors and woven fabrics decorated the space, brought back from the Fosters' annual trips to Mexico City, where Milo's mom grew up. It was cozy and comfortable. A refuge.

Milo went to the window and opened a crack in the blinds with his fingers. "What if whoever did this knows I'm involved? I was at Jake's house at the same time as you and Alex. Do you think they'll come here?"

"Milo, it could have *been* Jake," Evelyn said. "Maybe he heard us in the basement. Or somehow he knew we were coming." She glanced at Silvia.

"Don't look at me like that!" Silvia cried. "I didn't breathe a word of this to anyone!"

"Did you at least find out what happened to Jordan?" Milo asked.

"We didn't have a chance." *And the mirror is gone.* Evelyn couldn't bring herself to tell them.

"Evelyn?"

She rushed back to Alex's side. "I'm here. How are you feeling?"

"Okay, when I can see you." He touched her cheek with the back of his hand. "You have this *thing* around you. Around your head, sort of. It's nice to look at. Calming."

She managed a weak smile. "Well that sounds normal."

"But the other people," he said, "I mean Milo, Silvia … it's so much at once. I don't want to see in their heads but it's getting hard not to."

Silvia sucked in her lips. "Maybe we should go in the house. Give Alex some space."

"Yeah, I'd rather skip the mind-reading." Milo rubbed his hands together, still looking through the crack in the blinds. "We can put some sleeping bags in the living room. Silvia and I will stay there. But Evelyn—Whoever did this, I'm not saying it's Jake but *whoever*, might follow us here. I'm going to set the burglar alarm, so don't go anywhere."

"Good idea," Evelyn said. "Alex will be better by the morning." *Please let him be better.* She barely had any idea of what was happening to Alex or how much danger he might be in right now. But she would figure something out.

Milo and Silvia left the garage, and Evelyn relocked the door behind them. She peeked out between the blinds. No sign of anyone else. In another minute, Milo would have set the alarm and they'd be secure, if only until morning. After that, they'd have decisions to make. Too many decisions.

Alex had already crawled beneath the covers of the bed. Evelyn turned out the overhead light and reached under the blankets to pull off Alex's shoes. She climbed in next to him. Alex smelled of musk and sweat, but it was far from unpleasant.

He lay with his head on his pillow and watched her. There was a skylight over the bed, dusting Alex and the blankets with gentle iridescence.

"Are you okay?" she whispered. She wiggled in closer to him and put her hand on his neck, feeling the blood race beneath her palm. "We're at Milo's, miles away from Castle Heights. We're safe now. You know that, right?"

His chest rose and fell. "It was like looking in the mirror but inside of my head. I couldn't get away from it, even closing my eyes. I can still feel it there right now. Pushing at the edges of my brain, trying to get in. But when I'm focused on you it stays back."

His hand touched the air in front of Evelyn's face like he was brushing something away, or trying to catch hold of it.

"And you can see something around my head?"

Alex pushed up onto his elbow above her. "It's . . . *you*. It's pulsing in different colors in different places." His hand moved to the air above her ear. "Here it's sort of greenish. And here it's pale yellow." His fingers grazed her cheek. "Right here it's alternating between pink and blue. Wait, now it's . . . *oh*."

Something in his eyes unfolded in the dim light and grew brighter, like they were absorbing the moonlight.

"There are layers underneath. I'm just beginning to see them. You have no idea how incredible it feels."

Alex dipped his head and nuzzled into the crease between her neck and shoulder, his hand sliding along her side and under her shirt. His hand brushed over her ribcage and his thumb skimmed the bottom edge of her bra, then slipped just under the wire to run along the skin there. Evelyn gasped. The touch was so sudden and unexpected but also wonderful. In a dizzy kind of way, like the blood was flowing out of her head and filling up the rest of her, every nerve ending alive with it. If she moved, maybe she'd snap him out of wherever his mind had gone. But she didn't think he wanted her to do that. *She* didn't want to do it.

"I can see what you're thinking," he said. "I mean, not your *thoughts* exactly, not in single pictures or words, but all at once I just know. It's like hearing your heartbeat but feeling it inside me, too."

He rolled on top of her, covering the length of her body. Evelyn gently rested her palms on either side of his face and pulled him down until his nose touched hers.

"It's coming out of you in these waves of color," he murmured. "I can taste it when I breathe." He pressed his mouth into hers. "And when I kiss you."

Alex's hand went under her shirt again, up over the fabric of her bra and cupped her breast, and suddenly Evelyn's mind was as gone as Alex's seemed to be. She tugged at the bottom of his shirt, and he helped her lift it over his head. She arched her back so Alex could grip the edge of her top to pull it off. He kissed her bare collarbone, her shoulder. His nails brushed softly against her bare stomach and then her hip bone.

Evelyn lifted his chin with her fingertips and found his mouth again, wanting everything she was feeling to flood into him. He tilted back his head and closed his eyes, an involuntary shiver of pleasure catching in his throat. *More*, Evelyn thought. *Don't stop*. He nodded as if he'd heard her.

His hand reached behind her back and fumbled with the hooks of her bra.

Then Alex yanked his hand away and sat up, his eyes shining with hurt like she'd burned him.

"What's wrong?" Evelyn was still breathing fast, anticipating. It took a moment to make her mind work again. She tried to remember what she'd been thinking the moment before that might have upset him. She'd been so caught up with his skin and hands and mouth that all she could think was that she desperately wanted him.

But then she realized it: her mind had betrayed her without even a conscious thought. Underneath the desire was a splinter of pure, white-hot jealousy at an image hovering at the back of her mind. An image of Alex and Caitlin sprawled on a bed, doing what Evelyn wanted so much to do with Alex now.

"That never happened," he said. "We never even kissed. I swear, I would've told you."

"I know. I didn't even realize I was thinking it."

The pain in his eyes deepened. "You're still mad at me. About everything."

She was about to deny it, but he'd know she was lying.

He moved away from her and sat against the wall where it met the bed. "You *are*. You hate that I lied to you. You're not even sure if you can forgive me."

As he spoke, the hurt Evelyn had worked so hard to push down started to ache in her chest.

Alex covered his face with his hands. "Why didn't you tell me this? I know you said it was hard, but I didn't know. I've caused you so much *pain*."

She pulled Alex back down to the pillow. "It wasn't your fault. I just need time." She kissed his forehead, his nose, his scar. He closed his eyes.

"I love you, Evelyn. I've loved you for so long."

His words ran over her like a caress, even though he couldn't really mean it. "You're just saying that because of what *I'm* feeling right now. It's the effect of whatever you were injected with. You probably won't even remember this tomorrow."

He opened his eyes. They were glassy, shining like polished stones. "Tell me. Tell me you do, too."

"You know I do. I can't hide anything from you."

"I want to hear you say it. Please."

She brought her nose to his temple, to the little soft spot there at the side of his forehead. "I love you, Alex Evans," she whispered, her lips at his ear.

His eyelids dipped and he exhaled, nodding.

Evelyn lay her head on Alex's chest. She ran her hand down his stomach, feeling the soft give of his skin under her palm, and the firmness of muscle underneath. Within minutes Alex's breathing was regular and deep. Evelyn's eyelids grew heavy, carried away by the wavelike rise and fall of his chest. So much waited for them tomorrow. Too much. But for a few short hours, they could rest.

35

EVELYN OPENED HER EYES. SILVIA WAS STANDING over her. "Wake up," Silvia said. "Something's happened."

Alex was still sound asleep. Evelyn untangled herself from the sheets and crawled over him. She found her shirt on the floor and yanked it on. "What is it?"

"It's Ms. Foster. Milo's grandmother. Someone broke into her house last night."

"*What?*"

"It doesn't seem like they took anything, but they trashed her house. The police are there now. They don't even know how the person got in. Her doors were all locked. She was asleep upstairs the whole time."

Evelyn covered her mouth.

"Milo and I are heading over there," Silvia said.

Evelyn nodded, still dazed by the news. "Okay. We'll come too. Give us five minutes."

Silvia went for the door and then turned back. "Did you and Alex, um …"

"*No.*" Evelyn couldn't resist adding, "Unfortunately. Can we talk about this later?"

"Right. *So* not the time."

Evelyn went back to the bed, where Alex continued to sleep, unaware. She pictured Ms. Foster's beautiful house, all the treasures she'd collected—destroyed. Whoever did this might be the same person who attacked Alex the night before. But why would they go after Ms. Foster? They already had Ada's mirror and the antique key along with everything else that had been in her backpack. All that was missing was—*the letters.*

Ada's letters did reveal a lot of things: about the mirror, about Simon's sick plans, Walter's illness and his research... The thoughts spun in her mind like sharp, broken fragments of a stained-glass picture.

Slowly, the disparate pieces began to slide home.

Alex jumped when she put her hand on his arm. "We're at Milo's," she told him. "How are you feeling?" She'd roused him a couple times in the night, making sure he would wake up. But she wasn't sure if he was still sick from the injection. Or how much he'd remember.

He hesitated. "I feel normal. Mostly. But I can't stop thinking about Ada. I felt her in the tunnels last night. Her thoughts were all jumbled together, full of panic and pain. Awful." Alex put his hand over his eyes. "I think the same thing must have happened to Caitlin and the others. And you too, when you were a kid in the mine shaft. Your minds just couldn't handle it and shut down. But what I don't get is, why didn't I end up in a coma or catatonic too? Why do I even remember it?"

They were so close to an answer, even closer than Alex realized. But still the picture wasn't complete. Not yet.

"You weren't affected in the mine, either," Evelyn said. "When we were kids."

"That was only because you covered my face with your jacket." Alex reached up to touch her cheek. "It's always been you. Last night, if you hadn't been there, I couldn't have made it all the way through the tunnels. I know that for sure."

She put her forehead against Alex's. She didn't know if he was right, but it still felt good to hear him say it. That he needed her because in some small way she was stronger than he was. They were stronger together.

Hopefully, they'd be strong enough for what they had to do.

"Alex, someone broke into Ms. Foster's house last night. I'm sure they were looking for Ada's letters."

"But why—"

"Because the letters prove that there's a connection between Byrne House and what happened to Milo and the others. And to you, last night. The same person did all of this. Someone who has access to Walter Byrne's research, enough to replicate whatever experiments he was doing that ended up killing Elijah Stanton. And when you look at it that way ..."

She trailed off, not wanting to say it out loud.

Alex's mouth tightened into a straight line. "What about Jake? Jake had opportunity every time. It could easily have been him. Or Detective Tyson! He grew up in Castle Heights and has a whole history with Daniella and Darren. Maybe he wanted it to *look* like someone from the Byrne family, to get back at them."

"I don't know what Jake and Cliff Tyson might have to do with all this. But if Jake is involved, he couldn't have done it alone. Not the part with Walter's research, anyway. And does Detective Tyson seem like the science type?"

Alex got up, running his fingers through his hair. "I'm not a big fan of my family, you know that. But this is nuts. They're all in Fort Collins."

Evelyn was still sitting on the bed. She fingered the edge of the blanket. "So they said."

"We can't make accusations like this without something more to go on than century-old letters. We need real proof." Alex grabbed his shirt from the floor and yanked it on.

"I know." She'd already run through this in her own head, and she had only one idea of where to go. "I think the proof is somewhere inside Byrne House. We just have to find it."

36

Alex used Mrs. Lake's key. Inside, the mansion was dim and quiet. They made their way down the main hallway and paused in front of the staircase. It curved steeply upward and disappeared out of sight. Evelyn looked at Alex, and he nodded. They'd put this off long enough. They climbed the stairs to the third floor.

They came into a narrow hallway. The ceiling was lower here, their steps muffled by a thick maroon carpet. Every door was closed. But somehow, Evelyn knew: the door at the end of the hall. That's where they needed to go.

The tower.

Milo and Silvia had driven them here. Milo hadn't wanted them to go inside the mansion at all, but he finally agreed to fifteen minutes. After that, he was calling the police to spill every detail of what they knew. Fifteen minutes to find a smoking-gun piece of evidence in this giant house. She didn't have time to hesitate.

Evelyn turned the crystal knob and pushed the door open.

They were standing in a neglected but still elegant bedroom. A huge four-poster bed took up most of the space. The walls curved around the room, forming a perfect circle. Alex went over to a yellowed lace curtain and pulled it back, revealing the round window. They had a clear view of Evelyn's house from here. She imagined Milo standing in this exact place, looking out of this window. Why had he come in here? What had he been doing?

They made a circuit of the room. There was a closet still filled with outdated clothes. A spacious bathroom, which was a bit grimy at the corners, but the floor was tiled in delicate Victorian patterns. Alex kept looking around, while Evelyn picked up an old framed photo from a table. It showed a family of four smiling on Byrne House's front lawn. A man with thinning dirty-blond hair, a woman in a flowing maxi dress. And two children, a boy and a girl. Miniature versions of Darren and Daniella.

"This must have been the master suite," Evelyn said to herself. *Reginald Byrne's room.*

"In here," Alex said. His voice came from a nearby room. "Look at all this."

Evelyn went back out to the hall. Alex was in the next room over. He waved Evelyn inside.

It had once been a large study or classroom. There were desks shoved against the walls, covered with old textbooks and papers. A white board was mounted on the wall with faded scribbles of marker. Dust bunnies had collected in the corners.

But one end of the room had obviously been in recent use. There was a shiny, stainless steel work table and a shelf of gleaming beakers and graduated cylinders. A makeshift laboratory. Alex bent down to look through the glass window of a short refrigerator, where vials of brackish liquid sat in test tubes. A bubble popped from one as they watched.

"What exactly did Darren and Daniella major in at school?" Evelyn asked.

"Daniella's PhD was in some kind of science. Darren? I don't know. I don't think he finished college."

A tall bookcase stood beside the steel table. Evelyn glanced over the bindings of the books—dozens of titles on pharmacology, botany, and chemistry, and long words that she didn't know how to pronounce.

A drawer slid open behind her. Alex was looking through all the desks. He tried a deep bottom drawer, but it caught on something. Locked.

Alex found a letter opener and dug it into the top of the drawer, wiggling it back and forth. The tiny keyhole in the drawer slowly turned, and he pulled the drawer all the way open. He lifted out a stack of papers and handed them to Evelyn. She quickly scanned the pages, looking for anything that might be significant. It was easier said than done. Most of the papers were covered in diagrams and equations. A lot like Walter Byrne's journals in the library, except on newer paper and in different handwriting.

Alex lifted another stack of papers out of the drawer. "Evelyn, look."

At the very bottom of the drawer sat two faded and worn leather-bound journals. Alex picked them up and faced the bindings outward so they could read the handwritten notations. The dates spanned from 1899 to 1900.

Two more of Walter's journals.

Alex opened one and flipped through. He looked up from a page near the end of the volume, his eyes wide.

"January 31, 1900. Here's something. Walter is writing about 'observations of the subject.'" Alex's finger ran down the page. "'Subject ingested a highly-concentrated solution of the translucent crystal without my knowledge, I assume sometime between two and three in the afternoon. Initial attempts to give aid at five o'clock unsuccessful. Subject would not respond to verbal cues or other stimulation. Observed convulsions, vomiting, incoherent statements.'"

Alex looked up. "Then it says, 'I don't think I can save him. But the opportunity cannot be wasted.'"

"He's talking about Elijah." It was such a cold thing to have written about a dying nine-year-old boy.

Evelyn opened the next volume and started scanning. The handwriting was hard to decipher, but it got clearer as she kept reading.

"Here's one from the year before," she said. "'I once again located the source of the translucent crystals today, a vein in one of the oldest shafts. I have confirmed that this mineral is, indeed, the one I have sought. The explanation for my sickness. As I hold a crystal into the sunlight now, its internal structure seems to shift and move, exactly as I remembered.'"

Evelyn shuffled through more journal entries. "He's writing about different experiments with the crystals. And listen, 'The diluted serum has given me some measure of relief from my episodes. But the effects have diminished with every dose. I fear I will soon become entirely resistant.'"

Alex closed the journal he was holding and set it on the desk. "He was testing this serum on himself. He must not have realized how it would affect other people until Elijah took it accidentally."

"And after that, according to Ada's letters, he stopped looking for a cure. He created the mirror instead."

Evelyn's brain was going a mile a minute trying to puzzle it out. Somebody at Byrne House had been studying these journals. Doing experiments in this third floor lab. She still didn't understand why, but the implication was obvious: someone was trying to copy Walter Byrne's research. His experiments.

"We can't handle this on our own anymore," she said. She went to a window and peeked between the blinds. Milo's truck drove slowly past. "We need to go."

"But we don't have proof. It's just a science project and some old journals."

"We're out of time. We know enough. We need to tell the police."

Alex tossed the journals back into the drawer. A few papers scattered. "We can't just call the cops. Will would never forgive me. *My mother* would never forgive me, and we were just starting to be okay again. I need a chance to talk to my brother first."

"You're assuming he doesn't know already. What if it was William who did this?"

Alex made a dismissive gesture. "Maybe he's a jerk, but he's my brother. He's always bailed me out when I screwed up. You think he attacked me? Broke into Ms. Foster's house? Why would he be desperate enough to do something like that?"

She remembered what Darren had said yesterday. His warning. "Alex, is it true your family's in debt? That's what Darren told me."

"You've got to be kidding me. You were talking to Darren about my family? Behind my back?"

"Is it *true*, though?" She'd never wanted to have this conversation. But now, it was unavoidable. "Walter's research could be really valuable to whoever proves it's legit."

Alex turned around, digging his hands into his hair. "Yes, we're in debt! Things have been a mess since my dad died. But so what? My brother didn't do it!"

Evelyn didn't want to believe William capable of this. But she felt the same about Daniella and Darren, too. The Byrnes seemed odd at times. If any of them had the skills to replicate Walter's research, it would be Daniella. But dangerous? Evelyn couldn't see any of them that way.

"At this point, we have to suspect everyone," she said. "Family or not."

"Very easy for you to say, since it's not your family at stake."

"That's completely unfair. My family *is* at stake. Anyone who lives in Castle Heights could be at stake."

Alex rubbed his neck. "Evelyn, you're the last person I want to fight with. But I'm not backing down on this. I have to talk to Will first. No matter what, he's my brother. I owe him that much."

Evelyn was shaking her head, but she didn't know how to change Alex's mind. She jumped when Silvia's phone rang in her pocket. It was Milo.

"It's been twenty-three minutes. *Get out of there.*"

They jogged down the stairs to the first floor. In the kitchen, Alex hesitated. "You'd better go for now," he said. "Just give me a couple hours."

"But Alex—"

"I'm calling William. I'll use the landline. Please, just go." He turned on his heel and started back toward the main hallway.

He hadn't even said goodbye.

Evelyn wanted to go after him, but Silvia's phone was ringing again in her pocket. She ran out the back door and answered the call as she walked through the gardens toward the agreed pickup spot.

"Ev," Silvia said, sputtering, "your mom!"

"What about my mom?"

"I'm so sorry. She must have seen us driving around because she knocked on the door of the truck when we were at a stop sign. We couldn't just drive away. She demanded to know where you were. I panicked!"

Evelyn spun around, looking frantically for her mother's livid face. But she was still secluded in the gardens. Of course her mother wasn't here. "What did you say?"

"That I didn't know. She started freaking out and ran back into your house. I'm sorry!"

"*Crap.*" She was thinking much worse words right now, but didn't think Silvia needed to hear that. This wasn't really Silvia's fault. "Listen, I need to keep your phone for a while, okay Silv? In case Alex needs to reach me."

Milo spoke into the phone. "Where's Alex? What's going on?"

"Just go check on your grandma. But don't do anything or tell anyone until you hear from me."

Milo argued with her, but Evelyn made him promise. "You have to trust me, Milo. Please. Let me handle it."

She'd have to go home and tell her mother the truth. About all of it. It was going to be bad—probably worse than Evelyn could even imagine, and she was imagining some very dire consequences right now, far beyond grounding. But she needed help. Viv would know what to do.

Evelyn hung up and ran along the garden pathway. She was almost to the stable. She'd scale the fence and head straight for home.

Darren's stocky frame stepped out from behind an evergreen, blocking her path. "Evelyn! Thank God."

She stopped short to keep from bumping into him. Darren's eyes were wide and fearful.

"It's William," Darren said. "He's totally out of control. He kidnapped Daniella and left me stranded in Fort Collins, even took my phone. I have to find my sister."

Evelyn veered instantly toward Byrne House. "Alex is inside the mansion. He's alone!"

"There's no time." Darren grabbed her hand and yanked her backward. "Daniella's bleeding, trapped in the tunnels. We have to get her out before William comes back."

Evelyn held out Silvia's phone. "Call 911. I have to go after Alex!"

Darren wouldn't let go. His fingers were gritty, scratching her skin. And his other hand was deep in his pocket, searching for something.

He was pulling Evelyn toward the stable.

No. This isn't right.

She tried to pull away. "Stop. Let go!"

Darren looked back at her. An odd expression etched onto his face, all the fear gone from his now vacant eyes.

"I was trying to make this easier on you," he said. "But you're giving me no other choice."

His hand flew out of his pocket. He pushed a soft piece of fabric against Evelyn's mouth, suffocating her scream, and forced her to the ground. A chemical odor filled her head. She struggled to cry out, to fight, but her body wasn't working anymore.

Then the sun was gone, and she was deep inside her nightmares. Trapped in the dark.

37

Evelyn's head felt like it was stuffed with cotton, like her tongue was made of it. She opened her eyes and turned her face away from the sudden invasion of light.

She was lying on a large wooden table. Above her hung an oil-lamp chandelier, creaking slightly back and forth on its chain. She tried to get up, but straps of rough leather bound her hands and feet. A dry sound reached her ears. The scratching of an old-fashioned pen.

Darren was sitting at a paper-strewn desk. Next to him, the zipper open, was the backpack she and Alex had lost the night before. Ada's mirror lay on the antique desk beside it, along with three phones: Evelyn's, Alex's, and Silvia's. They'd all had their batteries and SIM cards removed.

Darren wrote furiously in a notebook, his head bent so close to the paper that his nose nearly touched it. *Scritch, scritch, scritch.*

Evelyn slowly became aware of the rest of the room. It was another lab, much dirtier and darker than the makeshift one on the third floor of Byrne House. Floor-to-ceiling shelves were laden with cloudy glass jars, like an apothecary straight out of the nineteenth century. Each jar had a yellowing label with faded, handwritten notations. More modern but still dusty equipment littered the tables—a microscope, hot plates, a whirring machine the size of a suitcase.

On one table, there were several wooden racks filled with vials of clear liquid. An open box of syringes lay next to them.

Evelyn's still-confused gaze drifted over the plastered walls and the vaulted ceiling. A red mountain bike leaned against one wall, and beside it, a closed, riveted metal door. She was in a basement. Or some other underground room.

There was a different noise, like a sigh. She turned her head.

Jake Oshiro was lying bound to another table beside her.

His glassy eyes were open, and he was staring in Evelyn's direction, but not quite at her.

Dead.

A wave of horror passed through her until his chest moved, taking in a ragged breath that whistled over his teeth.

"Jake," she whispered. His eyelids twitched but he kept staring, seemingly unaware.

A chair scraped against the stone floor. "You're awake."

Darren stood over her and held Evelyn's chin in his hand, turning her head gently to one side, then the other. "How do you feel? It might take a few minutes for the effects of the chloroform to wear off. If you had just come with me, it would have been much simpler."

She struggled to swallow, her tongue still swollen in her mouth. "What's wrong with Jake?"

"He's on a low dosage. He's going to be fine. I just need to keep him quiet for a while." Darren wiped a hand over his face. "This isn't how I wanted things to go."

"Why are you doing this?" Panic crept into Evelyn's voice.

Darren got up and walked over to her. "Just tell me where the journal is," he said. "That's all I want." This was spoken so calmly, so matter-of-factly that she had to pause a moment to process it.

"What journal? I don't know what you're—"

Darren slammed his free hand down on the table, making Evelyn jump. "You're wasting time!" His face crumpled, and he squeezed his eyes shut. After some deep breaths he said, "I'm sorry. I don't mean to yell. I just need to figure this out, and my head hurts so much it's hard to think. The micro-doses aren't helping anymore. So please, stop lying."

She struggled to stay calm. It was Darren who'd attacked Alex. And Caitlin and Jordan. Darren who must have taken Milo. But maybe there was a mistake, an explanation. Somehow, she could reason with him.

"Let me help you." Her voice sounded like a croak. "Let me go and I promise, I'll do whatever I can."

"I wish I could. If I could go back to a month ago, before any of this..." He shook his head. "No, you'd never have seen things my way. You don't have to live with this *thing* in your head like I do. You couldn't possibly understand."

"Let me try. *Please*, Darren."

He seemed to consider. He went back to his desk and picked up the mirror, examining the gilt frame. "Walter invented this. Didn't he?"

She nodded.

"Tell me how it works," he said. "I saw you using it in the gardens."

Evelyn tried to swallow again, but the sides of her throat stuck together. "Just hold it up," she said, trying to control the urge to cry. Giving in to panic wouldn't help. She had to think clearly. "Look into it, relax your focus and look at what's just beyond the mirror. Then you should see."

"See what, exactly?"

"It depends on the place. What happened there. The only way to know is to look."

Darren sat down at the desk and held up the mirror. He breathed out and his body loosened. After a moment, his expression froze.

The mirror had him.

"Jake? Can you hear me?"

Jake blinked and his mouth closed and opened again. He nodded, very slowly.

"Darren can't hear us right now. He's ... somewhere else. Are you okay?"

Jake blinked again. "Darren brought me here last night. He's been injecting me. I've been ... dreaming. Terrible dreams." His words were faint, slow.

"Do you know where we are?"

"I've been here before. With Darren."

She wanted to demand why, but they had no time for explanations. Evelyn didn't know how long the vision in the mirror would keep Darren in its sway. "Can you tell me where?"

"Walter Park. Underneath the statue."

"We aren't far from Byrne House." Was Alex still inside the mansion? Darren must not have gotten to him—otherwise Alex would be here too. She shifted her wrists, the leather straps chafing her skin. "How do we get out? Just the door behind me?"

"Other door."

Her eyes shifted up and she saw it, on the opposite wall behind Jake. It was closed like the other, probably locked. They'd need the antique key, which was on Darren's desk.

Evelyn tried to picture her map of the tunnels. "Do you know which door is which? Which one leads to Byrne House?"

"Neither does, exactly." Jake's eyes were clearing, his voice steadier. "They both lead into passages in different directions. The one behind me is the closest one to the stairs that lead to the stable in the gardens. That's the one Darren uses to come here, to the lab. The one behind you is blocked. There's a bunch of bricks and rock in the way. The passage must have caved in."

The pattern of the tunnels took shape in Evelyn's mind, the branches and curves. She added the lab to her mental picture, underneath Walter Park, across from Byrne House. There was a caved-in branch in the tunnels—so it led here, to this place.

Darren was moving again. Evelyn turned to look. His body shook in the chair. He jumped up, breathing heavy and fast. "That was incredible. My head..." He blinked, looking around the room. "My head doesn't hurt. That was no hallucination, was it? I saw Ada and Simon Byrne. They were as clear as if they'd been standing right in the room with us."

"What the mirror shows you—it's real."

"Incredible," he said again. "Walter wrote about an invention, but I didn't really believe. The crystal serum is nothing compared to this." He was pacing, muttering to himself. "Is it some kind of treatment? Something else altogether? The possibilities are vast. But I still don't get it. This doesn't make sense."

Panting, he stood over her. Drops of sweat clung to the tiny hairs at his temples. "Where did you get this?"

She saw no reason to lie. "The mirror? I found it in some kind of burial chamber, connected to the tunnels. The mirror was inside a secret compartment."

He eyed her skeptically. "And you just happened to find it? Then how did you know how it worked?"

"I don't know, it just ... happened. When I looked into it. At first I just saw things from my own past, in my own house. That's how I figured out what it could do."

He came closer, droplets of sweat falling from his chin onto Evelyn's shoulder. His hand touched Evelyn's bound wrist, and his voice turned pleading. "Look, I don't understand what interest you have in Walter's work, and I don't really care. But I need that missing journal. I need to know how this mirror thing fits into his research."

Walter's work. "You've been experimenting on them," Evelyn said. "You could have killed my friends. You could've killed *Alex*."

Darren's eyes went flat and cold. He walked over to the table. He picked up a glass vial from the wooden rack and held it to the light. "I'll offer you a deal. You tell me where the missing journal is, and I'll just let you go."

A tear slipped from her eye. "Darren, *please*, I don't know! I've only seen the ones at Byrne House—in the library and in the lab on the third floor. I swear!"

He unstoppered the vial and selected a syringe from the box. "You saw what the serum did to Alex last night. Who knows what your reaction will be. Every person is a bit different. After all, Jordan and Caitlin woke up on their own. Maybe their brains healed themselves after the drug wore off. You could hope for that. Of course, this will be a much more concentrated dose. It might not kill you. The massive dose I gave Alex didn't kill him, so who knows."

He dipped the needle into the liquid and started withdrawing the plunger, bit by bit, as the liquid filled the syringe's cavity. "But you're much smaller than Alex."

Darren held the syringe upright and moved toward Evelyn, the needle glinting in the overhead light. "Please, don't!" She struggled and cringed away, but the straps held her tight to the table.

"You've given me no choice."

"Help me!" she screamed at Jake. But he just squeezed his eyes shut.

Darren jabbed the needle into Evelyn's arm.

38

THE BURN OF THE LIQUID SPREAD IMMEDIATELY, scalding the insides of Evelyn's arm, then into her shoulder and through her chest. It overtook every nerve, every sensation, as the room began to pulsate. Then Darren and Jake and the tables and equipment grew hazy and transparent.

Evelyn blinked and another version of the same room came into focus underneath, like one photographic negative lain on top of another.

She sees Ada, lying face down.

And then she becomes Ada.

Looking through Ada's eyes, Ada looking through hers, Evelyn stares at the dusty stone floor. The stone is cold against the bodice of her gown. The toes of black boots stand inches away from her nose. Moments before, Simon threw her into this room from the open door at the base of the stairwell. She tripped over her skirts and hit the ground. She's terrified to think about what he intends to do next.

"Get up," Simon says.

"Where are we?" She pushes up onto her forearms, then her hands and knees.

"Don't you want to know where your husband spends his time? Take a look around. See for yourself what he's been up to."

She stands and rotates slowly in a circle, surveying the room. There is a low, straw-covered cot in the corner with a small nightstand next to it with books stacked on top. In the center of the room is a large wooden table, covered with more books and chemist's equipment. Surgical instruments lay parallel on a square of red cloth.

Behind the table, inside *the table, Evelyn sees Darren sitting at his desk. It is like looking through a reflective window at a faraway scene. Darren watches her, unblinking, from the other place. A cloud of confused emotions spills out of him—dark gray shot through with browns and yellows. She senses his fear, his guilt and his desperation. Sees flashes of the episodes he's endured since he was a child: first the debilitating migraines, then the terrible visions that make him scream and rave. Yet he never remembers afterward what he's seen. There are holes in his memory, time lost. It is the same illness that plagued Walter Byrne. He has prayed for a cure. He's come so very close, gone too far to turn back now. But while the visions brought Walter wild inspiration, they've driven Darren only toward madness.*

She sees a faded copy of Milo Foster lying on the same table where Jake lies now.

But Ada turns back to Simon, and Evelyn must follow.

"Why would he need this?" Ada asks through Evelyn. "His lab is in the house."

Simon walks around the room. He picks up a book from the nightstand, flips through the pages, and tosses it onto the cot, contemplating how to draw this out in just the right way.

"I don't understand half of what Walter does," Simon says. "You and I, we've always had that in common. He doesn't need *it, Ada. He wants a private space to do the real research he's been working on. Away from* you."

"Walter has shared discoveries with me that are greater than anything you could imagine. He's kept nothing from me."

Simon laughs. "I assumed you had learned something in the past years. Clearly I thought too highly of you. Walter confides in one person, and that is me. I know everything about his experiments, particularly the subjects *of his experiments."*

Simon picks up a scalpel from the table and traces it along the index finger of his other hand, though not hard enough to break the skin. His eyes shift up to meet hers. Evelyn feels the viciousness of his thoughts crashing into her like waves driven by a storm.

"Elijah, for instance."

An icy chill floods through her body as Ada recalls Henry's last visit and his biting words. "Never. You lie."

Evelyn knows he is not ... not exactly. Simon knows that Walter never intended to hurt the boy, even tried to save him. But in the end, Walter got the data he needed.

Simon smiles. "I admit I'm not the most forthright person in existence. But the beautiful thing is, I don't have to lie about this. Walter did it all himself."

Rage clouds over Ada's—Evelyn's—mind and she runs for the surgical instruments. Simon grabs her wrists and twists them behind her back. "Walter told me every detail," Simon whispers in her ear.

Now, Simon lies.

"Walter left his samples out for the boy to find. When he found Elijah, cowering in fear, Walter was pleased. He took notes. Observed the effects. You should have seen the darkness in his eyes when he described it to me. Even at the sight of Henry sobbing over his son's dead body, Walter felt nothing but pleasure. Except, I suppose, scientific curiosity."

Tears burn her eyes. "He could never be so monstrous. Walter is kind. Empathetic. He feels emotions more intensely than anyone I've ever known."

Simon sighs. "Yes, Walter's fits. Who do you think cared for him in the years before I brought you into this house? I sacrificed more than you could fathom to protect Walter from himself. I'm still *protecting him.* I'm the only one who understands him, and therefore the only one he truly loves."

Simon whirls her around to face him. She backs into the table and he presses himself close against her. She spits in his face, but Simon wipes it with his sleeve and wraps his hand around her upper arm and squeezes so hard she feels the circulation slowing. He pulls her by the arm into the corner with the trunk. He undoes the latch and lifts it with his free hand. He pushes her down until her collar bone is crushed against the rim of the open trunk.

"Look for yourself," he says. "This *is* your husband's research."

Inside the trunk, just below her chin, is the blue face of Mrs. Trilby, the housekeeper. Her open eyes stare at nothing, her uniform wrinkled and soiled. Her legs have been folded up with her knees to her chest so that she fits the length of the trunk.

Ada screams and struggles to escape. Simon lets her go, and she falls backward and scrambles away from the trunk. "You did this!" she screams. "You've killed her to blame it on Walter, to ruin him!"

Simon closes the lid of the trunk and slowly shakes his head. "If that was my plan, the authorities would already be here. I wouldn't be showing you the evidence first."

"But the candlesticks, they said she ran off with them."

Simon nods. "She did take the candlesticks. Walter found her in the garden, hiding until she could find transport away from Byrne House. She wanted to get away from me, presumably. Walter brought her here and gave her the concentrated drug he's developed. She died, much like Elijah, after days of suffering. He told me what had happened and asked for my help."

Evelyn knows that Simon lies. She sees it all, the nights Simon stalked Mrs. Trilby, how he terrorized her. And how, when Trilby dared to threaten him with the secrets he so foolishly let slip in moments of weakness, he rid himself of the problem. Simon smiles, thinking of how perfectly these pieces are coming together. As if he'd planned it.

Evelyn knows. But Ada does not.

Ada believes every false word, and the horror of it crushes her heart. She lays down and presses her forehead into the floor, unable to bear the pain.

"Why are you showing me this?" Ada moans inside Evelyn. "Why are you torturing me this way?"

"Because you and Walter took everything from me. You deserve to know the truth about the man you claim to love so that you can suffer as I have."

"If Walter did any of these things, it is because of you. Your corruption somehow infected him."

"I'm sure it would be easier for you to believe that. But Walter's plans far preceded my return. He's built his sickness into the very foundations of the house and underneath the idyllic community you've been hoping to create. I had nothing to do with that. He designed it painstakingly all by himself."

Evelyn sits up. Ada stares through her at Simon, trying to understand his meaning. His eyes brighten.

"You don't even know about the tunnels? Your lack of basic observation skills is truly astounding, Ada. Don't worry. I'll educate you. Even you must have noticed, these past years, Walter's growing paranoia? His rigidity? You only made it worse by insisting that he turn the estate into some sort of fairytale kingdom, building schools and *homes for the servants. How did you expect him to react? He couldn't simply let go of all that he's spent years creating."*

Simon turns to the metal door set into the wall.

"I think you might even like them, Ada. They're elegant, in a way. Unfortunately, these tunnels have taken on a life of their own in Walter's mind. I'm sure they've worsened his delusions. On more than one occasion, I've found him wandering around down here, practically lost in the maze he created to trap anyone who stumbled upon them."

Simon turns back to her. A smile slowly spreads his mouth into a crescent-shaped cut across his face. He is turning over a new plan in his mind, shaping it and examining it from all sides. *"It would be poetic, wouldn't it?"* Simon murmurs. *"Walter would appreciate that."*

Simon goes to the table and picks up a heavy key. He takes it to the metal door near the trunk and twists the key into the lock. When he pulls open the door, a rectangle of pitch black yawns into view. Before she can react, Simon yanks her by the shoulders into a standing position and pushes her through the doorway.

Darkness envelops her instantly. She reaches toward the light, but the gap is already closing. The door slams shut. She hears the echo reverberating.

Everywhere around her—so thick she can feel it crawling across her skin and coating the insides of her lungs when she breathes—is profound, absolute, blackness.

39

"Evelyn," the voice whispered. "Evelyn."

She lifted her gaze from the metal door, where Simon was still leaning back and smiling, enjoying Ada's screams. The dark haze over Evelyn's eyes cleared as she pulled away from Ada, and she found Daniella Byrne standing over her.

Daniella pulled at the straps holding Evelyn's wrists to the bed, her hands shaking. "We have to hurry. Darren went over to Byrne House but he'll be back soon. I saw him drag you into the stable and I followed you down here."

Evelyn could still hear Ada clawing at the other side of the metal door. She forced the sound to the back of her mind.

"Where's Alex?"

"I didn't have time to tell him. I wasn't even sure where Darren was taking you." Daniella freed Evelyn's hands and went to work on the straps at her ankles.

Evelyn lifted herself onto her elbows. A blackish-purple bubble hovered over Daniella's head, like a bruise that was fading to yellow-green at the edges. Evelyn spoke without thinking.

"You're lying."

Daniella looked up with shock. "Why would you say that?"

"Darren injected me with that *serum* you've been working on. You've been here before. Many times."

Her eyes widened, but she quickly recovered. "I suppose I did know, deep down." Daniella shook her head, pretending to clear it. "And I'll never forgive myself for it. I didn't realize he'd gotten so out of control."

She was harder to read than Darren had been. But there it was—another lie. "You knew exactly what Darren was doing down here."

Daniella's eyes pleaded. "I think he did something to our father, frightened Daddy so much that his heart gave out. And poor Milo Foster—I was afraid if I told anyone, Darren would kill me. But I didn't think Darren would do something like this. Over the past few days he's lost all touch with reality."

As Daniella spoke, the black-purple bulge shifted to cover the top of her head. Pops of lightning-blue appeared at its base. Daniella was saying whatever she could come up with to make Evelyn believe her.

But Evelyn could see the truth.

"You *knew*," she hissed. "About everything. Your father, Milo, Jordan, Caitlin. Even Alex last night. Darren told you everything, every time."

But Evelyn still couldn't understand why. Why had Daniella kept Darren's secrets?

"You don't understand," Daniella said, backing away from her. "I had a tyrant for a father. My mother couldn't stand it any longer, and I had no one but Darren. I've always taken care of him. I had no idea Darren would take things this far, I swear to you."

"Lies," Evelyn whispered. She saw it now. "You weren't protecting your brother. You were protecting *yourself*."

Daniella shook her head as tears streamed over her cheeks. But Evelyn could see the memories flying past, unbidden and unstoppable, in Daniella's mind. The unimaginable truth.

"You're the reason Darren is sick at all. *You left him down there.*"

Daniella cried out. She covered her mouth and turned away. The confusion of thoughts and emotions became a blur, too much for Evelyn to separate. But it had all started the day that Evelyn and Alex fell on the Byrne House grounds. Eleven years ago. So much came back to that day.

Then, Daniella's mind cleared. As if she'd decided to stop fighting. Evelyn watched the memory unfold.

Daniella was fourteen. She was supposed to be looking after the littler ones. She wasn't supposed to be spending time alone with her older cousin William, still boyish at nineteen but technically a grown man. But she saw him as an equal. None of her classmates liked her, much less understood her; she could talk to William. He listened.

Where were you? her parents had asked her afterward. *Why weren't you there when Alex and the neighbor girl got hurt?* As if they ever cared to know what she was doing, as long as she scored off the charts on every standardized test and aced her college-level classes. As long as she stayed out of the way and made them look good.

It was Darren who told on her. Her whiney, tag-along little brother who wouldn't let her have friends of her own. Her parents were livid. They blamed her, and even more they blamed William. They said she could never speak to William Evans again.

So a few weeks later, she made Darren pay.

One night, she made a rope ladder. The opening to the mine shaft was only covered with plywood. Easy to pry up. She tricked Darren into climbing down into the shaft. Then she pulled up the ladder and left him there.

From up above in the garden, she listened to his screams. He'd always been such a baby. Couldn't stand to be on his own. Well, this would teach him to be brave. She left him until morning so he'd learn his lesson well. Then she made him his favorite apple muffins, showing him all was forgiven. She went to let him out.

But Darren wouldn't wake up.

In the underground lab, Evelyn watched the colors around Daniella's head shift and pulsate.

"I didn't know what would happen to him," Daniella insisted. "How could I?"

"But you'd read Walter's journals by then," Evelyn said. "The ones in the library. You suspected they were more than just a lunatic's ravings. You were curious."

When he finally did wake up—weeks later—he remembered nothing. No one but Daniella knew that he'd been trapped underground. He began to suffer from bouts of a mysterious illness. Daniella's parents took Darren to every prominent doctor that their money could afford. But nothing helped. She became her brother's caretaker, soothing him after his episodes, crafting remedies for his headaches, watching over him whenever he fell into unconsciousness.

"I took care of him!" Daniella protested. "My father wanted to put him in an institution."

"You wanted him under your thumb," Evelyn said. "Someone to worship you."

Daniella shook her head. "You couldn't know what it was like."

Like Walter Byrne over a century ago, Darren would have uncanny insights whenever he was in the grip of a fit. He saw things that terrified him. Ghosts and monsters. But the thing that shocked him the most? His own sister's mind. Because with every episode, he would read the truth anew. He would remember that night underground and recoil from his sister, the one person he'd trusted. Mercifully—to Daniella, at least—he always forgot once the fit had passed. Every time, he awoke still adoring his sister. Never suspecting the truth.

But he couldn't stand the constant headaches, the isolation. No matter how many doctors he saw, no one could help. Friends wouldn't stay. Except for his sister, Darren was alone.

Like Walter before him, Darren began searching for an explanation for his illness. By chance, he read Walter's old journals—the ones that Daniella had always prized—and realized that there might be hope for a cure. If he could only complete Walter's work. He asked for Daniella's help in recreating Walter's crystal serum.

She was the one who showed her brother the tunnels and the underground lab. She herself had outgrown Walter's research—those journals had been her childhood obsession, but they were more madness than science. She had her doctoral work, a life at the university with students who admired her. But if Darren wanted to play around in that old lab, what did she mind? He could use the tunnels to sneak onto the Byrne House property as much as he liked. Their father would never suspect, and it kept Darren occupied. She was sure her brother's "research" would never go anywhere. Her secrets were safe.

But Darren managed to get further than she'd ever expected. Using Walter's instructions, he found samples of the crystal and recreated the serum. Like Walter before him, he began using micro-doses to soothe his episodes. But he grew more and more resistant to the drug. He needed a new breakthrough.

"You knew it all," Evelyn said to Daniella, "and you did *nothing*."

"No! I began to study the crystal myself. I created an antidote to Darren's drug. It worked on Milo, and then I made Darren set Milo free. And I helped Caitlin and the other girl, too! I only wish the antidote could've cured Darren, but his condition is too severe. I did everything I could."

On a nighttime foray into the mansion to search for more of Walter's writings, Darren had found his father's last will and testament. Reginald planned to give his share of Byrne House to the Evans family and disinherit his estranged children completely. When Darren told her, Daniella was furious. The mansion should be theirs. *Hers*. This was her birthright, the inheritance that she deserved.

Daniella asked her brother to fix it. So Darren used the concentrated crystal serum on their father.

Darren didn't expect the cleaning woman to get there so soon. And he certainly didn't expect Milo Foster to walk into his father's bedroom while Darren had been searching out every last copy of that damned will. Luckily, he'd had another syringe.

"You didn't care about your father or Milo or any of them. You only finally did something because Alex and William got involved—when Detective Tyson tried to blame us—and that meant it affected *you*."

Daniella braced herself against the desk. Tears flowed from her eyes, and her chest skipped with shallow, rapid breaths.

"You did nothing," Evelyn said, "and not because you were afraid. Because you wanted to see if Walter had been right all along."

She'd stood by while Darren tested increasing concentrations of the serum on the teens of Castle Heights. Let him keep experimenting even though his "research" had long since become madness. He hadn't come any closer to a cure.

Evelyn thought of Walter's expressionless face as he watched Elijah suffering in the tunnels. Ada's screams got louder in her head.

"You're wrong about me." Daniella finished releasing the restraints and helped Evelyn sit up. "I've been sabotaging my brother, taking equipment and notes from here every few days to slow him down. That's why he left here just now. He doesn't have what he needs to prepare your blood samples. But I was too scared to confront him, and for that I'm sorry. Please, let me get you out of here. We'll sort everything out later, even call the police if you want. I'll never forgive myself if you're hurt."

More manipulation. Daniella didn't want Alex, and by extension William, to get upset if Evelyn disappeared. She did love William, as much as she could love anyone. But Daniella had fooled William like she'd fooled everyone else.

"What about Jake?" Evelyn said. "He needs help too." Jake hadn't spoken, but he was following their conversation with a curious expression.

Daniella glanced over at Jake and set her jaw. "We'll get help as soon as we're safe. He's too confused from the serum. He'll slow us down."

This was the real Daniella.

"Do you hear yourself?" Evelyn said. "Do you even realize that it's wrong to look at a person lying there suffering and feel absolutely nothing for him?"

The bubble over Daniella's head shifted again and changed colors. She was running out of patience.

"You think I should be grateful that you're here to help me," Evelyn said. "Fine. Thank you. But I'm not leaving here without Jake." She swung her legs from the table onto the floor and started loosening Jake's restraints.

"Evelyn, think about this, you—"

A door closed nearby, and footsteps approached.

"Lie down," Daniella hissed. "Lie down!"

A key scratched in the lock. Evelyn jumped back onto the table, and Daniella re-fastened the straps without tightening them. Daniella stepped over to the desk and picked up Darren's sheet of notes as the metal door beyond Jake's table opened.

Darren stopped when he saw his sister. "Daniella. You came." The colors around him changed, brightening and stretching out. Daniella was the only person who'd ever accepted him. For so many years, she'd been his only reason to keep living.

Hatred swirled around Daniella's head, burning a deep maroon. It dripped along Daniella's body and sent out tendrils into the room. Evelyn turned her head to avoid breathing it in. Daniella had loved her brother, once. But it had been a very long time.

"You've been making so much progress. I can hardly keep up." Daniella walked from table to table, pretending to examine and arrange the equipment. She paused at the table with the wooden rack of vials. While Darren bent over his desk drawer, Daniella fiddled with something behind her back. She slipped whatever it was into her pocket and moved away from the table.

Darren stood, holding the mirror. "I've found something incredible. It will make all of this worthwhile."

"Are you sure this is the best time? William's been trying to reach us." Daniella feigned absentmindedness as she walked over to the table where Evelyn lay. Daniella put her hands behind her back and pressed something cylindrical into Evelyn's palm. Evelyn wrapped her fingers around the object and turned her hand to conceal it.

"You're worried about her overhearing us?" Darren said. "I'll do what I have to. I always take care of things for you. You know that."

Daniella started towards the door, pulling a key from her pocket. "But William's upset that we left Fort Collins without him. I need to go make some kind of excuse. He's getting suspicious."

Darren reached out and touched her elbow. "Wait. You'll want to see this, I promise." He handed her the mirror.

She turned the mirror over in her hands. Daniella's hatred and fear withdrew, replaced by eager curiosity. "What is it?"

"Walter's invention. The great discovery he kept referring to in his later writing, but we could never figure out. The subject of the missing journal."

Daniella looked up, her eyes on fire. "The missing journal? You've found it?"

"Not yet. But I will. I'll have it soon."

The fear evaporated from around Daniella, indecision now clouding her mind. A horrible realization washed over Evelyn.

Daniella wasn't going to tell anyone. Her feelings toward Evelyn had changed instantly when Darren mentioned the missing journal.

"Should I come back in the morning?" Daniella asked.

Darren took the mirror from his sister's hands. "Yes. I'll be ready then."

Daniella nodded and slowly walked to the door. She unlocked it with her key and glanced back one last time. She'd helped Evelyn the best she could. Evened the odds. Beyond that, she wouldn't interfere. She'd wait until morning to see who survived. Either way, she'd be sure to get what she wanted.

The door slammed behind her.

40

Darren came to Evelyn's side. "You've been watching us, haven't you? You hardly seem affected by the serum at all." He went back to his desk and jotted down a few notes. "Did you see Ada Byrne? Simon?"

"Yes," Evelyn whispered. Her fingers were sweaty against the object in her hand. "Ada Byrne. Simon ... did things to her. Horrible things. I keep seeing it happen, over and over, like it's happening to me."

"I know. The bit that I saw was awful." Darren frowned, gripping his pen. "But the *fact* that we saw it—don't you think that's breathtaking? This illness, it makes me hallucinate. At least, that's what Daniella has always said. Walter said they were insights into hidden things. But I never remember them afterward. What if, all this time, I've really been seeing the past?"

He walked back toward Evelyn, chewing on the end of his pen. "If that were true," he said, "then everything I've done would be worth it. This is bigger than us. Bigger than just a few small lives."

Evelyn moaned. "Please take me someplace else, anywhere. I'll do whatever you want, just don't make me stay here and listen to Ada scream."

"I could make it stop. My sister has an antidote. But you'll have to cooperate."

"I will. Please, just take me out of this room." Evelyn blinked, and a tear trickled onto her cheek. "I'll tell you where the journal is."

The notebook and pen fell to Darren's sides. He leaned in closer. "Where is it?"

Her hands were trembling, the cylinder in her fist almost hitting against the table beneath her. It was torture to keep lying there, letting him come closer. She steadied her hands and prayed they'd work when she needed them. Then she felt his breath against her neck. She couldn't take this another second. *Now.* Her arms shot up.

Evelyn drove the syringe into his side with both hands and pushed the plunger. He stumbled backwards, eyes blazing, the syringe sticking out from his shirt. He knocked the syringe away and it clattered to the floor.

Darren dropped to his knees. He moaned, clutching his ribcage where she'd injected him.

Evelyn rolled from the table and loosened Jake's restraints. After Jake was free, she scanned the room, running from table to table, searching for something she could use to hold Darren. She found a long piece of rubber in the box with the syringes.

Evelyn put her foot in the center of Darren's back and pushed. He flopped face-forward onto the floor. She wrenched his arms behind him and wrapped the rubber strap around and around his wrists. When the strap was nearly taut, she wrapped it around both wrists again and tied it in a double knot.

"Jake, let's go!"

She had no idea how Darren would react to the drug; how long he'd be distracted by Ada and Simon.

Or how long the band around his thick wrists would hold.

Jake's confusion and rage flowed out around him. He stood over Darren, contemplating whether he should kick Darren in the head or not. But they didn't have time for that. Evelyn grabbed the antique key from the desk, took Jake by the hand, and ran for the metal door.

"Not that one!" Jake said. "That's the cave-in!"

"I know."

They couldn't go the other way—Daniella might be waiting. But Evelyn hoped that if Darren tried to follow them, he'd think they went out the door to the stable. Evelyn frantically tried to make the key work, all the while glancing back at Darren. He was still lying on the floor, not moving. Lost in the past.

The key turned in the lock and she opened the door, pushing Jake ahead of her. The tunnel beyond was pitch black.

"There's a flashlight in the desk," Jake said. "The middle drawer."

She ran back to get it. Then she followed Jake into the tunnel and locked the door behind them. Darren clearly had his own key, and she didn't have time to search the lab to find it. But she just needed to slow him down.

She sensed Ada there, cowering against the far wall. Ada's terror tried to pull her in again, but Evelyn forced Ada out of her head.

They ran through the passage, the flashlight beam bouncing wildly ahead of them. It was like the other tunnels Evelyn had seen, but narrower and with a lower ceiling. Soon the flashlight hit upon a few stray bricks, and then more bricks scattered among pieces of wood and rock. Evelyn slowed down and brought the flashlight up.

A mountain of debris lay ahead, with a torn-open ceiling above. The vault had given way like an enormous trapdoor. Evelyn stepped carefully through the bricks and moved closer, seeing a wooden beam in the ceiling just above the pile. The beam formed the top of an inverted "U" shaped support, smaller than the ones in the other tunnels but obviously still strong. The support had kept the tunnel from failing entirely, but it narrowed the passageway at that point, allowing the debris to block the path.

Evelyn started climbing the sloping pile. It was surprisingly solid, having settled into place over who knew how many years. The corners of bricks and jagged edges of mortar cut into her skin, but they made good hand and footholds. She could hardly feel the cuts for all the adrenaline.

"What are you doing?" Jake asked. Fear emanated from him, hitting Evelyn's back. Like her, Jake could see and hear Ada all around them. He was afraid of her. He couldn't understand anything that was happening.

"I'm finding a way out of here."

Jake started to follow Evelyn up the shallow hill. She reached the top and saw a gap, over a foot wide, between the wooden beam and the heap of debris underneath. She wedged the flashlight between two bricks so that it lit the gap.

"Look out, I'm clearing space!"

Evelyn picked up bricks and threw them down behind her. They crashed at the bottom, sending out echoes into the tunnel. Jake yelped and he began scrambling up the slope. Evelyn sensed the change in his thoughts as the fog started to clear. He understood her plan. They shoveled the rocks and dirt away with their hands. Finally, the gap had widened into a circle broad enough for a person to fit through.

Evelyn poked the flashlight through the hole. There, on the other side, were the three tunnel branches she remembered. On her right, the two branches that led out into the labyrinth of passageways. And on her left, the tunnel leading back to the Byrne House basement.

The metal door behind them creaked on its hinges. Darren was already back on his feet. And he hadn't been fooled.

"Come on!" Evelyn whispered. She placed the flashlight on the downhill slope of the pile of debris to light where she was going, then pointed her legs toward the gap under the wooden beam. She pushed herself through it on her stomach. Bricks caught at her shirt and scraped the bare skin. Once she was through, Evelyn moved carefully to the side to make room for Jake.

They heard footsteps in the tunnel behind them. The footsteps sped up, another flashlight beam whipping through the air. Maybe they shouldn't have come this way. *If Darren catches up to us, we're trapped.*

"Jake, your turn! Hurry!"

Jake's feet came through the gap, then his thighs and hips. Evelyn grabbed his shins and pulled. His hands came through, and he tried to lift up his stomach to avoid scraping himself on the edges of the bricks. She pulled again at his legs as they flailed, his body jerking from side to side.

"I'm stuck! I can't fit my shoulders through!"

She climbed back to the top and pulled bricks and dirt away from either side of Jake's body.

"Evelyn, he's coming! I see him, he's getting closer! Help me!"

Darren panted as he climbed the cave-in, saying nothing. Evelyn moved another brick and pulled at Jake's right shoulder. It came through. He angled the other shoulder to get it past, and ducked his head under the beam.

Evelyn grabbed her flashlight and started working her way down the pile on her hands and knees and feet, pointing the flashlight down every few seconds as a guide. Then she looked back up.

Jake was still at the top, sobbing in gulps and hiccups.

"Jake, get going! We only have a few seconds!"

"Nuh nuh no. I can't. I ca ca can't."

Evelyn tossed the flashlight down to the tunnel floor as gently as she could. It hit the floor and rolled, shrinking into an elongated pool of light on the floor. She climbed back up and felt for Jake's wrist. When she found it, she yanked. Jake offered no resistance and fell headfirst on top of her.

They tumbled together down the slope of debris. Halfway down, Evelyn's leg slammed against something hard jutting from the pile. Air shot from her lungs. She felt first the twist then the pop inside her leg, and she landed with a dull thud. A blinding corona of pain emanated from her shin. Two seconds passed. Neither of them moved.

Then a brick cascaded down the hill.

Darren was coming through the gap.

41

SHE DRAGGED HERSELF TOWARD THE FLASHLIGHT, grabbed it and pointed it upward. Darren's feet wiggled in the light. He was trying to pull himself past the gap. Evelyn just hoped his large frame wouldn't fit through.

She braced one hand against the tunnel wall and pushed up onto her good leg. She tried putting a bit of weight on the hurt one. Pain rocketed from her shin up through her body, forcing a gasp out of her lungs. Jake looked up, rubbing his head.

"I'm hurt," Evelyn said haltingly. "I can't walk."

Jake hurried to Evelyn's side and put his arm around her. Leaning on Jake's shoulder, she took a step with her good leg toward the tunnel leading to Byrne House.

Then she stopped. Her mind, driven by instinct, was working faster than she could follow with logic alone. Something told her to go in the other direction.

"The other way," Evelyn told Jake.

He didn't question it. He'd turned over everything to her, trusting Evelyn completely to get them out.

They limped into the far left branch in the tunnels. Adrenaline pulsed through Evelyn anew, clearing her head from the pain. She put more pressure on her injured leg with each step. She kept the flashlight pointing forward, searching for what she knew would be just a few minutes ahead in the tunnel.

She listened for footsteps behind, but heard nothing except Jake's breathing and Ada's whimpers.

"Do you hear her?" Jake whispered.

"Her name is Ada." The question had been hovering in Jake's mind for a while. Evelyn knew Jake had seen much of what she had in the underground lab, but to Jake the conversation between Simon and Ada had sounded garbled, mixed with static. All he knew was that Ada was terrified. And very, very angry.

A wooden door appeared ahead out of the darkness. Evelyn stopped in front of the steps at its base.

"What is that?" Jake had never been this far into the tunnels.

"You'll see. Help me up."

Jake helped her to the top step. Evelyn turned the round handle on the door, and the metal bands started to move. She pulled open the door and limped inside, stepping over the ski boots and poles lying on the floor of the storage room. In the toolbox, she found a hammer and a box cutter. She gave those to Jake. Evelyn slipped the key out of her back pocket and replaced it with a screwdriver—she'd take any kind of weapon she could get.

Jake examined the smooth, inner surface of the open doorway. "We can't shut this. There's no handle on this side. Darren's going to find us."

The haze of terror began closing over Jake's mind again.

"Hey, stay with me. We won't be in here long." Evelyn hobbled over to the metal door on the other side of the storage room. She unlocked the door and guided Jake through into the dark basement.

Just before Evelyn closed the metal door, her flashlight beam caught the dark surface of an axe blade lying in a corner of the storage room. She grabbed the axe by its long handle and shut the door.

Evelyn shined the flashlight around the basement. There was a stacked washer and dryer unit, a furnace, and a water heater, and some shelves mixed in with a few wooden posts that supported the beams of the main floor above. A kayak leaned against one wall.

She closed her eyes and concentrated. The upper floors of the house were quiet. She sensed the people who lived here, a young couple in their thirties with a toddler boy, and before them, a widower with three grown children living in far-away cities, and other people too—visitors and repairmen and even a teenage runaway who hid in the house for a week when the family was away on a camping trip in Rocky Mountain National Park. But it was a calm, ambient hum, without the bright disruptions of a living person. It was safe.

Evelyn opened her eyes. Jake was sitting on the floor, cradling his head in his hands. What had seemed like white noise to Evelyn was an ocean of chaos in Jake's mind. She sat next to him and put her hand on his arm.

"Jake? You can filter all of this out. Imagine pushing it down away from you."

"I can't even hear my own thoughts. I don't know which thoughts are mine."

"You're exhausted. You haven't slept since Darren took you to the lab from your house. Right? Do you remember that? Milo was there before it happened?"

Jake nodded weakly. "I wanted to tell Milo everything. About how it had gotten completely out of hand. But I heard the noise downstairs and I knew Darren was there." Jake lifted his chin to look at her. "I'm so sorry, Evelyn. For what I said to you at the party, and how I acted at the dance."

She forced out a laugh. "Don't worry about it. That stuff doesn't matter now."

"It *does*." Jake reached out to caress Evelyn's cheek. "I thought I was going to die down there. I thought Darren was going to kill me, but then suddenly you were there with this golden glow all around you. It was the most beautiful thing I've ever seen."

"That's very sweet, but I need you to *focus*. I want you to go upstairs into the house. The family's not here right now. Find a phone and call 911."

Fear crackled through Jake's mind—he was afraid to call the police, though Evelyn couldn't tell why. She couldn't sort through it right now.

I need my mom and Alex, Evelyn thought. *Both of them. I can't do this alone.* But the idea of Darren coming after her mother next, injecting Viv with that serum ... No, Evelyn would never let that happen. Alex at least had some idea of the danger.

"Alex, then. I want you to bring Alex here." Evelyn took Jake's hand and dropped the antique key into his palm. She closed his fingers around it.

"Why aren't you coming?" he asked. "We should stay together."

"I can't. Not with my leg like this." Evelyn choked down the overwhelming, nauseating pain that kept rearing up inside her. "I don't think I can walk for much longer. Darren would have no trouble catching up to us. We wouldn't stand a chance."

"But he—"

"I'll be ready for him. Just get Alex here. He'll know what to do to help us."

"You love him." Jake squeezed his eyes shut. "Tell Silvia I'm really sorry. I should have—"

He closed his mouth and looked toward the metal door. His lower lip began to tremble. Evelyn felt it too. Darren was close. The locking mechanism shifted inside the metal door.

"Jake, *go!*"

As Evelyn watched him disappear up the stairs, she felt terror blanket Jake's thoughts again. Without her to calm him, the jumble of feelings and memories from inside the house had flooded back into Jake's mind. *Please Jake, remember what to do.* Evelyn crawled to the wall, switched off the flashlight, and sat with the axe clutched in her hands.

She waited.

42

THE METAL DOOR SWUNG INTO THE BASEMENT BY A few inches and then stopped. A flashlight beam shined from behind it, and then a hoarse voice.

"I know you're there."

She concentrated on her breathing, her heartbeat, trying to slow everything down. A layer of blank white formed over her thoughts like powdery snow covering a hillside.

"That won't work," he said. "I can see your thoughts before you even know what they are." The metal door opened farther into the room. Darren's silhouette appeared in the doorway.

"I see you, Evelyn. I know you're hurt. You can't hide from me."

She still sensed Jake's confusion upstairs. He didn't know where he was or where to go. Evelyn's panic and desperation grew, multiplying with Jake's. They had no hope. No chance.

Evelyn thought of her mother up there somewhere, trying desperately to find her. *Mom.*

Darren stepped cautiously into the basement. "That's it. Give up and call for Mommy. There's no way out. No point in fighting." He took a few more steps. He'd left the flashlight in the storage room, but he seemed to know exactly where Evelyn was crouched.

Her hands tightened around the handle of the axe.

Suddenly Darren ran forward. Evelyn screamed and swung the axe, aiming for his legs, but he jumped easily aside. The axe blade buried itself in one of the basement's wooden support posts instead.

Darren gripped the axe by its handle and pulled it from the wood.

Evelyn used the shelving unit next to her to pull herself up to standing. She tried to run but could only manage a stumbling limp. The pain in her leg sent starbursts of white across her eyes. Her leg began to give out.

Darren watched her struggle. Then he swung the axe. The blunt end of the axe head glanced off Evelyn's jaw, sending her spinning onto the floor. She crumpled to the ground, face up, the metallic tang of blood flooding into her mouth.

She could not get up.

Darren grabbed hold of Evelyn's ankles and started pulling her along the floor. She tried to kick him away, but excruciating pain tore through her broken leg. Evelyn screamed again, knowing there was no one to hear her, but unable to stop herself.

He dragged her into the storage room, where she collided with the toolbox. She put her arms up as skis fell onto her chest and face. Darren kept dragging her through the open doorway and down the steps to the tunnel floor. The back of Evelyn's head slammed against the bottom step on the way down, and darkness feathered at the borders of her sight.

Darren picked Evelyn up and slung her over his back.

He carried her through the tunnel. Her upper body swung back and forth. Drops of blood fell from her mouth onto the back of his pants. His pace was slow, his breathing labored. He was tired.

He was trying to figure out which way to go. Evelyn could hear him thinking as if he'd spoken out loud. Climb back over the pile of debris in the caved-in tunnel? Or go back through the Byrne House basement to the little passageway that linked with the stable? He longed to take

Evelyn through Byrne House and avoid the exertion of the climb, but it was far too risky. William could be there by now.

He would rest for a moment, then carry Evelyn up the slope and push her through the small gap to the other side of the caved-in passage. Gravity would roll her down the other side. He just needed her in a secure place, not necessarily in one piece. After he'd found the missing journal, he could use her to test a new version of the serum.

She'd done him a favor, really. He'd been too afraid to inject himself with the full concentration of the serum. But his mind was clearer than he could ever remember. He couldn't believe he'd wasted so much time longing for a cure. Wanting to be like everyone else. No, this was so much better.

His body was exhausted. But his mind? His mind was *invincible*.

Darren arrived at the three-way branching of the tunnels. He laid Evelyn on the floor and sat, panting, a few feet away. He kept the flashlight beam on her like a spotlight.

"There's one thing I don't understand," he said. "The journal should be at the surface of your thoughts, impossible to hide from me. But it's not there. How are you keeping that down, when I can see everything else?"

Evelyn kept her jaw clenched shut. She had a horrible feeling that if she opened her mouth, loose teeth would drop onto her tongue and lodge in her throat.

Darren crawled closer. "Oh, your mouth. I couldn't help that. I told you, I could see your next move coming a mile away. That's why it's so strange about the journal. If I can't get it this way, I'll have to find another way to make you tell me. Oh … oh, of course. Alex."

Her mouth still closed, Evelyn screamed again in fury and pain.

"I'll hurt him," Darren whispered. "Not like I'll mind, the spoiled brat has it coming. Maybe trap him down here alone with her? With Ada? You know Alex couldn't take that. Especially if I double the dose of the injection. It would be interesting to watch. Would he go insane from hearing Ada's screams inside his head? Or would he find a way to kill himself first?"

She wanted to strike out at him. To make Darren pay with pain. Shaking with rage, Evelyn pushed Daniella to the front of her thoughts.

Daniella trapped you in the mine shaft. She's the reason you're sick.

Instantly, his expression changed. "You're lying."

Evelyn recalled, in exacting detail, the story that she'd read in Daniella's mind. *All this time, your sister knew the truth. She's the one who's lied to you, again and again.*

Darren pressed his hands to his temples, trying to block the knowledge from streaming into his head. "That isn't true!"

She remembered the ooze of Daniella's hatred when Darren entered the underground lab. Evelyn used her entire being to amplify Daniella's emotions and project them at Darren.

"Stop it!" he screamed. He drove his forehead into the floor. "Stop!"

Evelyn snuck her hand around to her back pocket. *Your sister used you,* Evelyn said in her thoughts. *She gave me that syringe. Now that she has William, she only wants you gone.*

Darren lunged. He grabbed Evelyn's neck and squeezed. Her hand closed around the screwdriver in her pocket, and her arm shot up.

She drove the screwdriver into Darren's neck.

Black wetness sprayed the wall. Darren reared back, his mouth open, his eyes bulging. His hands flew to the wound. He fell back and thrashed on the floor and made a gurgling noise. Evelyn tried to crawl away from him. But her limbs wouldn't respond.

After several endless seconds, the noises and the movements stopped.

Evelyn opened her eyes and rocked onto her left side. The swelling in her mouth didn't hurt as much in that position. The beam of Darren's abandoned flashlight cast ghostly shadows through the tunnel, displaying the outline of his body against the wall.

Below Darren's shadow, there was Ada. Evelyn's mirror image, lying against the wall on her side. Ada was staring blankly back. Evelyn had no will left to struggle against her.

They lie for what feels like days, face to face on the floor. Evelyn hears nothing but the sound of their breathing, rising and falling in synchronous time.

Ada's hands are scarred from trying to find a way out. She long ago lost track of the metal door Simon had pushed her through. At first, she ran blindly through the tunnels, crashing headfirst into unexpected curves in the walls, struggling to find her way out of the dead ends. Her throat grew hoarse from screaming. For hours, she believed Simon would come back for her. Clara, my Clara, she thought. My daughter needs me.

Hunger and thirst started to gnaw at her. She realized Simon wasn't coming. Clara, she thought, my poor beautiful tiny girl. Ada sat and cried until the tears ran dry. She wandered for miles and everything was so very quiet. Quiet as death.

Finally, Ada laid down on the floor. The next time she woke, she didn't bother getting up.

Ada remembers her dear sister, so far away, and her mother and father in Heaven. They cannot see her here. Ada mourns for the husband and daughter she has lost. Ada thinks of the last time Walter truly saw her and spoke to her with love—on the day he gave her the mirror. She wonders if what Simon said was true and fears that it is. Every word. Part of her saw all of it unfolding as it happened, but she refused to acknowledge it. She let Walter slip away into his own dreams. Now she lies trapped inside of them, too. A Hell of her own making.

Evelyn listens to Ada's disjointed thoughts, sad beyond words that Ada has given up hope. Night doesn't last forever. But Ada can no longer remember the sun.

A man walks slowly toward them. Walter. He carries a lantern low by his side, a tiny glow in this unforgiving dark. He stops next to Ada and kneels beside her.

Ada's chest still rises and falls, a mechanical rhythm. Ada does not look up. Walter touches Ada's hair, her face, the cold dryness of her skin. Walter's body shakes with sobs as he lifts his wife's limp body into his arms.

Evelyn closes her eyes to the scene, although she cannot close her mind. She tries to focus on the ache in her jaw, the throb of her leg, the fatigue that stiffens every joint of her body. She pictures her Nana and her mom. They're sitting beside her, trying to hold back the dark with the sheer power of their love.

And she thinks of Alex—of the softness of his lips, the green-and-black intensity of his eyes, his lopsided grin. Of the warm weight of his body on hers the night before. The delicate thinness of his scar. The way he held her—saved her—when they were small.

She sees that day now like she's looking through a window: The tree as tall as the sky. The well as deep as the earth. The eyes that opened in the dusty walls, and the voices that began to whisper. The boy who comforted her, in spite of his own pain. I'm here, *he said.* Please don't be scared. I'm here. *A halo of colors swam out from him, trying to protect her in a soft, hypnotic glow.*

The light around Ada slowly drains away. But for Evelyn, the darkness holds no terror anymore. She's safe inside her memory. A long time passes in a single breath. Then something shifts in the passage.

Evelyn opens her eyes, and Alex is kneeling beside her. He bends down and a teardrop slips from his face onto hers.

Alex lifts her into his arms. Light shines all around him, and the light pushes away the sorrow of Walter and Ada. She shuts her eyes again and listens to the loveliest music. The boy's heart, beating against her ear.

43

EVELYN OPENED HER EYES.

Alex was sitting beside her, stroking her arm.

"Don't you ever move from there?" She asked. It was her second day in the hospital, and though she'd spent much of that time half-in and half-out of sleep, Alex had been there beside her every time she was awake, during daylight hours at least. Neither the "official" visiting hours nor Viv's dirty looks had fazed him.

"Yeah, when your mom makes me. But she's with your dad getting some lunch. I'm supposed to call them when you wake up."

"Are you going to?"

"In a minute."

Her mom and Alex seemed to have reached an uneasy truce. Viv wasn't happy that Evelyn had stayed out all night with Alex, but she also blamed herself for Evelyn's "rebellion," as she saw it. Ev had acted out because she'd been lied to for so long. It was much easier to let her mom believe that than explain what really happened. Viv had already been through enough.

After Alex brought Evelyn into Byrne House from the tunnels, he'd called the paramedics. She told them she'd been climbing a tree and fallen. If anyone thought the idea of a seventeen-year-old girl climbing a tree was odd, they didn't mention it.

They didn't test the blood on Evelyn's hands. They'd assumed it was her own.

As for Evelyn's dad, he'd rushed back to Castle Heights when he got the news that she'd been hurt. She still had mixed feelings about his return, and she didn't even know how long he'd stay. Viv, of course, refused to talk about the situation. Some things never did change.

Alex leaned over to kiss her gently on the nose. Her cheek and jaw were still swollen and bruised, but thankfully not broken. An oral surgeon had visited yesterday to check her teeth. All still there, her gums slowly healing. Silvia and Milo came by earlier that morning with milkshakes and homemade pudding.

"So what happened during my nap?"

"Your eyelids fluttered. You smiled, that was exciting."

Evelyn tried not to move her mouth as she giggled. "Anything else?"

Alex wrinkled his nose. "Jake stopped by. Again."

"Is he coming back later?"

"You actually want to talk to him?"

She folded down her blanket. "I feel like I should at least hear what he has to say. If it wasn't for Jake, I'd probably still be down in the tunnels."

Alex rolled his eyes. "Don't get me started on what the world would be like if Jake didn't exist."

She found Alex's hand. "I feel a little bit sorry for him. He's lost every friend he had."

"Exactly. We aren't his friends, so he doesn't need to keep coming around here. He's like a bad pair of socks that keep falling to the bottom of your gym bag and never get into the wash."

"Ew. Is that based on a true story?"

Alex grinned at her and lifted her hand. He kissed the end of each finger. "Oh yeah, Ms. Foster came by too. Half the neighborhood got together to help her clean up her house, and she got her new security system installed. Plus I'm pretty sure she's packing heat now—she has this jaded, 'I've seen it all' thing going. All she needs is the fedora."

Evelyn had considered whether she should tell Ms. Foster the truth: that Darren was the one who broke into her house, and now he was dead. She might sleep easier at night. The news had certainly made Milo feel better. But then Evelyn would have to spill the entire story to Ms. Foster, and no one knew that except for Alex and Jake. Even Milo and Silvia only got an abridged version.

"Have you heard anything from William?" Evelyn asked.

Alex looked down at her hand. He was still holding it, running his fingers up and down the inside of her forearm from her elbow to her palm. "Nope. Not a word. After everything he said to me, I'm not surprised. He blames me for the police showing up at our door and Daniella running away."

Milo ended up calling the police when he didn't hear from Evelyn. Of course, the cops didn't take his claims seriously—a bunch of old letters weren't proof of anything, and they weren't eager to break into a basement storage room to which Ms. Foster had no key. Within an hour, Milo heard that Evelyn had been found—injured, but safe—and so he clammed up when Detectives Penn and Tyson came with more questions.

But by then, the police had already made a visit to Byrne House as a courtesy to the Fosters. That spooked Daniella enough to make her pack her things and disappear. Without seeing the lab beneath Walter Park, though, the police had nothing against her. Daniella would realize that soon enough.

"She'll come back," Evelyn said. For the mirror.

Alex rested his head on Evelyn's pillow and stroked her arm. "You could tell the police what actually happened. Show them the evidence in that lab."

"What's the point? Darren's gone. It wasn't really Daniella behind the attacks, or at least we can't prove it."

Daniella had gotten what she wanted: Darren would no longer trouble her. And if Darren had survived the night instead of Evelyn? Then Daniella would have had the mirror and—so she might've believed—Walter's missing journal. Either way, she won.

Evelyn pushed the air out of her lungs. "It's just easier this way. For my parents, for Jake, for everyone. Nobody has to know ..." *What I had to do*, Evelyn finished silently. She'd told herself again and again that she'd had no choice. It was self defense. Darren would never have let her go free. But she still wished there'd been some other way. Darren had been a victim, too. Once upon a time, he'd been a child trapped in the dark. Just like her. But she'd had Alex; Darren had been all alone.

Alex's brows had knitted together when she'd mentioned Jake's name. "But you told *me* all of it, right?"

"As much as I could put into words." But that would never be all of it. Not entirely.

Alex stood up and went to the window. She could tell he was seething with jealousy and anger that he hadn't been the one down in the tunnels with her. Jake was the only person who truly knew what had happened to her there, at least up to the point that he ran for help.

But Alex was the one who'd saved her, even before he carried her out of the tunnels. Her memories of him had kept her safe from Ada's fate.

Someone knocked, and then the door swung open. Jake stepped in holding a small vase of yellow daisies.

"What do *you* want?"

"*Alex*." Evelyn frowned at him. "Can you let me talk to Jake for a bit?"

"You mean leave you alone with him?"

"Alex, please. A few minutes."

Jake bowed his head, remaining motionless as Alex glared at him on the way out.

"If I'm bothering you ..." Jake kept his gaze down, avoiding eye contact. He seemed like a different person from the boy who'd scoffed at her from his pool table a couple weeks ago.

Evelyn took the daisies and set them by her bed. "You're not. Did you want to talk?"

Jake went over to close the door. Then his face crumpled, and he covered it with his hands. "I'm just so sorry, Evelyn. If I had said something earlier, Darren would never have gone after you. He'd be in jail right now."

"It's not your fault." She'd said it automatically. But Jake did have something to do with it. "How did you get mixed up with Darren, anyway?"

Jake looked up, confused. "I thought you knew. Couldn't you see it in my head when we were in the tunnels?"

"Not in much detail."

"I guess everything started at the beginning of the summer. My dad ... he got *arrested*. It happened at work, so they were able to keep it quiet. But suddenly detectives were calling our house—like that a-hole Detective Tyson—saying my dad would be charged with fraud. Some business deal gone bad, my dad said. He agreed to be a witness against his boss. Like a whistleblower, you know? But the damage was done. My parents had just bought me a new car for my birthday, and now they were saying we might lose the house, lose everything. For a while I just tried to go on like nothing happened. I didn't even tell Silvia. When I met Darren at the Charity Club, I saw a way out."

"What did he ask you to do?" Evelyn tried to keep the contempt out of her voice, but it snuck in all the same.

Jake held her gaze intently. "You don't understand. Your family has lived here since ... I don't know, forever. I don't have your 'Castle Heights' pedigree. But we *earned* that house on Orran Avenue and our place in the Charity Club. And my parents were just ready to give up and go away? I wouldn't accept it."

He was right, she did not understand. But she was going to try. Jake squirmed in the chair, and then got up and paced around. Finally he rested his hands on the rail at the foot of the bed.

"I met Darren right after Milo disappeared. Somehow, he'd heard about my dad's problems. Darren told me if I was looking to make some money, he could help. Darren pulled this bottle of capsules from his pocket. He said it was an incredible drug, the result of medical lab research, and that it was completely safe with no negative side effects. He said it would give you a high like nothing else. It sounded crazy, but I was desperate."

Jake picked at the fraying edge of his sweatshirt as he spoke, pulling a thread away from the fabric. "Darren said I'd get a cut of the profits if I sold the drug to a select group of students, mostly the rich kids. People like Jordan Davis. I thought it was totally harmless, a win-win. The buyers seemed to like it. They said you could see colors around people's heads, feel somebody else's emotions like they were happening to you. I tried it too, and they were right. It felt good. Gentle, nothing like the injection that Darren gave us later on. For a while, I tried so hard to act like everything was normal. Silvia started to grate on me. She was so … naive. It was easier to avoid her than try to explain."

I was naive, too, Evelyn thought. She'd never suspected. "What happened at your party? How'd Jordan get sick?"

"The party was Darren's idea, to get some more people to try the drug. Darren said it would attract less attention if I invited most of the senior class, too. I swear I had no idea he would do that to Jordan. I didn't even know about it until afterwards, after she was already in the hospital. I confronted Darren. He said his experiment was going too slowly, he needed results sooner. He threatened me. He said that if I told anyone, he'd expose me as a drug dealer, and say I had something to do with Jordan's illness. Darren admitted what he'd done to Milo. He wanted to scare me, and it worked. But it was too late for me to tell the police. I stayed quiet. So many times after that, I unlocked my phone and pulled up Milo's number. But I never hit send."

"But you were going to tell Milo the truth, right? When he came to your house?"

Jake ruffled his once-glossy hair. Now it was dull and flat. In just the last few days, the black had turned ashy gray at his temples. He looked decades older than seventeen. "Even before Darren attacked Caitlin at the dance," he said, "I knew I couldn't keep the secret much longer. I even thought about telling Detective Tyson when he came to my house to interview my dad, for my dad's case. Darren must have figured it out. You know the rest already."

For a moment, Evelyn could read him as clearly as she had down in the tunnels—his despair, his shame. He felt it much more strongly here in the daylight, where he couldn't hide from what he'd done. But Jake couldn't bear to be anywhere else, either, with people who couldn't possibly understand.

"Jake ..." Evelyn held out her hand. "Thank you for finding Alex so he could help me. For a while, down in that basement, I didn't think you were going to figure out what to do. I should have had more faith in you."

Jake slid his fingers in between hers and held on tight. He touched his other hand lightly to her cheek. Evelyn turned slightly away.

"Alex will be back soon," she said. "We can talk later, okay?"

He nodded. Then he let go and backed away toward the doorway. "Bye, Evelyn. I'll see you."

44

A WEEK LATER, EVELYN HEARD THE KNOCK SHE was expecting. She got up from the couch, now her makeshift bed, and put on her coat. "It's open."

She grabbed her crutches and went to the entryway. Alex was standing there with his hand on the open door. Morning sunshine streamed through the doorway behind him. He had Evelyn's backpack, the one she'd left down in the tunnels in Darren's lab.

"It was all still there on the desk," he said. "Milo and Jake just left. They'll drop off Silvia's phone at her place."

"Was it ... bad?" If she hadn't been hurt, she'd have been there herself.

Alex rubbed his hands against his jeans. "What you'd imagine after over a week down there. Thankfully, with the three of us it didn't take long to get Darren wrapped up tight. Then we dumped him in the lab, I took his key and your backpack with the mirror in it, and Milo welded the doors to their frames on either side with his dad's blow torch. Simple. It's over."

"Almost," Evelyn reminded him.

"Yeah, except that. Almost over."

Evelyn hobbled out of the house. They headed toward Byrne House.

She had thought of the mirror a few times in the hospital, and again since she'd come home. She'd wondered if Daniella might come back to take it. But Evelyn didn't exactly feel relief to have the mirror back. When she thought of Walter and Ada Byrne, she only felt numb.

She had one last task for the mirror. After that, she didn't care if she ever saw it again.

Alex held open the gate for her. He helped her up Byrne House's front steps. Her crutches thumped on the wood floor of the main hallway.

"Is your mom awake?" she asked.

Alex's mother had flown in from New York City after William took off. Evelyn had met Lila Evans only once so far, in passing, and Lila had paid her as much attention as the furniture.

"She's still asleep. She's usually up around eleven for her pre-lunch Bloody Mary. So we're fine." Alex opened the door to the basement stairwell. "How do you want to handle the stairs? It would be easiest if I carry you."

Evelyn huffed, pretending to be annoyed. "I guess. If you have to."

Alex strung one arm through the holes in her crutches and lifted her up. Evelyn wrapped her arms around his neck. "I feel like I haven't kissed you for days," she said as they descended the steps. "My mom makes that grumbling sound every time you get close to me."

"What's stopping you now?"

She nuzzled into his neck and kissed just above his collar bone. Alex set her down at the bottom of the stairs and handed back her crutches.

"So what's your new room like?" Evelyn asked. Alex's mom had insisted he move into Byrne House with her. She'd even picked out a bedroom for him on the second floor.

"It has a bed in it. And a dresser. Other than that, it's hideous. It's like a flower shop vomited in there. And the pipes clank at night."

She laughed. "If it's any consolation, sleeping in the living room is awful. I can't wait until I can manage the stairs again. For one, all of my best clothes and books are up there. Plus I hear every car that passes on the street, and the ticking of that stupid clock in the kitchen sounds like a metronome. I can't sleep at all. I keep waking up thinking I'm supposed to be practicing the piano, even though I only took lessons the one year in second grade."

Alex grinned at her. "So what do you do all night instead?"

"Think scandalous thoughts about you. What else?" That wasn't exactly true. Sometimes, insomnia still came for her. The panic that squeezed her chest, wouldn't let her breathe. But no nightmares yet. Every night without them was a blessing, but Evelyn didn't really believe they were gone forever. *Forever* belonged only to fairy tales.

They came to the storage alcove with the metal door. Alex had already cleared a path, but Evelyn still kept running into chair legs and knocking clouds of dust into the air with her crutches. Alex unzipped her pack and fished out the key. He fiddled with it in the lock until it turned, then gripped the handle and pulled.

They walked into Ada's tomb.

The sarcophagus dominated the circular chamber. Directly beneath Ada's marble coffin lay the browned skeleton, dressed in rags.

Evelyn took the mirror out of the pack. Alex's arms circled her waist to hold her steady, and she lifted the mirror.

Walter stands before the sarcophagus, a husk of the man who was once a husband. He has come here each day for months, so many he's lost count. His beloved Ada lies in her final resting place. Walter put her there.

He remembers the day, not long after he found Ada in the tunnels, that he guided her to this room. After he found her, haunted and broken, he prayed for a recovery. He did everything he could think of to awaken her mind. But Ada never met his eyes. Never spoke. Never smiled. And two days before he brought her to this room—directly underneath the labyrinth maze that the workers were constructing in the garden above them—she had stopped eating. Then she refused even water.

Walter first saw the labyrinth in a vision during one of his fits years ago. He managed to remember the design long enough to scrawl it on a scrap of paper. He believed it a sign of something great and important, though he didn't understand what it meant. Walter pumped much of his fortune into transforming his old mine shafts to fit the pattern, building his vision into the very bedrock of Byrne House and the surrounding land.

But when he found Ada in the tunnels, he knew. All that time, Walter had been building a monument to hold her tomb.

That last day, he'd led her here and helped her up onto the table. She seemed to know exactly what he wanted her to do. Ada stepped inside the marble box that would be her grave. She did not blink as Walter injected his serum into her arm so that she could see him, and know his heart, one last time. The serum did its work. And finally, she looked at him.

Ada smiled.

Walter knew in that instant that his wife could see everything—the agony, the regret, the rage—that boiled unchecked inside of him. Walter and Simon were mirror images, both of them cracked and corrupted. Whether it was the mine's slow poison or some even deeper shared flaw, Walter didn't know. But where Simon chose easy cruelty, Walter had always struggled—sometimes blindly—for the light.

Walter placed his final gift in Ada's arms: the journal containing his design for the gold-framed mirror. It served as a promise, both of the love that inspired his invention and of the weaknesses that he will atone for. "I will be worthy of you and Clara again," Walter told her. "Soon." As for the mirror itself, he found it stowed in the housekeeper's room. Now he has hidden it so Simon will never take that too.

Ada closed her eyes and faded away, the smile still on her lips.

Now, so many months later, Walter rests a cold hand atop the sarcophagus. The garden labyrinth above, a replica of the larger one around them, is finished. Ada's statue will stand at the center just as he has envisioned it. He thinks of Ada, and his hatred for Simon subsides. Now he is ready to rest.

Walter lies down on the floor beneath his wife. He breathes. In. Out. He closes his eyes. He will not open them again.

Evelyn lowered the mirror and turned to bury her face in Alex's chest.

"Did you see them?" he asked.

She nodded. "You can too, if you want to know."

"Nah, the mirror's your thing. Do you want to tell me?"

She shook her head. "Can we go outside? I can't think in here."

They walked slowly upstairs, through Byrne House, and outside into the gardens. Tree branches rattled in a gust of wind. Alex put his arm on Evelyn's back and led her to a small gazebo near the rose garden. She set aside her crutches, and Alex helped her sit down on the peeling wooden planks of the gazebo floor. The gardens were quiet except for the sound of the wind humming hoarsely through the trees.

"My mom told me last night that this is only temporary," Alex said. "She only agreed to come here because I begged her to. She doesn't intend to stay. I'm still enrolled at my school back in New York, and she expects me to be there when the semester officially starts."

Not again. Sadness welled in Evelyn's chest. Would it always be like this? Always wondering how long they'd have until they said goodbye?

"Do you think you can change her mind?" she asked.

Alex seemed to consider it. He gritted his teeth. "I'm eighteen in a few months. I could stay here myself."

"Alone?"

"I wouldn't be alone. You'd be here with me. At Byrne House."

"You know what I mean."

Alex reached for Evelyn's hand, entwining his fingers with hers. "Do you know what *I* mean?"

She hoped Alex wasn't suggesting something that would change her name to "Evelyn Evans." She should have laughed at how ridiculous that sounded. Instead it just made her chest ache. He couldn't mean that. Could he?

For most of her life, she'd been looking for Alex without even knowing it. The boy who'd saved her. She refused to lose him again. If that meant fighting to be with him, then she'd fight.

The sun beat down with brilliant, golden light. Evelyn's eyes began to water. Byrne House loomed over the horizon, its face black with shadow, as if it had been burned away by the blazing sky. She watched as long as she could. When she turned her gaze away, she found Alex looking back.

Evelyn and Alex's story will continue in
DOORS OF GOLD AND RUST,
the conclusion to the Byrne House duology, coming Fall of 2020!

Thank you

I write for you, readers! Let me know what you think. I'd be so grateful for a quick review on Amazon and on Goodreads. It only takes a couple of minutes, yet reviews mean everything to writers like me. And if you'd rather not leave a review, leave a rating. Every single rating or review helps make this book more visible to other readers. Many thanks and happy reading.

More books by A.N. Willis

The Corridor

The Thirteenth World (*Corridor #2*)

A.N. Willis writes books for teens and adults—sometimes sci-fi, sometimes supernatural, always with heavy doses of action and romance. She loves the creepy, the suspenseful, the otherworldly. She blogs about writing in the Mile High City on anwilliswrites.com. Follow her on Instagram @morningcoffeeforwriters and on Twitter @anwilliswrites.

Acknowledgements

Alex and Evelyn's story has been through many transformations over the years, and several people have been with me every step of the way. To Carrie and Carolyn, who read that very first manuscript (and every major revision since), thank you for your enthusiasm and your patience as I figured out just how to best tell this story! I'm so grateful for your friendship. And to the rest of my wonderful writing group, who have borne with me through all the many versions of this book, thank you for your honest feedback, for your support, and for being so much darned fun. I love you all and can't imagine writing without you.

To my entire family, thank you for always encouraging and believing in me. I couldn't do this without you.

To all the rest of my varied critique partners, who've been kind enough to read versions of this book and give me your feedback, thank you! One of my favorite things about being a writer is discovering the incredible writing community that's out there. You've made a huge difference to this story, and I am always happy to return the favor on your next projects.

And to everyone who read *The Corridor* and *The Thirteenth World*, thank you for continuing to follow my writing. It means a lot.